A SUMMER
OF SECRETS

LORNA PEEL

Chapter One

Sophia knew Cathy wouldn't like it, but instead of driving her six-year-old goddaughter to her best friend Molly's house for a sleep-over, Sophia insisted that the two-mile walk through the frost would do them both good. It would also go some way to easing the Easter egg mountain in Cathy's stomach, and the new job butterflies in her own.

Walking back to town, Sophia decided to take a shortcut through the parkland of the Heaton Abbey Estate, hoping for the umpteenth time that she had done the right thing in accepting the position of tour guide there. She needed the job and she needed somewhere to live, and how many jobs came with accommodation these days? It wasn't as if she would be cutting herself off completely from family and friends by working and living at the abbey, she reasoned with herself. She'd only be five minutes away from them by car.

Parts of the park's ornamental lake had frozen over, thanks to the coldest Easter in years, and Sophia stopped to watch some birds sliding about on the ice in complete bewilderment before flying away. Picking up a stone, she flung it out, watching and listening as it slid across the thawing ice, which groaned and creaked. About to return to the path, she stopped, hearing a thud from the direction of the boathouse.

"Who's there?" she called but, not surprisingly, no-one answered.

Edging towards the wooden building, she peered in the window. Apart from one boat with outboard motor, it was empty. Sophia shrugged. She could have sworn she had heard something. She continued on around the building and walked straight into a man crouching down with a baseball cap covering his face and clearly hiding from her.

"Oh, God," she gasped, having to grab his shoulders so she wouldn't fall over.

"You're trespassing," he snapped without looking up.

"I know," she replied, letting him go. "I'm sorry."

"Well, go away, then."

Sophia didn't need to be told twice and hurried back to the path. She still had to buy a present for Cathy's parents, Michelle and Tony, as a thank you for allowing her to stay with them, so she had better get on with it.

"You're more than welcome back, you know?" Michelle gave her a hug and a kiss as Sophia prepared to leave the following afternoon. "If it's too bizarre. I've seen those programmes on television about country estates. I couldn't put up with all the bowing and scraping."

"This job is perfect for me – I love tour guiding – and I get my own flat, too. I couldn't have lived here forever."

"I know, but I've got used to you being here."

"Why, was I a problem in the beginning?" Sophia teased.

Michelle just laughed. "At least you're not going back to London."

"Everything depends on Mum."

"I know. Ring me?"

"I will," Sophia assured her, throwing her handbag onto the Mini's passenger seat, and getting into the driver's seat. "Give Cathy a kiss from me."

Michelle nodded and waved her off, shouting, "Remember – if it's too bizarre – come back."

Leaving her boxes in the car in what had once been the abbey's cloister garth – the grassy area around which the cloister arcades ran – she got out and took a long look around her. The grass had long been cobbled over and they were now covered with gravel. The cloisters had become stables and were now offices, while the lofts overhead had recently been converted into living accommodation. The estate manager occupied one flat, she was to occupy the second, and the third was still vacant.

Taking the computer printout of her tour and the map – kindly drawn by Lady Heaton – out of her handbag, she set off across the now redundantly-named stable yard towards Heaton Abbey House. The heart of the sprawling house had once been the monastic church, and opening a side door, she went inside.

This wasn't good, she thought ten minutes later, turning down yet another similar-looking corridor in the bowels of the house. Where on earth was she? Lady Heaton hadn't brought her down here the other day, had she? Weren't the signs to keep the public out of certain rooms supposed to have gone up by now?

A door to her right was ajar and she pushed it open. It was the library but the room was incredibly dark and gloomy with only one narrow window directly across from her. Anyone else would have retreated but she had always been intrigued by the contents of other people's bookcases and she wasn't going to resist delving into these, even if she could do with a torch. A whole room full of books – absolute paradise. The first shelf was rather disappointing containing large books on antiques, art history textbooks, a glossy coffee table-type volume on the various uses of herbs, and some new paperbacks on accounting, business management, and computers.

Further along, the shelves housed nineteenth-century novels by authors like the Brontë sisters, Mrs Gaskell, Thomas Hardy, and Jane Austen. Other shelves held classical prose and poetry but there were very few twentieth or twenty-first-century novels unless they weren't in keeping and were shelved elsewhere. Selecting a leather bound and rather dusty volume of Hardy's *The Woodlanders*, she opened the cover. Oh, that dusty, old booky smell. On the flyleaf, in spidery handwriting, she could just about make out an inscription…

"And you are…?"

Sophia almost jumped out of her skin and peered into a dark corner. It was Lord Thomas Heaton himself. Dark-haired and in his late thirties, he was stretched out casually in a leather wing-backed armchair, and she watched as he savoured a mouthful of what looked like whisky. One of his hands was resting lightly on the arm of the chair while the other held the glass of golden liquid as he waited for her to reply.

"Sophia Nelson. I'm the new tour guide."

His eyebrows rose in an 'Oh, I see' expression. "I must

correct you in that you are *the* tour guide. We have not had a tour guide here before unless you can count the few times Lady Heaton has shown guests around the house, that is."

"Lady Heaton is to bring me on another tour this afternoon," Sophia explained.

"During which she will no doubt tell you that this wing of the house is not part of the tour you will give."

Sophia closed the book and raised her eyes to his face again. He stared back impassively at her and she realised she was staring rudely at him.

"I'm sorry." She flushed, glad now for the gloom in the room. "I was trying to familiarise myself with the house and I seem to have got lost."

"You start tomorrow, don't you? As tour guide?"

What the hell must he think of her? The tour guide getting lost. "Yes. I know the, er…history, I just need to…er…place it in context."

"Context?" One eyebrow rose.

Oh, God, that had sounded better in her head. "Yes. I'm sorry that I disturbed you, my Lord."

Cringing, she replaced the book on the shelf and left the room. Michelle, not to mention her father, an ardent supporter of the Socialist Labour Party – 'Not that New Labour crap' – would have had a fit if they had heard her all but bowing and scraping. Mr Nelson was more than a little irritated at where she had found a job. Heaton Abbey House, a Cistercian monastery until King Henry VIII broke with Rome and found himself a bit strapped for cash, was situated just outside the Yorkshire town where she had been born and brought up.

A Sir William Heaton had bought the abbey and its lands

following the dissolution of the monasteries, modestly renamed the abbey after himself and remodelled the monastic buildings to suit his own domestic requirements.

A descendant was created a Baron in the early 18th century and more rebuilding took place, reflecting the family's elevation to the peerage. A further descendent made a fortune from coal mining, resulting in yet more rebuilding and restyling. A more recent descendent made a catastrophic business deal and had been forced to sell the mine and some land but, thankfully, the house with its mishmash of styles and five hundred acres of land remained unsold.

These were not the type of people her father wanted her associating with at all. The town's mining museum was more to his liking but that was before a malicious fire had burned it to the ground the previous January.

Sophia stood in the corridor for a moment before glancing at the library door. Lord Heaton. His voice – deep and without even a hint of Yorkshire in it… He was the man hiding from her at the boathouse.

"Ah, Sophia." Lady Heaton closed one of the doors to the drawing room and greeted her cheerfully in the enormous hallway, once the nave of the monastic church. "Welcome. Shall I show you the flat? It's finished at last."

"Yes. Thank you."

Wondering what on earth Lord Heaton was doing creeping around his own estate, Sophia followed his mother out the front door, around the side of the house, and back across the stable yard.

"Des' office is over there in the corner," Lady Heaton told her. "He is the estate manager. My son's office is there, and you are up here." Sophia followed Lady Heaton up a narrow metal staircase. The door at the top led straight into a large and airy kitchen-dining room-cum-living room. "The bathroom is through there, and the bedroom through there. The other room, you can either use as a second bedroom or a study, as it is rather on the small side."

"It's lovely."

"Yes, they did turn out rather well, didn't they?" Lady Heaton went to the window and opened it. "The smell of paint will go after a couple of days. If there is anything else you need, do let me know."

"I will."

"Oh, and if you happen to meet my son, I must warn you that he may be a little grumpy. He didn't want any of this, you see, a shop and tours of the house. But the house is impossibly big, as you now know and, well, it is either this or we would be in great difficulty."

"I see."

"Well, I'll leave you to settle in."

"Thank you. Oh, I did notice that the signs aren't up yet."

Lady Heaton nodded. "There's been a slight delay, they should be here and up tomorrow morning. Your keys," she added, passing a bunch to her. "The outside door, the flat door, here, and the side door to the house."

"Thank you."

The doors closed after Lady Heaton and Sophia peered around then up at the high ceiling. Two Velux windows added to the considerable light in the flat. She went to the bedroom and was pleased to see it was a double. The small bedroom-cum-study was empty and the bathroom contained both a bath and a shower. Compared to some of the flats she had lived in over the years, this was absolute luxury.

After sitting and then lying back on the double bed, and finding that the mattress was good and firm, she went back out to the living area. Making sure the fridge freezer had been plugged in, she attached the keys to her car key ring, then went downstairs to the stable yard.

Walking to her car to retrieve her belongings, she heard a raised voice coming from Lord Heaton's office.

"…No, I don't, and I will not lend him more money." It was Lord Heaton's voice and Sophia pulled an awkward face. "You've got a fucking nerve coming here. So take yourself, your wife, and your filthy disgusting habit back to Leeds. And you can tell your brother that he is a useless waste of space and I haven't a bloody clue what Stephanie sees in him. And if he comes anywhere near her again I will kill him. Do I make myself clear?"

Hurrying to her car, Sophia beeped open the central locking. She got in and belted up, watching over her shoulder as Lord Heaton threw a man out of his office. Heaton stood in the doorway, a thunderous expression on his face, as the man walked to a car before getting into the passenger side. Heaton then glanced in her direction and she flushed, started the engine, and drove out of the stable yard. It might be a good idea if she moved in later.

Taking the opportunity to go grocery shopping, she returned to the stable yard an hour and a half later. This time she parked right outside the door to the flat and began hauling her shopping bags up the stairs. Going back downstairs to the car for more, she saw Lord Heaton crossing the yard towards her. He hadn't got up from his chair in the library but despite this, she had seen he was at least six feet tall, with a muscular frame.

"Thomas Heaton," he said, halting beside the car and offering his hand. "But I think you probably already know that by now."

His dark brown hair was cut in a short and surprisingly modern style, not that she had expected him to be wearing a powdered wig, and his blue-grey eyes observed her with no hint of embarrassment. Now that was surprising, considering what she had seen and heard earlier, and she quickly banished her father's comment of, 'That sort don't care what we think about them,' to the back of her mind. Heaton was dressed in an impeccably neat black suit but his black silk tie looked as if it had been tugged at. Her own auburn curls were beginning to escape her ponytail and, dressed in an old pair of jeans and a polo neck jumper, she felt as if she'd just crawled through a hedge backwards in comparison.

"Sophia Nelson. I'm sorry if I intruded earlier," she said, shaking his hand. "I thought the signs would have been up by now but Lady Heaton told me that there's been a slight delay and they won't be here until tomorrow."

"Signs." He pulled a disgusted expression. "No entry here, private there. Here, let me help you with your shopping."

"Oh?" She watched him take four bags and go inside and up the stairs before following with the remaining two. "Thank you."

"Not bad." He put the bags on the kitchen worktop and walked across the room to the window. "I thought they might still smell of hay or something."

"I prefer hay to paint but I'll leave the windows open."

"Do you ride?" he asked.

"Only a bicycle," she replied.

He shrugged. "Just as well. This hasn't been a stable block in the true sense of the word for some considerable time now and soon the house will be full of tourists wandering about where they shouldn't despite all the signs."

"I will try to keep the visitors under control but unfortunately, the supermarket didn't have any stun guns."

It was out before she realised and cringed as he turned and stared at her.

"That's a pity. I could lend you a tranquilliser gun? We've got quite a few – Des uses them with the deer. You could take your pick?"

She just managed to keep a straight face. "Thank you, but I'd better say no. It might be less messy in the long run, litigation-wise."

He gave a short laugh and she blushed like a schoolgirl.

"That's true, but the offer is there."

"Thank you, I'll bear it in mind."

He nodded and glanced around the room again then grimaced as he caught her looking at his hair. It was completely at odds with the rest of his rather severe appearance.

"My sister's to blame."

"Oh, she's a hairdresser?" she asked, then winced. Stupid question.

"No, but I wish she was, she might have done a better job."

"Oh, but it's…"

"Awful, I know." He grimaced. "Well, I hope you have

everything you need. If not, the housekeeper should be able to help you."

"Thank you. Would you mind if I came to the house later and walked through my tour?"

"To put it in context?"

"Yes." She fought to control yet another blush. "If you don't mind?"

"No, not at all. Well, I'll leave you to it."

"Thank you," she said again, following him to the door. "It was you yesterday, wasn't it?" she added. He stopped and turned. "At the boathouse?"

"That was you?"

"Yes," she replied. "I'm sorry for trespassing."

He shook his head. "I apologise for...being rather short with you."

Still none the wiser as to what he had been doing there, she closed the door after him then went to the window and watched him walk back to his office. Moving to her right, she could see right inside and she saw him shrugging out of the jacket, pulling the black tie loose, and undoing the top button of his shirt before booting up a PC. He sat down, pulled a sheet of paper towards him, and began to type.

Sophia pulled at her bottom lip as she tried to make some sense of her completely unexpected response to him. When was the last time a man had turned her into a gibbering mess? Lee, at the beginning? Not really. Never, really. No-one, really. Heaton intimidated her big time, but there was more to it than that. He was what Michelle in her pre-Tony days would have called, 'A fine thing.' More's the pity. Why the hell couldn't he look like a Tim-nice-but-dim type or a floppy-haired Hugh Grant clone? And what grown man would allow his sister to take him out for a haircut? Things were getting more and more curious by the minute. Reluctantly turning away, she unpacked her shopping before returning to the car for her suitcases and boxes.

About to put a frozen lasagne in the microwave oven that evening, she went downstairs to answer a knock at the door, hoping it wasn't Heaton back again. She'd made enough of an idiot of herself for one day, thank you. To her relief, a stocky man of about fifty gave her a grin.

"Thought I'd come and introduce myself to my new neighbour. I'm Des Fields, Estate Manager."

"Fields?"

He chortled heartily. "I'm out in them every day."

She groaned. "Oh, God, sorry, you must get that every time. I'm Sophia, the tour guide."

"You've met his Lordship, then?"

"Yes, he kindly helped me with my shopping bags earlier."

"Bloody hell," Des muttered. "Shopping bags? It's a wonder he knows what they are. Helen gets everything delivered, and I mean everything."

"Helen?"

"Helen, the housekeeper," he explained. "And my wife."

"I must introduce myself."

"Do, she's looking forward to meeting you. Anyway, I hope you like it here. Don't mind his nibs, he'll get used to the tourists eventually. Hasn't got much choice, really. Have you seen the new website yet? Come and have a look."

She went with him to Heaton's office and waited as he sat down at the PC, connected to the internet and accessed a website.

"Wireless internet," he explained. "There's a mast on the roof of the farmyard apartments and a receiver on the roof here. The password is heatonabbeyhouse – all one word – if you want to try it out. Lord Heaton and Lady Heaton want to try and attract business people – you know – the type who can't go five minutes without checking their email."

Sophia smiled. "I do."

"I'm getting a laptop with wireless stuff on it soon. Though, to tell you the truth, I think I'll have to go on a course to learn how to switch it on. My old PC was pretty basic. Here we are." He turned the monitor around so she could read the description.

Heaton Abbey House – A Family Home
Heaton Abbey House is not a 'stately home' as is generally understood – certainly, its occupants are not stately. A former 13th-century Cistercian Monastery, dissolved by King Henry VIII, it is very much a lived-in and loved family home, something it has now been for almost 500 years. The public will see most of the house including several rooms used by the Heaton family. We hope visitors will feel more like guests, in a private home, rather than visitors to a public institution.

The gift shop sells locally produced crafts and the kitchen garden has over 600 species of herbs, with plants for sale in the garden centre.

Tours of the house and gardens: 2:30 pm and 4:30 pm daily, with an additional tour at 11:30 am on Sundays, £15 including tea, coffee, and home-made cakes.

"Who wrote it?" she asked.

"Lady Heaton and her daughter, why?"

"This bit." She pointed. "Certainly its occupants are not stately. I take it they were only referring to themselves when they wrote that."

Des grinned. "He is a bit intimidating all right, but you'll get used to him, don't worry."

I don't know about that, she thought. "A friend of mine works in the tourist office in the town. You should email them a link to the website."

"Not my department, I'm afraid," Des told her, disconnecting from the internet and putting the PC to sleep. "You'll have to speak to his Lordship about that."

"Okay, will do." She followed him out of the office, picking up a business card from a small tray on the desk as she passed.

After the awful rubbery lasagne, Sophia went to the house. Finding the side door open, and with only one wrong turn, she made her way downstairs to the kitchen.

"Helen?" she enquired, seeing a middle-aged woman kneading dough on a floury worktop. "I'm Sophia."

"The tour guide. Hello. Welcome to Heaton Abbey House. All set for tomorrow?"

"Almost," Sophia replied. "I'm going to do a walk-through of my tour to get it right in my head."

"Want a bun before you go?" Helen offered, nodding to some buns cooling on a wire tray. "You might need the energy."

She laughed. "Thanks, I will."

"I saw his Lordship speaking to you earlier. In a good mood, was he?"

No. "Well, I…" she began.

"He didn't want the house opened up to the public but didn't really have much of a choice," Helen explained. "It was either this or face the possibility of losing it all. So if he's a bit rude, don't mind him. He's had it rough when you realise what he's had to cope with. His father died not long after he'd left university so he couldn't have been much more than twenty-two or three. For umpteen years he's had the burden and responsibility of all this on his shoulders and it's taking its toll on him from what I can see."

"What happened to his father?" Selecting a currant bun, Sophia took a bite. It was delicious.

"Lung cancer."

"Oh."

"On the surface, he seems to have everything, but actually he's not been dealt that great a hand in life when you think about it. You can't really blame him if he appears to be a little irritable and unapproachable at times. We just have to have a lot of patience with him. He and Lady Heaton are not long back from a funeral. He doesn't like those either. Well, who does? And, of course with what happened to Stephanie last week… If he's grumpy…just don't take it personally, will you?"

"No," Sophia replied. "How is she? Lady Stephanie? I didn't know whether to ask."

"It's just Stephanie." Helen corrected her with a smile. "Baron's daughters or sisters aren't referred to as 'Lady'." Sophia flushed. She should have known that. Visitors could ask her anything. "She lost a lot of blood but she seems to be on the mend. Physically, I mean. Mentally, who knows? Losing a baby…none of us can understand why she won't

15

leave her boyfriend. It's not the first time he's hit her and it won't be the last, you mark my words."

Going upstairs to the marble-tiled hall, Sophia looked at her watch, then began the tour in her head. Starting with the basic history and layout, first of the monastery, then of the house and buildings modified and built on the site after the dissolution and in subsequent centuries.

Then get the visitors moving. In one door to the drawing room, out the other door, and into the dining room. Then bring them up the main staircase, past the portraits of the former Barons Heaton. On the first floor, they would see a bedroom with a seventeenth-century four-poster bed, a bathroom fitted early twentieth-century style, and the nursery, complete with vintage toys.

The servants' quarters were located on the second floor. Visitors would see two spartanly-furnished bedrooms before she would bring them down the back stairs to the enormous main kitchen where the tea, coffee, and cakes would be served by Helen and any questions answered.

After that, visitors would move on to the gardens where Jack Halewood, the head gardener, would take over before returning them to their coach or car via the gift shop and garden centre. Standing just inside the huge back door, Sophia looked at her watch again. Forty-five minutes. Good.

Returning to the main staircase, she went to the portraits. Lord Heaton's father was near the bottom and was a rather intimidating man, too, but without his son's scowl. She sat on the steps and re-read her tour before folding the sheets of paper and putting them in the back pocket of her jeans.

A door opened and she watched as, across the vast hall, Lady Heaton peered out of the drawing room. Clearly not having seen her through the ornately-carved oak bannisters, Lady Heaton slipped out of the room, clutching something in her hand. She hurried along the hall before turning down the dark corridor towards the library. Sophia stared after her then shrugged. What was it with the family creeping around the place?

"Is everything in context?" Hearing a voice, she twisted around. Lord Heaton was coming down the stairs and she got up. The black tie was gone, the jacket left open, and the white shirt was now open a couple more buttons but despite this, he only appeared marginally less intimidating than before.

"Yes, I think so."

"Would you like to see some etchings of the old abbey?" he asked. "They might help you in your description?"

"Thank you, that's very kind."

He nodded. "Follow me."

In the library, he retrieved a cardboard wallet from a shelf, and brought it over to a desk, before switching on the reading lamp.

"This is an aerial view," he told her, extracting the etchings, and placing them on the desk. "Showing the layout of the monastic buildings. You probably know that most Cistercian monasteries were built to more or less the same plan. It was quite a small abbey. This is the church and a view of the cloister. Then along comes King Henry VIII…"

He was very knowledgeable and seemed to relax when he spoke of the past but with a temper like his, his chances of being a good tour guide were very slim.

"You're from the town, aren't you?" he asked, returning the etchings to the folder.

"Yes, but I've lived in Leeds and then in London until quite recently."

"What brought you back? If you don't mind my asking?"

"No," she replied, giving him a weak smile. "My mother is ill. She had a stroke and is in Rich Hill Nursing Home. She suffers from dementia, so she couldn't live at home anymore. She kept wandering off and Dad couldn't cope. I didn't want to be too far away so I came back. To the mining museum originally, but then someone took a dislike to it."

He nodded. "I'm sorry to hear about your mother."

"Thank you."

"It must be very hard on your family."

She noticed a book on Renaissance women in the desk drawer as he opened it and placed the wallet inside. "I'm an only child but, yes, it is hard. She used to be such an active woman. She and Dad married late in life. When the mine closed, Dad—"

"The mine?" he interrupted sharply. "Your father worked in the mine?"

"Yes, he did. And when it closed, he put his heart and soul into the museum. I don't think there's a single family in the town that doesn't have a miner in their family history somewhere."

"I must have met him at one point or another. What's his name?"

"William Nelson. He gave a very long-winded speech when the museum opened a few years ago."

"I remember now." He smiled and glanced at her curls. "Red hair."

She grinned. "There must be Irish or Scottish in us somewhere."

"Could you give him and your mother my best wishes the next time you visit?"

"I will, but there are days that I could tell her I was the Queen of Sheba and she'd believe me." Don't cry, she ordered herself, but she couldn't stop the tears coming. "I'm sorry," she gasped and fled from the room.

She ran blindly through the hall – almost colliding with Lady Heaton – hauled the heavy front door open, and staggered out onto the steps before halting to catch her breath. Pulling a paper handkerchief from her pocket, she wiped her eyes. *Oh, God, what the hell will they both think of me now? A hysterical, nosy idiot who doesn't know when to keep her mouth shut, that's what.*

She blew her nose, took a few deep breaths, then turned and went back inside to grovel and apologise. Turning down the corridor to the library, she heard voices and slowed her pace. The door to the library was ajar and she crept forward, peering inside, and hoping she wouldn't tread on any loose floorboards.

"So my blood group gave me away." Lady Heaton was speaking quietly.

Heaton nodded. "I asked Dr Morrison whether it was unusual for both sibling and mother to not be suitable donors and he told me that with your blood group it was impossible that you could be my mother." He sighed. "I'm sorry, I didn't want you discovering I knew in this way."

"Well, now you know. I am not your mother."

"So who is? Who is my father? The postman?"

"No," Lady Heaton replied firmly. "Your father was your father."

"And Stephanie?"

"He was her father, too. Thomas, your father and I were married five years and we still had no children. I went to see a doctor about it who referred me to a specialist. It turned out that I am infertile. I would never have children. Your father desperately wanted children so I offered him a divorce but he refused. So we came to an arrangement."

"What sort of arrangement?" Heaton frowned.

"That your father would find a surrogate mother," Lady Heaton told him matter-of-factly.

Sophia's eyes bulged and Heaton gasped. This would have been before test tube babies or anything of the kind.

Lady Heaton gave him an icy smile. "I know. For my husband to father a child by another woman, he would have to do it the old-fashioned way, so to speak."

Heaton's face contorted in disgust. "With whom?"

"An unmarried young woman from the town."

"What is her name?" Heaton demanded.

Sophia strained her ears to hear then almost jumped out of her skin as a door closed frighteningly close to her and Helen began to hum to herself.

"Is everything all right, Sophia?"

Sophia turned and stared in consternation at the housekeeper while hearing footsteps approaching the door. It opened, and Heaton looked first at her, and then at Helen.

"How long have you been there?" he demanded.

"I've only just come up from the kitchen, sir," Helen replied.

He stared down at Sophia and she squirmed. "Come inside."

Silently, she followed him into the library, and the door was closed in Helen's face.

"I'm sorry," she began. "I only wanted to apologise for—"

"I suppose you heard everything?"

"Well…yes." There was no point in lying.

"Do you know Danielle O'Hara at all?"

"Danielle O'Hara?" Sophia repeated slowly.

"Thomas, stop it," Lady Heaton, seated in one of the leather wingback armchairs, snapped at him but he ignored her.

"Well, do you? She may be married now, of course?"

Sophia's stomach contracted and for a horrible moment thought she was going to be sick.

"Ms Nelson?" Heaton grabbed her shoulders to steady her.

"She was Mum's best friend. Her daughter is my best friend."

"Your best friend's mother?" Lady Heaton enquired. "How extraordinary. What a small world."

"Is she definitely my mother?" Heaton demanded, his hands leaving Sophia's shoulders, and sliding down her arms.

"Oh, yes," Lady Heaton replied. "When Stephanie was born we knew she would have to have another child, despite the cost."

"How much?" Heaton added.

"Five thousand pounds. Each."

"Our house cost three thousand pounds," Sophia whispered.

"Yes," Lady Heaton nodded. "It was quite a substantial amount back then but she gave us two beautiful children."

"And she just handed us over?" Heaton was incredulous.

"Yes. No baby, no money. Please believe me, Thomas,

that I love both Stephanie and yourself as though I had borne you myself."

"Were you ever going to tell us?"

"No," Lady Heaton told him. "Your father and I both agreed on that."

"But illnesses?"

His mother waved a hand dismissively. "You were both as strong as an ox. How was I to know that Stephanie would take up with a junkie? I take it that you knew?"

Sophia saw Heaton wince. "Yes, but I only found out on their last visit here."

"I see."

"Do not try and make me feel any worse than I do already," he snapped.

"I could say exactly the same thing," Lady Heaton replied coolly.

"So I have been working all the hours God sends for the past umpteen years to pay for my sister and myself?"

"I'm afraid so. We had to pay her enough to go through with it and then to move away. Your poor father did not have your head for business. We're now on an even keel, aren't we?"

"Just about; now that the farmyard has been turned into a holiday camp."

"Holiday apartments," she corrected him.

"How could you?" he cried, startling Sophia. "How could you stand knowing that your husband was fathering children with another woman?"

"Your father and I both wanted children. And your father needed an heir and thanks to her he got one. You."

With that, Lady Heaton got up from the chair and

calmly walked out of the room. After a moment's uncertainty, Heaton went to the door and let himself out.

Sophia stood in the middle of the floor and felt her cheeks with the palms of her hands. Her cheeks were burning. Her mother had hardly mentioned Danielle at all lately, even though they had been good friends at one time. Had she forgotten Danielle due to the dementia? Or was it because she had known and disapproved?

Sophia turned and fled from the library for a second time, only this time she didn't stop until she had reached her flat, slamming and locking both doors behind her.

Chapter Two

At a quarter past two the following afternoon Sophia was standing nervously at the front door waiting for the first coach party to arrive. She felt rotten. It had been well after four in the morning before she eventually fell asleep and then she woke at seven and didn't manage to get back to sleep again. With Michelle's mum going around and around her head it was little wonder.

"Ms Nelson?" Lord Heaton joined her at the door and she jumped. "I really must apologise for yesterday. It must have been appalling for you."

"No, I—"

"At the moment I seem to have all the tact of a rampaging elephant," he continued. "I am sorry."

"Well, it's understandable."

"I was very angry and I shouldn't have involved you. We'll say no more about it."

She looked sharply up at him. They couldn't just leave it like that. He was Michelle's half-brother. "But—" she began.

"Good." He gave her a bright smile. "Now, would you mind very much if I tagged along on your tour?"

She stared at him in horror, too tired to even try and disguise it. "Well, I…" She could hardly refuse. "No, not at all."

"Thank you. And don't forget, the offer of my tranquilliser guns still stands."

She smiled weakly, hearing the coach approach. Bloody hell. Michelle was right. This was proving to be completely and utterly bizarre. Maybe she should ring her and ask if she could have the bed in the loft conversion back?

An hour and a half later she returned to the kitchen after seeing the group out to Jack in the gardens following quite definitely the worst guided tour she had ever given. First tours were always bad but this had been something spectacularly awful. The group were Americans on their first trip to England and a lively bunch, to put it mildly. It hadn't helped matters that Heaton had stared intently at her all the way through, it seemed, except for a couple of alarmed glances at a woman who was intent on picking everything up. Sophia had to tell her politely that if she dropped something she would have to pay for it. By selling your house, she added silently.

Then, just when she thought that she was finally into her stride, Heaton's smartphone rang, even though she had specifically asked that the visitors please turn them off. The ringtone was the infamous Crazy Frog from a few years ago and she stared at him in astonishment at his lack of taste. Everyone shuffled in annoyance and she blushed and cringed before asking him to put the phone on silent. He turned a vivid shade of scarlet, swore at the screen under his breath and nodded at her, but thankfully did as he was asked. But that wasn't all. He then asked a question which she had to ponder for a moment before answering. What the real visitors had made of it all she could only begin to guess at but unfortunately, they took this as their cue to start questioning her.

"So, what's Lord Heaton like?" was the first question, of course, and her heart sank like a stone.

Sophia met Heaton's grey-blue eyes for a moment. "He's very pleasant. Shall we continue on down to the kitchen for some refreshments?"

"Is he married?"

"Er, no, he isn't."

"You hear that, May?" one woman called. "He's not married. He could be your fourth."

May laughed. "Only if he's rich and handsome. Is he?" she asked a startled Sophia, who glanced at Heaton again. He quickly turned to look at who he was being paired with.

Despite a trim figure, an obvious facelift and dyed blond hair, May was old enough to be Heaton's grandmother. Heaton's eyes bulged and his lips parted in horror. Sophia began to examine her hands and when she raised her head Heaton was gone and she politely but firmly ushered the group down to the kitchen for the refreshments.

Helen reached for a huge jug from a coffee machine and poured her another cup, as Sophia closed the kitchen door and sank down on a chair at the nearest table.

"So? Good? Bad? Indifferent?"

"Nerve-wracking. Lord Heaton came on the tour."

Helen's eyes widened. "Why?"

"I think he was testing me. Could you leave the coffee jug on the table, please? I'm probably going to drink it all."

"On your very first tour?" Helen added, setting the jug

26

down, and Sophia shrugged. "That's very unfair. I thought Lady Heaton had already been on a tour with you?"

"Yes, she has. And me with her. Anyway, it's over now and I can only hope he never does it again."

"Here." Helen passed her a plate. "Have a bun or two. You've earned them."

"Thanks." Taking one, she bit into it and sighed. God, she had earned that. Helen's baking was delicious. "Lovely," she added, with her mouth full.

"What happened yesterday?" Helen asked.

"Oh." She swallowed and took a sip of coffee. "It was just a bit of a misunderstanding," she said, hoping it sounded convincing. "I'm afraid Lord Heaton intimidates me like nobody's business."

"Don't worry." Helen gave her a kind smile. "You'll get used to him."

She saw Helen's smile fade and followed her gaze. Lord Heaton himself was standing in the doorway, looking around the enormous room at the flagstone floor and the wooden tables and chairs as if for the first time.

"It all went very well, didn't it?" he asked her.

No, it was bloody awful. "Yes, very well."

"Mrs Fields?" he added.

"Yes, sir, very well."

"Good," he replied, glancing at Sophia's cup of coffee.

"Would you like a cup?" she asked, seeing that Helen wasn't going to offer.

"Thank you, yes." Pulling out a chair, he sat down and watched her pour.

"Is her Ladyship in the gift shop?" Helen asked him.

"Yes, as far as I'm aware."

"Then, I'll go and see if she would like some tea. Excuse me."

"You didn't need a tranquilliser gun, after all," he said, stirring milk and sugar into the coffee, as Helen left the room.

"No, apart from the lady who couldn't leave anything alone, they were quite…interesting. Although, after you left, that lady did ask whether she could meet Lord Heaton. She had no idea that she'd just been standing next to you."

He frowned. "What on earth for?"

"So she could get her picture taken with you. I think she rather assumed you walked around in a suit of armour." He rolled his eyes and took a sip of coffee. "Then she asked where in the old abbey did the monkeys sleep?"

Curiously, she watched his reaction. He almost spat the coffee out. "The monkeys?" he repeated. "How did you keep a straight face?"

"Not very easily," she admitted. "Have a bun?"

"I think I will, thank you." He selected one and rolled his eyes again. "Monkeys?"

"Monkeys," she confirmed as he bit into the bun, chewed, and swallowed.

"I'm sorry about my phone. I thought I had it on silent but my sister has a habit of adding the worst ringtones she can find to it."

"Not from hospital, surely?" she asked as he took another bite and quickly finished the bun off.

"Knowing Stephanie, she's probably tunnelled out. So, how are you settling in?"

"Very well, thank you." *Considering*. She watched him take another bun. "Did you not have any lunch?" she asked before she could stop herself.

28

He shook his head before swallowing. "I completely forgot. I think Mrs Fields is rather annoyed with me. So, do you think you'll stay?"

She stared at him in surprise. "Yes. Why? Was I expected not to?"

"Well, the salary is ridiculously small."

"No, I mean about…?"

"Apart from that," he said, his eyes telling her not to continue with that subject.

"Well, I have a lovely flat," she said, fighting an urge to tell him not to tell her what she could and couldn't talk about.

"Good." He sighed and peered down at his half-eaten bun. "It's no use."

"What isn't?"

"These buns won't keep me going until seven o'clock," he explained. "I'm starving. I'm going to have to raid the fridge. Would you mind keeping watch?"

"Watch?" she echoed. He was a grown man in his late thirties, not a ten-year-old schoolboy.

He got to his feet before sitting down again. "The fridge is gone. It used to be over there by the sink before the room was done up to look antiquated."

"Is there a pantry or a scullery?"

"Yes, there is. I'll go and check." He got up again and left the room.

Ten minutes passed before she decided to go and find him, meeting him coming up the stone steps from the cellars with a furious expression.

"Did you find it?" she asked, despite knowing the answer.

"No. Where the hell can she have gone with a fridge? I

mean, all I want is a bloody sandwich."

"Come to the flat, I'll make you a sandwich."

He frowned at her and she almost regretted asking him. "There's really no need, I'll find the fridge eventually."

"By the time you've searched the entire house you might have died of starvation. I don't particularly want to find your corpse on tomorrow's tour. Imagine the kind of questions I could get about that?" She smiled. "I bought mature Cheddar cheese and a jar of pickle yesterday."

He pursed his lips. "I haven't had a decent pickle in years. Mrs Fields makes tomato chutney and to be honest, I don't particularly like it. Thank you, a cheese and pickle sandwich would be very nice."

He's shy, she realised, as they crossed the stable yard to the flat. While she made the sandwich he went to her boxes of books, which she had left on the floor.

"You need some shelves," he commented, crouching down. "I'll mention it to Des."

"Thank you." She watched as he held a book away from him to read the title, showing her that he was quite long-sighted. "I've got too many books but I didn't get a chance to get rid of some before I moved. Your sandwich." She put the plate on the dining table.

"Thank you." He sat down and demolished it. "Delicious," he proclaimed, pushing the empty plate away.

"Would you like another?" she asked.

"No, that really was delicious. Thank you."

"Well, I hope you find the fridge."

He smiled and she marvelled at just how much it transformed his face.

"I might just ask Mrs Fields, even though I could really

do with the exercise. I spend far too much time in front of the PC."

"Well, Lady Heaton has decided that Tuesdays are going to be my day off and she will do the tours on those days, so I'm going for a walk up on the moors tomorrow and blow the cobwebs away. You're welcome to come?"

He looked startled and she definitely regretted suggesting it. Was she overstepping the mark? She was 'staff' after all.

"Tomorrow? I don't know…"

"It will be the afternoon," she explained. "I'll be visiting Mum in the morning. Mornings are her best time."

"Do you not have any friends you could ask?"

"Yes," she replied and he stared at her, clearly realising who she meant. "But she works part-time and she has a six-year-old daughter to collect from school. My other friends are in London and told me I was daft to come back up here."

"But your mother?"

"Most of the time, my mum doesn't know who I am," she told him sadly.

He grimaced. "I've put my foot in it again, I'm sorry."

She shook her head and went to her bedroom, returning with a photograph. "Some days, she's as lucid as you and me but this is how I want to remember her after she's gone."

He took the photograph which showed her mother standing proudly beside her father who was in full mining garb, smiling at the camera on the day he retired, and held it away from him. "Yes, I remember your father now."

"He wasn't rude to you, I hope?"

"No, why?" he asked.

"He has certain…views on the…"

"Idle rich?"

31

She flushed. "Something like that."

"Well, I'm neither idle nor rich."

"I didn't mean to offend you. He was livid when I told him that I tended to vote for the Green Party."

"Why, is he a Labour Party supporter?"

"Socialist Labour," she told him. "He's not a big fan of the Labour Party and don't even mention the Conservative Party to him."

He smiled. "We all have our views on the Tories."

"Did you get to sit in the House of Lords?"

"Yes, I did. Once. Just before hereditary peers were kicked out back in 1999. I just wish I'd had the chance to go more often," he added, passing the photograph back to her. "So you'll be visiting your mother tomorrow?"

"Yes. I'll be back here around one to have lunch and to change my clothes."

He nodded and got up from the table. "Thank you for the sandwich."

"You're welcome." She smiled, reaching for the plate. "Oh, before I forget, that friend of mine works in the tourist office in the town."

"Tourist office?"

"Well, since the mining museum and gift shop went up in smoke there was nowhere for any tourists to get information on the area so a tourist office was opened recently. It'll be seasonal until they see how things go. They're setting up a town website, too, I just thought if you sent them some leaflets and the abbey's website address…?"

"I will. Thank you. What do you think of the abbey website, by the way?"

"Very interesting," she replied diplomatically.

"Good."

She saw him out then went to the window to watch him walk to his office. Usually, when she met a new work colleague or even a new boss, she quickly moved on to first name terms, unless they held an extremely senior position or, seemingly, if they had a title. Everyone, she noticed, called him 'sir' or 'his Lordship', or 'your Lordship', but never Thomas, Tommy, Tom, or, heaven forbid, Tommo.

How on earth could she change the rules? Should she even bother to try? How long could she stay here knowing what she did but forbidden to even mention it? In any case, she couldn't reply to his 'Ms Nelson' with a 'Thomas' without being invited to, could she? Apart from that, he was very shy, so teasing him wasn't a very good idea. With a temper like his, it wasn't a very good idea at all. And as to names, well, she had called him 'your Lordship' at their meeting in the library but since then she hadn't really called him anything at all. Her dad would be proud but how long could it go on for?

She went to the boxes of books to stack them neatly out of the way until she got some shelves and stared in horror. Heaton had left the book he'd been looking at on top of its box. It and the others in the box were steamy romance novels belonging to her mother. Mrs Nelson was incapable of reading them now, and Sophia had been reluctant to get rid of them, despite their – how could she put it – interesting content. She picked up the book and stared at its clichéd bare-chested hero on the cover. *Shackled by Love!* Oh, bloody hell. Putting it back in the box, she closed it, covered her face with her hands and shook with embarrassment.

Popping into the bank in the morning before going to the nursing home, she spotted Lady Heaton two ahead of her in the queue. When the older woman walked to the counter, Sophia saw her taking an envelope from her handbag and passing it across the counter. The clerk pulled an enormous bundle of banknotes out and begin to count them. Sophia tried not to stare but couldn't help it, there must have been a couple of thousand pounds there, and she had to be nudged from behind when her own turn came.

Sophia found her mother in her room with her father sitting beside the bed, the *Daily Mirror* on his lap. She watched for a few minutes from the corridor as her father turned the page before realising he and her mother weren't alone.

"Sally," her mother cried. It was clearly a day when her mother was thinking Sophia was her mother's sister and her dad was her brother, even though he was at least forty years dead.

"Hi." She went in and gave her father a kiss then did likewise to her mother. "Hello. I brought you some toiletries – deodorant, shampoo, soap and a few other bits and pieces. I found some fig rolls, too. You can have them with your tea later on. You look well today."

"You do, too. Have you started at Heaton Abbey yet, Sally?" her mother asked, assuming it was Aunt Sally starting work at the abbey and not Sophia. "I'm so glad you decided to come back up here to work. Cornwall always seemed like a million miles away."

"Yes, so am I," Sophia replied, deciding not to correct her mother and cause even more confusion. "I have my own small flat in what used to be the stable block."

"A flat?"

"Converted hayloft," Sophia clarified. "But it is lovely."

"While Lord and Lady Muck live in that huge house."

"I'm in that huge house nearly as much as them now, and the flats really are lovely. There's even wireless internet."

"What?" Her mother frowned.

"The internet without the need for a phone line," Sophia explained.

"They don't have any phones?"

"Yes, they do, but business people…" Sophia tailed off, seeing her mother shrug.

"I don't know what Father would have said to you working there for them."

She glanced sadly at her father, who just shook his head.

"I think you're forgetting that the Heatons owned the mines originally."

"I know they did," Mrs Nelson replied irritably. "But our father did an honest day's work."

"And what do you think I'm doing?" she retorted. "I like it there and I'm not leaving." She sighed. Why did they always end up rowing on her mother's good-ish days? What if she had no more good-ish days? "Have you and Mrs Hartley been watching the tennis?"

"Bits and pieces."

"How is Andy Murray doing?"

"Not bad," she replied, and Sophia smiled. "You've got Father's smile."

"I know. But I think I've got Mother's sense of humour, unfortunately."

Mrs Nelson laughed. "And that's bad, is it?"

"It is when I keep unintentionally teasing Lord Heaton."

Her mother grunted. "Only teasing? You should be taking the 'you know what' out of him. Let him and his like know that they don't rule the roost anymore. He went down the mine once. I remember John Davis giving him the grand tour but it didn't last long, Lord Muck got claustrophobic and had to be taken back up to the surface again. But the son went down instead and asked all sorts of questions, according to William. Must have been reading up on it. William was quite impressed but don't tell anyone that will you?"

"It is the son I'm talking about. Old Lord Heaton's dead."

"Dead?" Mrs Nelson frowned. "When?"

"Oh, a while back, so the son is in charge now."

"But he must be still at school?"

"No, he's in his late thirties."

"What?" Her mother stared at her and Sophia knew that the thick, thick fog was descending again. "How can that be?"

"Shall I get you a cup of tea?"

"…Tea…yes, thanks, Sally."

Sophia nodded and she sat with her parents while her mother drank the tea and ate some of the biscuits. When her father left the room in search of a wheelchair to bring his wife to the television room, Mrs Nelson grabbed her hand.

"What is it?" Sophia asked.

"I need to say something while he's out of the room."

"Okay," she replied hesitantly.

"Promise me that no matter how bad things get and that if you can't get a job, you won't sleep with someone for money."

Sophia stared at her mother in complete astonishment. Was her mother talking to her or to her aunt? "But—"

"Promise me." Mrs Nelson began to squeeze Sophia's hand with her good hand surprisingly tightly. "I've seen the damage it does. Promise me."

"I promise," she replied.

"Good." Her mother released Sophia's hand. "Now, I'll say no more about it."

"But who are you talking about?" she urged.

"I'm not saying anymore."

"Are you talking about Michelle's mum?" she asked and waited for a reaction.

"I'm not saying anymore," her mother replied stubbornly and Sophia sighed.

"You are, aren't you?"

"I'm not saying anymore."

"Okay."

"You are looking for another job, aren't you, Sally?" her mother added.

"I've got another job now."

"Where?"

"Up at Heaton Abbey. I'm the—"

"The abbey?" Mrs Nelson exclaimed. "No."

"Yes…What is it?" she cried as her mother began shaking her head violently. "Mum, stop it, don't do that."

"Not that place. Not that place."

"Mum." She tried to calm her mother. "Mum, stop."

"You get out of that place. You must get out of that place."

Sophia could hear feet running down the corridor and her father and a nurse rushed into the room.

"Mrs Nelson?" The nurse tried to soothe her.

"You must get out of that place. You have to get out."

"Sophia." Her father ordered. "Leave her."

"Why do I have to get out, Mum?" Sophia demanded. "Tell me."

"Sophia. Out. Now."

"Please?" the nurse begged.

Sophia got up and went out into the corridor, kicking the skirting board in frustration. A couple of minutes later her father followed.

"What the hell was that about?" he demanded.

"I don't know. She asked if I had got a job yet and I told her that I was at Heaton Abbey and she just started shouting and shaking her head."

"Right, well, you don't mention the abbey again to her. Do you hear me, Sophia?"

"Yes. I'll just lie as usual. Pretend I'm Sally one day. Pretend I'm her mother the next." She closed her eyes for a moment. "I'm sorry."

"I know," her father said quietly. "Let the nurse calm her down."

"All right."

"You like the abbey, then?" he asked.

"Yes. I did my first tour yesterday."

"What's Lord Heaton like?" Mr Nelson added. "Is he a recluse like everyone says?"

"I don't really know," she replied truthfully. "He seems to work very hard and he doesn't leave the estate much but I don't know if that makes him a recluse."

She drove straight back to the abbey, parking in the stable yard right outside the door to the flat. Stretching, she peered at her white face in the rearview mirror. By now her mother would have completely forgotten she'd been, whether it was in the guise of herself, Sally, or her grandmother, and would be complaining to the staff how she never received any visitors. Tears stung her eyes and she wiped them away before getting out of the car.

"Ms Nelson?"

Hearing Heaton's voice, she blinked furiously before turning to him with a weak smile. "Yes?"

"If you don't mind, I would like to go with you for that walk." Heaton stared at her. "Are you all right?"

"Not really." She gave him a wobbly smile. "But I'll be all right after a good cry."

"Your mother isn't…?"

She shook her head. "No, but—"

"Come into the office?" He extended a hand.

She went inside and he held the swivel office chair for her as she sat down. An invoice lay on the desk but he sat on it.

"She thought I was my aunt today," she explained. "At least I think it was my aunt. My dad is now her brother, she thinks Dad's dead," she added. "It's awful for him."

"Is that why you go up onto the moors? To try and walk and cry it all out of you?"

She glanced up at him in surprise but nodded. "If I don't catch hypothermia in the process."

"If you'd prefer that I didn't come…"

"No, I would like the company, but I mightn't be very good company for you, that's all."

"Well, if you're sure? I'm not exactly stimulating company myself at the moment."

"My mum knew," she announced. "About Danielle."

"Really."

"She's just made me promise never to sleep with anyone for money."

That took him aback a little. "I see."

"Do you? Because when the abbey was mentioned again, she started screaming and shouting and telling me to get out of there."

He grimaced. "She's not likely to…?"

"What? Blurt it out to someone else? I don't know. She has dementia. If I hadn't known, I'd have thought she was rambling – hoped she was rambling."

"I take it that none of Danielle's family know?"

She shrugged. "Not that I know of."

"Then, I think it's best for everyone's sake that this is kept quiet."

"But aren't you even a little bit curious?"

She jumped as the telephone rang. After two rings the answering machine came on.

"Heaton? I know you're there, Heaton, everyone knows that you live in that fucking office." Sophia glanced at the phone and began to squirm with embarrassment. "Pick up, Heaton, you—"

"Excuse me." Heaton leaned across her, picked up the handset and calmly pressed the end call button before putting it down again. "Sorry about that."

Giving him a little smile, she turned to the PC. The screensaver had taken over. It was a slideshow of various Renaissance paintings and he followed her gaze.

"I did History of Art at university," he explained.

"I did notice the book on Renaissance women in the drawer in the library."

"Do you like art at all?" he asked.

"I prefer literature, actually, but I could be persuaded." She cringed as soon as she said it but he nodded.

"Good. If only I had the time to read something worthwhile. I walk into the library and all the books seem to glare at me. If I get through *The Guardian* every so often, I'm doing well."

"You read *The Guardian*?"

"Yes, why?" he inquired lightly. "Should someone like me be reading the *Daily Telegraph*?"

She flushed feeling foolish and irritated that he was able to remain as cool as a cucumber, while she, normally the epitome of calm, was reduced to a red-faced gibbering idiot at the slightest thing. It was hard to believe that this was the same man she had seen in an intense verbal and physical rage. It was hard enough to keep up with her mother's frequent mood swings.

"I'm sorry. It's just that Mum and Dad used to read *The Guardian*. Now she can barely get through the *Daily Mirror*...Dad has to read it to her."

He pulled a sympathetic expression. "I'm sorry," he said simply.

Glancing around the office, she noted how spartanly furnished it was with the only decorative item being a calendar of Renaissance paintings. She squirmed as she caught him watching her.

"I'm sorry, I...er, I was looking for your...er, glasses."

He frowned. "My glasses?"

"I, um...I couldn't help but notice that, um...you're a bit, well, quite a bit long-sighted."

"Long-sighted?"

She nodded. "When you hold something away from you so that you can focus on it properly?"

"Oh, I see. Well, yes, that does seem to be getting worse."

"I think you need to get your eyes tested."

"You think I need glasses?" he asked.

"Well, I'm no optician but, yes, I think you do. Just for reading and close-up work. Has nobody mentioned it to you before?"

"No. I'd better make an appointment, then. Thanks for mentioning it."

She flushed. "Sorry, I didn't mean to—"

"No, I mean it. Thank you."

"Well, I'd better go and eat something." She got up and he slid off the desk. "Thanks for listening."

"Not at all. I'd better show my face for lunch today. I'll see you in about an hour?"

She nodded. "Don't wear jeans, will you? If it rains…"

"I'll find something."

Letting herself into the flat, she blew out her cheeks before going to the cupboard and retrieving a small tin of baked beans. She emptied the contents into a saucepan, turned the gas hob on, then heard her smartphone ringing. Picking it up and glancing at the screen her heart sank. It was Michelle and she swiped the screen to answer.

"You'll never guess who we had an email from at work?" Michelle laughed.

"Who?"

"Your boss."

"You expected him to be still writing on parchment with a quill, or something?" Sophia asked, pressing the speakerphone button and carrying on with preparing her lunch.

"No. Well, maybe not a quill. Did you give him the office email address?"

"Yes, why?" Sophia put two slices of wholegrain brown bread in the toaster and pushed the lever down.

"I just wondered what he was like. It's just that we're bringing out a glossy brochure. It might be the only brochure, glossy or otherwise. We'll see how it goes, but I was wondering if Lord Heaton would mind being interviewed? It would be a big plug for the place and a big scoop for us. Is he a bit…fierce?"

"No, not really," Sophia lied, opening the fridge and taking out a tub of low fat spread. "Well, not all the time. Actually, underneath it all, I think he's a bit shy."

"Shy? Great. He probably won't do it, then?"

"There's no harm in asking. Would you be doing the interview?"

Michelle laughed. "God, no. It'll be Vincent Graves, probably. The brochure was his idea. Pity, though. Is he good-looking?"

Sophia felt herself flush and stirred the baked beans. "Yes, I suppose he is."

"Excellent. Might even get him on the cover. I'll tell Vincent. So, how's it going up there?"

Don't ask. "Very well. The flat's lovely and the tours are no problem." Provided he doesn't come on them. "I've even got the use of the wireless internet connection."

"Have you tried it out yet?"

"No, I'm still unpacking."

"And Lady Heaton? What's she like?"

Where could she start? Best not to even try. Sophia's mind then went back to Lady Heaton's peculiar behaviour as she left the drawing room. And where had all that money come from? She shrugged. No, best not even try.

"She's been pleasant so far."

"You haven't got lost at all, then?"

She just laughed and said goodbye to Michelle as the toast popped up and the beans came to the boil.

She ate then changed into her walking clothes – combat trousers, jumper, and walking boots.

Closing the bedroom door, she saw Heaton crossing the stable yard. It was the first time she had seen him dressed in anything but a suit and she stopped and stared. He was wearing a brown wax jacket with a bottle green jumper underneath, khaki combat-style trousers similar to her own and brown walking boots. She sighed and shook her head. It looked as though he was one of those men who looked fabulous in everything they wore. She reached for her phone, pulled on a waterproof jacket, and grabbed her car keys before going downstairs to join him.

"You'll have to move the seat back," she said as she unlocked the Mini.

He got in and moved the passenger seat so far back that he might as well have been sitting on the back seat. She looked around at him, couldn't help herself, and laughed.

"Sorry. I wanted something small and cheap to run."

He pulled a comical expression. "I was looking to see if you had a sunroof that I could stick my head through. Maybe we should go in the Land Rover?" She nodded and he got out. "I'll just get the keys from Des."

She got out, locked the car, and saw him emerge from Des' office. The two of them crossed the stable yard to the huge Land Rover.

"You'll have to give me directions to where we start from," he said as they got in.

"I will."

Twenty minutes later, he pulled in at a small car park. "I haven't been up here for years. You don't walk too fast, do you?"

"No. There are two routes we can take. Up to what I call the big rock, which is eight kilometres there and back. Or up to the stone circle, which is five. Maybe five would be enough for today?"

He smiled. "I think so."

He locked the Land Rover, they climbed over the stile and walked up onto the footpath which ran through the heather.

"It's lovely up here, isn't it?" He halted after a few paces, hands on hips, and looked around them.

"If you need to stop and catch your breath just say."

"Thanks. I'm not very fit. Walking between my office and the house isn't really enough."

They set off again at a slower pace.

"Where did you go to university?" she asked.

"Cambridge. The Heatons have always gone there. I was halfway through my final year when I learned that my father had cancer. I still have no idea how I got through my finals. The last time I saw him, he didn't know who I was, so I do understand what it's like. Unfortunately, he had run the estate like there was no tomorrow. I went into his study the day after the funeral and found drawers full of bills, invoices, and tax demands. Some went back years. It took years to pay all the creditors and the tax bill was astronomical. I'm still struggling to make ends meet and when the idea was put forward of opening the house up to coach tour parties, well, you saw what I was like. I apologise if I was rude to you. It's no excuse, but I had to go to a funeral that day and I loathe funerals."

"I hate funerals, too, and I wouldn't like complete strangers traipsing through my home so I can sympathise. But there are tours booked for the next three months and Lady Heaton is scheduling additional daily tours because so many coach tour operators want to add the abbey to their list of stops. The way things are going, the abbey will soon have tours all year round."

He nodded. "I know, but I am not dressing up as a monk or in a suit of armour for anyone."

She laughed. "What do people say to you when they ask what you do for a living?"

"When people find out I have a title it is a bit of a conversation killer. I think some people have this idea that lords are all at least fifty, frequent gentleman's clubs, and hunt, shoot and fish. I do none of those things. I was twenty-two when I inherited the title; I've been working to keep the estate afloat ever since and I don't want anything to spoil that."

"It seems to be working, though."

"Yes," he agreed. "Just about."

"Mum and Dad remember when you went down the mine instead of your father when he became claustrophobic."

"Really?" He gave her an incredulous frown. "Good God, I must have been only about twelve or something. I wanted to go down with him but he wouldn't let me. Then, when he had to come back up I asked if I could go and he just waved his hand in agreement."

"Mum said that you asked lots of very good questions and that Dad was impressed. That is a huge compliment from my dad."

"Were you ever down the mine?" he asked.

"No, I was never allowed, and it's far too dangerous now. The nearest I got was the museum. I'd liked to have satisfied my curiosity but I much prefer the open air. Mum's grandfather was killed in a pitfall and I think she always worried that the same would happen to Dad. Now, most of the time she thinks he's dead." She burst into tears. "Oh, God, I'm sorry."

"Come and sit down." Taking her arm, he led her off the path. They sat down in the springy heather and she wiped her eyes. "You have to cry, and let it all out," he told her gently. "I've lost count of the number of times I've locked myself in the library and just…"

He pulled a comical expression as she stared at him. It was hard to imagine him crying his eyes out but who knows how he reacted when he left the library after learning that his real mother was a complete stranger.

"I used to cry for my family," he continued. "Me; the bills that still needed paying; the career I never had; the nightmare of possibly having to sell the estate; the fact that I have no life…that sort of thing. You have your cry then you dust yourself down and, in my case, head back out to the office."

"My friends in London didn't want me to come back up here." She fished a handkerchief out of a pocket and blew her nose. "But I had to, she's my mum. She and Dad are all I've got left and I know I'm quickly losing her. This morning she thought I was Sally, her sister. I'm really dreading a time when she forgets that I exist."

"Do you not have any other family?" he asked.

"Mum's brother, Martin, died when he was twenty," she explained. "Sally lives in Cornwall. They were never close, anyway. Dad was an only child."

"So why did you go to live in London?"

"I followed a man down there." She shook her head at her stupidity. "I thought I'd found 'the one' at long last and I thought I'd be able to persuade Dad to come and live in London, even though I knew deep down that he'd never leave Mum up here and he'd never move her down there. Anyway, needless to say, it didn't work out between Lee and me and I was packing up down there when I got a phone call telling me that Dad had fallen and badly broken his arm and he couldn't live on his own anymore. That was six months ago. He said himself that he should go into sheltered accommodation so he sold the house and he's in The Beeches Complex now. Finding a job which has a flat going with it is fantastic." She smiled. "Do you feel like going on?"

He returned a smile. "To be honest, I'd rather sit here and talk to you. I haven't had a conversation about anything but estate business in…I don't know how long."

"To be honest, I think you work too hard."

He nodded. "I think you're right. But I have to work hard. I'm not going to be remembered as the Heaton who had to sell up. And if that means coach parties and teas, then it means coach parties and teas."

"Did you find the fridge in the end?"

He rolled his remarkable eyes. "Yes. It's now built into the kitchen cupboards in the pantry. Integrated, I think Mrs Fields called it, so no wonder I couldn't find it."

"At least you can raid it now," she teased.

He shrugged. "There's no Branston Pickle."

"I can make you a sandwich if you get a craving."

"I might just take you up on that."

She smiled and looked away, hoping that he couldn't see her blush.

"I rang the opticians in the town," he announced and she turned back. "They gave me an appointment for tomorrow morning."

"Oh. Good."

"I hope I don't pick the most hideous frames there."

"Would you like me to come with you?" she asked, hoping she wasn't overstepping the mark, and he failed to hide his relief at her offer.

"Thank you. I'd welcome another opinion. Even if I could ask Stephanie, God knows what I'd end up getting."

"I suppose I should have mentioned it before," she began. "Properly, I mean. But I was sorry to hear about Stephanie. A friend of mine in London lost a baby. It was awful."

"I suppose you've also heard that it was because her boyfriend hits her?" Sophia nodded. "She won't leave him. I've begged her, Lady Heaton has begged her, her friends have begged her, but she won't. I'm terrified that one day he will kill her. She went home to her apartment the other day, refused my offer of coming here for a bit. Stubborn to the last."

"I take it she doesn't know?" she asked.

"No. And that's the way it's going to be." He sighed. "Look, I'm sorry you're caught up in all of this."

"I have to say this: I just can't help but feel you're burying your head in the sand over it all."

"Well, what can I do?" he demanded. "Turn up on your

friend's doorstep and introduce myself?"

"Her name's Michelle," she told him.

"Michelle's doorstep, then. Her whole family could fall apart. It sounds dramatic but if it's anything like what's happened between Lady Heaton and me—" He stopped abruptly realising he'd said more than he had intended to. "For now," he continued quietly. "I just want to try and get my head around it all and let sleeping dogs lie."

She shrugged sadly. "All right."

"We passed a pub about a mile back," he said, jabbing a thumb back in the direction of the road. "Would you like a coffee?"

"I would love a coffee, thank you."

"Good. I'm freezing."

"Why didn't you say?"

He just shrugged comically and they returned to the Land Rover.

There was an open fire in the pub and she chose the nearest table while he went to the bar to order the coffees. She shrugged off her jacket and hung it on the back of her chair then turned hearing raised voices.

"Yeah, well, I don't like your attitude either, mate," the barman retorted.

"All I want are two coffees," Heaton replied. "Now am I going to get them or do I have to contact the brewery to complain about their staff?"

"Fuck off."

"Do you usually swear in front of a lady?" Heaton demanded.

"A lady? Where?"

To her astonishment, Heaton lunged across the bar and

caught the barman by his collar.

"Hey, stop." She ran over to them. "Stop it. Let him go."

Reluctantly, Heaton did as he was told. "Sorry, but we'll have to go somewhere else."

"No, we won't. Go and sit down, please." She waited until he had sat down before smiling at the barman. "Sorry about that. Two coffees please."

"Sophia?" the barman asked and she frowned. "Remember me? Ed Sibley? We were in the same year at St Margaret's Grammar School."

She laughed. "Yes. God, you've grown a bit."

"So have you."

Charming. "So, could I have two coffees?"

Ed leaned forward. "You're not with him, are you?"

"We've just been for a walk and we're cold so, two coffees, please?"

"But you do know who he is?" Ed added.

She nodded. "Yes, and even lords are human and need to keep warm."

"Yeah, but—"

"Look, all we want is a bloody coffee each, not a debate on the class system."

"All right." Ed's hands flew into the air in a defensive gesture. "Keep your hair on."

"I'll try." She returned to the table and sat down. Heaton was holding his hands out to the fire. "It's all right, we're not going to get thrown out."

"Do you know him?"

"Unfortunately, I was at school with him. He didn't go on to A-Levels but quite a few other idiots did." The coffee tray was brought to them and placed on the table with a bit of a bang. "Thanks, Ed." He grunted and left them and she pulled a face. "Well, he won't be getting a tip. Milk and sugar?"

"Milk, one sugar, please," he replied and watched as she added them. "Thank you." He lifted the cup and saucer and stirred the contents.

"Do you usually try to strangle anyone who annoys you?" she asked as casually as she could.

He sighed. "No, not everyone. I'm sorry, that was a bit Neanderthal of me."

A bit? "Do you get that a lot?"

"I usually know where to avoid," he replied evasively.

"Are you warmer now?"

"Much warmer, thank you."

"Next week," she began. "Do you think you'll be up to the full five-kilometre walk?"

He put his cup and saucer down on the table. "You mean, you're willing to risk the other four and three-quarter kilometres with me?"

She smiled. "I might if you're up to it. I'd have to draw the line at giving you a fireman's lift back down off the moor, though."

"I don't think that will be necessary. And yes, I think I will be up to five kilometres as long as I wear some warmer clothes."

They finished their coffees and she got up to go and pay. "Won't be a minute."

"No, I'll pay," he protested.

"I think you'd better stay away from Ed, don't you think?"

A flicker of what might have been annoyance crossed his

face but he nodded and she went to the bar.

"You've got a strange taste in men," Ed commented as she passed him a five-pound note.

"Oh, I wouldn't say that. I turned you down, remember?" She followed Heaton outside and they drove back to the abbey in silence. "Have I offended you?" she asked as they got out.

"No, not at all."

"I sometimes speak without thinking."

"You've got every right to. No, it's me. I sometimes act without thinking. It's nothing you've done." He gave her a rueful smile. "I'd better go and change. I'll call for you in the morning."

Just as she thought she was, at last, bringing him out of himself, he retreats back into his shell. She watched him go into the house before crossing the stable yard to her flat. He was certainly explosive in a way Lee had never been, but did it worry her? She wasn't sure. Most of the time he seemed to hide behind what she was beginning to call his 'Lord of the Manor' persona. But there were occasional glimpses of a softer, more gentle side. Maybe she should do what her Mum, Dad, and practically everyone she knew would do and just judge him by his title and principles and have as little to do with him as possible. But she couldn't. There was now absolutely no denying that she found him incredibly attractive. Was it because of that or the fear of opening a huge Pandora's box that she was doing as she was told and keeping quiet? Both, probably, and that did worry her because she really didn't know what to do about it.

Chapter Three

Heaton knocked at the door of the flat at ten thirty in the morning. Sophia grabbed her handbag, went downstairs, and opened the door.

He gave her a weak smile. "I don't know why I'm nervous, it's only an eye test."

"I hate the dentist," she told him, stepping outside and closing the door. "But it has to be done."

"Yes." He pulled a bunch of keys from a trouser pocket. "I suppose it's an age thing. Getting glasses means getting old."

"Did your father wear reading glasses?" she asked, following him across the stable yard to the Land Rover.

"Yes, but he started wearing them when he was a lot older than me."

"Well, it still could be genetic. And glasses aren't that bad. Can be quite sexy, really." She bit the inside of her cheek in horror. *Shut up, Sophia.*

"Well, I'll take your word for it," he said, unlocking the Land Rover.

At the optician's, she went to study the frames display while Heaton went for the eye test, trying not to think about the female optician now gazing into his eyes. And getting paid for it. God, which frames? Ones which made him look like his grandfather's grandfather? Or ones which would probably make him look even sexier and slightly vulnerable and she wouldn't be able to look at him without dropping something? Was there something – anything – in between?

"You were right about my eyesight." She heard his voice, turned and he gave her a sorry smile. "Well, we'd better choose some frames." He reached for a plastic pair and put them on, peered at himself in the mirror and recoiled. "God, no."

"I think this is the Senior Citizen's section," she whispered. "Have a look at these over here."

"What about these?" He put on a large round pair and she clapped a hand to her mouth. "No?"

"Well, they're fine for Harry Potter."

"All right." He put them back, reached for some small silver metal frames, and put them on. "Well?"

"No. Too John Lennon. Not that there's anything wrong with John Lennon," she added quickly. "But…"

"But they don't suit me?"

Not in a million years. "Um, no."

"Okay, your turn." He swept an arm at the vast array of frames.

"Oh. Well." She reached for some black metal frames. "Try these."

Taking them from her, he turned them over. "Apparently, you can squash these and they bounce back into shape. Could be useful when I fall asleep face down on the PC keyboard." He put them on, turned to her, and she stared. Sexy yet vulnerable, what more could you want? "Ms Nelson?"

"They're very nice," she managed to get out. "Not too big, not too small, and…they bounce back into shape."

Turning back to the mirror, he pulled a comical face at himself, then turned back to her. "Yes?"

She smiled and nodded. "Yes."

"Good. Thank you for this." He gave her a relieved smile before taking the frames to the optician for measurements and to discuss the various types of lenses. Sophia tried on a few frames while she waited, thankful she had near-perfect eyesight. Seeing him approach in the mirror, she replaced some bright red frames on the stand which clashed terribly with her hair and turned. "Coffee?" Heaton suggested. "And I'll definitely pay this time." They crossed the street to a coffee shop. "What would you like?"

"An espresso, please," she said and walked to a table at the back of the shop.

He returned with two tiny cups and saucers and sat down. "Small but lethal. Thank God that's over."

"It wasn't that much of an ordeal, was it?" she asked.

"No, I suppose not," he replied as he emptied a sachet of sugar into his cup and stirred it. "Even if I did think I could look good in Harry Potter glasses," he said, glancing around the coffee shop. "Is this place new?"

"It's been here about a year, apparently."

He rolled his eyes. "I come into town to go to the bank and that's it. Shows, doesn't it?"

"I hardly recognised the town centre when I came back from London, thanks to the regeneration plan."

"Do you miss London?" he asked and took a sip of coffee.

"I miss being close to the clothes shops, bookshops, theatres, that sort of thing. It's a bit of a trek to Leeds from here but before I got the job I'd started to go a couple of times a month to get it out of my system. I'd walk around the shops instead of the moor for a change."

He gave a sad little smile. "I really need to get out more. People must think I'm a recluse."

Sophia replied with what she hoped was a dismissive smile and reached for her coffee cup.

That evening she unpacked her laptop, connected to the heatonabbeyhouse wireless network and went to her emails. The first was from Michelle.

> *Hi Sophia*
> *I'm at work and bored so I thought I'd drop you an email.*
> *I've just been on a tour of the net and I ended up on oldschoolfriends.com*
> *Guess what Jill Richardson is doing now? She's a nun.*
> *Email me sometime.*
> *Michelle*

A nun? Sophia rolled her eyes and clicked on 'Reply'.

> *Hi Michelle*
> *A nun, eh? Can't say that surprises me, she always was a sanctimonious cow. Hope it's a silent order.*
> *Bye for now.*
> *Sophia*

She did a search for oldschoolfriends.com and clicked on the Workplaces link and typed in Connolly's and Leeds. A kind person had added all the names of the employees between 1970 and 1980. Both her mother and Danielle were listed. Unfortunately, there were no photographs.

She got up and went to the fridge and poured herself a glass of orange juice. She had stuck Heaton's business card to the door with a magnet and lifted it off. She returned to the laptop and typed in the URL of Heaton Abbey House and clicked on the Contact Us link. The email address was a general info@heatonabbeyhouse.co.uk while on the card the email address was thomas.heaton@heatonabbeyhouse.co.uk. It must be his personal email address.

She opened a new email and typed it in then sat staring at it for at least five minutes before starting to type.

Dear Lord Heaton

Please find attached a photo of Danielle. It was taken at Michelle's wedding in 2009. Danielle is on the left in blue. The other lady is Tony's mother.

I don't know if you've ever been on the oldschoolfriends.com website but they have a section for Workplaces. Both my mum and Danielle worked in the office at an engineering firm called Connolly's in Leeds. No photos sadly.

If you have any questions, please ask, and I'll do my best to answer them.

Sincerely

Sophia Nelson

She attached the photograph, clicked on send and blew out her cheeks, hoping that she wouldn't live to regret it.

The following evening she was astonished to receive a reply from Heaton.

Dear Ms Nelson

Thank you for sending me the photograph.

I did have a look on the oldschoolriends.com site and typed in Danielle O'Hara's name but there were over 100 matches and I don't know where she went to school so that was a bit of a non-starter but thank you for your help, anyway.

All this is very hard for me, as you can appreciate, so thank you for being so understanding.

Kind regards

Thomas Heaton

Blood rushed into her face and she immediately saved the email to her desktop.

Sophia saw very little of Heaton to speak to over the next few days and he made no attempt to seek her out and speak to her. She wished that he had as she'd seen Lady Heaton behaving oddly again. She didn't really know what to do about that either, how to broach the subject, or even if she should at all.

Over a post-tour coffee in the kitchen, a visitor had asked if he could see one of the portraits again so she had taken him back up to the hall. While they were there, one of the drawing room doors had opened; Lady Heaton had stuck her head out and surveyed the hall suspiciously. Seeing Sophia and the visitor she had frowned, retreated and the door banged closed. The visitor had given Sophia a funny look and all she could do was shrug and hope that he would put it down to aristocratic eccentricity. Lady Heaton had never mentioned the scene in the library so, naturally, neither had she but this behaviour was down to something else. Clearly, Lady Heaton had expected her to be in the kitchen with the tour group and Heaton in his office as per usual. Why? What else was going on?

Like the angry telephone caller had said, Heaton did more or less live in his office and was often still there until well after midnight. On Monday evening, Sophia turned off the television and, as was becoming a habit, went to the window and peered out through the curtains. Yes, he was still there. She reached for a jacket, went downstairs and across the stable yard, and knocked at the office door.

"Yes?"

She opened the door and stared. He was wearing the new glasses. Oh, God, maybe he should have got the Harry Potter ones instead. "I, er…I was just wondering whether you ever slept?"

He smiled, took off the glasses, and rubbed his eyes. "Sometimes."

"Well, you should give it a try, which is why I didn't bring you a coffee. When did you get the glasses?"

"This morning," he replied, folding the arms behind the lenses, before putting them down on the desk. "They're terrific, actually. My eyes don't feel nearly as tired."

"Good. Well, I'd still give sleep a try. And I was also wondering if you were still coming to the moors tomorrow?"

His eyebrows shot up. "Tomorrow is Tuesday?"

She nodded. "Do you ever take a full day off?" He pulled a comical expression, which gave her her answer. "And when was the last time you had a holiday?"

"A holiday? You'll have to remind me what that is. When were you last on a holiday?"

"Five years ago," she told him. "Lee and I had a week in the Canary Islands."

"You were with him a while, then?"

"Six years in all. Too long."

He nodded. "You'll be going to see your mother in the morning?"

"Yes, and I'll be doing the five-kilometre walk in the afternoon. I'm very predictable."

"I don't know what that makes me, then." He got up and stretched. "I'd like to come to the moors very much. I'll try to keep my temper under control this time."

"I could bring a flask of coffee?" she suggested. "So we won't have to go near a pub. Ed was an idiot at school and it looks as though he hasn't changed a bit."

"That's still no excuse for my behaviour. It spoiled the whole afternoon."

"No, it didn't."

"Well…" he began but tailed off and shut the PC down. "The Land Rover again?"

"Oh." She laughed. "Yes, I suppose so. My car definitely doesn't have a sunroof."

"Thank you for your email."

She flushed and closed the office door. "Tell me if I'm interfering."

He gave her a weak smile and shook his head. "One thing you said has made me think, though."

"Oh?"

"What you said about every family in the town having an ancestor who was a miner. I can't very well meet her but I

61

want to try and find out about Danielle's family and ancestry. Will you help me?"

Her heart began to thump. "Are you sure you want to do that? Get your head around the fact that she's your mother, yes, but delve into her family and family tree? I don't know…"

"What, you think I'm such a snob that I'll hate what we'll find?"

"No," she exclaimed. "No, not at all. I just wonder now if it might be better to let sleeping dogs lie."

"I know she's my mother whether I like it or not." He sighed. "I just feel as if the rug has been pulled out from under my feet. And I am curious, I can't help it. I've always known where I've come from, who I'm descended from. But now…"

"Okay." She relented. "But we'll have to be careful. Michelle must never find out. Never." He nodded. "Danielle went to the same school as Michelle and me. St Margaret's Grammar School. It should narrow the Danielle O'Haras down a bit."

"Should do, I couldn't believe how many there were."

"Have you looked on the internet at all before?" she asked. "For genealogy in general, I mean? When Mum and Dad started the family tree, they interrogated Mum's aunt. You're supposed to start with the family to see what they know and what documents they might have but, well, in this case, it's impossible, so we'll just have to do it the wrong way and the internet seems the best place to start."

"I've never used the internet much," he admitted. "Surfing-wise, I mean. I only use it for emails, really. I put 'genealogy' into a search engine and millions of sites came up."

"It's second only to porn search-wise. You just have to be more specific."

He nodded. "I must look into it. How far did you get back with your family?"

"Well, Mum and Dad did it more than me. Once she was diagnosed with dementia she insisted on doing a family tree and telling Dad and me everything she knew. They eventually got back to the mid-eighteenth century before she had the stroke. We bought a genealogy computer program and I inputted everything and printed it out and had it bound nicely for them, documents and all. Who else uses this computer?"

"Why?" he asked, giving it a quick glance.

"Well, if Des uses it, he might wonder why you're so interested in Danielle."

"Oh, I see. Well, he does use the internet here sometimes. He's in between computers at the moment."

"We'd better use my laptop, then."

"Thank you." He smiled. "Where does she live? Danielle?"

"London. I'll tell you a bit about her. Her husband's called Don. They have a son and a daughter, Michelle and Peter. Michelle is the same age as me. Thirty-three. Peter is a year younger. Danielle moved to London from Leeds when she got married, not long after Mum and Dad married in October 1980. Michelle was up here all the time visiting her grandparents so eventually, she was sent to school here. She and Tony met at school. He was in the year above us."

"I was born in May 1976," he told her. "That's what it says on my birth certificate, anyway. But it has the woman I thought was my mother down as my mother, so I'm not taking anything as the truth."

She nodded. "I really don't know how Danielle kept it a secret."

"What do you think my half-brother and sister would make of me?"

"I have absolutely no idea," she replied truthfully. "Listen. You must also never forget the fact that what happened was illegal. We have to be very careful about everything."

He sighed. "I know. It's a bloody mess."

"Yes. We'll make a proper start tomorrow evening?"

He nodded. "Thank you. Goodnight, then."

"Goodnight."

Stopped at a red light while driving through the town to the nursing home the following morning, she saw Lady Heaton boarding a bus for Leeds carrying a large cardboard box. What was in the box, she wondered, as the light turned green?

Her mother was having one of her relatively good spells but how long it would last she didn't know. Every time she saw her she looked even more frail than the time before.

"I've picked some flowers for you." She placed the flowers in the vase on the windowsill, skipping over the fact that it was actually Lady Heaton who had picked them from the walled garden. "They're lovely, aren't they?"

"Yes, lovely. Have you started at the abbey yet?"

"I…" She shot a glance at her father, who pulled a face and shrugged. "Yes, I have."

"What's it like?"

"Lovely. I've taken some pictures of the house, gardens and flat. I've written what and where they are on the back of them." She left the envelope, which she was going to have given to her father, on the bedside locker. "Lord Heaton remembers you and Dad from the opening of the museum and sends his regards."

"Regards?" Her mother frowned.

"Yes. And I'm going walking with him on the moors this afternoon."

"Why?"

She smiled. "Because he needs the exercise." And I want to spend some more time with him.

"Well, be careful. The man isn't getting any younger."

Her smile faded. "It's not old Lord Heaton, Mum, it's his son."

"His son?" Mrs Nelson repeated. "How old is he?"

"He's in his late thirties."

"Thirties?" her mother exclaimed.

"Yes. How are you feeling in general?" Sophia asked in an effort to change the subject.

"All right, I suppose. Tired. How's Sophia? Haven't heard from her in months. That's London for you, I suppose."

"Sophia's fine," she replied.

"She's not still with that fool of a boyfriend, is she?"

Sophia shook her head. "No, they split up a while back."

"A while back? Has she a new boyfriend, then?"

"No," she said quietly. "There's no-one new."

She was filling the flask with coffee after lunch when she heard a knock at the door of the flat. "I won't be a moment," she called, putting the lid on the flask. She placed the flask in a rucksack, grabbed her mobile phone, jacket, and keys then left the flat. She found Heaton waiting outside.

"How was your mother?" he asked.

She shrugged. "She thought I was my mum's sister again. How many pullovers have you got on?"

He laughed. "Two."

This time they made it as far as the stone circle. They sat down behind one of the upright stones out of the wind; she opened the flask and passed him one of the plastic cups.

"It's coffee," she told him as she poured.

"Thank you."

"So, do you think you'll make it back to the Land Rover?" she asked, putting the flask down.

He gave a short laugh. "Yes, I think so. I've been meaning to do this for ages. Get fit, I mean. I used to smoke twenty to thirty cigarettes a day up until two years ago and unfortunately, I started again recently."

She stared at him in surprise. "But your father?"

"I know." He grimaced. "I get such cravings, though."

"I threw up after my one and only cigarette. I thought that if that's what they do to me only after a couple of puffs…"

"They're disgusting things but I can't help it." He drank the coffee and passed the cup back to her. "Thank you. Call of nature, excuse me."

He got up and she finished her coffee, returned the flask to her rucksack, and rested her head back against the stone.

"Have you ever fallen asleep up here?" She heard his voice and opened her eyes as he sat down again.

"Almost. Last summer I nearly nodded off. I bet you've often slept in the office."

He smiled. "Oh, yes, many times. I got a letter yesterday

from the local tourist office. They're bringing out a brochure to try and attract more tourists into this area and they want to interview me." He cringed. "It will be great publicity for the estate but I'm really afraid that I'll come across as an idiot."

"An idiot?" she repeated.

"I've never been interviewed before," he explained. "As Lord Heaton, I mean. I've no idea what I could be asked. I've opened the estate up because it needs the money, it's just that I don't really want the world to know that. I know that it needs to pay for itself in a different way now but...oh, I don't know."

"Well, say that, and tell them what it's like to have a title in this day and age. I know that they don't expect you to walk around in a suit of armour but tell them how hard you work."

"Then stop talking about myself and start plugging the place?" he finished.

She nodded then jumped as her phone rang. She pulled it out of her pocket and looked at the screen. It was the nursing home. Her heart pounded as she answered. "Sophia Nelson speaking."

"Ms Nelson, this is Fiona Mead at Rich Hill."

"Yes," she whispered.

"Ms Nelson, would it be possible for you to come straight here?"

She met Heaton's eyes. "Mum's dead, isn't she?"

"Yes, I'm afraid she is. I'm so very sorry."

"I'll be there as soon as I can." She ended the call, went to get up, but her legs wouldn't hold her. Heaton caught her and gently lowered her down onto the grass. "Mum's dead," she croaked.

The next few hours were a complete haze. How Heaton got her back to the Land Rover, she never knew, but he had taken complete charge of her, she realised, as she sat in her father's house with a glass of whisky in her hand. First, he brought her to the nursing home, where they had spoken to the clinical director, who informed them that her father had been with her mother when she died and had just left. Sophia saw her mother and kissed her goodbye before Heaton brought her to The Beeches. Her father struggled up from a chair and embraced her before staring rudely at Heaton.

"Dad, this is Lord Heaton. Lord Heaton, this is my father, William Nelson."

"My deepest condolences, Mr Nelson."

"Thank you."

"The funeral?" she said suddenly.

"Do you have a family undertaker?" Heaton asked gently.

She frowned. "A family undertaker?"

"Yes. What is the firm's name?"

"McKenzie Brothers," her father replied. "Buried my parents."

He nodded. "A good firm. They're our family undertakers, too. Would you like me to ring them and ask that someone call here in the morning? Or would you prefer to go to their office?"

"If someone could come here, please. The telephone and telephone directory are on the table in the hall."

"I won't be long," he said and left the room.

Going to her father, she crouched down and squeezed his hands. "I'm so sorry I wasn't there."

"Don't be silly, you couldn't be there all day every day."

"I know but…" She sighed. "Do you want a drink, too?"

"I don't think so, no. Sophia, you must promise me something?"

"If I can," she replied warily.

"Don't leave it too long before you have children. Your mum and I left it too late and now look."

"Dad…"

"I mean it." He was adamant. "We were old parents, more like grandparents."

"No."

"You'd have liked brothers and sisters, I know. You and Lord Heaton are being very kind. He's not really what I expected."

"No?"

They both looked up as Heaton came back into the room.

"Mr McKenzie will be here at ten in the morning."

"Thank you." She got up and gave him a weak smile. "I'll go and find the sleeping bag."

"No, you go back to the abbey," her father told her and she shook her head. She couldn't leave him here on his own.

"But, Dad?"

"I mean it, Sophia. I want to be on my own."

"No, Dad."

"Yes." He was insistent and her heart sank. "I'll see you in the morning."

Heaton accompanied her to the door of her flat. "I'll ask Mrs Fields to call over later to you with some dinner."

"Thank you," she said, pulling her keys out of her jacket pocket. "You've been so very kind."

"If you need anything, I'll be in the office."

She nodded and opened the door. She climbed the stairs to the flat, closed the door behind her, and wept.

Helen Fields called just after seven o'clock with a plate of steak and kidney pie. Sophia wasn't feeling at all hungry but it seemed as though Helen was going to sit and make sure she ate it all. She just about managed it, thanked Helen, then saw her to the door. Going to her bedroom, she sat on the bed with her phone and rang Michelle.

"Michelle?"

"Sophia? How are you?"

"Not good," she replied in a shaky voice. "Mum died today."

"Oh, God, no," Michelle exclaimed. "Oh, Sophia, I am so sorry."

"Thanks. Another stroke. Poor Mum."

"Yes. Would you like me to come over?"

She heard a loud sniff-like sound in the background as Michelle was speaking. "What's that noise?"

"Cathy. She's got a bad cold. Been off school the past three days."

"No, stay there. Poor little thing. Say hello from me?"

"I will. Do you need a hand with the funeral arrangements?"

"No, someone from McKenzie's is coming to Dad's in the morning."

"Okay. Soph, I'm so sorry."

"Thanks. Could you let your mum know? It doesn't matter if she can't come," she added quickly. "Just if you could let her know?"

"Yes, I'll tell her. They were good friends, your mum and

mine. Your mum was always so good to me. I'm so sorry."

"I know. I just can't believe she's gone."

At a quarter to three in the morning, she woke up needing to go to the bathroom. Switching the light on in the living area, she almost jumped out of her skin when she realised she wasn't alone. Heaton was fast asleep in one of the armchairs.

She went to the bathroom then back to her bedroom and retrieved a blanket from the top of the wardrobe. Carefully, she draped the blanket over him but he was so sound asleep he didn't even stir. She watched him curiously for a few moments, breathing slowly and deeply, a growth of dark stubble on his cheeks. How long had he been there? She went back to bed and switched off the light, feeling relieved and comforted that he was nearby.

She got up at half past eight in the morning, saw that Heaton was still in the armchair in the living area, and went to the electric kettle.

As if realising himself that he wasn't alone, he stretched and opened his eyes. "What time is it?" he asked groggily.

"Half past eight."

He nodded and fixed his eyes on her. She flushed, pulled her bathrobe around her, and switched the kettle on.

"I called here at eight last night. Mrs Fields was on her way out. I must have fallen asleep," he explained, peering down at the blanket with some surprise. "Thank you for this."

"Tea or coffee?"

"Whatever you're having."

She reached for the coffee jar. "I'm afraid I've only got cornflakes."

"Have you cried yet?" he interrupted softly, getting up and leaning towards her on the breakfast bar.

She nodded. "Yes, I have. Or would you prefer toast?"

"I really don't mind." She looked up at him in despair and he shrugged. "Toast, then."

She felt him watch her make the breakfast then he pulled out a stool and sat next to her at the breakfast bar.

"I can't remember much of yesterday afternoon so thank you for all you did." She began to smear low-fat spread onto a slice of toast. "And for staying last night."

"Not at all. Glad I could help. Where will your mother be buried?" he asked.

"St Margaret's Churchyard. Most of my family are up there."

"Is there anyone you have to notify?" he added.

"Mum's sister, Sally. Mum and Dad's friends at the rugby club. They were very good, going to see her regularly. Dad and I'll probably plan to have a few drinks there with them after the funeral."

And so it was arranged. After driving her father and herself to the church in a fabulous Jaguar which had belonged to his father, Heaton sat in a pew at the back of the church. Again, it was comforting to know that he was there with them. After the burial, he drove them to the rugby club where she and her father were quickly surrounded by their friends and her father's former work colleagues.

"…And then at the opening of the Mining Museum when you went on and on and on for twenty-five minutes." Gavin, an old school friend of hers, laughed.

Sophia and her father smiled at the memory.

"Who was it that had to go up and tell your dad that

Lord Heaton was making a speech, too?" Gavin asked.

"That was Mum," she replied. "I was still in London and don't think anyone else dared to."

"Your poor mum."

"Yes."

"What will you do now, Sophia?" Gavin asked. "Go back to London?"

"No." Following Gavin to the bar, she accepted a drink from him. "I can't leave Dad."

"I heard you were up at the abbey? Is that true?"

"Yes, I'm the tour guide."

"What did your dad say to that?"

She smiled and looked for him. He was walking with an old friend to two vacant stools further along the bar. "Not much."

"Not much of a fan of the Heatons, is he?"

She quickly glanced around for Heaton. She found him in a dark corner nursing what looked like an orange juice. Strangely enough, no-one seemed to notice he was there. "No, not really. But I like it there."

"You do?" Gavin's eyebrows shot up.

"Yes. I have a good job and a lovely flat."

"But the Heatons?"

"What about them?" she demanded. "Lady Heaton is very pleasant and so is Lord Heaton. Unless you know something I don't?"

Gavin shrugged. "He seems to be a bit of a recluse."

"He works very hard to keep the place going."

"He could give the place to the National Trust or English Heritage and buy a nice semi somewhere."

Somehow she couldn't really see Heaton in a nice semi-detached house anywhere. "It's been in his family since the dissolution of the monasteries, Gavin. I think it's the last thing he'd want to do."

"So it's coach parties, then?"

She nodded. "Yes, and they're proving very popular."

"I'd love to hear your dad's views on you working up there."

"Yes, well, I've got to have a job, haven't I?" she cried and everyone's head turned. She flushed. "Sorry."

"Ms Nelson?" She heard Heaton's voice and turned. "Are you all right?"

"What the hell is he doing here?" Tony muttered loudly from a little further along the bar and, beside him, her father coughed in embarrassment.

"Lord Heaton was kind enough to drive Dad and me today," she explained. "He's been very kind."

"I bet he has," another voice muttered.

She saw Heaton tense, quickly put a hand on his arm, and felt him relax.

"Tony, Gavin, this is Lord Heaton. Lord Heaton – Tony Giles and Gavin Vickery. Tony is married to my best friend Michelle. Michelle couldn't come as Cathy, their daughter, is ill. Gavin's dad used to work with my dad at the mine."

"I bet you've never been in here for a drink before?" Gavin asked him.

Heaton tore his eyes away from Tony. "No, I can't say that I have. My father used to go to The Swan occasionally."

"The Swan?" Gavin echoed. "Very nice. And what about you?"

"I'm afraid I don't really have the time."

"No, I don't really have you down as a pint of bitter man. Maybe a gin and tonic?"

"Whisky, actually," Heaton told him.

"Whisky, eh? Something like Glenmorangie? Laphroaig?"

Heaton smiled. "As long as it's a single malt, I don't mind."

"As long as it's a whisky, I don't mind," Gavin grinned.

She cringed and Tony shuffled uncomfortably. Further along the bar, her father just stared at them stony-faced.

"Can I get you one?" Heaton offered nevertheless. "Ms Nelson?"

"Thank you, but I'm fine with this." She held up her glass and gave Gavin a hard look.

"No, thanks," Gavin mumbled. "I have to drive home."

Heaton nodded. "Good to have met you both. Excuse me."

"This club is members only," someone said loudly and she looked over in the voice's direction.

"Well, in that case, I should leave, too, seeing as when I last checked I wasn't a member or a rugby player either."

She heard a harrumph and no more was said. She watched as Gavin's eyes followed Heaton back to the table in the corner.

"Well."

"Gavin?"

Reluctantly, he turned back to her. "Very nice." He laughed at her surprised expression. "You didn't know I was gay, then?"

She flushed. "No."

"He's not...?"

Her flush deepened. She hoped not but she had no idea. "I really don't know. It's not really the sort of thing you ask your employer."

"You could ask him on my behalf, though," he suggested.

"I don't think so, Gavin. I like my job."

"Sorry. Didn't realise I was treading on your toes."

"Gavin, for God's sake." She sighed, put her glass on the bar, and made a beeline for the door. Out in the car park, she took a few deep breaths to calm herself.

"Would you like to go home?" a deep voice asked anxiously.

She turned and stared at Heaton in his pristine black suit and tie. God, she hoped he wasn't gay. "Yes, but I can't. You go, I'll get a lift back."

"Sophia?" It was her father's voice. He stood behind Heaton and looked at them both before continuing. "You go if you want to. Tony's going to give me a lift home."

"No, Dad, it's all right."

"Sophia, go. Come and see me soon, though."

She nodded and kissed his cheek. He took a long last look at Heaton before going back inside.

She and Heaton got into the Jaguar but before he started the engine she spoke. "Thank you for all your help."

He smiled. "Not at all."

"No, I mean it. I was absolutely dreading all this; Mum dying, the funeral, the drinks afterwards, so thank you."

"Do you really want to go home?" he asked.

"Why?"

"Well, I thought that if you wanted to, we could go for a spin up on the moors?" he suggested.

"Do you think the car's up to it?"

"Well, as long as we keep to the main roads, yes."

She smiled. "I'd love that."

"Good." He started the engine and drove out of the car park.

She settled back into the leather seat, alternating her gaze between the moors and his face.

"This car doesn't get out much, does it?" she asked.

"No, a bit like me. So this will do us all good. It's a bit strange driving a car older than you are."

"Why, how old is it?"

"Nineteen Sixty-Nine."

"It's lovely," she told him sincerely.

"Yes, it is. My father loved it, taught me to drive in it, which was quite brave of him. The worst was having to do a hill start. I thought I was going to roll all the way back down to the bottom."

"I'd say it was a lot safer than the girly car I had to learn in."

"I don't know about that," he replied. "This car doesn't have any mod cons."

"Well, this is such an enormous tank of a car, if you did have an accident, you'd have been more protected."

He pursed his lips. "Yes, I suppose so. Did that man upset you?" he added suddenly.

"Gavin? No…well, a little. I shouldn't have allowed him to get to me." She glanced out of the passenger door window as the car slowed until he pulled into a gateway and turned the engine off.

"Have you given any thought as to what you'll do now?" he asked. "You came back up here to be near your mother."

She turned to him. "Unlike you, I've still got a father," she said, then closed her eyes for a moment and squirmed. "Oh, God, that was awful of me. I'm so sorry. I'll be back to work the day after tomorrow."

He shook his head. "That's far too soon. I could be a

stand-in, if need be, and bore them all silly."

Her eyebrows rose. "Are you suggesting that Lady Heaton and I are boring?"

He smiled. "I think I'd better rephrase that."

She laughed. "Well, we could always dress you up as a monk."

He stared at her and she froze with horror at what she had said.

"Not a suit of armour?" he suggested and she relaxed. "There is one somewhere."

"I don't know how you'd get up and down the stairs in one."

"Mmm. Better keep me as the very last resort, then."

"We will," she assured him. "I'd love to see the suit of armour, though."

"I think it might be in the attic somewhere. You haven't seen the attic, have you?" he asked and she shook her head. "I must show it to you, then. I haven't been up there for ages myself. I used to play hide and seek up there with Stephanie and Andrew."

"Andrew?"

"He's the son of Des' predecessor," he explained. "He managed to escape and have a career. Lives in Leeds now. Not far from Stephanie, actually."

"Oh, I see."

"He was the first to tell me that Simon was hitting Stephanie. Otherwise, I'd probably not have known until the miscarriage. We don't get on, Simon and I," he said with a humourless smile. "Never have. He claims to be an artist but he seems to be on a one-way ticket to self-destruction. Anyway, I will show you the attic, just remind me or I'll forget."

"I will," she replied. "I'm sorry about what I said about your father, it was awful of me."

"I heard what your father said to you about children." She flushed. "Oh."

"I hope you don't mind me saying this, but he has a point about not leaving it too long."

"At least you don't have a biological clock. Mine is rapidly counting down, according to Michelle, but considering my mum was forty-two when she had me, I think I have a bit of time yet. Do you feel under pressure to get married and have children?"

He shrugged. "It has never been mentioned. Especially now. It's just automatically expected of me. As if I didn't have enough to worry about."

"You mentioned something before…about you and Lady Heaton…oh, look, just tell me to mind my own business."

"No, it's all right. Lady Heaton and I rarely speak now, that's all," he told her, confirming what she had suspected.

"I'm sorry."

"You make it sound like it's all your fault." He smiled sadly, started the engine and drove them over the moors in a roundabout way back to the abbey.

Changing out of her navy blue suit into jeans and a jumper before cooking herself some pasta, she found herself relaxing a little. The funeral was over and neither Michelle nor Danielle had come. Sadly, she had been relieved. Evening sunshine was flooding into the flat and she opened the window fully. She ate then went for her phone, pulled one of the armchairs into the sunshine, and rang an old friend in London.

"Kitty, it's Sophia. How's the weather down there?"

"Sophia?" Kitty exclaimed. "How are you?"

"I'm okay. Mum died the other day, though."

"Oh, Soph, I'm so sorry. Look, Lee's here. Do you want to speak to him?"

Why the hell would I want to speak to him? "No thanks, Kitty. Lee and I are well and truly over."

"Does that mean you're not coming back to London?"

"I don't know," she replied truthfully. "How is London these days?"

"Oh, the usual. We all miss you, though. You sound as though you could do with a break. Can you come down for a few days?"

"Dad needs me and I have a job up here."

"Surely they could spare you for a few days?" Kitty asked.

"Maybe."

"Well, there's a bed here for you if you come."

"Thanks, Kitty. I'll think about it. I could certainly do with some serious retail therapy, anyway."

"So, what's it like on the man front up there in the frozen north?"

She laughed. "Quiet. They're not all like Sean Bean."

"More's the pity. Oh, there's someone at the door. Better go. I'll talk to you soon."

Sophia ended the call and rested her head back.

When she woke it was dark and cold. She got up and heard the phone fall to the floor. She retrieved it, left it on the chair, and went to close the window. Reaching for the handle, she looked over at Heaton's office and saw him fast asleep at the desk.

She closed the window, went downstairs and out into the

yard, leaving the door on the latch. Quietly, she pushed open the door of Heaton's office. He was using the PC keyboard as a pillow, his glasses halfway down his nose, but her eyes were drawn to the smouldering half-smoked cigarette in an ashtray beside his elbow. She sighed, reached for it, stubbed it out then saw the drawings laid out on the desk.

An excellent pencil drawing of a nude woman reclining on a bed. And a nude woman looking back over her shoulder. The third showed the same woman with a man in the throes of sexual intercourse, her face contorted in ecstasy. The dark-haired man was more roughly drawn but it was clearly a self-portrait. Either Heaton hadn't finished the drawing or he was solely concentrating on the woman. Her.

Chapter Four

Sophia gasped and backed out of the office into the stable yard, blood rushing to her face. Stopping in the middle of the yard, she stared up at Des' flat. Des and Helen were silhouetted against the curtains. They kissed, embraced, and disappeared from view. Des' office was directly under their flat but Heaton's was directly opposite and if she could see right into his office... Colour flooded her cheeks...those directional spotlights... What if he had seen her struggling with her aerobics exercises or getting ready for bed?

She spent the next half hour turning the lights this way and that, hoping it would solve the problem, before going to the window. Heaton was still asleep in his office. She sighed, went back downstairs and across the stable yard, and knocked.

He woke with a jump and peered at her bleary-eyed. There was an imprint of the keyboard down his left cheek and she couldn't help but smile.

"Go to bed," she told him slowly.

"What time is it?" He quickly gathered the drawings together and put them in a drawer.

"I don't know, I fell asleep in a chair myself." She found

a clock above the door. "One o'clock."

He sighed, took off his glasses, and rubbed his cheek before shutting down the PC. Then he saw her glance at the cigarette. "I needed one."

"Why?"

He looked startled. "I am trying to give up but it was a moment of weakness – a craving."

"Why now?"

He pulled an exasperated expression and she was sure that he was finally going to tell her to mind her own business. "I overheard your telephone call this evening," he said instead. "The window was open. I'm sorry."

"It's all right, it wasn't top secret. It was Kitty. I shared a house with her and a few others in London."

He made an 'oh' face. "So are you going back?"

She tried to meet his eyes but he could hardly bear to look at her.

"Do you want me to?" she asked quietly.

"Thomas?" There was a knock at the door and she bit back a curse. "Thomas?"

"Excuse me." Getting up, he went to the door and opened it. Lady Heaton stood outside wringing her hands. "What is it?"

"I've just had the police on the telephone. It's Stephanie."

"Tell me?"

"She's in hospital, Thomas. He's attacked her again."

"Christ."

"We're to go there." Lady Heaton's voice shook. "Now."

He nodded. "Get your coat, I'll get the car out." Closing the door, he inhaled and exhaled a shaky breath. "Christ."

"Is there anything I can do?" Sophia asked.

"If we're not back, then the tours and the shop," he said apologetically. "I'll have a word with Des before I go. I'm sorry that you may have to start them again so soon."

"Don't be silly. I should go," she said, going to the door. "I'm only getting in your way. I hope Stephanie will be all right."

She returned to the flat, saw him reverse the Jaguar out of the garage, then walk to the door of Des' flat. When he drove away a few minutes later, she peered out into the yard and saw light shining out from Des' office. She went downstairs and knocked at the door.

"Des? It's Sophia."

"Come in."

She went inside and found him sitting at his desk. "Do you know Stephanie at all?"

"Not very well," he replied. "She went off to university in London and now lives in Leeds. She works as a wedding dress designer and comes back here the odd time. The boyfriend is bad news. That was his brother you saw the day you arrived."

"Oh. What exactly does Simon do?"

"As little as possible, from what I can make out. His Lordship made the mistake of lending him some money a while back and now he keeps coming back for more. I think he might be a druggie. And so when he can't come, he sends his brother instead."

Given the circumstances, it wasn't going to be one of the best tours she had ever done but as she and her group made their way into the drawing room the following afternoon, it suddenly got a whole lot worse. The mantelpiece looked different somehow. How was it different? She racked her brains, acutely aware that the group were staring curiously at her. She smiled apologetically at them. She'd come back later.

Des was waiting for her as she passed the group on to Jack Halewood, the head gardener, with some relief.

"Sophia?" He smiled. "His Lordship has just rung me. Stephanie's going to be fine."

She clapped a hand to her face in relief. "Good."

"Yes. His Lordship said she was very badly beaten but that she'll be okay with some rest and recuperation here. Come to the kitchen for a coffee."

"Thanks. I'll be there in a few minutes."

She went straight back to the drawing room and stared at the mantelpiece. The figurine. The Royal Doulton figurine was gone. She glanced around the room. No, it hadn't been moved, it was definitely gone. Now what? Surely it wasn't some kind of test orchestrated by Lady Heaton to see whether she was honest or not? Surely such a test would have been done weeks ago? She would have to report it to Lord Heaton when he returned. As if she didn't have enough on her mind at the moment.

The following evening she saw the Jaguar pull around to the front of the house then went to the flat and made herself some dinner. Des gave her a wave from his office as she passed.

"Have you seen his Lordship at all since he got back last night?" he asked her in the morning.

"No, I haven't. I had an early night last night. Mum and the funeral and everything caught up with me."

Des pulled a sympathetic face. "How are you now?"

She smiled. "A good cry and twelve hours sleep did me the world of good. Was Lord Heaton supposed to see you about something?"

"No, no. It's just that Helen was wondering about the arrangements for Stephanie."

"I'll try and find him."

She went into the house via the side door and along the corridor to the library. She knocked and waited. Nothing.

"Lord Heaton?" There was no reply so she tried the handle. It turned and she went in. It was pitch-black in the room and it stank of cigarette smoke. She went to the window and opened the curtains before jumping violently. He was sitting in one of the leather armchairs watching her. He looked awful, his eyes were bloodshot, and the stubble on his cheeks was almost a beard. "Have you been here all night?" she asked gently and he nodded. "When did you last eat?"

"I don't know."

"Come with me, I'll make you breakfast."

"No."

"You must eat something," she urged. "Cigarettes can't make up for not eating. You're coming back to the flat with me. No arguing."

There was a ghost of a smile as he got up.

In the flat, she pointed to a chair. "Please sit down while I make you some scrambled eggs. You do like scrambled eggs?"

"Yes, I do." He watched her cook then joined her at the breakfast bar. "The first time you saw me, at the boathouse, did you ever wonder what I was doing there?"

"Yes," she admitted.

"Stephanie and Simon spent the weekend here but had gone out on Saturday evening to a nightclub in town. Steph came back without him, they'd had a row, and she told me that he was selling drugs in the club. I went a bit mad, I suppose. I ransacked their room and found ecstasy tablets and a small amount of speed in the wardrobe. I should have flushed them down the toilet but I just wanted the stuff as far away from the house as possible so I brought them down to the lake. Then I saw you coming. After you went, I dug a hole and buried it all. He didn't show up again until the Monday morning, saw that the drugs were gone, and was demanding money from me to buy more. I threw him out. Then his brother turned up. I threw him out, too. You saw me throw him out. God, if only I'd called the police and got Simon locked up instead of letting my temper get in the way."

She smiled sympathetically. "Eat."

He nodded and began on the scrambled eggs. She was relieved to see him finish it and passed him a glass of orange juice.

"When we got to the hospital, I couldn't recognise Steph, the swelling was so bad." He closed his eyes for a moment. "I couldn't even recognise my own sister."

Sophia shuddered. "I think Helen would like to speak to either you or Lady Heaton about the arrangements for when Stephanie comes here."

He nodded. "I'll speak to her. Thank you for this," he said, sliding off the stool. "It was very good of you."

"You're welcome. Oh, there's something I need to tell you. When I was in the drawing room with a group the other day I noticed that something was missing."

"Missing?" He frowned. "What?"

"A Royal Doulton figurine from the mantelpiece. I stand there when I tell groups about the length of the room and the décor and so I know what's on it...and not on it."

He sighed. "I see. Well, thank you for letting me know." He went out and she began to wonder if she should have told him about Lady Heaton's very odd behaviour. No, she decided, she was right not to. If it was a test of her honesty, surely Lady Heaton's odd behaviour in the house would end now? But even if it did, there was still the question of all the money she was lodging in the bank and what was in the box she was carrying onto the bus to Leeds. What on earth was going on?

Sophia met a tired but smiling Lady Heaton in the gardens that afternoon.

"Stephanie will be coming home in a few days. She was very lucky that her jaw wasn't broken."

"Have the police caught her boyfriend?"

Lady Heaton's nose wrinkled in distaste. "No, they haven't. Luckily, her room here is nowhere near where the tours go, so they will be able to continue."

"Yes, Lady Heaton."

"I'm sorry that you had to start work again so soon."

"I was glad to be doing something, actually," Sophia admitted. "And it was only a small group."

Lady Heaton nodded. "I hear you managed to persuade Thomas to eat. Thank you. He never liked Simon and considers himself to be a surrogate father to Stephanie on top of everything else, but she can be just as stubborn and refused to leave Simon. Until now."

"Love is blind," she said, thinking of Lee, and Lady Heaton nodded again. "I'm looking forward to meeting her."

"I was telling her about you and the tours and she is looking forward to meeting you." Lady Heaton looked at her watch. "The Australian group should be here soon."

"Yes, Lady Heaton." Sophia nodded and walked back to the house.

That evening, she went to visit her father. He was in surprisingly good spirits and full of gossip as she made them a mug of tea each.

"I heard from Reverend Jackson today that Stephanie Heaton was beaten black and blue by her boyfriend and ended up in hospital again," he told her.

"Yes, Stephanie's coming back to the abbey in a few days," she replied, stirring milk into the tea and passing him a mug. "Her boyfriend is still nowhere to be found."

"And what about Lord Heaton?"

She fought to control a flush and passed him one of the mugs. "He was very upset."

"Naturally." Her father took a sip of tea. "You do know the man fancies you, don't you, Soph?"

She swallowed and looked away, thinking of the drawings.

"I was watching him at the rugby club after the funeral," her father added. "He couldn't keep his eyes off you. Time you got out of the abbey, don't you think?"

"Why?" she asked.

"I'm not having my daughter as his fancy piece. Or worse."

"Worse?"

"His mother was nearly twenty years younger than the husband. Now, I was no spring chicken when I got married but at least I didn't cradle snatch your mum." He put the mug down. "I'm not having you being used as a broodmare, Sophia."

"Dad, for goodness sake. He's only a few years older than I am."

"You don't like him, do you?" he asked incredulously. "Fancy him?"

"Dad, he's been very kind to us."

"So you'll be repaying him in kind?" Mr Nelson demanded.

"Dad," she cried. "He's my employer."

"He's also a very good-looking man, according to Gavin."

"Yes, and thanks for not telling me that Gavin was gay. I felt a right idiot when he told me."

Her father gave a dismissive shrug. "He's very choosy as to who knows. Imagine if Neville and Brenda knew?"

Sophia's eyes bulged. "You mean everyone knows now except his mum and dad?"

"Yes, but that's of his own doing. Just promise me that you won't do anything silly?"

She kissed his cheek. "I promise."

"Good. Now." Mr Nelson went out into the hall and returned with a cardboard box. "These are a few things of your mum's I want you to have."

Sophia joined him at the kitchen table. In the box were some jewellery boxes, photos and – her heart pounded – diaries. "Dad, are you sure you want to give these away?"

"I'm not giving them away, I'm giving them to you. I'll never read your mum's diaries and what would I do with the jewellery?"

"If you change your mind and want them back, you just tell me?"

He smiled. "I won't want them back."

She drove back to Heaton Abbey via St Margaret's Churchyard. Crouching down beside her mother's grave, she began to read the cards attached to the wreaths.

A good woman. We won't see your like again. Neville, Brenda, and Gavin

To a good friend. Rest in peace. Danielle

Rest in peace. Sally

She smiled sadly then rose and stretched. She then saw a wreath a little way down the path between the rows of graves. It looked as though it had been thrown there as it had landed upside down. She went and picked it up and read the card. It had been simply signed Thomas Heaton and Felicity Heaton. She sighed and brushed grass and dried earth from the flowers before placing it back on the grave.

Straightening up, she turned and almost cried out in fright as Heaton emerged from behind a tall headstone.

"I'm sorry, I didn't mean to frighten you. I wasn't sure if you were alone or not."

"I am on my own," she told him. "I've just been to see Dad."

He nodded and they stared at each other for a few moments until she looked down at the grave.

"Thank you for the wreath."

"Not at all. I came to look for Danielle's parents' graves but I couldn't find them."

"They're not buried here. Danielle's family are Roman Catholic, they're buried over at St Mary's."

"Oh." He frowned. "Oh, I see. Well, that explains it, then."

"Would you like me to show you the graves?" she asked hesitantly. "I've been to see them with Michelle so I know where they are."

His face brightened. "Well, if it wouldn't be too much trouble."

He followed her to St Mary's Church in the Land Rover and they parked either side of the gates.

"I haven't been here since Cathy's christening," she said as she locked the Mini.

"Cathy?" he queried, holding the gate open for her.

"Michelle's daughter. Thank you," she said as they went in. "She screamed the place down. Cathy, I mean, not Michelle."

He smiled.

They walked up the gravel path towards the church, the O'Hara graves being immediately behind it. Then she heard a shout and saw three teenage boys appear from behind the church, followed by…

"Shit," she hissed, stopping abruptly.

"What is it?" he asked.

"Jeff, that boy in black, he lives next door to Michelle and Tony."

"He knows you?"

"Yes." She began to panic. "I lived there for months. God, I can't let him see me here with you." She glanced wildly from side to side. On her left was a fence about six feet high with trees growing at intervals along it. To her right were rows of neat headstones, too low to hide behind. In front of her, Jeff and the other boys were approaching. "Shit."

Heaton grabbed her arm and pulled her towards a tree to her left. "Quick, before he recognises you. I'll have to pretend to hug you, or something."

Heaton took one last look at the approaching boys, clasped her shoulders, and backed her into the tree. "Pretend" and "or something" went completely out of the window, of course. His arms went around her and he made an awkward pretence of hugging her before she felt lips on the side of her neck. She closed her eyes and felt them travel up to her mouth. He began to pull at her lips with his, his hands sliding up to hold her face. One of her hands was on his shoulder while the other hand crept up of its own accord and was half on the back of his neck and half in his hair and she found herself kissing him back.

"Need a hand there, do you?" one of the boys shouted, followed by a whistle of approval and encouragement from one of the others.

She felt Heaton tense and he turned her so that he had his back to the path, a hand in the small of her back holding her tightly to him, the other cupping her head and the back of her neck.

"Whoa." She heard Jeff's voice. "Shagging in a graveyard."

"They're not," one of the others told him.

"They will be in a minute," he assured them. "Shall we form an orderly queue?"

"Yeah, why not? I could do with a shag."

That was too much for Heaton and, before she could grab hold of him with both hands, he broke away from her and took the boy by the scruff of the neck.

"Would you like to repeat that, you little shit?"

"Hey, come on, it was only a joke."

"Well, I didn't find it very funny."

"Yeah, well, maybe you need to get out more," Jeff shouted, then looked across at her and did a double take. "Sophia?"

Face burning, she had to go forward. "Jeff."

"Fuck sake, Sophia. I thought Lee was a twat, but this one isn't even house-trained."

"Let him go." She pulled Heaton's hands off the boy's sweatshirt. "Now go," she told the boy. "You, too." She glanced briefly at Jeff. "Now."

They didn't need to be told twice and ran from the graveyard and the gate banged shut. She covered her face with her hands then dragged them down and took a quick peek at Heaton. He was rooted to the spot on the path. Taking a deep breath, she passed him, heading for the gate.

"I'm sorry."

She stopped and turned. "You might as well have put a full page advert in the local paper. How the hell am I going to explain all this? At least he didn't know who you were, so that's something."

"If there's anything I can do?" he said feebly.

"Yes. Stop trying to throttle people who annoy you. Bloody hell, they're not your feudal subjects."

"It was because he was making some derogatory comments about you. Maybe you were too busy to hear."

Even more blood rushed to her face. "I was too busy? You did say, 'or something', didn't you? Who couldn't even hug properly? Eh? Bloody hell, if I'd wanted more I'd have jumped on you up on the moors where there's nobody about." She cringed with horror as Heaton's eyebrows shot up in astonishment. Oh, God, is this what she did to Lee? Blurting out really, really stupid things all the time? No wonder he tried to put a couple of hundred miles between them, poor sod. "Look, I'm sorry… It's Mum and all that… I'm not thinking straight. I froze, I'm sorry. I didn't know what to do. We couldn't jump over that." She pointed to the fence. "And we couldn't hide behind those." She pointed to the gravestones. "I was stupid to offer to show you the graves without checking the graveyard out first, okay? Now I'll have to try and figure out what the hell to say to Michelle." He looked at his feet and she sighed. "You've got lip balm here…"

He raised his head and she gestured awkwardly to her own mouth.

"Here?" He attempted to wipe the pink smear away.

"No." Reaching up, she quickly wiped it away with her thumb. "There."

"Thank you. And I mean it; if there is anything I can do?"

They walked together to the gate then went their separate ways.

Returning to the flat, she put the cardboard box on the breakfast bar, went to the laptop and opened a new email.

She cringed and began to type.

> *Dear Lord Heaton*
> *Please find attached a photo of Danielle, Michelle, my mother and myself at Michelle's wedding at St Mary's in 2009. Danielle's parents are buried right behind the church.*
> *If you would like me to stop, please just say, and I'm sorry for shouting at you in the graveyard and being a general pain in the backside. I offered to bring you there, it's my mess, and I'll clear it up.*
> *Sincerely*
> *Sophia Nelson*

She attached the photo and clicked send then returned to the cardboard box and lifted out the diaries. They weren't yearly diaries, more of a journal where her mum had jotted down her thoughts. She counted the journals, there were seven in all. She put them to one side and brought out the jewellery; two necklaces, a bracelet and her mum's engagement ring.

She slipped the small diamond ring onto her finger. It was a little tight so she returned it to the box and took out the photographs. The first was Mum with her parents. The second was herself as a baby. A very fat baby. Sophia rolled her eyes and went to the third. It was a dinner party. She quickly picked out her mum then saw Danielle seated opposite. It must be one of Connolly's Christmas parties. She left it to one side so she could show Heaton then turned to the journals.

She opened one but the entry was dated October 1989.

S fell out of the apple tree and broke her arm. A clean break but S was very annoyed that it was her left arm and not her right.

Sophia smiled and reached for another. The entry was dated April 1990.

My menopause has definitely begun. Didn't really know how to tell W. We will just have to accept that S will be our only child.

A few days later an entry read;

W took it well, but deep down I know that he would have loved to have had a son.

Sophia snapped the journal closed and breathed in and out deeply to try and stop the tears coming. She picked up a third journal and opened it.

23 November 1974. D is pregnant. What can I say? How can I congratulate her knowing that she is only bearing those people's child for the money?

Sophia quickly flipped back a few pages.

12 November 1974. D finally told me what all the secrecy was about and why she's been off work pretending to be ill. I just can't believe it. It's like something from a film. She showed me a picture of

LH and he is handsome but under no circumstances would I do what D is doing.

Flipping forward in the diary, Sophia read on.

15 January 1975. D and I are in Blackpool. It's deserted and freezing. I tried again to make D see sense and to not sell her baby but she won't listen.

2 May 1975. D rang me late last night to tell me that she has had a little girl. LH is putting a brave face on it but what he wants is a son. They want her to have another child. I've begged her not to but she just won't listen to me anymore.

28 November 1975. D is pregnant again and is certain that this one will be a boy.

7 February 1976. D and I are in Blackpool again. If anything, it's colder than last year and we've just had the most enormous row and I told her that she would regret this for the rest of her life. I feel bad now because D ended up in tears and it can't be good for her or the baby.

12 May 1976. D rang me to tell me that she gave birth to a boy early this morning. L and LH are delighted. I bet they are. I tried one last time to make her see sense. This will be her last chance. If she gives this baby up too she will never see it again. But, no, she wouldn't listen. She's got her money, she's marrying DA even though the poor chap hasn't a clue what's been going on, and they're moving to London. I give up. That's it. Enough.

Her laptop jingled heralding the arrival of an email and she put the journal down.

Dear Ms Nelson
There is absolutely no need for you to apologise. I should be the one apologising. In fact, I'm a bit surprised you haven't lost your temper with me long before now. :)
My apologies and kind regards.
Thomas Heaton

She smiled weakly and returned to the breakfast bar, reaching for one of the later journals.

21 June 2010. With W to the opening of the Mining Museum. W's speech went on far too long so I had to go and put an end to it. He wasn't very happy. I then had to stand back and watch LH make a much shorter speech. I hadn't seen him for years, not since he went down the mine as a child. People say he's becoming a recluse up there at the abbey but he came to this so it's probably rubbish. He doesn't look like D but he rubbed the side of his nose exactly like D used to do, which startled me. Maybe his sister looks more like D. I hope they never find out. I wish S and M hadn't become friends but I wish that a lot of things hadn't happened. S rang. She's got a new boyfriend.

She picked up the newest of the journals and opened it. Many of the latter entries simply contained full names, telephone numbers, dates and even on one page a shopping list. She went back to the start of the journal.

> *30 May 2012. I think there might be something the matter with me. I met MG in Tesco and I couldn't for the life of me remember her name. I think I called the poor girl S twice. This evening I answered the telephone with Mum and Dad's old number. I'm having to write things down more. I hope it's just a sign of old age.*

Poor Mum. She closed the journal, not wanting to read of her mother's descent into dementia. She returned the journal to the box and got ready for bed.

All in all, it took less than twenty-four hours for Jeff to blab. Michelle rang her at lunchtime the following day.

"Just what haven't you been telling me?" Michelle demanded lightly. "Jeff from next door said, and I quote, 'Sophia was more or less shagging some posh bloke in a suit in St Mary's Graveyard last night and he nearly strangled Mike'. So, who was he and why the hell St Mary's Graveyard?"

Sophia took a deep breath and tried to get her story straight. Her dad's disappointment at not having had a son had gone around and around her head for hours the previous night.

"It was Lord Heaton and I wasn't 'more or less shagging him'. St Mary's was originally a grange, a farm belonging to the old Cistercian abbey, and we were just seeing how much of the old building was still there."

Michelle snorted. "And I'm supposed to believe that?"

"Well, I'd be bloody annoyed if you believed Jeff Bateson over me."

"So where did he get this 'more or less shagging' idea from?" Michelle asked.

"He was probably high on weed as usual plus the fact that Lord Heaton and I were trying to hide from him. It sounds pathetic but it's true. I knew Jeff would put two and two together and get ninety, so we tried to avoid him but it didn't work."

"So there is nothing going on between you and Lord Heaton?"

"Nothing," she replied simply.

"So why did he try and strangle Mike?"

"Mike was bloody rude. They all were."

"So you haven't got your own knight in shining armour, then?"

She forced a laugh. "No. He's not a knight, anyway, he's a baron. Doesn't really have the same ring to it."

"No, barons are usually the baddie, aren't they?"

"Yes." Unfortunately.

"Well, Sophia, I'm very disappointed."

"Sorry," she replied through gritted teeth.

That evening, she dropped her car off at Tony's brother's house in the town. He was a complete petrol-head and was going to service it for her. She walked back to the abbey through the parkland. The stable yard was deserted as she crossed it and unlocked the door to the flat. Des and Helen were out and even Heaton wasn't in his office. She opened the window, pulled off her shoes, then went to the fridge and poured herself a glass of orange juice. Closing the fridge door, she heard a voice.

"Andrew? It's Thomas. Have you time for a chat?"

Who was Andrew, she wondered, before remembering that he was the son of Des' predecessor.

She went to the window and peered out. Heaton was in the office, the window was wide open, and he was struggling with his jacket. He pressed a button on the telephone handset, put it down, and shrugged the jacket off.

"How's Steph?" a male voice on speakerphone asked.

"On the mend. She'll be home in a few days."

"Thank God for that. And Simon?"

"Crawled back under a stone. He hasn't been seen since." Heaton reached for a mug and took a sip. "If I see him again, I'll fucking kill him."

"If I don't do it first. How are you?" Andrew asked and Heaton replied with a humourless laugh. "That good?"

"That good." Heaton sat down in the office chair with the mug and put his feet up on the desk. "The place here is completely deserted except for yours truly. It's pathetic."

"Look, tell you what. I'll come down next week and I'll drag you out on the pull, yeah?"

"What happened to what's-her-name? Jessica?" Heaton asked, before taking another sip from the mug.

"Julia," Andrew corrected him. "Dumped me for some tosser of a lawyer with a flash car."

"Bloody hell, sorry. I thought that was going quite well?"

"So did I. So, fancy a couple of nights out on the pull, Lord Heaton?"

"Maybe."

"Fucking hell, Thomas. When was the last time you had a night out?"

"Don't you start. I get enough of that from Stephanie."

"Well, she's right. Christ, Thomas, you're forty next Tuesday. How the hell are you ever going to meet someone stuck in that bloody office day in, day out? And now I'm sounding like your mother."

"Don't mention my fucking mother. She doesn't give a toss." Heaton roared, swinging his legs down from the desk and Sophia jumped violently. He heaved a sigh to control himself. "Sorry."

"All right," Andrew replied surprisingly calmly. The poor sod must be used to it. "Let's cut the crap. Tell me what the matter is."

Heaton took such a long time to answer that Sophia's heart began to thump. He wasn't going to tell him, was he?

"It's the tour guide. Her name's Sophia."

"Excellent. And…?"

"There isn't an, 'And'?" Heaton snapped.

"Why the hell not?" Andrew demanded. "Is she a lesbian, or blind, or something?"

Sophia rolled her eyes. No. Not even, 'or something'.

"No. No, but she's the tour guide."

"And that's it?" Andrew asked, sounding incredulous. "Jesus. What's she like?"

"Stunning," he replied miserably and Sophia's cheeks began to burn.

"Then, what the hell is the problem?"

"Every time I'm with her, I act like a complete moron. If I'm not practically beating up people she knows, I'm acting and speaking like something out of the Dark Ages. I can't even call her by her first name…it's just hopeless."

"No, it's not," Andrew replied patiently. "Can you actually hold a conversation with her?"

"Yes. We've even been walking together on the moors…but she's the tour guide, Andrew."

"So bloody what? I know you didn't want one but now you've got one I think you should make the most of it, eh? Does she fancy you?"

"What?"

"It's a simple enough question," Andrew said patiently. "Does she fancy you?"

Yes, Sophia wanted to scream. Yes, I bloody do.

"Well…I don't know…I mean, she's been very kind and all that, but why the hell would she fancy someone like me? Oh, fuck it, I don't know."

"If you just shagged her would it help? Get her out of your system?"

"I don't want to just shag her, Andrew. She works here. She bloody-well lives here, too. If it didn't work out, it'd be far too bloody awkward, so it's best just left as it is."

"What, with her just seeing you being 'His Lordship' all the time and not Thomas Heaton, a bit repressed, but a nice guy and a good mate when you get to know him a bit?"

Heaton gave a short laugh. "Thanks for that; the cheque's in the post."

"Don't bother, the last one bounced."

"Fair enough." He sighed. "I just don't know what to do, Andrew."

"Is it possible for you to just be friends with her, then?"

"I don't know. I'm just too fucking attracted to her. I

mean, I just keep wanting to…"

"Kiss her?" Andrew prompted.

"I have kissed her. It's a long story. Complicated. But I have kissed her. Once. Completely unromantic."

"Make love to her?"

"Oh, God Almighty." Heaton groaned, which she took as a yes. "What I mean is, to draw her. It's pathetic. I've loads of drawings of her in the desk here. I bloody-well hope I'm never burgled."

"Why, are they a bit…?" Andrew tailed off.

"Some of them are. She's got a fantastic figure. All curves. Jesus, it's…and I just keep wanting to…"

"Yeah, you said. Look, you have to decide whether this is a crush, lust, or something more. Spend more time with her, try and figure out whether she fancies you or not. We only live once and even if it doesn't work out, you'll have at least tried. Okay?"

"Yeah."

"Good luck, mate."

"Thanks, Andrew."

"Give my best to Stephanie, yeah?"

"I will. Bye."

Shaking a little, Sophia watched as he ended the call, reached for his mug again, and drained it. He wheeled the chair closer to the desk and put his glasses on before unlocking the drawer and lifting out some sheets of paper. Resting his head on a fist, he began to look through them. They must be the drawings of her. Suddenly, he gathered them all up, returned them to the drawer and locked it. He booted up the PC, reached for the mouse, and opened a program. He sat back in his chair and ran a hand across his jaw before leaning forward, elbows on the desk, and his head in his hands. He might as well have shouted out, "It's just hopeless."

A couple of hours later Sophia opened her eyes hearing a car approach. It must be Des and Helen coming home. Turning over in the bed, she looked at the clock radio – half past midnight – then rolled onto her back. It was a car being driven at speed into the stable yard and sliding to a halt on the gravel. Then there was an almighty crash and the car sped away down the drive. She leapt out of bed and ran to the living room window. The light was on in Heaton's office but the window was completely smashed and Heaton was getting to his feet shaking glass from his hair and brushing it from his front.

"Jesus," she whispered. Slipping her feet into a pair of trainers, she grabbed her bathrobe and ran down the stairs pulling it on. She flung open the outside door before running across the yard to his office. "Are you hurt?" she demanded.

"You're here?" Heaton stared at her in surprise. There were cuts on his cheek and chin. Blood from the cut on his face was beginning to trickle down his cheek and he reached up to wipe it away. "I thought you were away or something."

"I left my car to be serviced in town and walked back." There was a brick at his feet with something wrapped around it. "Your face needs seeing to," she told him, looking him up and down. "Are you hurt anywhere else?"

"No." Bending over, he picked up the brick. He pulled off a sheet of paper attached to it with a rubber band, read the contents, and smiled humourlessly. "From Simon, surprise, surprise."

He threw it onto the desk and she read it.

You owe me, Heaton. Tell Stephanie I'll see her soon,
won't you?

"Come with me." She eyed the glass lying on the floor, the desk, the PC and the telephone, and glistening in his hair. "Sort this out tomorrow."

He nodded, turned off the light, and closed the door before following her upstairs to the flat.

"I was fast asleep," he murmured. "Didn't even hear them drive into the yard."

She went into the bathroom and returned with cotton wool, antiseptic lotion, and sticking plasters and found him shaking.

"Shock," she said softly. "Come and sit down." She went to the table, pulled out a chair, and sat him down.

"Stephanie will be here in a few days. What the fuck is he going to do to her?" He blinked, clearly realising he had sworn. "Sorry."

"Doesn't matter." She tilted his face up. "This will hurt." She dabbed at the cuts and he winced. She applied the plasters then poured him a glass of red wine. "Drink this. I've nothing stronger, sorry."

"Thank you." He held the glass in fingers which still shook and she gently took it from him and held it to his lips. He sipped the wine then sighed. "Thank you."

"Are you going to ring the police?"

He shook his head. "I know I should, but if it got out that there was even a whiff of something to do with drugs up here, all the tour companies would cancel. And Simon would make doubly sure that there was more than a whiff, believe me. I just don't know what to do about Stephanie. He's never openly threatened her before."

"She'll be safe enough in the house, won't she?"

"Yes, but I can't keep her under house arrest." Taking the glass from her, he drank deeply before setting it down on the table. "And she hates being told what to do."

"We could both keep an eye on her?" she suggested tentatively. "But, as you said, you can't stop her going out. But she probably won't be leaving the estate for a couple of weeks, anyway."

"No. Thank you, yes, we'll both keep an eye on her."

"You've got glass in your hair." She retrieved a comb from the bathroom and passed it to him. "Comb your hair onto the table and I'll get the dustpan and brush."

He combed out his hair and she deposited the glass fragments into the bin.

"You must think I'm an awful bloody nuisance," he said, running his fingers through his hair. "Don't answer that, but at least have a glass of wine yourself?"

She smiled. "I think I will." She brought a glass and the bottle to the table and topped up his glass before pouring herself one. "I don't think you're a bloody nuisance. I'm probably the bloody nuisance."

"No," he replied quietly. "If I didn't have you to talk to, I'd have gone mad by now."

Hearing a car approach, they both looked towards the window. He quickly got up and turned off the light then fumbled for her hand and led her to just to the right of the window, where she usually stood watching him.

"They can't get into the house, can they?" she whispered.

"No, the door's locked but the alarm isn't on yet."

They waited, hearing the car approach until it drove into the yard, and did a circuit, before stopping. A door opened and they heard Des' voice. Heaton squeezed her hand before releasing it, going to the light switch, and turning it on.

"Des?" He went downstairs to the stable yard and she followed.

"What the hell happened?" Des asked.

"Simon left a calling card attached to a brick."

"Are you hurt?" Helen asked anxiously.

"A couple of cuts. Ms Nelson kindly patched me up."

"Have you rung the police?" Des went to Heaton's office, switched the light on, and surveyed the damage.

"How can I? I can't risk it getting out that drugs are involved." He sighed. "I should have told you before but the weekend Simon was here with Stephanie, he had drugs with him, was selling them in the nightclub in town. To cut a long story short, I found out, found drugs in their room, and I brought them down to the lake and buried them behind the boathouse. Now he claims that I owe him for them. I can't go to the police because he'll make sure that it's known that the estate is connected with drugs and what do you think that will do to visitor numbers?"

Des grimaced.

"The other thing is," Heaton continued. "He's threatened Stephanie, and she'll be home in a few days. It might just be his way of making me sweat and pay up but we need to keep an eye on her all the same."

They all nodded.

"Does Lady Heaton know?" Helen asked.

"She knows nothing about Simon and drugs and she

109

hasn't heard a thing tonight by the look of it. I want to try and keep it that way."

"Yes. I'll find something to board up the window. It's supposed to rain later." Des turned away, Helen following.

Sophia watched them go. "I think I'll turn in."

Heaton caught her arm as she went to walk away. "Thank you for your help."

"No more sleeping in the office, I hope?"

"I can't promise anything but I'll try not to now."

"That's something, I suppose." She smiled and he let her go.

Chapter Five

Over the next few days, the glass in the office window was replaced, the office itself tidied, and there were no further emails. It also looked as though Heaton wasn't going to take Andrew's advice.

Sophia stared at the birthday card. A nameless Renaissance beauty. She had bought it the previous week, knowing Heaton's birthday was approaching. The book lay on the breakfast bar: *Art Treasures of the Renaissance*. She'd found it in a charity shop but should she be buying him presents and giving him cards? No-one had mentioned his birthday, Stephanie being uppermost in everyone's thoughts, but even so, this would be his fortieth.

She signed the card and put it in its envelope, wrapped the book, and placed them carefully in her rucksack along with the picnic. He had been visibly relieved that morning when she had mentioned she was resuming her walks on the moors and had gladly accepted her invitation to come along if he wasn't doing anything else?

They sat in the stone circle and she took a deep breath, forcing the phone call about her mother to the back of her mind, then opened the rucksack.

"Happy birthday." She passed him the book and card.

He flushed. "You didn't have to."

"Well, I don't know if I should be saying this but, I kind of got the impression that everyone had forgotten what day it was."

He carefully unwrapped the book and smiled before opening the card. "Thank you," he said simply.

"And I hope you didn't eat too much for lunch because I made a few sandwiches and..." She opened the Tupperware box and showed him the muffins she had made but more especially the one with a candle in the middle. "I have matches here somewhere."

She began to rummage in the bottom of the rucksack before glancing up. He had turned away and she watched as he got to his feet and stood with his back to her, his hands on his hips. Oh, God, she'd made him cry.

She put the rucksack to one side and got up. "I'm sorry."

He shook his head. "Everyone had forgotten." He took a deep breath to calm himself. "But that's nothing new, really." He turned and gave her a little smile, his eyes bright with tears. "So, thank you."

"How could they forget your birthday?" she whispered.

"Lady Heaton hates fuss. She usually gives me a card and a book token. Stephanie's better present-wise. A little bit more imaginative. She started buying me clothes a couple of years ago. She hates the suits I wear. She bought me these, actually." He pulled at the combat trousers he wore. "So it's usually clothes. I can't remember when I last had a cake."

"It's a muffin," she said miserably.

"It's the thought that counts. The book, the card, the cake – thank you."

"Are you hungry?"

He nodded. "I forgot about lunch. Again."

"I made salad sandwiches. We'd better eat them before they get too soggy."

They sat down and devoured the sandwiches and she was delighted to see him laugh as she finally found the matches and lit the candle.

"Make a wish before it goes out." He did and blew it out. "They're chocolate chip. We've three each."

"I'll never manage three."

"Well, bring two back to the office and eat them when you forget about lunch again."

"Thanks, I will," he said, taking a bite. "It's delicious."

Biting into the muffin, she chewed and nodded. "Mmm, they are."

"I lay in bed this morning and I seriously considered staying there all day. I'm glad I didn't now."

"So am I. I don't think I could go back to doing this walk on my own."

"You mean that?" he asked incredulously.

"Yes, I do."

"Good. Because, sad as this may seem, going walking up here with you has become the highlight of my week."

"You really need to get out more," she teased.

He laughed. "I'm doing my best."

She smiled and reached for the flask. "Coffee?"

About to settle down for an evening in front of the television, she went downstairs to answer a knock at the door. Michelle was on the step.

"Okay, you've got twenty minutes or Tony's going to go nuts."

"Eh?" Sophia looked past her and Tony gave her a wave from the car.

"Cathy's at Molly's and there's a disco on at the rugby club. You're coming with us, so chop-chop." Michelle marched her up the stairs and paused at the top. "Nice flat. Bedroom?"

"Over there." She pointed to the door.

"Good, come on." Michelle marched her on into the bedroom.

"Yeah, but you don't want me tagging along with you."

"It's not too soon, is it?" Michelle asked, rummaging in the wardrobe.

"No, but—"

"Good, then this will do." Michelle threw a long skirt, a blouse and a jacket at her. "These boots, too, I think," she added, taking them out and throwing them at her feet.

"You're putting all those television stylists to shame, you know," she said, kicking her jeans off.

"What the hell do they know? Hurry up," Michelle shouted from the depths of the underwear drawer.

"Okay, okay."

"Oh, and this, too."

A push-up bra landed on her head. She pulled it off and stared at it in amazement. "I'm not wearing this."

"You've never worn it, have you?"

"Do I look like I need to?" she retorted. "Unless this is a really subtle way of telling me that they're starting to sag?"

"I wouldn't dare. Just wear the bloody thing, will you? Make the most of what you've got, eh?"

"All right." She tugged her top off and unhooked her bra.

"Make-up?"

"No, not if we're in such a rush, I'd look like a clown."
She reached for the push-up bra and put it on. "Anyway, do
you really think men are going to be looking at my face
now?"

"Hair, then?"

"Shaggy ponytail will do," she replied slipping the blouse
on and doing up the buttons.

"Bloody hell, you'll look like a horse." Michelle passed
her the skirt and she stepped into it, pulling up the zip and
doing up the button.

"Thanks."

"Sorry, you do have nice hair."

"Hmm." Sophia sat on the bed and pulled the boots on.
"Well?"

Michelle looked her up and down as she gathered her
hair into a ponytail. "Not bad for no time at all. Must see
what sort of talent is there now."

Shrugging on the jacket, she and Michelle went
downstairs, and out to the car. "Thanks for this, Tony." She
climbed into the back of the car, clutching the jacket to her
throat.

"No problem. Michelle thinks you're sliding into
spinsterhood."

"And you think the man of my dreams is going to be at
the rugby club?"

At the rugby club, Sophia and Michelle found a table
while Tony went to the bar. The place was surprisingly
packed.

"So where's my sign?" Sophia asked.

"Sign?" Michelle was puzzled.

"I thought you'd have made a sign to hang around my

neck with 'Desperate – Please ask me to dance' on it."

"It wouldn't fit in my bag."

She smiled and looked away, only to see Gavin elbowing his way towards her.

"My mum and dad are here, please dance with me?"

"Gavin, for God's sake, I'm trying to find Sophia a husband," Michelle cried.

"Please?" Gavin pleaded and Sophia got up. "Thanks, Soph."

"I really think it's time you told them."

Poor Gavin looked horrified. "You know, I'd rather crawl naked across a field of broken glass."

"They're not that bad, surely?"

"They are," he replied. "They still call gay people 'queer'."

"Ouch. Even my dad's not as bad as that. But dancing with me really isn't going to help."

"I know but…I'm not usually such a wimp, it's just…don't take this the wrong way but your mum was, and your dad being oldish like mine…"

"There's no 'ish' about it."

"What?" Gavin strained to hear.

She smiled. "I know what you mean."

"So how's your love life?"

"What love life?"

Gavin laughed. "Sorry. You wouldn't be dancing with me if you had one."

"True."

"He's here, you know?" he added.

"Who?"

"Lord Heaton."

Sophia's jaw dropped. "Here? Where?"

"Saw him out in the beer garden earlier on with some other bloke smoking."

"You sure?"

"Oh, yes. Actually…" Gavin peered over her shoulder. "He's at the bar right now…not sure if he's seen you…we could, kind of, dance in that direction?"

She shook her head. "No. Leave it."

"Why?"

Sophia couldn't think of anything to say and another couple banged into her as she stood staring at Gavin.

"Ow, sorry."

"Come and have a drink." Gavin took her hand and began leading her towards the bar.

"No." She tried to shake it off but he wouldn't let go and to shake it even more would just cause even more of a scene. Thankfully, they ended up at the end of the bar nowhere near Heaton.

"What'll it be?" Gavin shouted at her.

"A white wine spritzer, please."

"What the fuck are you doing, Sophia?" Someone bellowed at her from behind. It was Michelle. "Has Gavin suddenly decided that he's not gay or what?"

"Shut up, will you?" Sophia urged. "His parents are here."

Michelle nervously looked around them then started bellowing again. "I've never seen so much talent here and what are you doing? Dancing with him."

"He's a friend."

"Yes. And that's all he can be. Gavin." Michelle greeted him with a grin, lifted the glasses from his hands, and passed them to Sophia. "I'll dance with you. Let Sophia suss out the talent, okay?"

"Oh, okay." Gavin allowed himself to be led away.

Sophia found herself standing at the bar with a glass of spritzer in one hand and a pint of Guinness in the other. She watched Gavin and Michelle being swallowed up by the crowd then yelped as someone trod heavily on her foot. "Ow." She almost dropped the pint. "Watch it."

"Sorry." The person turned and she stared up into Heaton's face.

"Oh, hello."

"Hello." He frowned, glanced at the glasses she was holding before his eyes rested on her cleavage. Her cheeks burned and he quickly raised his head. "Sorry, I, er…I didn't expect to see you here. Here with friends?"

"Yes. You?"

"Andrew dragged me out for my birthday. Come and meet him."

She opened her mouth to make an excuse but he had already turned away and was making a path for her up towards the far end of the bar. She cringed and followed.

"Andrew? This is Sophia Nelson. Ms Nelson, this is Andrew Hardy."

She put the glasses down on a table and shook his hand, feeling his eyes on her, clearly comparing what Heaton had told him on the telephone with what his eyes were actually seeing in front of him.

"Good to meet you. Thomas has been singing your praises."

"Oh. Good."

"You like it at the abbey, then?"

"Yes, I do."

"Excellent. Well, it's Thomas' birthday so I thought it was high time he was dragged kicking and screaming for a night out."

"Oh. Happy birthday," she said, pretending that she hadn't known.

"Thank you."

"He works far too hard," Andrew went on. "Hasn't been out in ages."

"He does work very hard, yes."

"Should have been an art critic or something similar. Now he has to humour bloody tourists."

"I think you'll find that it's Ms Nelson who has to humour bloody tourists," Heaton clarified. "And very good she is at it, too."

Andrew suddenly leaned towards her with a grin and whispered as loudly as he could, "And do you call him Lord Heaton?"

Blood began to rush to her face again. "Um, yes, why?"

"Andrew," Heaton said as quietly as he could over the din. Andrew shrugged knowingly and reached for a glass. "Do you dance?" Heaton asked her, startling her.

"Dance?"

"Yes. Look, I won't hear the last of it from Andrew if I don't dance with someone tonight and as I don't know anyone else…"

Out of the corner of her eye, she saw Andrew roll his eyes at the ham-fisted invitation. Heaton himself then began to shuffle awkwardly.

"Actually," she told him. "I'm so bad I make Mr Bean look like Rudolph Nureyev."

"That's perfect because I'm hopeless too." With that, he held out a hand. Sophia stared at it for a moment before taking it. He led her out onto the dance floor, again clearing a path for her, but then kept on going. Out in the beer garden, he finally stopped. "Sorry, but I really am hopeless. I just wanted to say thank you again for this afternoon."

"I bet Andrew didn't make you cry."

"No, but he didn't make me muffins either."

She smiled. He was still holding her hand and she made a concerted effort not to look down in case he let her go.

"Who are you here with?" he asked.

"Well, Michelle practically kidnapped me from the flat. So I'm here with her and Tony and we seem to have acquired Gavin as well."

"Gavin?"

"A friend from school," she explained. "His dad and mine were miners. He was at Mum's funeral; you thought he'd upset me. He hadn't, he was just being Gavin."

"It's not too soon for you to be out?"

"No, I'm okay. Thanks for asking."

"Do you like rugby?"

She shook her head. "You?"

"I played it at school but, no, not really," he replied before his head jerked up suddenly.

"What?"

"I haven't heard that song in years…"

"Come on, then." Grabbing his other hand, she guided it to the small of her back, and they began to dance. "So you can tell Andrew that you really did dance. Well, kind of swayed."

He smiled and they swayed until the song ended and rap

music boomed out through the doors. He let her go and nodded inside. "We'd better go back."

"Yes," she replied reluctantly.

"Thank you again for today. For this afternoon and for this."

She smiled then turned and reluctantly went back inside. She sat down beside Gavin. "So, have I missed anything?" she asked him.

"Nope. Sussed out the talent?"

"Talent?" She caught a glimpse of Heaton's head as he made his way back to Andrew. "What talent?"

Stephanie Heaton arrived at the abbey two days later but it was a further week before Sophia finally met her in the gardens. Stephanie's face was a disturbing shade of purple and it was almost impossible as yet to see whether she looked like Danielle.

"They've allowed me outside at long last. You must be Sophia. Thomas has told me about you."

"Oh." Not all, I'll bet. She gave her a polite smile. "I hope you're feeling a little better."

Stephanie shrugged exactly like her brother. "I feel better, I just look like crap."

"The bruises will be gone in a week or so."

"I hope so." Stephanie nodded. "Mother says you've been feeding Thomas on and off. And reminding him to get a life, too, I hope? He might as well put a bed in that office and move in there permanently."

"He does seem to work very hard."

"There's no 'seem' about it. Poor Thomas, to be lumbered with all of this." Stephanie swept her arm around dramatically. "He says you're from the town originally. He told me about your mother, too. I'm very sorry."

"Thank you."

"Have you been in the chapel?" she asked eagerly. "I found a key. I haven't been in there for years."

"No, I haven't."

Stephanie took her arm and began leading her off the lawn. "Come and have a look, then."

A few of the monastery buildings remained intact, including the former 'stranger's chapel', the chapel near the gates of the monastery which was used by lay people, travellers and pilgrims. After the dissolution of the monasteries, the Heatons had retained it as their private chapel and burial place. Always kept locked, Sophia followed Stephanie and watched as she went to unlock the door with an enormous key but found it open.

"Thomas?" Stephanie called. "Is that you in there?"

"Yes."

"Tell us if you'd prefer to be alone?"

"No, come in." Sophia saw him look past his sister and at her. "You've met. Good." They joined him at the tomb. "Our father," he told her. "I'm not sure where I'll be put, it's getting rather full in here now."

"That's not really for you to worry about, is it?" Stephanie laughed.

He smiled. "No, I suppose not, but there's a lot to be said for cremation. Mother wanted to include the chapel on the tour but I said no. People now see where we live, I don't particularly want them to see where we're put when we die. What do you think?"

"It might appeal to the ghoulish side of people's nature,"

122

Stephanie mused. "But, then again, I think you were right. What do you think, Sophia?"

"I'd rather not take sides."

"No, of course not." Stephanie walked up to the altar. "I haven't been in here for years. Do you come in here a lot, Thomas? I thought you lived in the office?"

"I don't have anything else apart from this, Steph," he roared and they both jumped. "Father died when I was barely finished at university. I was completely on my own. Mother was a mess and you were in London. I didn't know what the hell I was doing half the time. I still don't know how I haven't lost the place. People think it must be fucking fantastic being Lord Heaton. All they see is the title, the estate, the big house. Everyone's out to get you. You can't have any proper friends. It's so fucking lonely and a lot of the time I bloody hate it here. But what else is there? If I packed it all in, a lot of people would be out of a job. And, anyway, now I don't know how to do anything else. And people here wonder why I'm such a bastard."

Sophia stood in silence desperately wanting to put her arms around him, but not daring to.

"You're not a bastard," Stephanie told him. "Well, not all the time. Take a chill pill, Thomas."

He glared at her then strode out of the chapel, banging the door behind him.

Sophia examined her hands and heard Stephanie shuffling awkwardly.

"Bugger. Shouldn't have said that. He gets so worked up that Simon gave him a small bag of...anyway, this is the family chapel."

Sophia just managed a smile. "Excuse me."

She hurried to his office and walked straight in without knocking, and as he went to boot up the PC, she squeezed in front of him. "You need to get out of here. Even if it's only for a few hours. You really can't go back to work today."

"So what do you suggest?" he asked shortly.

"Well, you were kind enough to take me for a drive after Mum's funeral and I'd repay the compliment only you don't fit in my car and I'm not insured to drive yours and I don't really think I'd dare to, anyway…"

He finally smiled. "Where would you like to go?"

"I'll leave that up to you."

He unlocked a drawer and she saw the drawings face down, a DVD-RW labelled 'website photographs', and a small sealed plastic bag full of powder. He saw her look at them before taking out some keys. He locked the drawer, held the door open for her and they went to the garage. They got into the Jaguar and he drove out of the stable yard. He sped up onto the moors before reversing the car into a gateway from where they could look down on the town and the estate in the distance. They sat in silence for a few minutes. She watched him, wishing that she could read the expression on his face. Then he turned to her.

"Are you cold? I think there's a rug in the back." He twisted around and groped for it, his shoulder brushing hers. "Here we are." He draped the rug carefully over her knees.

"Have you cried yet?" she asked. Startled, he stared at her wide-eyed. "You asked me, so I'm asking you. You need to cry. Properly. Stephanie is fine but I think you need to get it all out. Bottling stuff up is bad for you, trust me."

"I know that I need to cry. But, to be perfectly honest, I think if I cried properly I don't know when I'd stop. I shouldn't have shouted at Stephanie. I shouldn't have tried to throttle that boy in the graveyard." He sat back in his seat with a sigh. "And I'm dreading Simon turning up again."

"You think he will?"

He nodded. "I'd put money on it. If I had some to spare."

"Tell me to mind my own business, sack me or whatever, but what was that powder?"

"Speed. Courtesy of Simon."

She gasped. "I thought you'd got rid of it all? You haven't taken any, have you?"

He looked away. "A bit. Not recently. I didn't like what it did to me. That's why I'm back smoking cigarettes."

"Please get rid of it," she urged.

"Mrs Fields found it in Stephanie's room the other day – in what used to be Stephanie and Simon's room. Do you know where it was?" She shook her head. "Behind the shutters. One wasn't folding back away from the window properly and she found the bag in the gap. Simon wanted to get me hooked. You get it for nothing in the beginning and then—"

"Just throw the stuff away," she begged. "Please?"

"Steph's had a go at me, too. When she and Simon rowed, Simon told her about the speed he had given me a while back. Claimed that he had me in his pocket. Well, he bloody doesn't. And when he comes—"

"You'll just ask him to leave," she interrupted calmly.

He sighed. "Yes."

"Why speed?" she asked and he frowned at her.

"I'd spent the night in the office and must have looked like death warmed up. His internal cash register must have rung or something. He's just an out-and-out bastard and I'm just so sorry that Steph had to find out like this. I'll get rid of the stuff, don't worry."

"He didn't try and get Stephanie hooked on anything?" she added.

"Yes, but she wanted none of it and it looks as though their last visit here was the beginning of the end for them. How are you coping?" he asked suddenly, startling her in turn. "I meant to ask when we went for our walk but I completely forgot. I'm sorry. Selfish of me."

"No. I'm glad you forgot or there'd have been two of us in tears up there." She gave him a little smile. "I'm fine, coping quite well. Michelle rang the very next day about St Mary's."

"And?"

She shrugged. "And I had to tell her it was you. I'm a terrible liar. I told her that we were looking at St Mary's Church seeing if there was anything remaining of the old monastic grange. I couldn't think of anything else."

"Did she believe you?"

"Yes, I think so, eventually. I shouldn't have shouted at you in the graveyard. I know you said that I didn't need to apologise but I was very rude. I'm sorry."

He shook his head. "I deserved it. There's none of the grange left at St Mary's, by the way. I looked it up in the library. My guess is that they reused the stones to build the church."

"Oh. Well, I'll be able to bore Michelle with that if she asks again."

"Sorry, I tried to make it sound interesting." She shot a glance at him but saw him smile. "How long were you living there?" he asked. "With Michelle and her family?"

"Four and a half months. When I came back from London I was on Dad's sofa for a bit but then Michelle took pity on me."

"And Jeff?"

"Jeff has a big mouth and likes Metallica," she replied, rolling her eyes. "So I went from not being able to get a decent night's sleep on Dad's sofa to not being able to get a decent night's sleep at Michelle's thanks to Jeff. We had 'words' about it on a few occasions."

"And?"

She grinned. "I threatened him with Radio 2 every morning after a night of Metallica. The prospect of listening to James Blunt at full volume at half seven in the morning terrified him, thank goodness."

"I don't know who James Blunt is, but I do know Metallica and if I played Metallica at home at full volume, it would be barely audible in the next room. My grandmother was quite deaf towards the end of her life and used to listen to *The Archers* more or less at full volume. It was only when you'd open the door to her sitting room that the noise would hit you."

She smiled and they looked out at the view. "This is what I missed most in London," she said. "Being able to come up here and just walk and walk and walk."

"You will be going walking again on Tuesday?" he asked.

"Yes, I'm hopelessly predictable."

"May I come?"

She looked at him. "Yes, I meant what I said the other day, but there is one condition."

He frowned. "Oh?"

"That you stop smoking. There's no point in you coming

walking with me and trying to get fit if you go and light up the minute you're home."

His eyebrows rose and she wondered if she had offended him.

"You're right, but I can only try. And, maybe, we could somehow squeeze in a bit of research on the O'Haras without Steph finding out?"

"Somehow is the question, but we'll try." They sat in silence for a few moments before she spoke again. "Dad has given me some of Mum's things. Photos, jewellery and her journals. She definitely knew what Danielle was doing. She tried both times to talk some sense into Danielle but Danielle wouldn't listen. Mum told her she'd regret it for the rest of her life then gave up. I don't think they ever spoke to each other again. Whenever Michelle wanted to come to stay with us it was me who would have to pass on Mum's yes or no."

"You never thought that that was a bit odd?"

She shrugged. "It had always been like that. One of the photos was of one of Connolly's Christmas dinners. Mum and Danielle are sitting opposite each other. I'll bring it to your office so you can scan it."

"Thank you."

"It was strange," she admitted. "Reading the journals. I kind of felt like I was intruding – stupid really. But they are answering a lot of questions. Some that I wasn't all that keen on having answered."

"Like what?"

She sighed. "Dad wanted a son but all he got was me."

"He's bloody lucky to have you."

She gave him a grateful smile. "I just hated seeing it

written down like that. I flipped through all the journals but I'm wary of reading them from cover to cover."

"Maybe it's too soon. Give it a few months?" he suggested and she nodded. "Have you got enough shelves?"

"Loads, thank you. The small bedroom looks like a library now. It's fantastic. I've never had a library before."

"Every home should have one."

Three hours later she was washing up after dinner and hoping that there was something worth watching on TV when there was a knock at the door. Going downstairs, she found Stephanie outside.

"I know I shouldn't say this as I'm here for a lot of R and R but I am bored out of my mind. Mother is visiting a friend, darling brother is in the office as per usual, so I was wondering what you do here for a bit of fun?"

"Fun?" Sophia echoed.

"Yes, you know? When you enjoy yourself?"

"Ms Nelson's mother died recently, Stephanie." They heard Heaton's voice and turned. "I hardly think that she is eager for fun."

"Ms Nelson? Bloody hell, have I travelled back in time, or what? Sophia, meet Thomas. Thomas, meet Sophia."

She and Heaton stared at each other.

"Can I call you Sophia?" Stephanie asked. "Or do you actually prefer Ms Nelson?"

"No – I mean – yes, call me Sophia."

"Good, that's that sorted out. Now, fun anyone? I know a nightclub is out of the question, a) because I look like something from Doctor Who, b) Thomas only has a vague recollection of what a club is, and c) poor Sophia is in

129

mourning, so that leaves the cinema or we do something here?"

"Well, I've got quite a few DVDs?" she ventured.

"Oh, at last. Thomas, be a darling and go and find a bottle of wine while Sophia and I choose a DVD for us to watch."

"Steph, I'm busy," he told her irritably.

"No, you're not. I was watching you draw something a few minutes ago, so off you pop."

Heaton flushed, Sophia quickly turned away, and she and Stephanie went upstairs.

"Oh, these flats are lovely." Stephanie went to the window and peered out at the stable yard. "What a transformation. Now, let's have a look at your DVDs. I'd better choose something that won't send Thomas to sleep."

Stephanie eventually chose *The Last of the Mohicans* after going through the entire collection and leaving most of them on the floor.

"I hope Lord…Thomas hasn't seen it."

"He won't have," Stephanie replied confidently. "The last complete film Thomas saw was *E.T.* It was my birthday treat. He cried at the end but don't tell him I mentioned it." Leaving the DVD on top of the Freeview box, she went to the door. "That you, brother of mine? Come up, then." Heaton came in and Stephanie took the bottle of wine from him. "Australian, good choice."

"Shall I open it?" Sophia suggested.

"Thomas can do it. Find him a corkscrew."

She went to the cutlery drawer and passed it to him then went to look for three wine glasses.

"Sorry about this," he whispered, pulling the cork out of the bottle.

"It's all right, I wasn't really doing anything. Were you busy?"

"It's nothing that can't wait. Here." He passed her the opened wine.

"Thanks." She poured them each a glass of the wine then sat down on the sofa beside Stephanie, leaving Heaton the armchair.

"Okay, are we ready?" Stephanie pressed play.

Sophia had seen the film countless times so she was able to alternate her gaze between the television and Heaton's face. He sipped at the wine and seemed to be genuinely engrossed in the story. When the film ended, Stephanie wiped her eyes.

"It always makes me cry," she sniffed. "So, Thomas? Better than *E. T.*?"

"They're very different films, not that I've seen many recently…"

"No, you haven't. Do you actually watch any television at all, Thomas?" Stephanie demanded.

"The news. Documentaries, and some crime drama."

"Thomas, darling, how old are you?" Stephanie added.

He frowned. "You know how old I am."

"This is for Sophia's benefit. She must think you're at least a hundred and two, not forty."

"I'm busy, Stephanie."

"You're always busy," she snapped. "Whether you're actually busy-busy or just drawing pictures, I don't know. I mean, look at you. Those bloody suits. Everyone knows who you are, so why do you have to dress the part, too? They make you look like Grandfather, especially when you're wearing your glasses. Just wear something that will tell people that you're still young, for God's sake."

"I don't have to listen to this." He got up and put his glass down on the breakfast bar. "I can only apologise for Stephanie's behaviour, Ms Nelson. Thank you for a pleasant evening."

Stephanie rolled her eyes. "Good God, he's back to Ms Nelson again. I know you've got some decent clothes, Thomas, I bought them for you. Wear them," she shouted after him as he left the flat. The door slammed and Stephanie rolled her eyes. "Doesn't he irritate the hell out of you, Sophia?"

"He's my employer…"

"I'll take that as a yes, then. Bugger, though. I shouldn't have teased him about his drawings because they are quite good. Have you seen any?"

Sophia flushed. "No," she lied.

"I'll get him to dig some out for you. It's nice and cosy here, isn't it? The house is bloody freezing. I'd forgotten that it was only about one degree warmer than Siberia. I bet you've never gone to bed in P.J.'s with thermals underneath and a bathrobe over them?"

"No, I can't say I have."

Stephanie laughed. "God knows what Thomas wears in bed. Sorry, that image will probably give you nightmares. I'd better be nice to him, though, I want to ask if I can move into the flat next door while I sort myself out."

"But there are fifteen bedrooms in the house?" Sophia frowned. "And it's the middle of May."

"I know but I just…oh, I don't know…I suppose I want some independence while I sort myself out but want people I know close by, too. I had to crawl downstairs to the phone when Simon…I knew that even if I screamed, no-one would come."

"I'm sorry."

Stephanie shrugged. "Nobody wants to get involved these days. They don't want to have to go to court and all that. I just hope that Simon doesn't turn up here. Thomas would kill him. I'm not exaggerating, he'd kill him. How secure are these flats?"

"Well, the outside door and the door, there," she pointed, "at the top of the stairs are pretty sturdy."

"Yes. Sorry. I'm just a bit paranoid. I don't usually talk so much crap."

"It's all right, it's understandable…I mean…sorry, I didn't mean that you—"

Stephanie roared with laughter and she laughed in relief.

"It doesn't matter." Stephanie squeezed her arm. "You got a boyfriend?"

"No."

"Sore point?"

Sophia shook her head. "No. My ex was from Leeds. We met at university there, and I was stupid enough to follow him to London even though I knew that the relationship wasn't going anywhere. Anyway, I had to come back up here because of my parents."

"And now?"

"Dad's in sheltered accommodation," she explained. "He's happy there, and I'm happy here."

"What are the tours like? I mean, are people really interested?"

She nodded. "They seem to be."

"Mother used to take people around who asked."

"Lady Heaton took me on one of her tours then I took her on mine then Lord, um, Thomas came on a tour."

"Thomas did?" Stephanie looked and sounded incredulous. "I thought he was dead against it?"

She shrugged. "Well, he came, anyway."

"Poor Thomas," Stephanie mused. "He's got no life at all, really. I know I tease him about it but I thought he would have done something about it by now."

"I suppose you get into a routine and habits?" she suggested.

"Yes. I must try and bring him out of himself while I'm here. Will you help?"

"Me?" She fought to control a blush. "Well, yes, if you think it will help."

"Thank you." Stephanie got up. "I'd better go. Thanks for letting us invade this evening."

"I enjoyed it."

"Good. We'll do it again."

She closed the door after Stephanie then brought the wine glasses over to the sink. She washed them out then heard a knock at the outside door. She went downstairs and found Heaton on the step.

"I think my phone fell out of my pocket."

"Oh. Come up."

"Thank you." He followed her up the stairs and went to the armchair. "It's here." Retrieving it, he put it in his jacket's inside pocket. "I'm sorry about Stephanie. She can be a little overbearing."

"I enjoyed the evening. Didn't you?"

"Yes. I thought the film was interesting."

"What were you drawing?" she asked as casually as she

could. "Stephanie told me you were quite good."

"Quite good? That is a compliment. I draw...the house...people...anything that interests me."

"Can I see some? If you show them to strangers, that is?"

He smiled. "You're hardly a stranger. Yes, I'll dig some out for you."

"Thank you. I wish I could draw but I can't draw a straight line. I did a photography course a couple of years ago, that's about it for me on the visually creative front."

"Photography?" His face brightened. "Do you have any photographs I could see?"

"I have a portfolio somewhere. I haven't looked at it since London. I think I know where I put it." She went to a box in the small bedroom and returned with the portfolio. "Some of them are a bit pretentious."

"They're good." He halted at one of Lee. "Your ex-boyfriend?"

"Yes. I was going to do some more in black and white but it never happened." She flushed as he came to some of her. "We had to do some self-portraits...talk about being self-conscious."

"They're very good, don't put yourself down. I do like black and white photography myself. There was an art exhibition on in Leeds a few years ago that I went to and across the road there was a photography exhibition which I enjoyed more."

"Faces and Features?"

He stared at her in horror. "You were there?"

She nodded. "Some of them were very interesting. I think my tutor would have thrown me out of the class if I had tried some like that, though. He wasn't very broad-minded, to put it mildly."

"Just portraits, poses and places?"

"Very demure portraits, poses and places. You've never been photographed or painted properly?" she asked.

"Good God, no." He laughed. "My father had it done – the portrait – when he turned fifty. I have a bit of time yet."

"It's just that people have been asking about you," she explained. "There are photographs in the drawing room but the one of you looks like it was taken while you were still at school. If there was another, more recent one, to go with the ones of Lady Heaton and your sister?"

"You want to photograph me?" he asked doubtfully.

"Unless you'd like to draw a self-portrait?"

Again, he looked horrified. "I don't know."

"Think about it."

He nodded. "I've decided to agree to the interview and feature on the estate for the tourism brochure."

"Good."

"I don't know about that but Stephanie said once that any publicity is good publicity, or something, can't quite remember exactly... Not sure that I agree with her now, though."

"Why don't you ask her for a few tips?" she suggested. "I take it that you haven't told her about it?"

"No, I haven't...I don't know...She helped with the website and I ended up sounding like I should be put in a museum." Sophia flushed. "I'll ask her but whether I'll take her advice, I don't know. Are you still going walking tomorrow?"

"Yes, and you're still welcome to come."

"Thank you. And thank you for showing me these."

"You're welcome. Look, I know it's late but shall we finally make a start on the O'Haras while you're here?" He nodded. "Good. I'll get my laptop." They sat at the table as the laptop booted up and she opened a new family file. "Right. We'll start with Danielle. She was born in 1950. What year was your father born?"

"1935."

"Okay." She typed it in. "I have no idea how to describe the relationship between Danielle and your father, so…" She scratched her head. "I'll put 'other'. When was Stephanie born?"

"Second of May 1975. I was born on the twelfth of May 1976." He watched as she typed in both Stephanie's and his own details. "Right. Danielle O'Hara married Don Armstrong in Leeds. I don't know the year but Michelle was born in September 1983 and Peter was born in November 1980. He isn't married but Michelle married Tony Giles in March 2009. Cathy was born in August 2010."

He smiled. "How can you remember all this?"

"Michelle's my best friend," she told him "I was her bridesmaid and I'm Cathy's godmother. Now, Danielle's mother was called Helen. She died in 2005."

"What about her father?"

"He's dead, too. His name was Thomas O'Hara."

Heaton paled. "Must be a coincidence. When did he die?"

"I can't remember the exact year but it was in the mid-1990s."

He nodded. "O'Hara…was there an Irish connection?"

"Way back somewhere, yes. Are you okay?" she asked gently.

He gave her a little smile. "It's just all a bit strange."

"I'm afraid that that's all I remember off the top of my head. We'll have to go back to St Mary's sometime. Maybe at six in the morning or ten o'clock at night. With a bit of luck, the gravestone inscriptions will give us an age at which they died and from that, we can get an approximate date of birth. Then, we hit the internet and the record offices."

"Right. Okay."

"If you don't want to go on, all you have to do is say."

He nodded. "It's strange. I don't know and never knew any of these people. They're just names to me and yet they are my family."

"We'll try and flesh things out, find out what they did for a living, try and find a photograph somewhere. Other than that…" She tailed off.

"It's difficult, I know. Thank you for this."

"No problem." She smiled as they got up. They went to the door and she opened it. "Goodnight."

"See you tomorrow."

She closed the door and returned to the portfolio. She looked at the photographs of Lee again and put them to the very back, before closing the portfolio and returning it to the box. She couldn't help but smile. If 'Faces and Features' had been a film, it would have been a Certificate 18 at the very least. Even Michelle had been embarrassed at some of the pictures. She shut down the laptop and went to bed.

Chapter Six

Stephanie met her the following morning as she was preparing to go and see her father.

"Thomas has just told me that he's asked if he could go walking with you this afternoon. Any room for one more?"

Her heart sank but she smiled. "Of course."

"Good. I bet Thomas is as fit as a tortoise."

"We won't go too far," she replied instead of answering.

"How far is not too far?"

"Five kilometres."

"Oh." Stephanie gave her a relieved grin. "Not too bad."

Sophia watched Heaton's face as he saw both Stephanie and herself waiting at the Land Rover at two o'clock that afternoon. A flicker of irritation crossed his face then he grimaced.

"I'm not going to regret this, am I?" he asked.

"We'll break you in gently," Stephanie told him, climbing into the back.

"You'd better."

Sophia gave him a little smile as they got in and was thrilled to see him return one.

"Nice to see you out of a suit, by the way." Stephanie

laughed. "You look quite good in combats."

"Thank you," he replied dryly and started the engine.

"I'm impressed," Stephanie proclaimed as they reached the stone circle forty-five minutes later. "You're not as unfit as I thought, Thomas."

Sophia stepped into the stone circle and stared at where she and Heaton had been sitting when she had received the phone call about her mother's death. Would she always think of her mother up here now?

"I haven't been up here for years." Stephanie was still speaking. "Do you do this every week?"

Sophia turned. "Yes."

"Good for you. You wouldn't mind Thomas tagging along, even if I wasn't able to come?"

Sophia looked at him, he was eyeing her solemnly, clearly knowing why she was standing where she was. "No, I wouldn't mind."

"Good. It's lovely up here, isn't it? Cold, but…"

"Christ, Steph," Heaton roared and they both jumped. "Do you ever shut up?"

Stephanie stared down at her hands and for an awful moment, Sophia thought she was going to cry.

"Yes," she whispered.

Heaton closed his eyes for a couple of seconds. "Sorry. I didn't mean to shout."

"No? I was only trying to make conversation. What the hell must Sophia think of you?"

He looked at her and Sophia pulled an apologetic face.

"I'm sorry," he said.

"Don't worry about it. Shall we start back?"

They walked back to the Land Rover and travelled back

to the abbey more or less in silence. At the stable yard, Stephanie stomped off into the house while Heaton swore under his breath. Sophia turned to go back to the flat.

"Ms Nelson?"

She glanced back. "Yes?"

"I'm sorry about all that."

"It doesn't matter. Really."

"I've only had five cigarettes today," he explained. "I don't know if…well, it is probably why I'm so…I don't know…"

She smiled. "Coffee?"

He gave her a wry smile in return. "I would love a coffee, thank you."

"Come up, then, but I must warn you that caffeine is an addictive substance, too."

He laughed and followed her up the stairs. "It's not quite as harmful, though."

"That's true."

"I was thinking about the photographs," he added.

"Oh?" she asked, opening the door to the flat.

"Well, if you're sure that it wouldn't be too much trouble?"

"No, not at all," they went in and she shrugged her jacket off. "When?"

"Oh…whenever it suits you."

She nodded and hung the jacket over the back of a chair. "I know you wanted me to have a quiet moment at the stone circle. Thank you."

"For completely ruining it by shouting at Stephanie?"

She shook her head. "Blame the cigarettes or lack of."

"Thank you."

She felt him watch her make the coffee. "Black and white or colour?" she asked.

"Sorry?"

"The photographs?"

"Oh. Oh, whatever you think…you mentioned black and white…and it'll go with the other snaps in the drawing room."

Snaps? They were portraits. "Black and white it is." She passed him a mug. "This evening? Or tomorrow sometime?"

"Oh, well, as it's such a good day, perhaps this evening?"

"The weather doesn't really matter, I can rig up some lights."

"Lights?" He frowned at her. "I thought it was going to be a few snaps of me at the front door?"

"And I thought it was going to be a decent studio portrait to go with the others in the drawing room?"

"A studio?"

"Well, I thought the flat next door?" she suggested.

"Oh…yes, of course. But a portrait?" He looked sceptical.

"It's up to you?"

He took a sip of coffee. "No, you're right, a portrait to go with the others. I just hope that I'm not putting you to a lot of trouble?"

She shook her head. "I need the practice. I'll dig out the camera and some film."

"Film?"

"Yes, the camera I'll be using isn't a digital camera. Could you open the flat, please, so I can have a go at the lights?"

"Yes, of course."

She spent an hour after dinner fiddling with the lighting

in the flat. Luckily, it also had directional lights and she brought a couple of her own lamps in and set them up. Returning with her camera and tripod, she saw him cross the stable yard and heard him climb the stairs to the flat. He watched as she set them up.

"Where would you like me to stand?" he asked.

"A little to the left so I can check the lights…there. Thank you. Now." She went to him and brushed imaginary fluff from the shoulders of his black suit, feeling him tense. She smiled up at him. "You're not in front of a firing squad."

"Sorry, I…"

"Just try and relax a little?" She returned to the camera. "Ready?"

"As I'll ever be."

She laughed. "Okay." She took some full-length then a few head and shoulders pictures. "There. Done."

He almost slumped. "Is the film full?"

"No, there are a few left. Why, do you want me to take some more?"

"No, I was just wondering if you could show me how to take a proper photograph?"

She smiled. "I'll show you."

His eyes almost glazed over as she explained about f-stops and shutter speeds. "Is there no automatic switch?"

She pressed it. "There. Have a look now."

He peered into the viewfinder. "I can't see a thing. Could you stand there?"

"I'd rather not."

"Please?" he asked again and she went and stood in front of the camera, watching him peer through the lens. "I'll never be David Bailey."

She smiled then heard a click. "You took one?" she cried. "I look a complete mess."

"Nonsense. Just one more?"

"Of me? Oh, no."

"Just one?"

"What's all this?" someone asked and Sophia jumped. Stephanie was standing at the door.

Heaton straightened up. "Ms Nelson was kind enough to offer to take a photograph of me to go with the others in the drawing room."

"But you hate having your photograph taken."

"It didn't take very long."

"Nice camera." Stephanie walked to the camera and began to examine it. "Was he a good subject?"

"I've had worse."

"Can I see the photographs in the camera?" Stephanie asked. "Is it possible with this one?"

"No, sorry, it's not digital and rather ancient."

"How many pictures are left on the film?"

"Four," Sophia told her.

"Hmm, well, if I know Thomas, he would have stood completely to attention. Back over there, please."

"What?" he cried. "No."

"The stiff ones can go in the drawing room but it's Mother's birthday in a couple of weeks; how about one of you looking almost normal?"

He glared at her. "Normal?"

"Natural, then. Over you go." Reluctantly, he went back. "And take the tie off." He did as he was told and Stephanie took it from him. "Hmm, undo a couple of buttons. Come on, it won't kill you." He undid the buttons then flinched as she began to run her fingers through his hair. "Better," she proclaimed, standing back from him. "Isn't it, Sophia?"

Sophia had been staring at him, marvelling at how a couple of open shirt buttons and slightly ruffled hair could make a complete difference. He stared back at her sheepishly.

"Yes…"

"You'd better do it now before he runs for it."

Sophia went back behind the camera. "I'll take two full-length pictures and two head and shoulders," she told him. "Is that all right?"

"You'd better ask my agent," he replied and she laughed.

"Try and stand casually, Thomas," Stephanie urged. "Put your hands in your pockets or something."

"I feel like a complete idiot."

"Well, try not to. And stop glaring at me, just look at the camera."

Sophia saw him swallow his irritation and turn to her.

"That's fine, like that, good." She took the photographs and wound the film back.

"Do you develop them yourself?" he asked.

"I used to. Well, we had to on the course, but I don't have the equipment or a dark room. I'll bring the film into town tomorrow."

He nodded and picked his tie up from the floor, where Stephanie had dropped it. "Well, thank you, it was…interesting."

"Bloody hell, Thomas, she wasn't pulling all your teeth out with no anaesthetic."

He just gave Stephanie a glare and went out.

Sophia began to dismantle the lights while Stephanie walked around the flat.

"I must grovel to him now so that he lets me move in here. So, um, where did you learn photography?"

"London. I did a course. I needed the practice, I hadn't taken a proper photograph in months."

"I always leave the lens cap on."

"A lot of it is just practice." Sophia brought the lights to the door then went back to the camera and took it off the tripod. "You learn from your mistakes."

"Hmm, one being don't tease your brother when you have to grovel to him soon after," she said and Sophia smiled. "You do know he fancies you?" Stephanie added casually, and Sophia almost dropped the camera.

"What?"

"I was watching the two of you for a couple of minutes. I don't think I've ever seen him look at someone the way he looks at you." Blood flooded into Sophia's face. "Oh, God, I'm sorry. I've embarrassed you, but I know you fancy him, too. I could have powered a small industrial town with all the electricity surging between the two of you."

Sophia put the camera down on the floor before she did damage it.

"Why hasn't he asked you out?" Stephanie asked.

"I don't know."

"Well, why haven't you asked him out instead?"

She sighed. "Because he's my employer. I've always had a rule that I never get involved with my boss."

Stephanie frowned. "But I thought Mother interviewed you?"

"Your brother pays my salary. Anyway, I don't think my dad would approve."

"Of Thomas?" Stephanie's eyebrows shot up.

"My dad is very set in his ways; he was a miner, he supports Socialist Labour…"

"Sophia, this is the twenty-first century. Women don't have to do what their fathers tell them to do these days."

"I know, but even so, it's too awkward. I'd better hand in my notice."

"Let me speak to Thomas?" Stephanie urged.

Her jaw dropped. "No."

"Why not?"

"Just don't. Please?"

"Only if you promise not to leave?" Stephanie begged. "I'd go stark staring mad here if I didn't have you to talk to. And, to be honest, I think Thomas would, too. He keeps mentioning you, even though he doesn't realise he's doing it."

"But if it's so obvious, it's going to be so awkward."

"Please?" Stephanie asked quietly.

Sophia closed her eyes. "All right."

"Thank you. Think you could put up with me as a neighbour?"

She smiled and nodded.

An hour later, she crossed to the window of her own flat. Heaton was in his office, his head resting on a fist and wearily listening to Stephanie, who was talking animatedly, her arms flying about all over the place. He hadn't taken his glasses off, clearly hoping his sister wouldn't stay too long. Sophia watched as they slid down his nose and he pushed them back up impatiently. Suddenly he pulled them off, got up, left the office and headed in the direction of her door. She heard a knock and went downstairs.

"Could I speak to you for a moment, please?" he asked.

"Yes, of course. Come in."

He followed her upstairs and into the flat. "Stephanie has asked me whether she can move into the flat next door until she sorts herself out. I was just wondering whether you'd have any objection to having her as a neighbour?"

"No, none."

"You don't have to be polite."

She laughed. "I'm not."

"You really don't mind?"

"No, not at all."

"Good." He both looked and sounded relieved. "Thank you. Look, I'm sorry about earlier, it was quite embarrassing for me and I'm sure it was for you as well."

"A nice photograph will be a lovely present for Lady Heaton."

"It will stop Stephanie from asking any awkward questions, anyway. Well, I'd better give her the good news. And if she's noisy, please tell her."

"I will."

Stephanie spent most of the following day moving in before coming to the kitchen after the final coach party had gone, flopping down in a chair, and accepting a cup of coffee.

"Those stairs. Still, it'll be worth it. When will the photographs be ready?"

"In a week," Sophia told her.

"A week?"

Sophia sighed. There was something else missing from the drawing room. A small box containing three silver spoons. She would have to speak to Heaton again. Had he even done anything about the figurine? Oh, God, what if he and Lady Heaton were selling them to raise cash and were too ashamed to tell her? Could that be it?

"Sophia?"

She turned back to Stephanie. "Sorry. Black and white photographs are rare these days, not everyone can develop them."

"I suppose not."

"His Lordship is in the library." Helen stood at the door. "He's wondering if you could join him." Stephanie went to get up. "His Lordship meant Sophia, Stephanie."

Stephanie's eyes widened for a moment before she gave her a knowing wink.

Nervously, Sophia went to the library and knocked.

"Come in." Heaton was at the desk. "I've dug out some drawings for you to look at. If you've time?"

"Yes." She closed the door and went to him.

"The only two subjects I liked at school were History and Art."

"Where did you go to school?" she asked.

He grimaced. "Eton."

"It wasn't that bad, surely?"

"It had its moments, I suppose. Where did you go to school? I know you told me but…"

"St Margaret's Grammar School in town," she told him. "It had its moments, too."

He smiled. "When I was bored in class, I would draw caricatures of the teachers."

"So, you prefer to draw people?"

He pursed his lips then shrugged. "Not really. I do buildings, too, but not landscapes, I'd need to be able to paint decently for that. Now, guess who this is?"

He passed her a sheet of paper then watched her face. She roared with laughter. It was Stephanie – a manic Stephanie.

"Oh, my God, it's her. It's perfect."

He laughed. "She doesn't know about it, so don't tell her."

"I promise."

He pulled out another of Lady Heaton wearing her glasses on a chain, the glasses having slipped halfway down her nose. She was peering intently at something.

"Oh, please don't make me laugh at Lady Heaton," she begged.

"She's attempting *The Times* crossword and not getting very far. Why she doesn't try the simpler one, I don't know." He extracted another and she stared at a man of about sixty, wearing what looked like tweed, and a rather bemused expression. "My father. I always remember him as looking like he wasn't quite with us. Like an absent-minded professor, or something."

"Have you ever attempted a self-portrait?" she asked.

He looked horrified. "Good God, no," he exclaimed. "Do you think I should?"

She nodded. "And then put it up in your office as a subtle way of telling people that you're not scary and that you do have a sense of humour."

"You think I'm scary?"

She flushed. "I don't, no, but…"

"You want me to take the 'you know what' out of myself?"

"Definitely."

He laughed. "I'll have a go, then."

"You'd better not have one of me… You do, don't you?"

"Well...I...yes, I do." He pulled the drawing out and handed it to her. "I tried to imagine your expression when you were asked where the monkeys slept."

She was wearing an expression of astonishment, hilarity, and pity. She was holding a hand to her forehead with her lips slightly parted in consternation. She had to admit, it was her to a tee.

"I've offended you, haven't I?" he asked quietly.

"No," she replied. "It's me. But I want to see the one of you."

"It's a deal."

"You're very good."

He pulled an embarrassed expression and returned the drawings to a drawer. "It's just a hobby."

"And that was a compliment."

"I know, I'm sorry. I don't get complimented very often. Thank you. Did Stephanie mention the photographic exhibition to you?"

"No?"

"Oh. Well, it's on in Leeds. It's a collection of turn of the last century photographs of the county. She mentioned that the three of us could go?"

She watched him nervously run his fingers along the edge of the desk.

"I'd love to go, but it would have to be Tuesday."

"Yes, of course. Would it interfere with anything?" he asked. "You visiting your father, I mean?"

"No. I'll visit him the evening before."

"How is he?"

"He's very well, considering. Thank you."

"Good." He smiled. "Oh, a Vincent Graves is coming

tomorrow to interview me, take some photographs, and to look around. He'll probably want to go on the tour." She nodded. "You know him?"

"A little. Don't worry, he's okay."

"I asked Stephanie for some tips. She said for me to just be myself." He rolled his eyes.

"She's right. It'll be worse if you put on an act."

"I suppose so," he mused. "But I'll be glad when it's over."

"I think you should know that something else has gone missing from the drawing room," she told him. "A small box containing some silver spoons."

"My grandmother collected spoons. No member of the public is allowed inside the house unless on a tour and then there's the burglar alarm. I set it myself every evening."

"Who knows the code?" she asked.

"Myself and Des." He sighed. "I'm not even going to suspect Des. Or Helen. They've been here since my father's final days, through the very worst of things. Someone must be getting into the house during the day."

"But I close the front door after admitting each group. Sometimes the tour leader doesn't go on the tour but they go straight to the kitchen and Helen's there with them all the time."

"Well, someone is getting in," he said.

"Who has a key to the side door?"

"Myself, Lady Heaton, Des, Helen, you. And now Stephanie." He closed his eyes tightly and shook his head. "No. She couldn't be so stupid…I don't suppose you have a video camera?"

She shook her head. "No, I'm afraid not."

"I think Des has. I'll ask if we can borrow it. It'll have to be next week, though."

Next week? She frowned and he smiled wryly.

"I do allow them the occasional holiday."

She flushed. "Sorry."

"We'll both keep an eye on things, yes?"

"Yes."

She sighed as she returned to the flat. It wasn't his sister, it was Lady Heaton. How could she tell him? She sighed again. She could only hope that Lady Heaton was caught in the act on camera, though what the repercussions would be, she had no idea.

Someone knocked on the flat door that evening and Sophia quickly closed the lid of her laptop before going downstairs to answer it. She had been going through her photographs for more pictures of Danielle and Michelle to attach to an email to Heaton.

"I've got a bottle of whisky on the go." Stephanie smiled. "Flat-warming of sorts. Thomas is choosing a CD so it could well be Wagner. You have been warned."

Sophia followed her next door. Thankfully, an Annie Lennox CD was playing and Heaton was pouring whisky into three tumblers.

"No ice, sorry," he told her. "Would you like water in it?"

"No, thanks, it's fine as it is." She took one.

Stephanie picked up the second glass and Thomas the third. "What shall we drink to?" she asked. "I know. New beginnings. Well, for me, anyway."

"New beginnings." The three of them touched glasses and drank.

"So we're all set for next Tuesday, then?" Stephanie

added. "God, I so need to get out somewhere. Even if it is to a photographic thing."

"It'll be interesting, the exhibitions there always are," Heaton said.

"So interesting you ended up across the road at the dirty photographs exhibition the last time."

Heaton flushed with annoyance and gulped the whisky.

"I went to it with a friend," she told Stephanie. "It was a bit too strong for her. But I thought it was interesting." She pulled a comical expression and Stephanie laughed.

"But not art?"

Sophia shrugged. "I'm not sure."

"Thomas?" Stephanie called. "Are dirty photographs art?"

"I suppose it depends on what context you look at them in. If you looked at them on the internet, for example, they could be considered pornography. But in the context of an exhibition, I think they can be considered art."

"Bloody hell. A yes or no would have done, you know?"

"A yes or no wouldn't have been enough," he snapped.

"So-rry. Here, have some more whisky and chill out a bit." Stephanie picked up the bottle and sloshed more whisky into his glass. "It's not single malt but hey. Sophia?"

"Thank you." She held her glass out and Stephanie added more whisky.

"Oh, I love this song." Stephanie turned the stereo system up and began to dance around the room, the bottle in one hand and her glass in the other.

"I think she's had a head start on the whisky," Heaton murmured and retrieved the bottle from her. "You don't have to stay, you know?"

Sophia smiled. "I know, but it's interesting."

Heaton shrugged comically. "You don't have to be polite."

"I'm not. If you want to go, I'll keep an eye on her."

"What are you two whispering about?" Stephanie suddenly demanded. "Come and dance."

"I think we'll just watch," Heaton replied. "Thanks all the same."

"You're no fun."

"So you keep telling me."

"But you don't take any notice." Stephanie sank down into an armchair. "Have you ever been drunk? I bet Sophia has."

Sophia spluttered and began to laugh. "Thanks a lot. I have, but not for a while."

"So, Thomas?"

Heaton pulled a face. "Yes," he replied shortly.

"When? In a previous life?"

"Stephanie," he warned and her hands flew up in a mock defensive gesture.

"I'm just asking when?"

"At university," he told her.

"That's twenty years ago."

"I can bloody count." He gulped his whisky down and poured himself another.

"That's the spirit." Stephanie laughed then laughed again at her pun. "Pour Sophia some more, too."

"Just a little," she said, holding her glass out and watching as he poured. "Thank you. So you like the flat, Stephanie?"

"I love the flat. All hail darling brother for allowing me to move in."

Sophia left as early as she could without being rude. She went back to her laptop, attached a photograph to the finished email, and clicked on send.

Dear Lord Heaton

Please find attached a photograph of Danielle, Michelle, my mother and myself taken on the day Michelle and I started school. I'm afraid this is the last photograph I have of Danielle on my laptop. I have an album with Michelle's wedding photographs but I don't have a scanner, unfortunately.

Regards
Sophia Nelson

She went to the fridge starting to feel quite light-headed thanks to the three enormous whiskies. About to open the door, she heard the jingle on her laptop announcing the arrival of an email. It was from Heaton. She went to the window and saw him at the desk in his office leaning on a fist at the PC.

Dear Ms Nelson

Thank you for sending me the photograph. Stephanie has now retired to bed so I hope she doesn't snore. If she does, just bang on the wall. :) I have to apologise for our behaviour this evening, we behaved like school children. I'm sure the last thing you wanted to hear was Steph telling me how boring I am. I know I am, I just don't particularly like hearing it. I just hope it won't put you off going to the exhibition with us on Tuesday. We'll try to behave. :)

Regards
Thomas Heaton

She clicked on 'Reply'.

Dear Lord Heaton
> *There is no need to apologise, you're not boring,*
> *and I am looking forward to Tuesday, believe it or*
> *not. I must be a glutton for punishment.* :)
> *Regards*
> *Sophia Nelson*

Five minutes later, her laptop heralded another email.

Dear Ms Nelson
> *I'm not boring? Thanks for that! But, yes, you*
> *must be a glutton for punishment if you don't mind*
> *listening to a brother and sister bickering. I hope she's*
> *not snoring yet? Remember, just bang on the wall. I*
> *think I had one too many whiskies. I usually have*
> *just enough spare time to savour one glass of single*
> *malt in the library, not three enormous glasses of*
> *cheap stuff. So ignore me if I'm rambling.*
> *A rather sloshed Thomas Heaton*

Sophia laughed and clicked on 'Reply'.

Dear A rather sloshed Thomas Heaton
> *I don't think I've ever had single malt so I can't*
> *really compare it with the cheap stuff. All I know is*
> *that cheap wine causes the most bloody awful*
> *hangovers as Michelle and I discovered after her hen*
> *night. Thank God it wasn't the night before the*
> *wedding as I'm not sure how our green faces would*

*have gone with her ivory dress and my burgundy one.
I looked like Widow Twanky as it was. I hated my
dress. Really hated it. Talk about making me look
like Ten Tonne Tessie. The slip underneath was
nicer than the dress. But, of course, I was too polite
to say anything. :(But everyone is meant to look at
the bride not the great lump behind her and Michelle
did look fantastic and she and Tony are very happy.
One girl I was at school with split from her husband
after three weeks.*

*I don't know about you, but I think I had two
too many whiskies.*

Very Sloshed Sophia Nelson

A reply arrived very quickly

Dear Very Sloshed Sophia Nelson

*From what I could see of the picture you sent of
the wedding, your dress was a bit meringuey. Not
your fault. Maybe you should have just worn the slip
but then you would have completely upstaged the
bride. Was it the same colour as the dress?*

*I'm attaching a picture of me in full regalia in the
House of Lords. It was my one and only attendance.
Absolutely not sexy. Try not to laugh too much.*

*Is there such a word as meringuey?! I don't know?
Hope you know what I mean. :)*

Thomas

She opened the photograph and smiled. He looked very
young and rather uncomfortable. She saved the photograph

to her desktop and began a reply.

> *The robes were, how can I put it? Interesting. Not sexy? Hmmm. Depends on what was underneath! As for meringuey? Brilliant word! The slip was the same colour as the dress. I wish I'd had the nerve to tell Michelle. I mean, leg of mutton sleeves. What was she thinking?*
> *Sophia*

Shaking her head, she clicked on send and waited impatiently for a reply.

> *Interesting? I looked like an idiot. What was underneath? One of my infamous suits. :(So categorically not sexy. I wish you'd had the nerve to tell Michelle, too. You know, I find myself writing emails to you a lot. I never send or save any of them, sometimes I don't even finish what I start. Pathetic isn't it?*
> *And now I'm very, very, very sloshed.*
> *Thomas*

Oh, God, what was in those emails, she wondered, clicking on 'Reply'.

> *The next time you're debating whether to email me, please do. I mean, if I don't like what you've written I can reply and say please don't send emails like that again. We don't even have to speak about it so no harm done.*
> *Sophia*

She clicked on send then disconnected from the internet, shut down the laptop and went to get undressed and into a pair of pyjamas. While in the bathroom about to brush her teeth, she heard an almighty crash from next door. She threw the tube of toothpaste into the sink, ran to her bedroom, and just managed to pull on a pair of trainers without falling over. She staggered down the stairs and out into the yard. There was darkness in Stephanie's flat but Heaton was still in his office. She went across the yard and threw open the door. He looked over at her bleary-eyed.

"Sorry, I just heard a crash." She tried to enunciate each word but they still sounded slurred. "From Stephanie's flat."

He quickly reached for some keys and, with a struggle, managed to unlock a drawer and take out another bunch.

"Master keys," he told her slowly. "For emergencies."

They crossed the stable yard and he slowly and precisely inserted the key into the lock, opened the door, and they climbed the stairs to Stephanie's flat.

"Steph?" he hissed, switching on a light. "Steph, what've you done now?"

The door to the large bedroom was ajar and Sophia pushed it open. Stephanie lay on the floor beside the bed.

"She's fell…fallen out of bed. Give me a hand."

With a struggle, they lifted her back onto the bed and covered her.

"Should we tie her to it?" he asked and Sophia giggled. He closed the door and accidentally kicked over the empty whisky bottle which rattled across the floor. "Shit." He picked it up with a groan and put it in the sink. "Christ, a one-litre bottle between three of us…no wonder we're completely sloshed." He leaned back against the breakfast bar and she saw his eyes scrutinise the strappy top of her pyjamas before resting on her cleavage.

"And what are you looking at?" she asked with a smile.

"You. Your breasts."

"My breasts?"

He shook his head slowly. "Ignore me, I'm drunk. It's not right, I said so in my email."

"Which one?"

"You probably haven't got it yet."

"I got your others."

Again, he shook his head slowly. "Shouldn't have."

"What?"

"Told you…fuck…why did you have to come here?"

"Hmm?" she murmured.

"I mean, have you any idea how much I want to touch you?"

"Have you any idea just how much I want you to touch me?"

He heaved himself away from the breakfast bar. "Come here, then."

She walked forward, he lifted her onto the bar and stood between her legs staring down her cleavage.

"It's rude to stare."

"Hold your arms up, then." She did as she was told and he pulled the top off. "You're so beautiful," he whispered, reaching out to hold her breasts in his hands. She watched as he smoothed a thumb over each nipple then bent his head to kiss them. "Like that?" he asked softly as she sighed.

"Hmm."

"Hmm yes, or hmm no?"

"Yes."

"Good. That slip, have you still got it?"

She laughed. "No."

"Pity."

He watched while she slowly undid the buttons of his shirt, drew it apart, and pushed it off his shoulders.

"Very nice," she murmured, running a finger down his chest.

"For a slob who smokes and doesn't exercise enough."

"True."

He bent his head and kissed her mouth, down her neck, and to her breasts. She closed her eyes, running her fingers through his hair as he pulled at her nipples with his lips. Then, there was another crash, and they both jumped violently.

"What the hell was that?" he gasped.

"Stephanie?"

"Stay there." He went to the bedroom door and she saw that his sister was on the floor again. "Bloody hell," he muttered.

"Come on." She slid off the bar. "Middle of the bed this time."

They hauled Stephanie into the bed and as Sophia covered her with the duvet, she caught Heaton staring at her.

"What?" she asked softly.

"Go back to your flat," he whispered and her heart sank.

"But—"

"We're drunk and I want you too much, but not... drunk...and I'm your boss." He smiled sadly.

"But—"

"Please?" He went out, returned with her top, and passed it to her. "Please put it on. Now." Taking it from him, she pulled it on. "Thank you." He held the bedroom door open and she went back out to the living area. "I'm sorry."

"You're always bloody sorry," she blurted out. "And you keep pushing me away. I'm sick of being pushed away. My mum and dad did it. Lee did it. And I'm sick of it."

He frowned. "Why did your parents push you away?"

"They wanted me to be independent because they knew that there'd come a time when they wouldn't be there for me. No wonder I wouldn't let Lee go. No wonder I followed him all the way down to London and made a complete idiot of myself. And now you're doing it. Well, I'm sick of it."

"Well, how the hell do you think I feel?" he demanded. "Apart from anything else, I can't sleep with you because I'd hate for you or anyone to think I was only sleeping with you so that you would keep quiet about Danielle."

"'Anyone', being Lady Heaton, I take it?" She shook her head. "Well, she can fuck off."

He rolled his eyes. "If only it was that simple. I'm sorry, but sleeping with you now would be a mistake."

"Would it. Is this how little you really think of me? A mistake. Thanks a fucking lot. Fine. Just push me away like everyone else," she threw at him, turned and began to make her way to the door of the flat. "One night, that's all. I mean, we're drunk. We can blame the cheap whisky. We can do the whole corny, 'last night was a mistake' thing tomorrow." He made no reply and she smiled and nodded bitterly. "God, what a slapper, eh?"

"No."

She opened the door. "Yes. Lee called me a 'clingy bitch' and he was probably right." She went out and slammed the door behind her.

Chapter Seven

She woke with a thumping hangover, which two black coffees, one straight after another, began to eliminate. She stared at the laptop on the table. A notepad with 'meringuey' written on it lay beside it and she couldn't help but smile. Glancing out of the window, she saw Heaton walk to his office with a mug in his hand. In the office, he put the mug down and rubbed his eyes. She blew out her cheeks, remembering his lips pulling at her nipples. Fresh air was called for so she reached for her jacket and went out, just managing not to look in Heaton's direction, and walked as briskly as she could to the end of the drive and back.

Returning to the flat, she found an envelope on the mat. She put the kettle on for a third coffee and opened it. It was an official letter from Heaton, written on Heaton Abbey House headed notepaper.

Dear Ms Nelson

Please accept my sincere apologies for my behaviour last night, both in person and online, which was completely inappropriate. I would like to assure you that it will not happen again and I have deleted the emails I received from you.

If you feel that my behaviour constitutes sexual harassment and wish to make an official complaint, I will completely understand.

Should you wish to discuss this matter further please contact me so that a meeting can be arranged at which Lady Heaton or Mrs Fields can be present if you so wish.

Again, I apologise unreservedly for my behaviour and any embarrassment, offence or distress it may have caused.

Yours sincerely
Thomas Heaton

She threw the letter onto the worktop, reached for her phone, and rang Michelle at work. "It's Sophia. Can you talk?"

"Yes, what's up?"

"I need to talk to you about something."

"Oh? You sound…angry, is everything all right? Is your dad okay?"

"Dad's fine," Sophia assured her. "I need a chat about me. Can I come round sometime?"

"Yes, of course, you can. Look, Tony's going out with the lads tomorrow evening. Come then? Or is it more urgent?"

Tomorrow? She pulled an exasperated expression. She needed to talk now. "No, tomorrow evening's fine."

"About eight?"

"Thanks, Michelle. I'll see you then."

She sighed and went to her laptop. Two emails downloaded. Both were from Heaton.

I know I shouldn't be emailing you like this but I've had too much to drink and the image of you in that slip keeps going around and around in my mind. Steph thinks I was born middle-aged but I think you know that I wasn't, at least I hope you know. One thing you might be glad to know is that the suits will be banished to my wardrobe unless they are really necessary. I really, really want to tell you what I feel for you but I don't think it would be appropriate as I'm your boss.

I know you probably don't care about me one bit so I would be very happy if we could just be friends?

She clicked open the second email.

How the hell can we just be friends when I've just told you that I care for you? Please forget I said any of it, it was very unprofessional of me, I apologise.

You've gone to bed now so I'll stop.

Sophia sat staring at the screen for a long time until she re-read all his emails then sadly deleted them one by one. She then opened a new email.

Dear Lord Heaton

Thank you for your letter.

I, too, would like to apologise for my behaviour and the embarrassment, offence and distress it must have caused you. I also apologise for shouting at you again. All in all, it was very unprofessional of me.

I have deleted all of last night's emails and will
not be taking any further action.
Sincerely
Sophia Nelson

She clicked on 'Send' and swore.

Her tour, a group of twenty Americans with Vincent Graves in tow, passed without incident. So far, nothing further had been taken from the drawing room, she noticed with relief. Vincent remained behind in the kitchen as she saw the group out to the gardens and was helping himself to another cup of coffee when she returned.

"Excellent tour." He smiled.

"Thank you."

"Get asked any daft questions?"

"A few."

"So, what is Lord Heaton like?"

Behind her, Sophia saw Helen look over with a frown.

"Very pleasant. As is Lady Heaton, and Stephanie. Lord Heaton works very hard here."

"Is he a recluse?"

Helen cleared her throat with great disapproval at this line of questioning.

"No," Sophia replied simply.

"No?"

"No. As I said, he works very hard here, but that does not make him a recluse."

She ended on a note of finality and Vincent nodded and turned as Heaton himself stood at the door looking none the worse for wear.

"Lord Heaton."

"Thomas, please."

"Vincent." They shook hands.

"Would you like to come out to the office or would you prefer to take some photographs first?"

"The photographs first, while it's dry?"

Heaton nodded and extended a hand out into the corridor. He looked over at her as Vincent went out, flushed, and she gave him what she hoped was an encouraging smile but was probably more of an embarrassed one.

"What an awful man," Helen hissed.

"I wasn't rude, was I?"

"No. I hope his Lordship keeps his temper."

"So do I. I told him that Vincent was okay. Me and my big mouth."

Sophia went to her flat and kept an eye on them out of the window. The two men crossed the yard about half an hour later and went into Heaton's office, emerging after a further half an hour. When Heaton returned to his office she went across the stable yard, took a deep breath, and knocked.

"How did it go?" she asked hesitantly, opening the door.

"All right, I think. I'm just glad it's over."

"How's Stephanie?" she added. "I didn't see her this morning."

"She's fine. Even apologised, which was a first."

"And how's your head?"

"Okay now. Not so okay at eight this morning. You seem to have escaped relatively unscathed."

"Just about." She smiled. "I'm not green in the face, anyway."

"Thank you for your email. I don't get drunk often," he added quickly.

"I know. Neither do I."

He nodded. "Thank you for being so understanding."

"I wasn't. I was anything but understanding and I'm sorry. I should never have said what I did and I wouldn't blame you if you sacked me."

"I'm not going to sack you," he told her, much to her relief. "We both behaved inappropriately and I think we should both try and put it behind us. Yes?"

She nodded. "Yes. Thank you. You won't mind, then, if I send meringuey to the *Oxford English Dictionary*?"

He frowned for a moment then just managed to keep a straight face. "Do you think they'd take it?"

"Maybe."

"You'd better send it, then."

She was at Michelle's at eight o'clock on the dot that evening.

"Come in." Michelle smiled. "I've just put the kettle on." They brought their mugs of coffee into the living room and sat on the sofa. "So what's up? You sounded like you were about to strangle someone yesterday."

"Lord Heaton," she replied simply.

"What, he's a pain in the arse?"

"Yeah, and the rest."

"What?" Michelle's eyes bulged. "Oh, my God, you don't fancy him, do you?" Sophia looked away. "Sophia?"

"I don't know what to do," she said miserably. "I need to leave but I can't because I need the money and I need the flat but…"

"Heaton," Michelle finished and Sophia smiled sadly and nodded. "Okay, tell me what's been going on."

"Everyone thinks he's a recluse. He isn't. I mean, he doesn't go out much but it's not like he never leaves the house or anything. I mean, we've been going walking together for weeks now—"

"Walking?" Michelle interrupted incredulously. "Hang on. Hang on. Rewind. You go walking together?"

"It came up that I go walking and I asked if he'd like to come. He said yes after a bit and we go walking on the moors. Stephanie comes too at the moment, though."

"His sister?" Michelle asked.

Sophia swallowed. "Yes."

"Okay. Go on."

"I fancied him from the start. Bloody hell it's so corny but he's tall, dark and handsome. But he's got an awful temper and he smokes."

Michelle shrugged. "You can't have everything."

"No. We just…talk. He's shy and he's lonely. He hates to admit it but he is. Everyone just treats him like 'Lord Heaton' and it's like he's become this character and he has to keep on playing it. I mean, he continually calls me Ms Nelson. He's never once called me Sophia."

"And what do you call him?" Michelle frowned.

"Lord Heaton," she replied. "It sounds ridiculous but he's never once asked me to call him Thomas."

"And you never once thought to ask him to call you Sophia?" Michelle added and Sophia shrugged. "Does he fancy you?"

"Yes."

"What?" Michelle had reached for her mug but had to put it down again. "How do you know?"

"He, um, draws people. He's got drawings of me."

Michelle stared at her until the penny dropped. "He draws dirty pictures of you? Yuck. Don't you find that creepy?"

"Creepy? No. I don't think they're dirty pictures, anyway. If I didn't feel the way I do about him, then, I probably would find it weird, yes."

"Bloody hell." Michelle picked up her mug and took a gulp of coffee.

"And I've overheard him on the phone to a friend. Talking about me."

"Oh?" Michelle put the mug down. "And?"

"He's shy," Sophia told her. "And he says he's my boss and all that."

"What did the friend say?"

"To go for it, you only live once."

"But he hasn't?"

Sophia sighed. "Stephanie's moved into the third flat in the stable yard. She had a kind of housewarming. We all got drunk on cheap whisky and to cut a long story short, Heaton and I ended up together in the living room of Stephanie's flat."

"And?" Michelle asked eagerly.

"And we kissed a lot, he took off my top, I took off his shirt, we kissed a lot. Then Stephanie fell out of bed."

Michelle pulled a disbelieving expression. "What?"

"I'd heard a crash earlier," she explained. "Heaton and I went back up to her flat to see what was wrong. She'd fallen out of bed. That's why we were alone there together."

"Okay, right." Michelle nodded. "So she fell out of bed again…"

"And Heaton came to his senses, kind of, and made excuses. He said he didn't want me drunk and that he was my boss. I shouted and swore at him a bit and he shouted back at me and then I left. But then I got a letter from him the next morning all typed and official, apologising for his behaviour the previous night; that it was highly inappropriate and that if I wanted to go to a tribunal or something that he would completely understand. I don't want to go to a fucking tribunal, I want to pull all his clothes off him and go to bed with him."

Michelle began to laugh. "Oh, God, sorry. Jesus, you have got it bad. Write him a letter and say that. Maybe not quite like that but…"

"He'd sent me emails, too. He says stuff in his emails that he can't say face to face and he was drunk that night."

"So they were a bit…?" Michelle waggled her head from side to side suggestively.

"They were very…for him, you know what I mean?"

"Have you still got them?"

She shook her head. "No, he deleted mine so I deleted his."

"Great."

"I just don't know what to do, Michelle." She sighed.

"Do you like it there? Apart from him?"

"Yes. The job's great and so is the flat. And I can see right into his office from the window of the living area."

"Okay, ask yourself this: is this lust or love?"

Sophia grimaced. "Heaton's friend said more or less the same thing to him."

"And what did he say?" Michelle asked.

She shrugged. "He didn't really answer."

"Well, you answer me. What is it? Try and forget that he's your boss."

"Love," she replied quietly. "It was lust but not now."

"Do you think it would work out? I mean, he's a lord. Your dad will go nuts."

"Dad knows he fancies me," she said. "He saw it at the funeral. But all he can see is the 'lord thing'."

"The 'lord thing' is all a lot of people will see," Michelle told her quietly.

"I know," she replied miserably.

"Do you think he'd ever make the first move?"

"No, I doubt it."

"Then, it's up to you, girl." Michelle squeezed her arm. "That's your mission should you choose to accept it. I just hope he's a better man than Lee. I don't want to see you hurt again."

"Thanks. And thanks for listening. I needed someone to just talk it all out to."

Michelle smiled. "And what will you do?"

"Try and pluck up the courage to go for it."

Sophia collected the photographs the following Monday, sat in the car, and pulled them out of the wallet. She sighed. In every photograph, Heaton smouldered, even in the ones orchestrated by Stephanie. If things got really bad, there would definitely be work for him as a model.

She drove back to the abbey, went straight to his office, and knocked.

"Yes?"

"The photographs," she announced, opening the door.

He pulled a pained expression. "Are they awful?"

"No, they're very good, actually." She passed the envelope to him and watched as he pushed his glasses up his nose and went through them, stopping at the photograph of her. She tried her best not to blush.

"It came out," he exclaimed.

"Unfortunately."

"I think it's very good, considering that it's my one and only attempt." He groaned as he came to the last few. "Oh, my God. Stephanie really expects me to give Lady Heaton one of these?"

"I think that one is the best." She extracted it and put it on the desk.

"Why that one?"

"Because it is the least self-conscious one of you. You could give that one to Lady Heaton and not be embarrassed. What are you working on?" She nodded to the sheet of paper which he'd turned over when she came in.

"Me. And it's been agony."

"Is it finished?"

"More or less."

"Am I allowed to see?"

He grimaced and turned the sheet of paper over.

She clapped a hand over her mouth. He had demonic eyes, it looked as though his tie was choking him, his eyebrows were almost together in a frown and there was smoke coming out of his ears.

"That's brilliant."

"Thank you very much," he replied. "I had thought I was being a bit too hard on myself." She couldn't help but laugh. "I've had Vincent Graves on the telephone," he went on. "There's going to be a launch of the tourism brochure on Friday evening. I've been invited, and I can bring a guest, too. I was wondering if you'd come along and help me plug this place?

Apparently, someone from the local paper is going to be there, too. And seeing as you're the tour guide...?"

"Where is the launch?" she asked.

"The town hall. Look, there's bound to be lots of boring speeches, you don't have to come."

"I don't mind."

"Oh?" He stared at her in some surprise. "Oh, okay, then. Good."

Back at the flat, the first thing she did was to ring Michelle. "Are you going to the tourism brochure launch?"

"Me? No, I'm only part-time. Full-timers and big wigs only. Why?"

"Lord Heaton's been invited and he's asked me to go, too," she explained.

"Really? I hope you said yes?"

She blew out her cheeks. "I did, but I'm kind of regretting it now. I thought you'd be there. Oh, well, it'll only be for a couple of hours. Have you seen the brochures yet?"

"I have. They were delivered this morning. They've printed a picture of you, too."

She rolled her eyes. "Oh, no."

"But it's a lovely picture – you and a load of Americans."

"What about the rest?" she asked.

"Well, you neglected to tell me just how seriously gorgeous Lord Heaton is, which I'm very annoyed about. Handsome doesn't do him justice at all. Women will be flocking to the place just to get a glimpse of him."

"And then having to make do with me," she muttered.

Michelle laughed kindly. "Let me know how it goes, won't you?"

Heaton knocked at the flat door at seven thirty on Friday evening and she checked her appearance for the hundredth time before going downstairs. Ignoring her navy blue suit which would now be forever linked to her mum's funeral, she had opted for her brown pinstripe trouser suit and a white blouse. Dressy but not too dressy.

Heaton was in a brown suit she hadn't seen before but, then again, he probably had a wardrobe full of the things.

"The taxi's here," he said unnecessarily as it halted behind him.

"Right."

"Let's just hope this isn't too boring."

The taxi deposited them outside the town hall and they made their way up the magnificent central staircase to a large reception room. Once inside the room, Heaton stopped dead and grabbed her arm. Puzzled, she looked to where he was staring at in horror. Bloody hell, it was a huge enlargement of the brochure, and he was on the front cover. Standing at the front door with a slight smile. God, it was almost life size.

"Oh, no," he hissed. "He never said that I'd be going on the front."

"Lord Heaton." The mayor rushed across the room to them. "You're very welcome."

"Yes." Heaton tore his eyes away from the enormous front cover. "Thank you."

"Impressive, isn't it?" The mayor nodded towards the display.

"Er." She saw Heaton fighting to gather himself together. "Sorry. I didn't realise that it would be my picture on the cover."

"Oh, I see." The mayor laughed. "And this is…?"

"Sophia Nelson," she said, putting out a hand. "I'm the tour guide."

"Excellent." He shook it. "Come and have a drink."

"This is going to be bloody awful," Heaton muttered as they followed the Mayor across to a table laden with glasses and bottles of wine and sparkling water.

"Sorry, I had no idea."

"Try and get a look at the article, will you please?" he begged.

"Red or white?" The mayor asked.

"Red." They answered at the same time and the mayor laughed. Heaton glared at him before taking a glass and passing it to her.

She made her way to the stand and picked up a brochure, flipping through the pages until she came to the feature.

Heaton Abbey House Opens its Doors to the Public

She quickly scanned through the feature and sighed with relief. If Vincent had done a hatchet-job she would never have forgiven him but that would have been like cutting off his nose to spite his face seeing as the Abbey House was now the biggest tourist attraction in the area.

"Well?" Heaton joined her. "Dare I read the article?"

"Yes, because you come across very well. Vincent did a good job."

"Well, that's a relief because that," he looked up at himself with disgust, "is bloody terrible."

"Try and ignore it. We'd better mingle."

"Yes, I suppose so."

She made her way across the room to Janice Brown who worked with Michelle in the tourist office.

Janice greeted her with a smile. "His Lordship doesn't look happy."

"He didn't know he was going to be on the cover."

"Well, it was either him or the mayor and as the whole idea is to attract people here and not frighten them away…" She tailed off and Sophia smiled. "So, how are things up at the abbey?"

"I like it there."

"And what's he like to work for?" Janice asked.

"Fine."

"Only fine?" Janice's eyebrows rose.

"I have no problems working there," she elaborated. "Both he and Lady Heaton are very pleasant."

"But he's gorgeous."

Sophia could feel herself beginning to blush. "He is better looking than the mayor, I'll give you that."

"That wouldn't be bloody hard," Janice smirked.

"He's not giving a speech, is he?" Sophia asked. "The mayor?"

"Of course he is, you know he loves the sound of his own voice. Oh, here we go." Janice groaned as the mayor made his way over to the display, a clearly reluctant Heaton following.

"My Lord, ladies and gentlemen," he began and laughed.

Heaton rolled his eyes and Janice sighed. "Asshole," she muttered.

"I'd like to thank you all for coming this evening to launch the town's first, and hopefully first of many, tourist brochures. As you know, since the destruction of the town's mining museum we have been without a major tourist attraction in the area. However, with thanks to Lord Heaton, here, we now have Heaton Abbey House and gardens open to the public – a major attraction right on our doorstep…"

The mayor rabbitted on for a further ten minutes before the photographer from the local paper began taking photographs.

Janice nudged her. "I think they want you over there for a photo."

"Oh, no." She trudged across the room.

"Ah, Sophia." The mayor beamed at her. "You stand here." She stood uncomfortably between Heaton and the mayor and grimaced as the photographs were taken. "All done?" He asked the photographer, who nodded. "Excellent. Thank you all."

"Are you okay?" she asked Heaton once they were alone.

"Not really." He threw a glare at the mayor's back. "Did you see me standing there like a complete arse?"

"The mayor is the complete arse, not you."

Finally, he smiled. "Another drink, I think. Red or white?"

"Red, please. I'll be back in a couple of minutes."

She went out into the corridor in search of the ladies toilets. Spotting a sign, she headed in that direction, only to almost collide at the corner with the mayor coming out of the gents.

"Ah, Sophia Nelson. Anything to Willie?"

"No, he's a country and western singer," she replied briskly and went to go past him.

"What's the hurry?" He stepped in front of her.

"I thought that was obvious. Now, excuse me."

"You're very pretty."

Oh, yuck, go away. "I said, excuse me."

"Your mum was very pretty, too," the mayor added.

"I beg your pardon?" She stared up at him.

"I was your mum's first boyfriend, her first kiss."

"Really."

"We were stepping out for a long time," he explained. "Then she met Willie."

"His name is William," she told him tightly.

"Dropped me like a stone, she did. For Willie bloody Nelson."

"I see. Right. Well, excuse me."

"You're not like that, are you, Sophia?" he asked. "Planning on dumping anyone soon? Lord Heaton would be a good catch and by the way he was sizing you up earlier I'd say he'd be in your knickers quick as a flash if you let him."

She slapped his face hard. "You're drunk."

"Not drunk enough to get a kiss off of you."

Before she could react, he had grabbed her shoulders, and thrown her up against the wall.

"Hey?" She heard a shout and feet running towards them. Someone began to haul the mayor away from her. "Get away from her." It was Heaton. She managed to escape and watched as the mayor was thrown against the wall. "If I ever catch you near her again, I will kill you."

"Quite a threat, your Lordship." The mayor laughed.

"I mean it."

"Yes, well, I am the mayor and you are...what? Baron Heaton. A useless title. Can't sit in the House of Lords anymore so what's the point of you? When I was a lad you lot owned the mine. Now you have to rely on coach tours to survive. Oh, how the mighty have fallen, eh?"

Heaton gave him a good shake then let him go. Sophia shot a glance down the corridor towards the corner and the reception room beyond. Miraculously, no-one had heard. Heaton took her hand and led her towards the staircase. Halfway down the stairs, she stumbled and he had to grab her other arm to stop her from falling. He got her to the bottom and onto a bench.

"Are you hurt?" he asked.

She shook her head. "He said he knew my mum."

"I know, I heard."

That meant he had heard the comment about getting in her knickers, too. "I didn't think he was that drunk."

"Drunk or not, he should bloody-well know how to behave."

"Yes."

"Well, this has been a fantastic evening, hasn't it?" He sighed.

She spluttered a laugh. "I have had better. Thank you for rescuing me."

"It was nothing."

"No, I mean it. I couldn't move." Looking down at her hands, she saw they had started to shake. He gently took them in his own hands and held them tightly.

"Did you follow me?" she asked.

"The mayor followed you. I followed the mayor."

"How?" she added. "He was coming out of the gents?"

"By the time you found the toilets, he had more or less run the circuit of that floor and was pretending to come out of the gents," he explained.

"Oh. No-one's ever done that to me before."

"I should bloody-well think not. Do you look like your mother?" he asked.

"Yes, a bit, but she had brown eyes and I've got Dad's blue eyes."

"When I was small, people used to tell me that I had my mother's eyes." He shrugged and smiled wryly. "Let's find a taxi and go home. We'll have a proper drink in the library."

Twenty minutes later, she accepted a glass of whisky from him and went to one of the library's two armchairs. "Thank you. Was he at Mum's funeral?" she asked. "Did you see him there?"

"I honestly don't know." He brought his glass to the other armchair. "I'm sorry."

"My mum's first boyfriend, bloody hell." She sipped the whisky. "And it seems she went out with him for a while."

"Yes, but she saw sense in the end, and that's the main thing."

She laughed. "Mum and Dad courted for six years before they got married. Six years."

"My father courted Lady Heaton for six weeks before proposing."

"Six weeks?" she echoed.

He nodded. "I suppose he thought, what's the point of dragging his feet if she's the right woman? He clearly must have loved her deeply seeing as he didn't divorce her when no children came along. There's a wedding photo here somewhere." He got up and went to the desk. He put his glass down and began to rummage in a drawer. "Here it is."

She joined him at the desk and stared at Lady Heaton. She had been a stunning bride. Her husband – actually smiling in this photo – was tall, dark, and handsome and had bequeathed his looks to his son.

"You look very much like your father," she said.

"Well, as long as I don't turn into him, I don't mind. I'd hate for my children not to have really known their father."

"Lady Heaton was very beautiful," she added.

"Yes, she was. She could have had her pick of husbands but for some reason, she chose my father, twenty years older than her."

"Was her father an old father?" she asked.

"Yes, he was getting on when she was born. Why? You think she was trying to replace her father?"

She laughed. "Oh, I don't know. We'd better not over analyse, I think I've watched one too many daytime talk shows."

When they finished their drinks, he walked her across the stable yard to the door of the flat.

"You're all right?" he asked softly.

"Yes. Thank you again." She reached up and quickly kissed his cheek. "Goodnight."

There was a knock at the door while she was at her breakfast. She went downstairs and opened it, expecting Heaton, but found Stephanie on the step instead.

"So, was it really boring?" Stephanie asked.

"Yes and no. Come in."

"What happened?" Stephanie followed her up the stairs and into the flat.

"The mayor made a pass at me. Well, more of a lunge. He threw me up against a wall."

Stephanie's chin almost hit the floor. "Bloody hell. What did you do?"

"Nothing. I couldn't move. Luckily Lord – um – Thomas rescued me."

Stephanie rolled her eyes in relief. "Were you hurt?"

She shook her head. "No, just a bit shocked. Usually men run away from me, not towards me."

"Don't be silly. Have you been to the police?"

"No. Would you like some coffee?" she asked.

"No, thanks. You are going to, aren't you?"

Sophia shrugged, sat down at the breakfast bar, and patted the stool beside her. "I'd have to make a statement."

Stephanie sat on the stool. "Yes, so?"

"Thomas threatened to kill him."

Stephanie rolled her eyes in a 'nice one, Thomas' way. "Thomas didn't hit him or anything?"

"No, but the threat was enough. Anyway, I doubt if the mayor will do it to another woman."

"How come?"

"He was drunk and getting his own back at my mum for dumping him," she explained. "He was her first boyfriend and she left him for my dad."

"Wow, he's not one to bear grudges, is he?" Stephanie asked and Sophia shrugged. "Are you still coming to Leeds on Tuesday?"

"Yes, I'm really looking forward to a day out, actually."

"Good."

Heaton greeted her in the stable yard half an hour later as she crossed it to the house. "How are you?"

"I'm fine." She smiled. "I've just told Stephanie."

"Oh."

"She wanted me to go to the police," she added.

"Are you going to?" he asked.

"No. It was Mum, through me, he wanted to get at."

"Are you sure you don't want to go to the police?"

She stopped at the side door. "You threatened to kill him."

He flushed. "I'm sorry."

"Don't be. If you hadn't been there…"

He nodded, opening the door. "I've borrowed the camcorder from Des," he told her. "Shall we go and set it up in the drawing room?"

She smiled and they went inside.

They set the camcorder up opposite the door to catch whoever came in.

"Let's hope it doesn't fall over now." She pulled a curtain to one side and began to check around the window for draughts.

"Well, if it doesn't, someone has to sit and watch the recording each evening."

"Someone?"

"Well." He smiled. "I could watch half and you could watch half?"

"You'd better ask Helen to put on vats of coffee for us, then." She let the curtain fall back into place.

"I was wondering if you've time if you wanted to go to St Mary's?"

She smiled and nodded.

An hour later, they walked through the graveyard in search of Thomas' grandparents, having first made absolutely sure that it was deserted.

"They're over here." She brought him to a plot under a tree behind the church and read out the inscription. "In loving memory of Thomas O'Hara. Born 1915. Died 1995. Erected by his loving wife Helen. Also his wife Helen O'Hara (neé Granger). Born 1920. Died 2000. Lovingly remembered by their children and grandchildren."

She wrote down the inscription then looked at him as he stared at the gravestone.

"What would they have made of Stephanie and me?" he murmured and turned away. "There are more O'Haras over here."

They found three more O'Hara gravestones and one Granger gravestone, the last one being right at the back of the graveyard. Heaton sat down on the grass and gazed over at the church.

"We'll have a look at the 1901 Census on the net later and see where those second O'Haras fit in," she told him. "If at all." She sat beside him and he turned to her.

"Where did she go?" he asked. "Danielle? Where did she go when she was pregnant? Pregnant twice? Where did she live before her marriage?"

"Just before she got married she definitely lived in Leeds, and when she was working she definitely lived in Leeds. Mum was working in Connolly's and Danielle went to work there after doing a secretarial course after leaving school. They worked together for four years. Whether Danielle stayed on in Leeds when she was pregnant I have no idea. She and Don then went to London when they got married."

"She met Don in Leeds?"

She nodded. "Yes, as far as I know."

"What about her brothers or sisters? The gravestone said 'children'."

"Danielle has a brother called John," she told him.

"Where does he live?"

"In town, in Campion Street." She flipped through the pages of the notebook. "I've been writing this down as it's come back to me. His wife is Fiona and they have two children Barbara and Kevin. Kevin's wife is Sarah and they have three children – Yasmin, Chloe and Jack. Barbara is married to John Tarrant and they have two children James and Simon." He sighed. "Don't worry, I'll put them all on the laptop for you."

"Thanks." He gave her a weak smile. "I don't suppose you have any other photographs?"

"I have some school photographs with Michelle in. I also have some old school yearbooks somewhere with photos of the various years in. Michelle, Peter and I went to the same school but the others went to St Michael's. They're in the boxes in the flat. We'll have a look on the internet. Maybe oldschoolfriends.com will come up with something more? The next time I'm over at Dad's, I'll have a look and see if there are any photos of Mum and Danielle," she promised. "I'd be amazed if there isn't."

"Thank you. You would tell me if you're finding this very boring?"

She smiled. "I would, honestly. But I'm not. Tell me if you want to stop."

"I don't. Shall we get back, then, so we can digest all this?"

A search in the 1901 Census placed all the O'Haras in the town on census night. Two O'Hara brothers were miners but whether one of them was Thomas' great-grandfather was yet to be determined.

"They're miners," he murmured. "They worked in the Heaton Mine."

"You want to be descended from a miner, don't you?" she asked him bluntly.

He turned to her and she met his eyes. "Yes. It sounds daft, but I feel so isolated sometimes. I just feel that I have nothing in common with anyone here. I want to feel connected."

"Your family has been here for nearly five hundred years."

"And not one of them did a proper day's work in their life," he told her.

"I think you're making up for that, don't you?"

That raised a smile. "I think so."

"We'll have to go to the County Record Office sometime and look at the church registers. Let's have a look on oldschoolfriends.com then call it a day."

At the flat, she brought up the page for St Michael's School and scrolled down the page for Barbara and Kevin O'Hara but sadly there were no notes and no photos. They called it a day.

Chapter Eight

Stephanie talked all the way to Leeds, not caring if anyone was listening. Two rooms had been given over to the exhibition and when Sophia was three-quarters of the way around the first room, she noticed that Stephanie had disappeared. Heaton was walking towards her with an irritated expression.

"A friend of Stephanie's rang her. They're going to meet up and go shopping. She'll take the train home. I couldn't stop her."

Oh, Stephanie! "This was too interesting for her?"

He smiled. "It wasn't the word she used. What do you think of this photograph?"

She glanced again at the miners emerging from the pit. "My grandfather started working in the mine in 1903. He probably knew some of those men."

They continued on into the second room.

"What do you think of this one?" She pointed to a photograph of Heaton Abbey House.

"There's one very similar to that at home somewhere."

"Want to see what's on across the road?"

He nodded. "Then I'll buy us lunch somewhere."

They crossed the road to the shop being used as a temporary exhibition space and she pulled an embarrassed expression. It was a display of corsets and crinolines. Still, it was better than 'dirty' photographs.

"This should be interesting," he said dryly as they went inside.

"You should have seen the things my grandmother used to wear. No, actually, you shouldn't, they were horrendous."

"The ones that look a bit like straitjackets?"

"Exactly. Poor Grandad. Look at this one," she pointed. "No wonder they used to faint all over the place."

"I must show you some photographs of my great-great-grandparents. My great-great-grandmother's waist is hideously tiny."

"Worse than this?" She motioned to a mannequin.

"Much worse. It must have been agony."

They wandered around separately. She put her head around a screen and came face to face with a man dressing a headless mannequin. "Sorry."

"It's all right," he assured her. "We've only got the one room."

"Well, I'm impressed. Where did you get them all from?"

"Some were donated and some are reproductions. You ever worn a corset?" he asked with a cheeky grin.

"No, never."

"Well, you're welcome to try?" he offered.

"You cheeky git."

He laughed. "Well, it was worth a try. All we've had in here so far are grannies cooing over the Old Age Pensioner section as I call it, going, 'Oh, do you remember those?'" She laughed. "What do you think of this one?" He held up a gorgeous black lace corset. "Suzie will give you a hand with it?"

"Why me?" she asked.

He shrugged. "Because I'm a cheeky git and because I need a couple more photographs of gorgeous curvy women in corsets."

"You have got to be joking," she laughed. "People I know could come here."

"It would only be the corset, not your face, I promise."

"But I'm with someone," she added.

"Boyfriend, girlfriend?"

She smiled. "Boss."

His eyes widened. "Your…no, I'd better not ask."

"He is, honestly."

"Which one is he?" He peered around the side of the screen.

"The tall man in the black jacket."

"Bloody hell, that man could scowl for Great Britain at the Olympics."

"He's a bit shy and hides behind that." She looked at the beautiful corset then across the room at Heaton. "I suppose I'd better tell him that I've just gone mad."

Heaton saw her approach and the scowl was exchanged for a smile. "I thought you'd nipped off to Harvey Nichols, too."

"Can't afford to. Look, um, I hope you don't mind but I've just been asked to model a corset."

He stared at her in astonishment. "You're not going to do it, are you?"

She smiled comically. "If you want to go home, I can get the bus back."

"You really think I'm going to go off and leave you with a complete stranger? Where is this person?"

"Behind the screen."

He crossed the room and walked straight behind the screen. "I'll be watching you," he warned.

"Oh, yeah?" the man retorted. "You going to dress her, too, are you?"

Heaton flushed scarlet. "No, of course not."

"Well, neither am I. I'm not a bloody pervert. My name is Peter Wilson. Suzie, there, is my wife and is going to help."

"Actually," Sophia began. "I'm not sure whether this is such a good idea."

"Because your boss doesn't like it?" Peter asked and she squirmed. "I take the photographs, you can see the previews, and if you don't like them they get wiped. Deal?"

"Okay," she replied and, without looking at Heaton, went behind a dressing screen.

"He's really your boss?" Suzie whispered as Sophia began to undress.

"Yes."

"Well, boss or not, he fancies you like mad."

"I know," she replied miserably.

"Leave your jeans on," Suzie told her. "This can show that corsets can be just as fashionable these days. Now, tell me when to stop pulling. Hold onto that door frame."

Feeling like Scarlett O'Hara, she held on as Suzie pulled the strings at the back. "Oh, there. Stop."

"Can you breathe?" Suzie asked.

"Just about." She turned around and Suzie grinned.

"That's quite a cleavage, his tongue will be hanging out."

"Shh."

"You want him to notice you, don't you?" Suzie asked. "Show him what's on offer?"

"Yes. But this is really teasing him."

Suzie just gave her a wink and they stepped out from behind the screen. Heaton stared in disbelief then flushed.

"Wow." Peter whistled and nudged Heaton knowingly.

All Heaton could do was stare so she had to make a point of not looking at him.

After taking the photographs, Peter brought her over to the camera. He had been true to his word, even though the photographs looked like those unintentional headless shots her grandmother used to take.

"You wouldn't consider doing a spot of modelling sometime?" Peter asked Heaton cheekily.

"No, I bloody wouldn't," he snapped and Sophia went back behind the screen to remove the corset.

"I think that worked a treat," Suzie whispered, untying the strings. "Bloody hell, all that passion. Get him into bed, girl."

"He's my boss," she replied miserably.

"That didn't stop me. Life's too short for all that crap."

"Hmm." She held the corset out but Suzie shook her head.

"We can't afford to pay you. Just put it to good use, eh?"

"I'll try," she said, getting dressed. "Thank you."

"Will it fit?" Susie asked as Sophia put the corset in her bag. "Yeah, good. Surprise him soon."

She saw Suzie wink at Peter, and him return one.

"Well, you can be nosey again here anytime," he called after her as she and Heaton left the shop.

Out on the pavement, she awkwardly did up her jacket.

"Lunch?" Heaton asked simply.

"Oh. Oh, yes please."

They walked along the street in an uncomfortable silence until he stopped outside an Italian restaurant.

"Do you like Italian?"

"Love it, yes."

"Good." He opened the door for her and they were seated at a window table. "Mrs Fields' culinary skills are excellent but very English. The tagliatelle is very good here, by the way."

"Oh. Good. I'll have that."

He nodded and ordered two tagliatellis and a jug of water and they lapsed into silence once more. She glanced at her bag. With the corset inside, it had only just zipped closed. She stole a glance at Heaton's face but it was unreadable as he watched life go by outside.

"Do you think Stephanie's bought most of Harvey Nichols?" she asked eventually and he turned back to her with a weak smile.

"Not too much, I hope. She still has to get it all either to her apartment here or home on the train." He poured them a glass of water each.

"If you want to go straight home I don't mind."

A glimmer of disappointment crossed his face. "Have you ever been to the Central Art Gallery?" he asked. "They've got a landscapes exhibition on."

"Sounds interesting."

"We'll go, then?"

She smiled and nodded, relieved that he didn't want to go home yet and get her out of his sight. The meal was delicious and she had to turn down his offer of dessert.

"We'll have a coffee and something with a million calories in it later, then," he suggested.

She laughed. "You're on."

At the gallery, he brought her straight through to the landscapes exhibition. "Choose a favourite," he whispered.

Slowly, she circled the room then sat down beside him on the bench in the centre of the room.

"That one." She pointed to a painting to their left.

"Why that one?" he asked.

"I like the clouds. They're like the clouds up on the moors."

He nodded. "They are."

"So, which is your favourite?"

He smiled. "That one."

"It's not?" she replied.

"It is. It's like lying on your back up on the moors and seeing nothing but sky. Shall we go on and see something else?"

She nodded and they went into the next room. Of course, the first painting they saw was that of a nude woman.

"Do you think I was wrong to pose for those photographs?" she asked him bluntly.

He gave a brief frown then shook his head. "It was up to you, but thankfully they weren't gratuitous. They gave you the corset, didn't they?"

"Yes."

"It's beautifully made. There are corsets and the like in a trunk in the attic but nothing like that one. Was it very uncomfortable?"

"No, not really, but I wasn't wearing it for very long."

"So something like this wouldn't embarrass you, then?" He gestured to the painting.

"No, I'm not a prude. She doesn't look very comfortable, though. I hope she didn't have to pose like that for too long at a time."

"No, could have caught her death of cold," he murmured and they moved on.

When they returned to the car it was starting to get dark.

"Stephanie's credit card has probably gone into meltdown," he said and started the engine.

"As long as she enjoys herself. Retail therapy can work wonders."

The car wound its way across the moors in the dark until it slowed.

"What the…?" Heaton muttered as it ground to a halt.

"What is it?"

"I'm not sure. What the…? There's no petrol? I filled up only yesterday." He threw open the door, went to the boot, and lifted out a torch. She got out and watched as he got down on his hands and knees, switched the torch on and pointed the beam under the car. "Doesn't seem to be a leak or anything. Could you steer while I push the car onto the verge?"

When the car was safely on the grass verge, he extracted his phone from his jacket's inside pocket. In the dark, she heard him swear.

"The battery must be dead. Do you have one?"

"Yes." She opened her bag and took out the corset, passed him her phone, then put the corset back. He sighed. "What?" she asked.

"Yours isn't working either."

"But I charged it last night. Turn the torch back on." He did as he was told and she opened the back. The sim card was gone. "Open yours."

He opened his but with the same results.

"For fuck sake, Stephanie." He swore viciously. "We're bloody miles from anywhere."

"She stole the petrol from the car?" Sophia asked in disbelief.

"She probably fluttered her eyelashes at someone to syphon it out. I am so sorry about this."

"I hate being without contact with Dad. That's why I gave him the office and house numbers."

"I know. I'm so sorry."

"Well, do we stay here or do we start walking?" she asked.

"We're miles from anywhere. It's probably best to stay here."

"Okay," she replied apprehensively.

"Christ, I hope Des sets the burglar alarm otherwise there'll be nothing left anywhere."

"I'm sure he will," she said.

"The camcorder is still in the drawing room and will probably be found now. We'd better stay in the car, it's getting cold." They got in and he turned to her. "The rug is on the back seat. I hope it will be warm enough."

"It doesn't matter."

"If we're going to be here all night, it does. Stephanie is going to end up living in a tent on the front lawn for this."

That made her smile. "She means well."

"She just has all the tact of a herd of stampeding buffalo. Are you cold?"

"Well, I've been warmer," she admitted.

"Why don't you stretch out on the back seat?" he suggested.

"What about you?"

"I'll be fine here. I'll keep an eye out in case there's a car."

She climbed into the huge back seat and pulled the rug over her. That was a bit better. If only he'd sit still, the leather squeaking and groaning was making an awful racket.

"Look," she said a few minutes later. "There won't be any cars up here at this hour."

"So what do you suggest?"

"That you get out and sleep on the bonnet, it might be still warm."

"What?"

"That was a joke." She sighed. "I'm freezing; you must be too, and you're obviously uncomfortable and I'm not going to get any sleep with all that noise the leather is making. So what I recommend is," she began, "that…" She took a deep breath and continued in a rush, "That you come and join me here on the back seat."

Silence.

After what seemed like a century, she heard the leather on the driver's seat squeak and groan for a final time as he got out of the car. He closed the driver's door, and opened the back door, before getting into the back and sitting beside her on the Jaguar's back seat.

He still hadn't spoken and she squirmed. "It that better?" she squeaked.

He stretched out and sighed. "Yes, much better. Lean back against me."

She did and he pulled the rug over them then put his arms around her. It was all non-sexual so far but then she felt his hands around her waist as he pulled her into him so she moulded into his body. She lay there, trying desperately to ignore the sexual tension building volcano-like between them.

"Warmer now?" he whispered and she felt his breath on the back of her neck.

"Yes," she whispered back. "You?"

She felt him laugh. "Thank you, yes. So you enjoyed the day?"

She laughed this time. "Yes, I did. And if I embarrassed you this morning, then, I'm sorry."

"Embarrassed me? No, not at all. Shocked me, yes. Frightened me, yes." He exhaled a long sigh. "When you emerged from behind that screen," she felt him shake his head, "you looked incredible. And that shocked and frightened me – how every time I see you, you look even more beautiful than the time before."

She opened her mouth to say, "Oh," but nothing came out.

"I'm sorry, I've embarrassed you now."

She shook her head vehemently and he sneezed.

"Sorry," she croaked and he laughed.

"It doesn't matter."

In the distance, she saw the headlights of an approaching car and felt him tense.

"Do you want me to get out?" he asked softly.

"No," she whispered and he relaxed.

They watched the car pass them.

"You do know that I've been in love with you ever since you walked into the library that afternoon, don't you?" he said.

She swallowed. "Yes. So why didn't you say or do something? While you were sober, I mean?"

"I could ask you the same question."

"I'm a member of staff, as you kept reminding me."

He sighed. "Well, it's not as though you're a serving wench currently in favour with the master, like in one of Stephanie's appalling historical novels. I'm not going to use you then cast you aside But I was worried. What if I had made what you saw as a pass at you and you didn't reciprocate it? I mean, what happened in the graveyard…those emails…Steph's flat… That's why I had to write that bloody awful letter. I can't afford to go to a tribunal. I'm absolutely amazed that there wasn't a tribunal."

"There won't be any tribunals," she told him. "Ever."

She felt him give a little smile.

"No-one's dared speak to me the way you have."

"Is that a good thing?"

He spluttered a laugh. "Oh, God, yes. No-one else has told me that I work too hard, that I need my eyes tested, that I need to get some sleep. No-one else is worried that I'm back smoking cigarettes. I hope that it's because you care."

"You know that it's because I care about you. I love you."

He exhaled a long breath. "It's been a long, long time since I've felt like this and I'd be lying if I said it didn't scare me. I've worked so hard that there just hasn't been time for relationships so if that is what you want, you'll have to have patience with me."

"I'll be patient," she said softly and she felt him smile again.

She felt his hands on her waist as he turned her around so that she was sitting on his legs. He kissed her, gently at first, pulling at her lips with his, then more intensely, harder and harder until it almost hurt.

"I thought you wanted me to be patient?" she asked.

"Sorry."

"It doesn't matter. Anyway, there's something I need to know."

"Oh?"

"Yes, the small question of what do I call you?"

He laughed. "Thomas. Just Thomas. It's never been shortened."

"Well, hello, Thomas, I'm Sophia." He laughed before pulling her towards him for another kiss. "Still going to exile Stephanie to the front lawn?"

"I should do, but…"

For a while they were content just to kiss, then, he slid his hands down her back until they reached her buttocks and he pulled her close against him. She felt his hands slide under her jacket, under her top and up her back until they reached her bra.

"Undo it," she whispered.

He fumbled a little with it before pulling her jacket, top and the bra off then lifted her close to him again. She closed her eyes, gasping as his lips found and pulled at her nipples. She began to moan and couldn't stop. His mouth returned to her lips and he kissed her until she was disorientated.

His hands explored her upper body before stopping at her jeans.

"Undo them," she whispered.

"Are you sure?"

"Yes. I have a packet of condoms in my bag."

"I have condoms in my wallet." She felt his arm brush her breasts as he reached into his jacket's inside pocket to retrieve the wallet. She heard him fumble with it and felt his arm again as he returned the wallet to his jacket. "Okay."

"Good. Undo my jeans."

He felt for and undid the button, lowered the zip, and she struggled out of them and her panties. If she hadn't wanted him so much it would have been hilarious. She heard him grunt impatiently as he battled with his own clothes and the condom before reaching for her hips.

In the cramped space and pitch black, she needed his hands to guide her as she straddled and sank down onto him. Any self-consciousness and embarrassment was quickly forgotten. She exhaled a long breath as she felt him fill her while he gave a soft grunt of pleasure. She lifted herself then slowly slid back down onto him, feeling his hot breath on her breasts as he gasped. Slowly, she lifted herself again, trying to memorise every second. Lowing herself onto him, he groaned, his breath beginning to quicken, and he tried to lift his hips in an effort to dictate the pace. She ground her pelvis against him, forcing him back down onto the seat. She moaned as her own breath and pace began to accelerate. Waves of pleasure washed over her. She cried out as he made a low, inarticulate noise deep in his throat and, clasping her face in his hands, lowered it to his own. When their mouths met in the darkness it was, for her, simply exquisite.

"So much for patience," he panted and she felt him laugh. "Thank God my father wasn't a Mini enthusiast."

"What's your bed like?" she asked, her fingers locating and undoing his shirt buttons.

"Big," he replied as her hands began to explore his chest.

"Not a four poster?" she added as his hands slid under her breasts. He lifted them and she exhaled as his tongue began to lap one nipple and then the other.

"Like that?" he whispered and she murmured in agreement. "No, it's not a four poster. I did sleep in the four poster once, though. When I say sleep, it was more a case of trying to find a spot in the mattress with no lumps. And failing. No, I have a modern bed."

"For the odd time you sleep there and not in the office," she teased then gasped as he ran his thumbs over her taut nipples.

"It will be more than the odd time now," he said, allowing her breasts to gently drop, and ran his hands up her back. "You're cold…"

"Mmm." She climbed off him and somehow they managed to dress.

She slept seated between his legs, his arms around her tightly. When she woke it was bright outside. She climbed slowly out of the car and stretched then looked back inside. He peered at her bleary-eyed before stretching.

"What time is it?" he asked and she glanced at her watch.

"Just after eight."

"Ms Nelson?" he began and her heart sank.

"Yes?"

"The next time I lick your nipples, I really want to be able to see what I'm doing."

She stared at him for a moment then he grinned and she laughed in relief.

"Want to keep an eye out for a car or shall we live here permanently and enjoy nights like that every night?" he added.

"Hmm." She pretended to mull it over. "Well, actually, I want to see this bed of yours. Not that I'm saying that last night wasn't good."

He smiled and got out. "It's still cold, here." He draped the rug around her shoulders. "I also want to see you in that corset again," he whispered in her ear and kissed her neck.

"I need help with it."

"That can be arranged."

Half an hour passed until a Royal Mail van pulled up and the driver agreed to take Thomas to the next village to get petrol. An hour later they were on their way home.

Pulling up in the stable yard, he put a hand on her knee. "I'm going to nip across to see Des, make sure everything's all right, then I'm going to see Stephanie. Pretend that nothing's happened? That you've just come back from a walk?"

She smiled. "This I have to see."

Stephanie opened the door to them and smiled nervously. "Thomas? Where the hell have you been?"

"In a garage. There was something wrong with the car so I sent Ms Nelson home on the bus. You got home all right?"

Stephanie looked dumbfounded. "Yes, fine."

"Did you buy much?" Sophia asked.

"A pair of shoes...you?"

"Nothing but I was so tired that I fell asleep in an armchair. I must go for a shower. What was wrong with the car?" she asked Thomas.

"Leak in the petrol tank."

"Dangerous?"

"Yes, it had the potential to be. Must get my phone repaired now. Or should I get a new one?" he asked Stephanie. "You know all about these things."

"Well, you have had it a while," she said and he nodded. Stephanie looked him up and down. "Where did you sleep?"

He smiled and Sophia began to smile, knowing that he was about to put his sister out of her misery.

"Stephanie, do you believe absolutely everything I tell you?"

"Well…I…what do you mean?"

"I mean, from now on, the Jag is going to be locked in the garage and if you want to go anywhere you'll just have to get the bus. Have you any idea how cold it was last night? If Sophia and I hadn't kept each other warm I really don't know what might have happened."

Stephanie stared at him then the penny dropped. "Oh, my God."

"And now, could we please have our sim cards back?"

Stephanie grinned. "Only if you come in and let me cook you both breakfast? I suppose it's the least I can do?"

"It is." He took Sophia's hand and they went inside. "So we want smoked salmon and caviar at the very least."

"Look, I'm sorry." Stephanie turned. "But I just didn't know what the hell else to do to give you both a kick up the backside and just get the hell together."

"Hmm." Thomas held out his hand. "Sim cards? Sophia doesn't like being out of contact with her father."

"Oh, God, I'm sorry. I never thought." Stephanie ran to her bag and extracted the two sim cards from her purse.

"Thanks." Sophia took her sim card and put it back in her phone. Switching it back on she was relieved to see that there were no missed calls. "It's okay."

"Scrambled eggs? Poached eggs? Boiled eggs? I'm afraid I've only got eggs."

"Scrambled eggs?" Sophia looked at Thomas, who raised his head from his own phone and nodded. "And coffee, please."

"Dare I ask how you kept warm?"

"No," Thomas replied lightly but firmly. "But suffice to say it worked."

"At bloody last."

As Sophia stood at the front door that afternoon, a hand suddenly rested in the small of her back. "Need the tranquilliser gun?" a voice whispered in her ear and she smiled.

"What, just in case? Where am I supposed to hide it, just in case?"

He laughed. "Everything is fine, nothing missing as far as I can tell. See you later."

"That is a man in love," a large American woman told her categorically. "You lucky girl."

I know. "Thank you."

"Is he the manager?"

"Er, no, that was Lord Heaton."

The woman's eyes bulged. "No? Are you Lady Heaton?"

She flushed. "No, I'm not."

"Well, you're still a lucky girl."

Oh, I know. And about time, too.

That evening, she was curled up in the armchair with her phone and pressed 'send' on a text message to Michelle: *Re. Heaton – mission accomplished* :) when she saw Thomas cross the yard towards her. She went downstairs to let him in.

"Sorry." He kissed her lips. "Dinner took ages, then I spoke to Lady Heaton."

"And?"

"Well, I'd be lying if I said that she wasn't a little surprised."

"Surprised?"

"Yes," he replied, climbing the stairs after her. "I think she was beginning to worry that I was going to remain celibate for the rest of my life."

"And you're not?" she enquired as he put his arms around her.

He laughed. "No." She felt his hands slide down her back and onto her bottom and he pulled her body against his. "You are beautiful," he whispered. "Fancy coming back to my place? We'll set the camcorder again then have a drink."

They made their way across the stable yard, into the house via the side door, and up the stairs to the drawing room.

"If only the doors could be locked, but they don't lock, and, if they did it would completely give the game away. Come to my living room."

He brought her to a room two doors down from the library. She stared. It was about as different from the drawing room and library as it was possible to be. Two black leather sofas stood at right angles to each other on the varnished floorboards. The only floor covering was a black rug on which stood a wooden coffee table. A laden bookcase stood along one wall, a drinks cabinet along another, and a widescreen television and DVD player stood against a third.

"I don't use this room as much as I should, considering the effort I put into it," he told her. "The library is so dark, I usually end up going in there for a nap. I do like 'old' but there are times that I just crave 'modern'." He gave her a little smile. "You hate it?"

"No," she cried. "No. It's the last thing I expected, but no, it's lovely."

"Lady Heaton hates it. Never comes in here."

"What's her living room like?"

"Sitting room," he corrected with a grin. "Flowers, frills, clutter everywhere. Claustrophobic. Whisky?"

"Yes, please. Look, there's something I need to tell you."

"What?" He looked anxiously at her from the drinks cabinet.

"It's Lady Heaton. I don't really know how to explain, it's just that I've seen her behaving very strangely."

"What do you mean, strangely?"

She sighed. "The first day I was here, I'd just gone through the tour and I was sitting on the stairs. It was just before you came down and asked if I wanted to see the etchings of the abbey. Lady Heaton opened the door of the drawing room. She looked around but didn't see me. She walked out of the drawing room. I'm almost positive that she had something in her hand. Then there was the time I was showing one of the portraits to a visitor and she opened one of the drawing room doors and stuck her head out and looked around. She saw me and the visitor and withdrew and banged the door closed. She was expecting no-one to be there."

"You think she's a thief?"

She flushed. "At first I thought it was some kind of test of my honesty but now I don't know. Maybe I've got an overly suspicious mind. I'm sorry, I just didn't want to keep it from you anymore."

He nodded and she saw that she had really shocked him.

"Well, I'm going to need some proof." He passed her a glass.

"I've also seen her in the bank in town lodging an awful lot of money."

"How much is an awful lot?"

She shrugged and sat down on the sofa. "An envelope full of twenty-pound notes, it looked like. I've also seen her getting onto the Leeds bus with a large box. That mightn't be anything, though, because I didn't know that Stephanie lived in Leeds then."

He nodded and sat on the other sofa. "We still need proof. I can't go accusing her."

"I know. I hope it's nothing. When did you have the room done?"

"I started six years ago on here and my bedroom. My grandmother had used this room as a sitting room. Father had furnished it exactly the way she wanted it, and it was appalling. Even Lady Heaton didn't want the furniture when Grandmother died, so it stayed here and I began using the room as my sitting room until I just couldn't stand it anymore and Des and I took it all outside and burned it. Gradually, I furnished the room, whenever I could afford it. I eventually finished it last year, when I went completely mad and bought the widescreen television to replace Grandmother's black and white portable."

"When did your grandmother die?" she asked.

"When I was seventeen. She was eighty-seven. My grandfather died when I was eight. He was eighty. I'd love to have known him better. Spoiled Stephanie and me rotten. He fought in World War One. Ran away and lied about his age. His uniform is in the attic somewhere."

"You never did show me the attic." She smiled.

"Tomorrow, I promise. I take after him, my grandfather, so if visitors do expect me to dress up, I suppose you could dress me in his uniform? While I lace you into that exquisite corset."

"I think you liked that corset."

He laughed. "I did, but I much prefer what's inside it. Those beautiful curves I was exploring in the dark, which I'd very much like to explore again, and see what I'm doing this time."

"Flattery will get you everywhere."

"Good." He put his glass down. "Come with me."

He led her up the main staircase and along a corridor into the east wing, a part of the house she had never ventured into even when 'lost'.

"Here we are." He opened the door and switched the light on.

Again she stared. It was a huge room, dominated by a vast king size sleigh bed. Although the furniture was modern, it did not jar. "Is the bed big enough for you?" she teased.

He smiled. "I'm six foot two, I need a big bed. Now, where were we?"

"I think you want to make up for lost time."

"I'll be completely honest with you, I hadn't thought about sex in a long time until I met you. I know men are supposed to have sex on the brain but I've either been too busy or too tired, usually both. I'm sorry, we don't have to."

She quickly covered his mouth with her fingers. "I want to."

He smiled, picked her up, and carried across the room to the bed.

Although he claimed to be very unfit, his body did not show any evidence of this as he quickly undid his shirt buttons while she sat on the bed undoing her blouse with full view of his broad shoulders, strong arms and flat stomach.

"Can I?" he whispered and knelt down. He undid the rest of the buttons and eased the blouse off her shoulders. Again, he fumbled a little with her bra but gasped when he removed it and saw her breasts. "You are beautiful," he said again. "A real woman."

"A real woman?" she echoed.

He grimaced. "Please don't take that the wrong way…what I am trying to say is that you are feminine, curvy, and beautiful, not stick-thin and gaunt. Renaissance artists knew that curves and softness, not boyish angles and hardness, are the characteristics that people naturally associate with the feminine ideal."

"So I was born five hundred years too late?"

He smiled. "I don't think so. Titian, for example, putting the symbolism aside, created his works of art as consummate expressions of womanly beauty. I just wish that I could paint you."

"Not just now, I hope?"

He shook his head. "I'd never be able to do you justice."

They lay down together and he moved down her body to kiss and caress her breasts then he moved his hands steadily down her body. He eased her legs apart to stroke her and she arched her back in response to the deep pleasure it gave. She reached out for him and found him hard. Running her fingers along his length, she smoothed her thumb over the tip and he exhaled a long groan.

"Like that?" she whispered.

He nodded. "But I want to be inside you and I need a condom." He rolled over and got off the bed. She watched as he walked around the bed with no evidence of self-consciousness at all, his huge erection bobbing up and down.

He pulled open the drawer of a bedside cabinet and extracted a condom. He closed the drawer and ripped open the packaging. He rolled the condom on then turned to face her.

When he climbed onto the bed and over her, she couldn't help but wonder whether he would be gentle or rough through inexperience. Her curiosity was quickly replaced with a feeling of warmth and security as he pushed into her slowly but firmly. She relaxed and opened her legs wider, inviting him in deeper. He pushed in further, she savoured every extra inch, and they both groaned. He pulled out and pushed in again, only this time faster and deeper, pushing his whole length into her. The waves of pleasure began to build again as he thrust into her, his hips finding a rhythm. Her moans became louder and louder as she contracted around him as she came and felt him tighten and shudder as he climaxed.

They lay panting in each other's arms. Sophia was shocked at the intensity of her responses and she felt herself blush.

He opened his eyes and kissed her lips. "Don't worry, no-one can hear us. The walls are four feet thick, remember?"

"That's a relief."

She wanted to have woken first so she could look at him while asleep but he was already awake and looking at her. He ran a hand across her stomach, up to her breasts, and cupped one.

"Down boy." She smiled. "What's the time?"

He rolled over and back. "Half past eight." He sighed. "I should get up but I don't want to."

"Then don't, you deserve a lie in."

He gave her a grin. "I won't, then."

"When did you last have a lie in?" she asked curiously.

"I can't remember exactly, but I think John Major was still Prime Minister."

Michelle rang her later that morning. "Hi, Sophia, how are you?"

"I'm fine. Well, more than fine, actually. Especially now."

"Now?" Michelle prompted.

"Thomas and I are an item at long last."

"Really?" Michelle exclaimed. "What happened?"

"Didn't you get my text message?"

"My phone didn't survive a hot wash and spin cycle yesterday. I'm getting a new one tomorrow. So what happened? Tell all."

"Oh, you know…but we're on first name terms now."

"And the rest, I hope?"

She laughed. "Oh, yes. I need to go shopping later this evening, I'll call in on the way home."

"I'll have the kettle on. See you, then."

"The attic awaits." Thomas stood at the door of the kitchen as Sophia finished a well-earned cup of coffee following a tour. "What is it?" he added when she didn't reply.

"One woman tried to pinch the new photograph of you in the drawing room. I saw her trying, and failing, to zip up her anorak. Would you object to roping most of the room off?"

"I hoped that we wouldn't have to but, no."

She followed him into the drawing room. "If we move this table in a little bit, we can run a rope, along here, so groups can still come in that door and out the other and still be able to see the whole room."

"What's this?" Lady Heaton came in after them.

"A lady tried to steal a photograph of me," Thomas told her.

"And a few others kept picking things up," Sophia added. "I had to ask one woman to put things down three times."

Lady Heaton nodded. "Some visitors can be persistent. Well, I have no objection to roping most of the room off. If visitors want a souvenir, they can buy one from me in the shop."

Sophia smiled.

"All right then, ropes in this room." Thomas nodded.

"What if it's my fault?" she said, as they climbed the stairs to the attic. "When I have a large group it's hard to keep an eye on all of them."

"We'll see if the ropes make a difference. Here we are."

He opened a door and switched on a light which flickered on. The roof space was enormous but full of clutter. *The Antiques Roadshow* would be able to spend an entire series up there.

"What's in all the chests?" she asked.

"Clothes, papers, letters, toys, you name it. Come, and I'll show you the suit of armour." The armour was already dressed on a mannequin. "Apparently, my great-grandfather stood it in the hall and used it as a hat and umbrella stand until my grandfather banished it to the attic."

"It's a shame to have it hidden away up here. It should be on display. Was it Sir William Heaton's?"

"I really don't know. It's just always been here. I won't fit into it, will I?"

"No, definitely not. Where's your grandfather's uniform?"

"Over here, I think." He went to a chest and opened it. "Yes, it's here." He lifted out the cap and jacket. "Still in very good condition."

"Are there any other old clothes?"

"Yes, loads. Come and see the corsets." He opened another chest and lifted one out. "This belonged to Great-Great-Grandmother Catherine. It really must have been agony."

"Yes," she replied simply, letting her hands drop to her sides.

"What is it?" he asked, putting the corset back.

"I don't know where to start. All of this should be on display."

"I know but I don't want to turn the house completely into a museum. It's not damp up here so nothing is going to disintegrate. We'll display the suit of armour and see how it goes, yes?"

"Yes." She smiled. "All we ever had in our attic at home were old suitcases, bits of carpet, and boxes of my old Enid Blyton books."

"Famous Five or Secret Seven?"

"Both. I think I had every book she ever wrote."

She drove back to the abbey from Michelle's, having left as quickly as she dared to – not particularly wanting to go into detail about sex with Thomas – and found the brochures being delivered. Four large cardboard boxes stood outside Thomas' office and Thomas himself was signing for them.

"At last." She followed him as he carried one of the boxes into the office. "I was beginning to think they had forgotten about us."

"There was some problem at the printers but at least the brochures are here now." He set the box on his desk, reached for a pair of scissors, and sliced the box open. He lifted a brochure out and cringed at his picture on the cover. "Urgh. We'd better get these over to the shop. I hardly ever go in there so at least I won't see them."

"I'll take a box."

"All right." He kissed her lips. "See you later."

She went out, picked up a box and saw that Des had seen the kiss. She flushed as he fell in step with her as she crossed the stable yard.

"Want me to take that box?" he offered.

"No, it's okay, thanks."

"So, er, how long have you and his Lordship…?"

"Not long."

"Well, I'm glad to see that he's got taste and picked a local girl."

She gave him a relieved smile. "And me a local boy?"

He laughed. "Well, nearly five hundred years does make him local, I suppose." He gave her a wink and headed in the direction of the kitchen and she continued on to the shop.

"Oh, good grief, they've put Thomas on the cover." Stephanie groaned as she lifted a brochure from the box.

"He looks very well," Lady Heaton murmured. "As does the house. I think I'll keep one of these for myself. Has he seen it, Sophia?"

"Yes, he's going through it now."

Lady Heaton took a brochure and went out as Sophia offered Stephanie another.

"Want one to keep?"

"What, with Thomas as cover boy?" She laughed. "Oh,

go on, then. You'd better give me one for Des and Helen, too. Hopefully, there'll be enough left for the visitors."

Stephanie followed Lady Heaton out of the shop and Sophia began to place some brochures beside the leaflet rack.

"Sophia?"

She jumped and turned to look at Lady Heaton. "Sorry, I didn't hear you come back in."

"Thomas has told me about you and him."

"Oh, I see."

"I hope you care for him as much as he cares for you. Please don't hurt him."

"I love him if that's what you mean?" she said, a little harsher than she had intended. "I've never gone lightly into any relationship."

"Have you had many?"

"No. My previous relationship lasted six years. Do you not approve of me, Lady Heaton?" she asked bluntly.

"Good heavens, yes." Lady Heaton laughed. "I'm just being rather overprotective, that's all." She lowered her voice. "I may not have given birth to him but he is still my son. Even if he won't admit that anymore." She smiled sadly. "Has your father met Thomas?"

"Not recently, no. I'm going to see him in the morning to tell him."

On being told, her father remained silent for what seemed like an age. "So how long has it been going on for?" he asked finally.

"Almost a week."

"Does he love you?"

"Yes."

"Well, he would say that, I suppose." Her father shrugged.

"Dad, he's not the sort of man who'll say that to—"

"Get you to sleep with him…?" Mr Nelson suggested.

"No," she replied quietly.

"Well, I hope you know what you're doing."

"Dad, we can't help who we fall in love with."

"I want to meet him properly," her father said firmly.

"Okay, I'll organise something."

Returning to the abbey, Sophia found Thomas standing back to look at the now roped-off drawing room.

"It looks good." He smiled at her. "Hopefully, that rope will do the trick, but Des said that there's no hurry with returning the camcorder."

"Good. Right, I'm going to the flat for some lunch and I'm off up the moors with or without you, at two."

"I'll be on time."

"The door's open," she called an hour later, hearing footsteps on the stairs. The door opened and closed and she turned. Her heart lurched when she saw a stranger, not Thomas. "Who the hell are you?"

"Where's Stephanie?" he asked instead of answering.

"You're Simon?"

"Ten out of ten. Now, where's Stephanie?"

"I don't know."

"Do I have to look for her?"

"If you want but you won't find her. She went out early this morning and she's not back yet."

He nodded. "I'll just have to wait, then." He went to an armchair and sat down. "Who are you?"

"This isn't Stephanie's flat."

"So she lives in one of these flats?"

Sophia could have kicked herself. "Could you please leave? I'm going out."

"I asked who are you?"

"Get out."

"Not until you tell me who you are." He crossed his legs.

"My name is Sophia. Now get out."

"Ready?" They heard Thomas' voice from below and Simon leapt out of his chair.

"You're his girlfriend? I heard that he was shagging someone at long last. Well, well."

"Get out."

"Sophia?" Thomas called.

"Thomas." She half-screamed as she saw the knife.

"Shut up." Simon went to the door and turned the key in the lock. "He owes me for all that stuff he chucked away."

"He hasn't got any money."

"Sophia?" Thomas was outside the door at the top of the stairs.

"Don't you even think of breaking it down," Simon ordered. "Or I'll cut her throat."

"What do you want?" Thomas demanded.

"You owe me five grand, Heaton."

"Don't be bloody ridiculous."

"Finally getting your leg over, eh?" Simon laughed. "Better late than never."

"Police." Sophia heard his voice, presumably speaking into his phone. "Yes, my girlfriend is being held hostage. Heaton Abbey. Yes, a knife, I think. My name's Thomas Heaton."

"You shouldn't have done that, Heaton," Simon called casually.

"Then let her go before they arrive."

"How much is she worth to you, Heaton? More than five thousand quid?"

"Let her go," Thomas repeated.

"Is he a good shag?" Simon asked her conversationally. "You know, I was getting quite worried about him. Public school can do that to a chap. Poor Thomas, at school he wouldn't say boo to a goose."

"You were at school together?" she stammered.

"Didn't he tell you?"

"No."

"Oh, yes," Simon laughed. "We were very close. I mean, a lot of us experimented, not just with drugs, but you're the first shag, male or female that poor old Thomas has had in years."

"He's not bisexual."

"Isn't he?"

Simon had walked to the door and Sophia saw her chance. She raced to the bedroom and slammed the door. She turned the key in the lock and dragged a chair across the floor, wedging it under the handle.

"Bitch," Simon roared.

"Sophia?"

"I'm in the bedroom," she screamed, opening the window.

She heard Thomas thundering down the stairs and running outside. From the window, she saw Des running across the stable yard with a ladder and in the distance, she could hear police sirens. She threw open the window as the ladder was propped up against the wall. She was about to climb out when the bedroom door burst open, sending the chair flying, and she was pulled backwards. The last thing she knew was falling backwards with Simon before everything went black.

Chapter Nine

When she came to, a complete stranger was leaning over her. She had to blink a few times to reassure herself that it wasn't Simon. Somewhere in the background she heard raised voices.

"What's going on?" she asked groggily.

"You're in hospital. I'm Dr Healy. Let's take a look."

"I meant out there?" she added.

"Your father and your boyfriend are arguing."

"Sophia?" She heard her father's voice and he came into focus. "How are you, love?"

"Sore. Is that Thomas?"

"He's gone, love, don't worry."

"Gone?" she repeated. "What've you said? Dad? Thomas, are you there?"

"I'm here," he said in a low voice.

"Come here."

"Never mind him now," her father protested. "Let the doctor take a look at you."

"In a minute. Thomas?"

"How are you?" He bent and kissed her forehead.

"A bit groggy."

"I'm sorry."

She gave him a wobbly smile. "It wasn't your fault."

"No?" He kissed her lips this time and straightened up. "I'd better let the doctor examine you. I'll see you later."

After being examined, she was told that she would have to remain in hospital for twenty-four hours for observation due to slight concussion. She thanked the doctor then turned to her father, sitting in a chair beside her bed.

"What did you say to Thomas, Dad?"

"Not now."

"Yes, now," she replied stubbornly. "What did you say to him?"

"That you won't be going back to the abbey."

"What?" she cried, her head beginning to throb. "Don't be ridiculous; of course I'm going back. For God's sake, Dad, I'm thirty-three years old."

"And if you stay there any longer you mightn't make thirty-four."

"Was Simon arrested?" she asked.

"No."

Her heart pounded. So he was still out there somewhere? "What happened?"

"Never you mind for now. You just rest."

"No, tell me now, or I'll go and ask Thomas."

Her father sighed. "All right. Simon jumped out of the window."

She stared at him. "He's dead?"

"He and Heaton fought in the stable yard but he managed to get away before the police got there."

"Is Thomas all right? He looked all right to me."

"Yes. Now rest."

She did and woke feeling less groggy and with her father still sitting beside the bed. "Did you go home at all?"

He smiled. "I did. You've been asleep for sixteen hours."

Sixteen? "Right, can you get a doctor to look at me so I can go home?"

"Sophia…"

"Dad. Please."

An hour later she was in the process of being discharged but not so she could go home as she lived alone. She would have to spend the next twenty-four hours at her father's.

"Are you Sophia Nelson?"

She turned. A nurse was approaching her with a scrap of paper.

"Yes, I am."

"Thomas Heaton asked me to give you this note."

"Oh." She took the note. "Thank you."

> *Sophia*
>
> *Your father has ordered me to keep away from you, hence the note. I'm upstairs in the Intensive Care Unit. Simon went straight to Steph's apartment in Leeds and when she refused to give him five thousand pounds, he stabbed her before killing himself. She was in surgery most of last night and things were a bit touch and go but she's stabilised in the last couple of hours. I'll come down to you if I can but your father was naturally very upset so don't worry if you don't see me.*
>
> *Love you.*
>
> *Thomas*

"Ready?" her father asked.

She folded the note and put it in her pocket. "When were you going to tell me about Stephanie and Simon?"

He rolled his eyes. "That note was from him, I suppose?"

"Yes, and I'm going upstairs to see him. Then…" she added as he opened his mouth to argue. "Then you can take me back to The Beeches."

She stepped out of the lift and followed the signs to the Intensive Care Unit. She pressed the intercom and asked to speak to Thomas.

The door opened five minutes later. "Sophia." Gently, he clasped her face in his hands and kissed her lips. "How do you feel?"

"Sore. How's Stephanie?"

He went to a bench, sat down heavily, and she sat beside him. "Her spleen had to be removed. The doctor said it went well, the operation."

"I'm glad."

"The police want to speak to you whenever you're up to it."

"Okay. Simon killed himself?"

"Yes. Do you really have to go home now?"

"Yes, she does," her father replied and she jumped, not having heard him follow her. "Sophia has concussion and needs rest."

Thomas nodded and kissed her forehead.

"Ring me?" she said, taking the note out of her pocket. "Have you a pen?" He pulled one from his jacket's inside pocket and passed it to her. "This is Dad's number," she added, scribbling the number down. "My phone is still at the flat. I'll be back in the morning, I promise."

He nodded again and took the pen and note from her. She kissed his lips then reluctantly followed her father back to the lift.

She opened her eyes and looked at the clock. Eight o'clock. Despite being back on her father's uncomfortable sofa, she'd slept for twelve hours with no interruptions. She quickly washed and dressed before opening her father's bedroom door and looking in at him. He was still asleep, snoring a little. She wrote him a note then went to the telephone. There were no messages. She sighed and left the flat. Deciding to get the police over and done with first, she went to the police station where she was questioned and made a statement. That done, and taking the shortcut from the town via the ornamental lake, she made her way back to the abbey.

"Sophia?" Des opened the door of his office as she crossed the stable yard. "How are you?"

"My head is still a bit sore but I'm fine apart from that. Thanks for helping."

"I'm just sorry police didn't get the bastard."

She nodded. "Did you hear about Stephanie?"

Des nodded. "His Lordship rang me."

"Has he rung you since last night?"

"No." He frowned. "What've you heard?"

"I spoke to him just before I left last night. Stephanie's spleen had to be removed." Des winced. "The last I heard, she was stable. I'm going to the hospital now. Have you the keys to my flat?"

"They're in a drawer in my office. Should you be driving?"

"Probably not, but I'm going anyway."

"The police want to speak to you at some stage," he said, going to his desk and retrieving the keys.

"I've just come from the police station. Thanks, Des."

She took the keys from him and climbed the stairs to the flat. Someone had been inside to tidy up. She took a few gulps of orange juice straight from the carton in the fridge then grabbed her car keys.

Approaching the hospital entrance, she saw Thomas light up a cigarette and inhale deeply before spotting her and stubbing it out. He looked terrible, even worse than the previous evening, his face grey with exhaustion.

"How is she?" she asked as he held her in his arms.

"On the mend. She regained consciousness last night. She's sleeping now."

"Thank goodness for that. And you?"

He shrugged. "Not good. I'm absolutely exhausted."

"When did you last eat?"

"Haven't a clue."

"Right, come on." She took his hand. "There's a café just past the lifts." She bought them coffee and scrambled egg on toast and they ate at a corner table.

When they went up to the Intensive Care Unit in the lift and the lift doors opened, Lady Heaton was standing outside.

"I was about to come looking for you, Thomas. Stephanie has woken up."

"Good," he replied simply and walked past her.

Sophia shot an apologetic look at Lady Heaton before following him.

Outside the I.C.U., she halted. "I'll wait here."

"No, come in."

"No. I won't be allowed," she protested. "It should be you and—"

"My 'mother'?"

"For now, yes. Go and see Stephanie. I'll wait here."

He nodded and went inside.

"Is he all right?" Lady Heaton approached her.

"Relieved," she replied.

"And how are you?"

"My head still aches a little bit but apart from that I'm fine, thank you." She went to the bench and sat down. "I'll wait here."

Half an hour later, Lady Heaton emerged from the I.C.U. "Stephanie wants to see you, Sophia."

"Oh." She got up. "Thank you."

A nurse showed her the way and Thomas rose from a chair beside the bed as she opened the door to Stephanie's room.

"Come and sit down here."

She walked around the bed and sat down. Stephanie looked tiny in the bed and Sophia eyed all the tubes attached to her chest and the drip attached to her arm.

"I had a tube down my throat," Stephanie croaked. "So I sound awful." Sophia smiled sympathetically. "My spleen, eh?" She rolled her eyes. "Wasn't quite how I planned to lose a bit of weight."

"Would you like me to bring you in some magazines for when you're up to a bit of reading?" Sophia offered.

"Yes, thank you. Doesn't matter what. I'm not fussy. I just wanted to say sorry."

"Sorry?"

"Simon could have killed you too," Stephanie explained.

"We Yorkshire girls are made of strong stuff."

Stephanie grinned. "Didn't even know what a spleen did until he," she nodded at Thomas, "explained it to me. Now, go home the both of you. Sleep. You look almost as bad as I do."

"We'll be back later." Thomas kissed her cheek.

"And shave," Stephanie croaked after him.

Lady Heaton got up from the bench as they left the I.C.U.

"Stephanie's starting to order me about so she's definitely on the mend and we're going home," Thomas informed her. "Are you staying here?"

"You look exhausted, Lady Heaton," Sophia added. "I think you need to get some sleep."

Lady Heaton nodded. "I'll just tell Stephanie. I'll follow you down to the car."

"Come on." Thomas took Sophia's hand and they walked to the lift. In the lift, he rubbed his eyes. "Ideally, I need to sleep for twelve hours."

"Then, why don't you? I'll come and wake you later."

"Will you?" He smiled.

She laughed. "Yes."

"Then, Lady Heaton and I need to talk."

At half-past eight that evening, Sophia drove back to the abbey from a shopping trip. She unpacked her groceries and went into the house by the side door to wake Thomas. Closing it, she stopped, hearing raised voices. She crept up the stairs towards Lady Heaton's sitting room. The door was open and Thomas was standing with his back to her, listening to Lady Heaton.

"Stephanie is going to know that there is something wrong…"

Lady Heaton tailed off and stared at her. Sophia flushed as Thomas turned.

"Sophia. Come in."

"No, I just—"

"Come in," he repeated. "Lady Heaton and I were just discussing how to continue to keep Stephanie in the dark."

"I sincerely hope Miss Nelson is fertile," Lady Heaton said and Sophia flushed with indignation. "We wouldn't want to have to go through all this again."

"You leave Sophia out of this," Thomas snapped.

"I've been watching you since you told me about your relationship. You can hardly keep your eyes off her. The funny thing is that your father was just the same. We had a very short courtship before he told me that he loved me and that he wanted to marry me. When Heaton men love, Sophia, they love quickly and deeply. And he did the only thing he could do at the time in order to give us children with Heaton blood. Hate us if you wish, Thomas, but Heatons have lived here for almost half a millennium and your father and I did not want to be the ones who brought that to an end. If you wish to shout at me again later, I shall be in the garden."

Sophia quickly turned and followed her into the hall. "Lady Heaton?"

"Yes? Sophia. I'm sorry for casting aspersions on your fertility."

"There is nothing wrong with my fertility as far as I'm aware," she told the older woman stiffly. "Did Danielle have to sign a secrecy clause?"

"No, the agreement was that she have the baby, hand the baby over, and then leave."

"So was Thomas born in town?"

"No, she came here for the birth."

"Was there never any hesitancy on her part?"

"No," Lady Heaton replied, sounding a little surprised. "You cannot understand how a woman can sell her children?"

"No, I can't understand, because if I were to have children it would be with a man I loved."

"Not Thomas?"

"Lady Heaton—" Sophia began but the other woman interrupted her.

"Sophia, if you cannot love him, tell him now. He needs to marry and have children."

"Was Danielle allowed to contact you?"

Lady Heaton frowned. "Why do you ask?"

"Did you not worry that she may turn up here? I mean, she often visits Michelle."

"I wondered if she might. But so far she hasn't been here. Go to Thomas, but remember, if you do not want children, tell him now then leave and don't come back."

She found Thomas seated in an armchair in the library and sat on his lap.

"I'm sorry," he said quietly. "She had no right to speak about you like that."

"I set her straight."

He closed his eyes for a moment and nodded.

"Thomas? Thomas, where are you?"

Hearing Lady Heaton's voice, they hurried out of the room, finding her at the telephone in the hall.

"It looks as though I spoke too soon, Sophia. Danielle is at the hospital demanding to see Stephanie. She is being quite aggressive."

"Aggressive?" Thomas asked.

"She is drunk, apparently," Lady Heaton replied, wrinkling her nose in distaste.

"I'll get the car."

"I'll get my coat." Lady Heaton turned to go.

"No," Thomas snapped. "Sophia and I will go."

Sophia shot an apologetic glance at Lady Heaton before running for her coat and handbag.

They were halfway to Leeds before Thomas spoke. "Will she recognise you?"

"Yes. She visited while I was staying at Michelle's. Don't rush into anything, will you? I don't really know what to do when we get there. I don't know if her husband or children know where she is."

"Well, what do you expect me to do?" he asked harshly. "Ring them myself? 'Hello, you don't know me, but...'"

"No. I'll try and calm her."

Her stomach was in knots when they emerged from the lift. Danielle was seated on the bench outside the I.C.U. with a security guard standing over her. She looked terrible, hair and make-up all over the place.

"Sophia?" she wailed then caught sight of Thomas. She made an "Oh," sound and clapped a hand momentarily to her mouth. "You're Thomas."

Thomas was staring in consternation and couldn't reply.

"Come on, Danielle." Sophia took her arm. "Michelle will be wondering where you are."

"I want to see my baby."

"No." Sophia was firm. "You're not seeing Stephanie while you're in this state."

"Is this your mother?" the security guard asked her.

"No, mine," Thomas murmured.

"We're taking her home," Sophia assured the security guard. "Sorry about this."

"Need a hand with her?"

"No, we'll manage, thank you." Thomas gripped Danielle's other arm.

"You're my baby, too, aren't you?" Danielle asked him.

"Let's get you into the lift," he replied instead of answering.

Somehow they managed to get Danielle into the back of the Jaguar, where she curled up and fell asleep. At the abbey, Thomas parked right outside the flat and he had to carry her up the stairs.

Sophia immediately rang Michelle. "Michelle, I met your mum in town this evening."

"Oh? I didn't know she was coming up."

"No? Oh. Well, it's just that she, um…had had a little bit too much to drink, so I have her here at the flat. Just in case you wondered where she was."

A long silence followed. "So she's back on the booze, is she?"

"Michelle, I didn't know she—"

"Well, it's not the sort of thing you want to broadcast, is it?" Michelle interrupted.

"I thought I was your friend?"

"You were in London," Michelle snapped. "Then you had your mum and dad to look after."

"Michelle, I'm sorry. Look, she's fine here until the morning."

"Thank you but I'll come and fetch her."

"She passed out, so you'd better bring Tony to carry her."

Michelle exhaled a long sigh. "A little bit too much to drink?"

"I'm sorry."

"Tony's out, but I'll get someone to mind Cathy and then I'll be straight over."

Sophia ended the call and glanced at Thomas. He hadn't spoken since the hospital and was staring intently at the woman sleeping in the armchair.

"Go back to the house. I'll come across to you when she's gone."

He nodded and walked out.

Fifteen minutes later, Michelle pulled up in the stable yard and Sophia went downstairs to let her in.

"Okay." Michelle pushed past her and went up the stairs. "Let's fetch her."

Sophia quickly glanced around the stable yard before following her, but thankfully it was deserted and dusk was falling.

Somehow, they managed to get Danielle down the stairs and into the back of Michelle's car.

"If you find her drunk again, Sophia, please ring me immediately," Michelle told her as she got into the driver's seat.

"Michelle, I'm sorry, I—"

She watched Michelle drive away and rolled her eyes. She turned and walked across the stable yard to the house, finding Thomas in the library.

"Whisky?" he asked.

"Yes, please. Please don't judge Danielle on today."

He laughed harshly. "Don't judge her? She turns up drunk at the hospital, demanding to see one of the children she sold."

He passed her an enormous whisky and brought his over to the window. "Does she have a drink problem?" he asked.

"Yes. Michelle said something like, 'So she's back on the booze, is she?'"

"Terrific." He took a sip of whisky. "It just gets better and better, doesn't it?"

"How are you?"

"I think I'm still in shock," he admitted. "I almost lost my sister and now I feel as though I've really lost my mother, too. I mean, I have, because Lady Heaton is not my mother. But now that I've seen the woman who really is my mother…" He turned. "This sounds awful but I feel like I've lost fifty pounds and found fifty pence. How am I supposed to forget that my first sighting of my real mother was when she was drunk?"

Sophia grimaced. "Michelle wasn't very pleased with me. She didn't want me knowing about her mother."

"Danielle might not even remember where she was today with a bit of luck."

"So you don't want to see her again?" Sophia asked.

He curled his lip and looked away. "It might be for the best and it would save a lot of problems. And the transaction was, as you said before, illegal. At least I've seen her now. But I still feel so…"

"Lonely?"

He nodded then put his glass down. She did likewise with hers and went to him. He pulled her to him, his hands holding her shoulders so tightly it hurt, but she put her arms around him and held him as he sobbed.

When he raised his head she reached up and gently wiped his tears away. "Better?" she whispered.

He nodded. "Stay with me tonight?"

She lifted a hand to his cheek where another tear was trickling down. She rubbed it away gently with her thumb. "Are you sure?"

"Yes," he whispered hoarsely. "Please?" She nodded. "I told you you'd have to be patient."

"I'll be patient," she said softly and he smiled.

"Thank you for letting me cry all over you," he said softly then bent his head and kissed her. "Will you move in with me?" he asked softly.

She swallowed. "I'd love to…"

"But…?" he prompted.

"Dad. Lady Heaton."

He sighed. "I'm going to have to have a long hard talk with her."

"Don't be hard on her. Imagine finding out that you're infertile."

"Imagine standing back and allowing your husband to service another woman. They probably breed racehorses with more care."

"How do you think she'd take it?" she asked. "The possibility of me living here?"

"I don't understand?" he frowned.

"In her eyes, I'm a member of staff."

"Well, to me you're not." He pushed curls away from her face. "I really thought Simon had killed you."

"What happened with him?" she asked.

"He jumped out of the window. I caught him as he ran

236

across the yard. We fought for a few minutes but he punched me in the stomach, winded me, and got away. Des had managed to get up to your flat and found you in the bedroom. He called me up there and…" He inhaled and exhaled deeply. "And for a moment I thought you were dead."

She knocked on her skull with her knuckles. "Wood. Simon said that you were at school together."

"Yes, but that's something I'd rather forget."

"Why?" She frowned.

"Because he was an idiot then and he didn't change one bit since."

"He mentioned drugs."

He gave her a humourless smile. "I bet he did. How about alcohol?" he asked and she shook her head.

"Not alcohol."

"It's a wonder we weren't expelled. We nearly got caught once. Cannabis. I told him to get rid of the stuff. He refused. We argued and had a fight. I knocked him out. He retaliated and spiked one of my drinks with something. I woke up in a corridor completely naked. I didn't speak to him again for years. You can imagine how I felt when he and Stephanie started going out together."

"Was he bisexual?" she asked bluntly.

"What?" he exclaimed then frowned. "What did he say to you?"

"Something along the lines of that you and he were very close. That a lot of you experimented, not just with drugs, and that I'm the first shag, male or female that you've had in years."

"I'm not bisexual," he roared and she jumped. "I don't

care what he said, I'm not bisexual. The lying bastard. Bloody hell." He fought to control his temper. "Why the hell didn't you say something before this? You've been wondering all this time?"

"No. Well, yes…I knew I should ask you but…" She sighed and rubbed her eyes. "There just never seemed to be a right time, not that there is ever a right time to ask something like that. I'm sorry."

"I don't know if he was bisexual but as far as I know, he never tried anything with me. The only time I can't answer for is that night." His face contorted in disgust. "Surely I would have remembered something? Felt something?" He clapped a hand to his mouth. "Oh, God, I feel sick."

"Come outside." She took his hand and they went outside and onto the front steps. "Take a few deep breaths." He did as he was told. "Feel better?" she asked softly.

He nodded. "A little." He sat down on the top step hugging his knees.

"Thomas." She sat beside him. "I had to ask about him, I'm sorry."

"No, I'm glad you felt that you could."

"For what it's worth, I think he was lying. Trying to stir things."

"Well, we'll never know for sure, will we?" he replied quietly.

"Well, I still love you. Nothing has changed there."

He looked at her and gave her a little smile. "Come up to bed."

"I'll just get my phone and lock the flat. I'll be ten minutes."

By the time she returned to the house, locked the side

door and set the alarm, he was already in bed and watched as she got undressed.

"Look at you," he whispered.

"Hmm?" She frowned. He nodded at her and she looked down. There were bruises on her right breast and waist. "I hadn't even noticed."

"Bastard. If only I'd—"

"Hey?" She climbed into the bed. "Stephanie is going to be okay, I'm fine, and we're going to forget about our previous conversation altogether."

He smiled gratefully. "I just don't know if I can tell Stephanie about our mother. Or lack of. But she's not stupid, she's going to notice something is not right."

"I know. Worry about it when she comes home, yes?"

He nodded, leaned over and kissed her breast. "You're beautiful," he whispered.

"So you keep telling me." She smiled as he kissed the other one.

"Please move in with me?"

"I need to talk to Dad. Look, as soon as it's convenient, I'll cook a meal for the three of us. All he can see at the moment is your title."

"Does he know you're sleeping with me?" he asked.

"Yes, I think so."

"You think so?" he repeated, drawing back from her.

"Thomas, he's my dad," she tried to reason with him. "And he's quite old for a dad. And he's very set in his ways and outlook on life." She sighed. "I will tell him. He needs to get rid of the notion that once you've bedded me you'll abandon me."

"Oh, good grief." He rolled onto his back. "When I

mentioned the master and the serving wench thing I was joking."

She laughed. "I know you were. Did your father ever talk to you about women?"

"Yes." He put an arm behind his head. "I was told about the birds and the bees."

"I meant marriage," she added. "You told me once that it was just automatically expected of you. Did he never speak to you about it?"

"No. But Stephanie has."

She was astonished. "Stephanie?"

"Yes. She told me only to marry if I loved the woman in question, not to marry someone because they are 'suitable', or would make a good wife. What's brought this up?" he asked, rising onto an elbow.

"Lady Heaton told me that if I couldn't love you or if I didn't want children, to tell you and then leave and not come back. But I do love you and I do want children sometime."

"She's probably wondering why I haven't proposed yet." He sighed. "She knew what she was marrying and marrying into. I deliberately haven't mentioned marriage because I don't want to frighten you away. I love you and if we were to marry, I'd be marrying just you. You would be marrying me, a title, and all of this." He indicated the house and estate with the sweep of an arm. "That's why I suggested you move in with me. Don't think that I've never thought about marrying you because I have. I'd marry you in the morning if you'd have me, but would you marry me and all that comes with me? The need to provide an heir? The need to keep coming up with ways of keeping this place going without turning it into the Heaton Abbey Theme Park? The need to somehow deal with the fact that I am one of two children your best friend's mother sold? The need to realise that you could end up with not just one but two mothers-in-law if Danielle decides she wants to see her 'babies' more often? It's a mess and do you really want to marry me, all this, and a mess? Think about it."

He lay down again and turned over with his back to her. She sighed. He was right.

"I'll think about it," she replied, kissed his shoulder, and lay down with her back to him.

Chapter Ten

She woke to find herself alone in the bed. Downstairs, she peered into the breakfast room but it was empty, and so was his office when she crossed the stable yard.

"His Lordship's gone to the hospital," Des told her from the door of his office.

"The hospital? Is Stephanie…?"

"No, no, she seems to be well on the mend," he assured her. "He said he wanted to beat the traffic."

"Oh, I see."

"The tours start again today, don't they?" he asked.

"Yes, so I'd better get on. Thanks, Des."

There were twenty-five Americans on her first tour that afternoon all listening intently except for one woman who was staring at the photographs on the table in the drawing room. Halfway up the main staircase, she realised that the woman had gone.

"I don't believe it," she whispered, then added; "Did anyone see where the lady in the green jacket went? Some of the rooms are private…" She tailed off hearing a roar.

"Can you not read, woman? It says private. And how dare you start looking in the drawers. Give those to me. Please leave this room immediately and re-join the tour. Now."

Sophia raced down the stairs and across the hall then halted as Thomas appeared, leading the woman firmly by the arm. She hadn't known he was back from the hospital.

"One of your group, Ms Nelson?"

"Yes, Lord Heaton."

He nodded, looked up, and she followed his gaze. The rest of the group were leaning over the bannisters agog.

"Excuse me." He turned and walked back to the library.

"That's Lord Heaton?" The woman's mouth fell open. "Do you have any postcards of him?"

Sophia frowned. "Postcards? Of Lord Heaton?" In a strop?

The woman nodded vigorously. "Ones like that picture in there." She nodded towards the drawing room.

"Oh, right. Well, I'm afraid we don't, but I'll suggest it. Could I please remind you all that the Heaton family do live here and therefore some of the rooms are private."

She continued with the tour and was gasping for a coffee by the time they reached the kitchen. The tour leader was munching a currant bun, having decided not to go on the tour, and probably relieved to be free of the group for three-quarters of an hour.

"You been wandering off again, Lydia?" The leader asked the woman casually.

"Yeah, but I got to meet Lord Heaton."

"No!"

"Got yelled at, too, when I looked at his drawings." The woman grinned. "My, he is handsome." The grin faded. "But they got no postcards of him."

When the group had been shepherded out to the gardens,

and Sophia had gulped down a cup of coffee, she went in search of Thomas. She found him in the library smoking a cigarette.

"I'm sorry. Apparently, she wanders off a lot."

"Does she."

"You made her day, anyway."

An eyebrow rose. "She likes getting shouted at?"

"I don't know, but she thinks you are very handsome and wanted to know whether we had any postcards of you."

He shrugged in incomprehension and lifted the cigarette to his lips.

"How is Stephanie?" she asked.

"Starting to complain as well as order me about."

Sophia laughed. "That's good."

"For Stephanie, yes. She'll be back to shouting at me soon."

"The woman was looking at some of your drawings?"

"Yes," he replied shortly. "Bloody nerve."

"New ones?" she enquired and he nodded. "Can I see them?"

He stubbed out the cigarette before going to a drawer in the desk and pulling out a cardboard folder, leaving it on the desk for her.

She opened it. There was quite a bundle of drawings but the first was herself reclining naked on a bed. The second was herself again as *The Birth of Venus*. The third was herself in the throes of sexual ecstasy, the drawing she had seen on his office desk. Bloody hell, had the woman been looking through these?

"You're disgusted?" he asked quietly.

"No...I don't think so." She went on through the

drawings. The fourth was of herself up on the moors looking into the distance with him watching her. It was a beautiful drawing with Thomas doing justice to himself at last. "I love this one."

"Yes, you're beautiful in it."

She smiled. "I meant you. There's no caricature, just you."

"And the others?" he asked. "Of you?"

"Well, I'll never be able to look at *The Birth of Venus* in quite the same way again."

He grimaced. "I have embarrassed you, I'm sorry."

"No. Um, it's just that I try not to look at myself naked."

"Why not? You're beautiful."

She shrugged. "Others would see me as...well-built."

"Well, you're not and it's my view that counts, doesn't it?"

"Yes," she had to admit.

"I'm sorry about last night. I think I was trying to put you off me. Or at least play up the downside to being Lord Heaton. If that makes sense."

"I can see what being Lord Heaton has done to you," she said softly. "And I think you need someone to share the burden with. We just need to convince my dad that I'm not mad."

He finally smiled. "When do you want to invite him over for dinner?"

"Tomorrow?" she suggested. "It's my day off so I can go shopping and prepare the meal. I was thinking roast beef and Yorkshire pudding?"

He nodded. "And for dessert?"

"Which you'll only get when you've cleared your plate."

She laughed. "I don't know…ice cream?"

"I love ice cream." He ran his hands down her back to her buttocks. "But not as much as I love you."

He bent and kissed her until they heard someone clearing their throat at the door. Lady Heaton stood watching them.

"I'm sorry to interrupt but I heard from Helen that one of this morning's group wandered off?"

"Yes," Thomas replied. "Despite Sophia's threats with the tranquilliser gun."

"I'm sorry?" Lady Heaton asked, looking taken aback.

"A joke," Thomas explained. "The woman wanders off a lot, apparently."

"Oh, I see."

"I escorted her back to the hall and she re-joined the group," Sophia told her.

"Good. Any news on Danielle?"

Sophia felt Thomas tighten his grip on her.

"Not since her daughter took her home, Lady Heaton," she replied.

"Good. Well, I'll…" Lady Heaton tailed off and left the room, closing the door after herself.

"I'm going to have to go and see Michelle," Sophia told him. "She's my best friend."

"I know."

"I'll go now," she decided. "She'll be back home from picking Cathy up from school."

Twenty minutes later, she rang Michelle's doorbell and waited nervously for the door to open. Michelle opened the door and stared at her for a moment.

"Sophia," she greeted her in a flat tone.

"Can I come in?"

Michelle nodded and Sophia followed her down the hall to the kitchen. "Coffee?"

"Yes, please. Look, I'm sorry. I didn't really know what to do…"

"With your best friend's alcoholic mother, I know," Michelle finished harshly. "She went home this morning. I poured her back onto the train."

"Oh, Michelle, why didn't you tell me about her?"

"What happened to your mother wasn't her fault," Michelle cried. "What's happened to my mother is her fault."

"How long has she been drinking?"

Michelle shrugged and switched the electric kettle on. "Since before I was born. She's never turned up here drunk before, though, that's a first."

"How is your dad coping?"

"Badly."

"What about Alcoholics Anonymous?" Sophia suggested.

"She went once. Years ago, and arrived home in floods of tears. Went on a bender almost immediately and swore she'd never go back. She's killing herself and doesn't seem to care." Michelle smiled bitterly and went to a cupboard for the coffee and lifted down a jar. "Anyway, how's it going with Lord Heaton?"

"Very well." Sophia went to the fridge for milk and passed the carton to Michelle.

"You'll have to introduce us." Michelle sloshed milk into two mugs then added a teaspoon of coffee to each. "I want to make sure he's good enough for you." Sophia just managed a smile. "It is serious, then?"

"Yes."

"So I could be making instant coffee for the next Lady Heaton?" Michelle asked as the kettle clicked off and she poured boiling water into the mugs.

"You never know. Dad isn't too keen on the idea."

"And you're surprised?" Michelle added.

"No, but I just want him and Thomas to try and get to know each other a bit."

"Good luck." Michelle passed her a mug. "So, what is he like, Lord Heaton? When he's not being 'Lord Heaton'? Apart from being gorgeous?"

"Shy."

"Shy?" Michelle repeated. "Yes, you mentioned something. Is that why he doesn't go out much?"

"He works very hard."

"And the sex?"

Sophia blushed. "It's good."

"Only good?"

"All right, it's fantastic," she admitted.

"Better than Lee?"

She smiled. "Infinitely better than Lee."

"Wow. A lord, extremely gorgeous, and fantastic at sex. What more could you want?"

"To try and make my dad understand that there is a man behind the title."

The following morning, she went on a shopping expedition to the local butcher and supermarkets. Returning to the abbey, she saw Thomas crossing the stable yard towards her.

"Need any help?" he asked, lifting two bags out of the boot of the car.

"Can you cook?"

"Not really, no," he replied apologetically. "Well, not a roast, anyway. But I wouldn't mind watching you."

She smiled. "Come on, then."

At half past six, she went to collect her father, leaving Thomas watching the vegetables as they began to simmer on the hob.

"Hungry?" she asked him as they climbed the stairs to the flat ten minutes later.

"Very." Her father laughed before sobering as Thomas opened the door of the flat for them.

"Dad – Thomas. Thomas – my father." She introduced them again nervously.

"Lord Heaton."

"Thomas, please, Mr Nelson."

"William."

The two men shook hands and she sighed with relief and went to see to the gravy. Leaving it to simmer, they sat down to the starter – prawn cocktail.

"Delicious," her father proclaimed.

"I agree." Thomas smiled at her, William Nelson watching him intently.

"So you love my daughter, then…Thomas?"

"Yes, I do," Thomas replied. "Very much."

"Is there any point in me asking what you can offer her?"

Thomas put his spoon down. "Well, yes, there is."

"Are you rich, then?" her father asked bluntly.

"Dad, for goodness sake."

"No." Thomas squeezed her hand. "No, I'm not rich, William. Running a house and estate like this costs a fortune – maintenance, heating, insurance, staff – we all work very hard just to keep the place afloat. Both the house and gardens are now open to the public. There is a shop and a small garden centre. The old farmyard has been converted into holiday accommodation. To be honest, I wanted none of it. This is my home and the way things are going I don't know where it's all going to end. I don't really want to have to start doing Bed and Breakfast but if that's what it takes…"

"So what can you offer Sophia?" Mr Nelson asked again. "I mean, she's going to have to give you children, whether she likes it or not."

"I want children, Dad," she protested.

Mr Nelson sighed. "God, I wish your mother was here. What does your mother make of all this?"

Thomas looked startled. "My mother?"

"Yes. I bet she's not too happy about you carrying on with a miner's daughter from the town. I'd have thought she'd have lined up some heiress with piles of money for you."

Thomas smiled. "No. And even if she had, I couldn't marry her unless I loved her. And I don't believe that I am 'carrying on', as you put it, with Sophia. I love her and I am completely astonished that she will even look twice at someone like me."

Sophia flushed and got up from the table. "I'll see to the main course."

"Did your parents marry because they loved each other?" Her father was persistent.

"Yes." Thomas nodded. "They did."

"Your father was a lot older."

"Yes, by nearly twenty years. You married…later in life?"

"I did," Mr Nelson replied. "I wanted to put a bit of

money away first. I worked bloody hard and I had enough for a deposit on a house by the time Sophia's mother and I wed. How old are you?"

"Forty."

"Up in the town they think you're a recluse," her father told him and Sophia winced.

"I spend too much time in my office but that doesn't make me a recluse. I'm round and about here all the time."

"You were down the mine once?" Mr Nelson asked.

"Yes, when I was eleven or twelve."

"Could you have worked down there?"

"No," Thomas replied at once. "I don't think I could."

Sophia turned around with two plates in her hands and saw her father nod.

"At least you're honest," Mr Nelson conceded.

"Would you want to run this place?" Thomas challenged.

"No chance."

Both men smiled and she put a plate down in front of each of them before going back for her own.

"Enjoy your meal," she told them and sat down.

"I will," her father replied. "This looks wonderful."

"It tastes wonderful, too," Thomas added.

"Proper Yorkshire pudding," she said. "Not stuff out of a packet."

"A packet?" Thomas queried.

"You'd be amazed what you can get in a packet," her father told him. "Grocery shopping is an education these days. You can even buy ready-made pancakes."

"Oh." Thomas pulled a disgusted face. "I don't think I'd like them ready-made."

"No, they taste like rubber. Sophia makes lovely pancakes."

"Thank you." She smiled. "But it's ice cream for dessert."

"And not until we clear our plates." Thomas grinned and her father laughed.

The two men not only cleared their plates but had second helpings of beef and Yorkshire pudding and still had enough room left for the ice cream.

"Sophia, that was an excellent meal, thank you," her father declared.

"Hear, hear," Thomas added.

"Thank you."

"Do you like whisky, William?" Thomas asked. "I brought a bottle of single malt across with me."

"Well, I wouldn't say no."

"Good." Thomas smiled and accepted two tumblers from Sophia.

"Poor Sophia, you deserve a drink after all that effort."

"I'll have some later, Dad," she assured him as Thomas poured the whisky. "After I've brought you home."

"Fair enough."

"Why don't you go and sit in the armchair?" she suggested.

"I think I will." He sat down and accepted a glass from Thomas. "To Sophia."

"Sophia."

She bobbed a quick curtsey and, after pouring herself a glass of orange juice, she sat down on the sofa. Thomas sat beside her and smiled at her father.

"What do you think of the whisky?"

Mr Nelson took a sip and raised his eyebrows. "Good stuff."

"It is."

"I like these flats," Her father added, glancing around the room.

"Thank you, yes, they did turn out well. Des Fields, the estate manager, and my sister live in the others."

"How is your sister?" Mr Nelson asked.

"Well on the mend and starting to complain of boredom."

"Always a good sign."

"Yes," Thomas replied. "She feels that she's wasting valuable shopping time."

"What does she do?"

"She designs wedding dresses."

"Have you ever had to look for a job?" her father inquired. "I mean, would you have to tell them you're a lord?"

Thomas shook his head. "I'm afraid my father died when I was just out of university so this place has been my full-time job ever since. But Stephanie did work for other companies before setting hers up. One knew already, but the other only found out after she had been there over a year. I was at school with a duke and two earls, so I was a long way down the pecking order. But, like I told Sophia, my family have lived here for almost five hundred years and I don't want to be remembered as the Heaton who had to sell. That's why I work very hard at it. My father remembered his grandfather after he sold the mine off. He really felt as though he'd failed."

"We were lucky with the mine," Mr Nelson mused. "It survived the Miners' Strike by five years."

Thomas nodded. "It was the end of an era."

"It was. And we don't even have the museum anymore now. Bloody vandals."

"Have you tried for a lottery grant or something?" Thomas suggested. "To try and re-open it?"

"No." Her father perked up at that. "I must look into it."

"And not just the lottery, there must be other grants available."

He nodded. "Sophia comes from mining stock on both sides, you know?"

"I know, she told me."

Mr Nelson finished his whisky and put his glass to one side. "It's time I was going. It was good chatting with you, Thomas."

"And you, William. We must do it again."

"So?" Sophia asked as she drove him back to town.

"A nice lad. Quiet, and a bit shy, as you said. But a nice lad all the same. I think your mother would have liked him, too. I'll nip down to the library in the morning and see what I can find out about these grants."

She arrived back at the flat to discover that Thomas had washed up. He poured her some whisky.

"Thank you." She took the glass from him and kissed his cheek. "Dad likes you."

"I like him. My father was always rather distant. I wish I'd known him better but I was away at school and then university and then it was too late. What did Michelle say when you went to see her?" Sophia pulled a face. "Sophia?"

"Danielle has been an alcoholic since before Michelle was born. She tried A.A. once and never went back. Michelle knows that she's killing herself."

"Does Michelle's father not wonder why his wife started drinking?"

"I don't know," she shrugged. "Michelle never mentioned it."

"Danielle is going to give herself away one day, isn't she?" Thomas asked her.

"Yes, I'm afraid she is," she replied quietly.

After waving off the latest tour group, Sophia went to find Thomas. He was in his office surfing the internet.

"I'm turning into an internet nerd as well as a 'recluse'."

She smiled. "Come up to the flat, I have a bottle of wine in the fridge."

He nodded. "I'll be up in a few minutes."

She opened the wine then went into the second bedroom where she had stored all her boxes. She went through three boxes before she found her school yearbook and photograph album, left them on the sofa and poured the wine, hearing Thomas coming up the stairs. She passed him a glass and followed him to the sofa.

She opened the photograph album and went through the pages until she came to Michelle's wedding.

"There's Danielle," she pointed and he leaned over. Danielle was dressed in a pale blue suit. Thankfully her hat did not cover her face. "That's Don," she added. "And that's Peter. That's Andrew and his wife. Barbara and her husband, and Kevin and his wife." She turned the page. "The women. Michelle, Danielle, Tony's Mum, Danielle's Mum, me, and the flower girl."

"It's a lovely photograph."

"Yes. And it'll be here for whenever you want to look at it." He nodded. She closed the album and reached for the yearbook. She flipped through it until she came to her old class. "There's Michelle."

"And where are you?" he asked.

"There." She pointed and cringed at her grin, displaying the ugly braces on her teeth.

"I had braces, too," he told her. "At primary school. Worse than those."

"That's not possible."

He laughed. "They have to be seen to be believed."

"I shall expect evidence then." She turned the page. "Peter's class. That's him, there."

"Didn't want his photograph taken by the look of it," Thomas murmured, pointing to the scowl on Peter's face.

"No." She put the album and yearbook to one side and picked up her glass, seeing him smile. "What?"

"What do you think Jerry Springer would make of all this?"

"Jerry Springer?" she exclaimed.

"Mmm. I saw one of his shows once. Unbelievable. Or so I thought."

She laughed. "Sorry, but I just can't visualise you watching Jerry Springer. Or Jeremy Kyle. Or any of them, really."

"Oh, really?" His eyebrows rose playfully. "So what do you actually visualise me watching on television?"

"I really have no idea, now that I know you've seen *The Jerry Springer Show*."

"Are you mocking my choice of programmes?" he teased. "I mean, you're probably glued to the soaps every evening."

Her mouth fell open in mock-outrage. She quickly put her glass on the floor and hit him with a cushion. He fended her off and managed to pin her down, helpless with laughter, on the sofa.

"I love you," he whispered, starting to undo her blouse.

256

"I don't know what I would have done without you these last few days. So let me make love to you," he said, concentrating on undoing the last button before slipping the blouse off her shoulders. "Come with me." He took her by the hand and led her to the bedroom and across to the bed.

"You don't have to reward me," she said softly as she climbed onto the bed and felt his hands unfastening her bra. "But having you make love to me would be lovely, thank you."

"Good," he replied, taking it off and dropping it onto the floor.

"But we'll have to be quiet," she told him as he eased her onto his lap with her back to him.

"Quiet?" He slid his hands under her breasts and held them in his hands. "There's no-one next door."

"Well, quieter. The walls aren't four feet thick here."

"All right, quieter." He ran his thumbs over her nipples. "I love your breasts," he whispered in her ear, as he began to massage them, and she rested her head back on his shoulder. "I love you. Look at us."

"Hmm?" She raised her head and saw them reflected in the wardrobe mirror. His hands cupping her breasts, her skirt up around her thighs and her legs already wide open. She quickly began to close them.

"Don't," he whispered. "Don't hide yourself." She opened them again and felt hot breath on the back of her neck. "I'm hard already. Feel." He shifted position slightly and she felt his erection through his trousers in the small of her back. "And I want to be inside you. Do you want me inside you?"

"Yes," she replied and smiled as he kissed her neck then

lifted her off his lap and onto the bed before getting up.

He undid his trousers and pushed them and his briefs down, grunting as his erection sprang to attention. He pulled his shoes off then stepped out of them, shrugged his jacket off, then began to unbutton his shirt.

"Wait." She got up and began to undo the buttons, standing so close to him his erection was pressing into her stomach. She pushed his shirt off his shoulders then began to undo her skirt button.

"My turn." He smiled and undid it and lowered the zip. He eased both the skirt and her panties down her legs and lifted her out of them. He reached for his jacket and pulled a condom out of his wallet, tore open the packaging and rolled it on. "Kneel on the bed?" he asked.

"Kneel?" she echoed and he nodded. She climbed onto the bed and he positioned himself behind her, turning her so they were facing the mirror again.

He took her hips and bent over her, kissing her back, from her neck down to her buttocks. Holding her hips steady, he eased himself into her, grunting his satisfaction. He pulled out slowly and she raised her head and watched his expression in the mirror, the wondrous and almost painful satisfaction she was giving him evident in his face.

He pushed in again deeper and she let out a small moan. He pulled out almost completely and when he entered her again more quickly, they both groaned. Pulling out, he pulled her back into a hard thrust, then did it again, with a loud grunt each time his groin met her buttocks.

She didn't want to come yet, didn't want him to ever stop so she pushed herself up, bringing her back up to his chest, angling her hips so she could fit even more of him inside her. His hands slid upwards from her hips to her breasts and he kneaded them as he thrust upwards into her, finding a rhythm after a couple of moments. He was hitting a spot inside which was setting her on fire. As she grew close to her climax, he slipped one hand between her legs and she felt his fingers stroke her, the movement enough to send her over. He continued to stroke through her orgasm, until with one final thrust, he came with a muffled groan.

When she opened her eyes she saw them in the mirror, almost moulded to each other, his arms around her holding her tightly against him. He bent his head and kissed her neck.

"I love you," he whispered.

"And I love you," she replied.

Waking early, she heard him slip out to the kitchen to make a hot drink and rolled over to watch him. There was barely a sound as he put the electric kettle on. He found the teapot, tea and mugs and stood waiting for the water to boil. Looking around at the simple furnishings, the pictures of her parents on the wall, photos stuck to the fridge with magnets, the table with a vase of wildflowers in the middle. He was clearly thinking how homely it was, how warm and friendly, and of his own life in a huge mansion isolated from the town and normal life.

Sophia silently followed him out of bed and stood at the door to the living area. She watched him as he peered at one of the more casual black and white photographs she had taken of him stuck to the door of the fridge.

He sensed her presence and turned around. "Why on earth have you stuck that on here?"

Sophia walked over and took a closer look at the photograph. He looked good enough to eat, both in the photograph and in the flesh.

"I hate having my picture taken," he protested. "I look like an idiot."

"No, you don't. And I'm thinking of using it for a postcard like that American woman wanted." She laughed and dodged him as he tried to grab hold of her. "Fifty pence a card, we'd make a fortune."

"Frighten people away, you mean." The kettle came to the boil and clicked off and she watched him make the tea. "See?" he said as the tea brewed. "I'm not completely undomesticated."

"Did I ever say you were?" She smiled as he poured the tea and took a mug, realising how very little she knew about him, and yet how much. "Did you have a flat or a house when you were at university?"

"A flat. And I did all my own cooking and cleaning. So coming back here was a shock in more ways than one; no more wandering about at seven in the morning completely naked making tea. So, like I said last night, I don't know what I would have done without you these last few days. I'm shy." He smiled comically. "And because I'm shy, I'm lonely, but people think I'm either a snob who doesn't want to mix with them or a hermit. So thank you for being persistent and patient with me."

She put the mug down and put her arms around him. "I love you," she whispered. "You're neither a snob nor a hermit. Come back to bed and tell me about university."

They picked up their mugs and got back into bed.

"I had a flat ten minutes from the college," he told her.

"I shared with two others. I went a bit wild the first year but knuckled down to my studies after that. Then in my final year, Lady Heaton suddenly turned up. Father had had a persistent cough. She eventually managed to persuade him to go and see a doctor. He referred Father to a specialist. Advanced lung cancer." He took a gulp of tea. "I wanted to drop out but she wouldn't hear of it. I managed to get through the rest of the year, coming back up here at weekends, somehow managed to sit my finals, then moved back here and I've been here ever since. Thank God I had that first wild year."

"A lot of wine women and song?" she asked and he laughed.

"Beer, girls and drunken renditions of Oasis songs mostly. I have to go with Lady Heaton to see Stephanie today." He grimaced. "We have to go together sometimes otherwise Stephanie is going to think there's something wrong."

"What's going to happen when she comes home?"

He sighed. "I have absolutely no idea. One thing is for sure – she won't be going back to the flat for a while. She'll be in the house with Lady Heaton whether she likes it or not. And whether I like it or not."

Sophia found her father watching cricket on television later that morning, but he turned it off and smiled at her as she closed the living room door and shrugged off her jacket.

"Tell Thomas that I went to the library. I went surfing the internet and I found out all about grants."

"I will." She smiled. "What did you find out?"

"Oh, the different types available. A couple of

organisations are sending me some information. Do you think Thomas would give me a hand with some of the forms?"

"I'll ask, but I'm sure he will."

"Good. He's a nice lad. Fancy a cuppa?"

"Yes, please," she replied and he went out to the kitchen.

She went to the sideboard and opened the doors. Her mother had neatly numbered all the photograph albums and she pulled out 1974-75. Her mother had been working in Leeds with Danielle and Sophia flipped through the pages until she came to photographs of what looked like the company's Christmas dinner dance.

She sat cross-legged on the floor and picked out her mother and father immediately but where was Danielle?

"What's this?" Her father put a mug of tea down on the floor beside her. "Ah, Connolly's Christmas do."

"Was Michelle's mum not there?" she asked.

"No, she was ill. Your mum was disappointed that she couldn't go. There's a nice photo of your mum with you and Danielle with Michelle." Sophia turned a few pages and he pointed. "That one," he said before returning to the sofa.

Sophia turned back to the beginning of the album and went through all the photographs until she came to one of her mother and Danielle on the promenade in Blackpool. It was out of season as the promenade was almost deserted. She stared, trying to remember what her mother had written in her journal about the trips to Blackpool. Despite being wrapped up warm, Danielle was holding a large bag in front of her, the way some television actresses do when trying to conceal their own pregnancy even though everyone knows they are pregnant. Except not everyone had known that

Danielle was pregnant. But her mother had. Two pages later was the Christmas do. It was 1975. Thomas was born in May 1976. No wonder Danielle didn't go, she would have been pregnant at the time. In the Blackpool photograph, Danielle was pregnant with Thomas.

"Dad, can I borrow this album? I want to make copies of a couple of photos."

"Course you can,"

"Thanks." She reached into the sideboard again and pulled out 1973-74. Going through the pages, she came to another photograph taken in Blackpool. This time, her mother was seated on the beach in a deckchair while Danielle was crouching behind. "Mum and Michelle's mum seem to have liked Blackpool," she commented. "Did you take these?" She held the album up so her father could see the photographs.

"No, it wasn't me. Your mum and I were never in Blackpool."

"Can I borrow this one as well?" she asked.

He nodded. "How can you copy photos?"

"Thomas has a scanner, I can scan them."

Her father looked none the wiser and she took a sip of tea.

"If he asked you to marry him, would you say yes?" he asked.

Sophia looked up at him. "Yes, I would," she replied quietly. "Would that upset you?"

"All I want is for you to be happy." He sighed. "And he is a nice lad. Loves you – he made that quite clear at the hospital. If only he wasn't a lord. You must try and get him out more."

"Dad, he's not a recluse."

"I know that but others don't."

"After I've been shopping, and lunch, we're going walking on the moors," she told him.

"He likes the moors?"

"Yes, he does. And he needs the exercise."

Back at the flat, she left the two photograph albums on the sofa while she brought up her shopping and made herself some lunch. Munching on her salad sandwich, she looked through the photos again.

"Can I come up?" She heard Thomas' voice below.

"The door's open," she called and heard him coming up the stairs.

"How is your father?"

"Fine, thanks. He's been looking into grants and is hoping that you'd help him with some forms?"

"Me?" He looked and sounded astonished.

"It's an enormous compliment."

"Oh. Well, of course, I'll help. What have you there?"

"Photographs of Danielle," she told him. "When she was expecting Stephanie and you." He froze. "Come and look." Slowly he walked across the room and sat down. "This one is the first and it was taken in Blackpool," she explained. "It's sometime in winter 1974. She was expecting Stephanie. This one is Blackpool again. Winter 1975."

"She was expecting me," he whispered.

"Yes. I'll scan them and I'll put them on the laptop with the other details." He nodded. "There's a clearer one of her...here...Michelle and I were born within a week of each other."

"Thanks for finding these. Your father wasn't a bit…strange, about you borrowing these?"

"No, which is why I don't really think he knew. Mum and Dad married in October 1980. Danielle and Don married in August 1981. Mum moved back here from Leeds when she married. Danielle lived on in Leeds then moved to London when she married. I don't think there was much opportunity for Dad to get to know her much at all. Michelle came back up here to school but, even so, it was mostly Mum and me and Michelle and her mum who mixed."

He nodded. "It's strange. I thought Father would pick someone who looked like Lady Heaton but Danielle doesn't really. Maybe they did, but Danielle was the only one who would go through with it." He blew out his cheeks and went to the window. "God, there are times I'm glad that I know and then there are times that I wish I didn't know. I don't want Stephanie to know but she's going to find out. Lady Heaton and I spoke about three words all morning and even they were a struggle. I don't think Stephanie noticed, she was just happy to see us."

"How is she?" Sophia asked.

"Still weak but walking a bit further every day. She says thanks for the magazines."

"No problem. I'll just get changed. Could you make the flask of coffee?"

Seated out of the wind in the stone circle, she poured the coffee and handed him a cup.

"Thank you." He took a sip and smiled. "I love it up here. I can almost forget everything when I'm up here with you."

"Good." She leaned over and kissed his lips.

He finished his coffee and lay down, closing his eyes. She closed the flask and lay down beside him, running a finger lightly over his lips.

He opened his eyes and stared solemnly at her. "Marry me?" he whispered and her heart somersaulted. "No, you don't have to answer immediately but the proposal is there. Take as long as you need." She nodded. "And remember all the other things you need to take into consideration, too." She nodded again and he lifted her hand and kissed it.

"Will you come out with me tonight?" she asked. "You've just asked me to marry you and we haven't even been on a proper date."

He rolled his eyes. "I know. Where would you like to go?"

"The cinema?" she suggested. "And a couple of drinks afterwards?"

"I haven't been to the cinema since…"

"*E.T.*, Stephanie told me. I'm afraid they don't have those courting seats at the Odeon anymore. Actually, you might have a job squeezing into the ones that are there now. Legroom-wise, I mean."

"Only midgets go to the cinema these days?" he asked.

"I wouldn't call them midgets. I just wish they'd turn their phones off and shut up."

"What's on?"

"Oh." She shrugged. "It's bound to be something extremely violent with lots of car chases."

"Oh." His face fell.

"We'll see. And if all the films look terrible, we'll just go straight to the pub."

They walked into town and stood outside the cinema weighing up what was on offer, eventually choosing a reasonable thriller, emerging two hours later.

"I don't know about you, but I miss the courting seats." Thomas rubbed his knees. They had been forced to sit some way along a row and even she had found it uncomfortable after a while. "And those two behind us were kissing so noisily that I was on the point of asking for the sound to be turned up. I don't kiss like that?" he asked anxiously.

"No. Oh, God, no. He sounded like he was unblocking a sink with a plunger."

He smiled. "I haven't been on a date since the latter part of the twentieth century so, a drink?"

"Yes, please."

They went into The Swan and he ordered two whiskies.

"Father used to come here," he told her as he brought the glasses back to their table and sat down.

"Did he ever bring you out for a drink?" she asked and he frowned. "For your first pint or something?"

"No," he replied in a surprised tone. "Why? Were you brought out?"

"Yes, but not for a pint. Michelle and I had a joint eighteenth birthday party. First legal drink and all that."

"I don't think I knew my father at all." He took a sip of whisky. "I had a twenty-first birthday party but it was mostly relatives who came. It was like an Agatha Christie novel. Without the murder, but you know what I mean. The lord, the major, the maid, the butler, all the clichés were there."

"When did the staff leave?"

"We had two house-parlourmaids, a butler, and Mrs Fields...Helen. The maids left to get married about a year after father died and MacDonald, the butler, retired a couple of years later. I decided not to replace them – I couldn't afford to replace them." He pulled a comical face. "Sorry, I'm supposed to be chatting you up, aren't I? Trying to get you into bed?" he added in a low voice.

"Excuse me, but I have never slept with anyone on a first date," she replied in an equally low voice.

"Sophia?" She glanced up. It was Gavin.

"Hello, Gavin. You remember Thomas, don't you?"

"Lord Heaton."

"Thomas, please."

"Thomas, then. I went to see your dad the other day," Gavin turned back to her. "He's looking well."

"Yes. He's looking into possibly getting a grant or something to try and open the mining museum again."

"A grant?" Gavin echoed.

"Thomas mentioned it."

"Oh, I see. Well, let's hope he can get one, then. Nice one, Thomas."

Thomas smiled. "It's worth a try."

Gavin returned to the bar and she smiled at Thomas. "Another whisky?"

"Yes, please."

She went to the bar and ordered the drinks.

"Your dad told me about you and his Lordship," Gavin told her.

"Oh, Gavin, please just call him Thomas?"

"All right, all right. I'm probably just jealous of you. He's definitely not gay, then?"

"Absolutely definitely not gay, Gavin," she replied without hesitation.

"Bollocks."

"Bye, Gavin." She smiled.

"Everything all right?" Thomas asked as she returned with the drinks.

"Fine."

"So why does he keep staring at me?"

"He fancies you," she told him and he almost inhaled his drink. "But I told him that you were absolutely definitely not gay."

"Bloody hell."

"Sorry, I didn't mean to give you a fright."

"No, it's all right. I just can't quite believe that you find me attractive, let alone anyone else." He groaned. "Oh, God, I need to get out more."

"Yes, you do."

"So, can I take you out again sometime, then?"

"Oh, I don't know, I'll have to think about it."

"Choosy who you go out with, are we?"

"Extremely. How about you?"

"Well, I'd been celibate for over twenty years but a few months ago I met this beautiful woman. She just wandered into the library without knocking and started to go through the books. The cheek. I was sitting in the corner and all I could do was stare. I fell in love with her at first sight."

She smiled. "I knew I was in trouble from the very first moment I saw him. He was sitting in the corner staring at me. I have to be honest and say that it wasn't love at first sight, but it was definitely lust. The trouble was, he was my employer. We spent weeks tiptoeing around each other until his sister took pity on us and set us up together. He's been very lonely so I've been trying to bring him out of himself."

"And is it working?" he asked softly.

"I think it is. There's a lot going on in his life at the moment but I think it is."

"And is he good in bed?"

Her eyebrows rose and she smiled. "He is unbelievable in bed."

He pulled a comical face. "Well, that's done it for us, then. How can I possibly compete with this other man?"

"I know. I mean, that woman you've been going on about, she sounds far too good to be true."

He laughed and leaned over. "Shall we go home?"

She nodded and they went out to find a cab.

When the cab deposited them in the stable yard and drove away, Thomas shrugged. "So, what happens now?"

"Well, I could invite you in for a coffee…?"

"Ah, yes, the famous, 'Would you like to come in for a coffee?'"

"My only concern is that you'll start going on about this fantasy woman again."

"Well, why don't I invite you in for a coffee instead? Provided that you don't bore me to death about this other man? I mean, how can I possibly compete with someone who is unbelievable in bed?"

"Very well, I think, especially if you've got a big bed. Do you have a big bed?"

"Well, now you come to mention it…" He held out a hand and she took it. "But I thought you didn't sleep with anyone on the first date?"

"I could be persuaded."

Walking up the stairs, they heard a door close. Lady Heaton appeared at the top of the stairs, gave them a long look and Sophia squirmed.

"I'd like to speak with you in the morning, Thomas. About me moving out. I think it's time, don't you?"

"This house is enormous, it's not as though we are living in each other's pockets."

"No, but I still think it is time."

"What about Stephanie?"

"We will speak in the morning."

They watched her continue along a corridor then Sophia turned to him.

"I'm sorry."

"Whatever for? You're not pushing her out, or anything of the kind. If she wants one of the flats or one of the apartments, even, then she's welcome to one. Just not right now. Come on," he added softly and they went to his bedroom. He went to the window and closed the curtains. Shrugging out of his jacket, he slung it over a chair. "I might as well go and tell Stephanie right now," he said and Sophia shook her head. "Then, what?"

"I don't know. But surely Lady Heaton would want to keep it from Stephanie for as long as possible?"

"This is Lady Heaton, we're talking about; the woman who stood back and allowed her husband to fuck another woman."

"Who would the estate have gone to if your father had had no children?"

"His brother. Who worked in a bank." He rolled his eyes. "And who would have sold this place within a week. I can't win, can I?" He sat on the bed and held his head in his hands. "Sorry, we can't even forget about it for one evening."

"I'll be back in a couple of minutes," she said, opening the door to the landing.

She went to the bathroom and opened the cabinet above the wash-hand basin. Inside was shaving paraphernalia, aspirin, dental floss and a very old and rather sticky bottle of baby lotion. She smiled and returned to the bedroom with it and a towel. He looked up and frowned.

"What's that?"

"Baby lotion. I'm going to give you a massage. Clothes off, please."

He smiled and did as she asked then lay on the towel watching as she got undressed and straddled him. He gave a little moan of encouragement as she poured on a little of the lotion and her hands started to knead and rub at his muscles, applying firm pressure where necessary. She moved over his shoulders and his neck, stroking, squeezing, working the tension away, then down his back. Her soothing fingers brought forth more groans and murmurs until she wiped her fingers on a corner of the towel and lay down beside him.

"Good?" she asked.

He nodded. "Fantastic. Thank you. Can I put you on twenty-four-hour call for that?"

"What, you'd dare to interrupt the tours?" She pretended to be shocked and he laughed and leaned over to kiss her lips. "So, what do you think of dating?"

"Not sure. Can we try it again sometime?"

"Mmm. What would you like to do?"

"Dinner? A drink? Make love?"

"Sounds good, I'll hold you to that."

As she brought the latest tour group up the main staircase the following afternoon she heard raised voices and a door slamming. Thomas' meeting with Lady Heaton was clearly not going well. A couple of people raised their eyebrows and she began to flush.

"Looks like we arrived at a bad time," one woman commented.

"No, not at all." Sophia pulled herself together. "Please follow me."

When the group left the house, Helen approached her. "His Lordship asked if you could join him in the library."

"Thanks, Helen," she said and went up the stairs and along the corridor. "Thomas?" She knocked at the library door.

"Come in."

"What happened? I could hear you both on the tour."

"Yes, sorry about that. Well, it went spectacularly badly and the upshot is that she's moving out today."

"Today?" Sophia echoed in dismay. "What about Stephanie?"

"When she comes out of hospital she'll go and live with her until she's well enough to return to the flat or go back to Leeds. Like I said last night, I might as well go and tell Stephanie everything right now."

On her way back to her flat, Sophia detoured and knocked at the door of Lady Heaton's sitting room.

"Come in? Oh, Sophia?"

"May I speak with you, Lady Heaton?"

"Yes, I suppose so. Sit down."

"Thank you." Sophia went to an armchair. "Thomas told me your meeting didn't go well."

One of Lady Heaton's eyebrow's rose. "That's an understatement if ever I heard one."

Sophia took a deep breath. "Lady Heaton, do you really

need to move out? I mean, there is more than enough room for you to have your own apartment here. Unless you really want Stephanie to know sooner rather than later?"

"You think she's going to find out?"

"Of course she will, she's not stupid."

"I am going to tell her as soon as possible."

Sophia's jaw dropped. "What?"

"It is better I tell her now. I do not want her to find out by accident like Thomas did. He says that he's asked you to marry him."

"Yes," she replied.

"But you haven't accepted yet."

"Lady Heaton, please, if you're going to tell Stephanie, at least wait a little while, and don't move out, please?"

"But as you said yourself, she's not stupid, she is going to know something is wrong."

Sophia rubbed her forehead. "Just see how long it takes her to notice anything. When she asks, then she will have to be told."

"Are you going to marry Thomas?"

"I need to speak to my father."

"Why?"

She gave Lady Heaton an incredulous frown. "Because he's my father." She got up and went to the door. "Thank you for seeing me," she said as she opened the door.

"What does he think of Thomas?"

"He likes him as a person."

"But not the title? Does he not want a daughter married to a baron?"

"Not particularly," she admitted.

"How strange…Well, Thomas loves you. I knew he would."

Sophia shrugged. "I'm sorry, I don't understand what you mean."

"I narrowed the applicants for the tour guide position down to three," Lady Heaton explained. "The first was called Kylie, which is fine for a pop singer, but not a baroness. The second was almost anorexic. Which left you. You have a lovely name and you are...how shall I say...curvaceous. I knew Thomas would love you...the amount of time he's spent pouring over paintings of curvaceous Renaissance women...I knew you would be exactly what he was looking for. But whether he would be exactly what you were looking for was another matter. But if I let the two of you spend as much time in each other's company maybe something would happen. And I was right, wasn't I?"

Sophia felt furious heat creep up her neck towards her face. "You set us up."

"Well, it was Stephanie who actually got you to...whatever it was you did in the car on the moors to keep warm. But, yes, I chose you."

Someone began to push the door open from the corridor and Sophia had to step to one side. Thomas stood in the doorway looking as furious as she felt.

"What the hell will you not stoop to?"

"Thomas—"

He held up a hand to silence her. "Not only do you choose my mother, you choose my girlfriend, too. I want you out of this house today. There is an empty apartment at the farmyard. Start packing your things and get out." He turned and left the room.

"Hadn't you better follow him?" Lady Heaton suggested calmly.

Sophia went out, slamming the door behind her. She stood in the corridor for a moment her hands covering her face before taking a deep breath and hurrying to the library. Thomas was downing an enormous whisky.

"I didn't know, I promise," she began.

"Want one?" He held up a glass and she shook her head.

"I have to drive, I have to go and see Dad."

"To tell him you're leaving here?"

"Leaving?"

"Well, you can't possibly want to stay now?"

"You want me to go?"

He drained the glass and poured another helping. "I don't know what I want."

"Please don't get drunk," she pleaded.

"I think I need to let go a bit, don't you? For almost twenty fucking years I've done exactly what's been expected of me. Right down to choosing you for my wife. So, please, just leave me alone. Now."

Sophia jumped and retreated into the corridor. She went back to the hall and sat on the stairs, watching wearily as Lady Heaton came towards her.

"Danielle was the best of a bad lot, Sophia."

"Like me?"

Lady Heaton smiled. "Could you stand back and watch Thomas father children with another woman?" Sophia's face contorted in disgust, despite trying hard not to. "It's all in the breeding, Sophia."

"So it didn't bother you one bit that your husband presumably had to do it numerous times to father two children?"

"No. It was something which had to be done."

"I don't believe you."

Lady Heaton waved a hand dismissively. "Believe what you like, Sophia."

"Well, if breeding is so important, why the hell didn't you just put an ad in *Country Life* or *Horse and Hound*?" Sophia stared at her, realising why. "Because you think he's tainted goods, anyway. The Heaton name is there but the breeding isn't. His mother will never be good enough. Her ancestry can't be traced back to someone who came to England with William the Conqueror." She smiled humourlessly. "You are unbelievable."

"If you say so," Lady Heaton replied crisply and left her.

Sophia sat on the bottom step of the stairs and began to chew her knuckles; something she had thought she had long grown out of. "Shit," she whispered then got up from the step, left the house, and went to her flat.

Chapter Eleven

What do you do when the man you love is intent on getting as drunk as possible and the woman you thought was his mother but actually isn't his mother but chose his mother actually chose you to be his wife? Scream? Run? Sophia flopped back onto the bed and groaned. She couldn't very well go and see her father now. What could she tell him without having to lie? Nothing, she concluded, closing her eyes.

When she opened them it was dark. Sliding off the bed, she went to the door but hesitated. Should she go back to the house? If she did, what sort of a state would Thomas be in? She sighed and went out.

She crossed the stable yard and let herself into the house via the side door. It was pitch dark and she fumbled for a light switch. Turning it on, she went up the steps and along the corridor to the library before hesitating again. She couldn't hear a sound from inside. Opening the door, she turned the light on.

Thomas was slumped in the leather armchair, an empty crystal tumbler balanced precariously on the arm. She put it on the desk before tilting Thomas' face upwards. He opened his eyes and with an effort focused his attention on her.

"There's none left."

She glanced across the room at the empty whisky decanter. "Good. Try to stand up."

"Why?"

"You're coming back to the flat with me."

"I've thrown my so-called mother out."

"I know. Try and stand up. Come on." Thomas heaved himself out of the chair, wobbled, and she steadied him. "Good. Lean on me."

Slowly, they made their way out of the house and she locked the side door. The chilly night air sobered him a little and he groaned.

"Take a few deep breaths," she instructed.

"I need a cigarette."

"No, you don't. Breathe in and out." He did as he was told and coughed. "Good. Come on."

She helped him up the stairs to the flat and straight through the living area to the bedroom, pulling back the duvet and sitting him down on the bed. Kneeling down, she proceeded to undress him. About to lie him down, he took her hands.

"Sorry."

"Shh."

"I mean it."

She nodded. "Sleep."

"Are you coming to bed?"

"Yes. Now sleep."

He lay down and she covered him with the duvet. She got undressed, turned out the light in the living area, before getting into bed beside him. She lay for a few minutes watching him sleep before leaning over and gently kissing his lips then turning off the light.

She was woken when he woke with a jump. She rolled over and saw him gape wildly around him before realising where he was and relaxing.

"Sorry," he whispered.

"Are you okay?"

"Hangover."

"I'll make some coffee."

She got out of bed, put her bathrobe on and went out to the kitchen, hearing him slowly getting out of the bed and groaning. Making the coffee, she felt him watching her from the bedroom door.

"I behaved like a complete bastard last night. I'm sorry."

She turned and gave him a little smile. "How much do you remember?"

"Just drinking. And drinking more. And more and more until the decanter was empty."

"You don't remember me coming over to the house to fetch you?"

He frowned. "I remember us walking across the stable yard. It was freezing."

He went into the bathroom and she brought the mugs over to the table.

"I didn't do anything stupid, did I?" he asked, walking from the bathroom to the bedroom, and pulling on his trousers.

"Apart from getting drunk, no. Come and drink some coffee."

He did up the trousers then came to her. "I'm sorry," he said again, squeezing her hands.

"I know. And I don't blame you for being angry."

"You mean you're not?"

"I was very angry with Lady Heaton last night. I felt manipulated and used. Now, I don't know. She knew you would find me attractive but she didn't know whether I would find you attractive or even like you. I mean, a workaholic who intimidated me, smoked, called me Ms Nelson until it made me want to scream, who had a terrible temper, hated having his photograph taken…need I go on?" She smiled. "But every now and then, you'd let me see past all that, and I wanted to see more. Thank God I've got patience. And thank God Lady Heaton picked me. Drink your coffee while I have a quick shower."

She went into the bathroom, slipped out of the bathrobe and turned on the shower, waiting until the water ran warm.

"Is there room for two?" Thomas asked from the doorway while undoing his trousers.

"It might be a tight squeeze."

He smiled. "Good," he said, following her in and closing the doors. "I love you," he whispered, smoothing wet hair back off her face.

"I know," she replied, standing on tip-toe and kissing his forehead. "Now stand still," she instructed, reaching for the shampoo.

"Yes, madam. Thank you for rescuing me last night. I don't think I deserved it."

"Don't do it again?" she asked quietly. "Please?"

"I won't."

Thomas came down to the kitchen when the day's final tour group left the house. Helping himself to a cup of coffee, he kissed her cheek.

"Lady Heaton's gone," he whispered at the same time.

She nodded. "Bun?"

"No, thanks, just coffee. No wanderers?"

"No, none."

"I'm going to start offering herbal tea," Helen announced. "And decaffeinated coffee. Two women asked and it's lucky I had some."

"Decaffeinated coffee." Thomas rolled his eyes. "Well, whatever you think."

"And low fat spread for the scones."

"Why don't we just offer bread and water?"

Helen laughed. "Because someone will ask whether the bread is gluten free and whether the water is still or sparkling."

"Well, at least one of us has the patience of a saint. Because I find your teas, coffees, cakes and buns delicious."

"Thank you, sir."

Thomas smiled then turned to Sophia. "Come to the library."

"When did Lady Heaton leave?" she asked, following him up the stairs.

"Very early this morning. Des is bringing her belongings to the farmyard."

"When will you tell Stephanie?"

"Tomorrow. Will you come to the hospital?"

She smiled and nodded.

Stephanie was delighted to see them.

"I was beginning to think I'd been forgotten about."

"How do you feel?" Sophia passed her some magazines before sitting down beside the bed.

"Thank you. I was going to try and see if I can make it down to the shop in the lift. But, according to Fiona, over there, all they've got is old women's magazines."

"And celebrity ones." Thomas retrieved a second chair and sat down.

"I'm not that desperate."

"Fine. It will have to be old women's magazines next time, then."

Stephanie rolled her eyes exactly like Thomas. "So, how are things chez Heaton?"

"Mother has moved out." Thomas came straight to the point.

Stephanie's eyes bulged. "Where to?"

"The farmyard."

"When did this happen?"

"This morning."

"Why?"

"Because I have asked Sophia to marry me," Thomas explained, "but not to answer me until she is absolutely sure."

Stephanie stared at her at first in surprise before sighing. "I suppose it is a huge step. You're not just marrying Thomas, you're marrying everything. Don't let him rush you, take your time."

Sophia nodded.

"Well, Mother obviously thinks you'll say yes. It will be very strange not to have her living in the house. When they let me out of here, will I have to go and stay with her for a bit?"

"That is up to the doctors, whether they think you are capable of living on your own. If not, then probably, for a little while."

"A couple of weeks will be all I can stand if that."

"Do as the doctors tell you, Stephanie," Thomas warned and she pulled a face.

"You'd never know I was the eldest, would you?"

Sophia smiled. "I took Thomas out to the cinema the other night. We saw an okay thriller and went to the pub afterwards."

"Good grief, Thomas."

"Let's get all the jokes out of the way now, shall we?"

"What jokes?" Stephanie asked. "I'm completely flabbergasted. Thomas on a date."

"And we're going to do it again sometime," Sophia added.

"I should think so, too, considering he's asked you to marry him."

From the hospital, they went to the County Record Office and began to plough through the registers of St Mary's Parish. After two hours, they took a break and went to get a coffee and to take stock of what they had discovered.

Thomas' great-grandfather was another Thomas O'Hara born in 1881. His wife was Sarah Price born in 1886 and he was one of the O'Hara brothers listed as a miner on the 1901 Census. Thomas O'Hara's father was yet another Thomas O'Hara, an agricultural labourer, and his wife was a Margaret Milmoe. Their baptisms were not to be found in the parish records but their marriage was, having taken place in December 1879.

"Thomas was a miner and I think we've found the Irish connection," she told him, typing the information into the genealogy program on her laptop. "I think we should look at the 1881 Census next."

The 1881 Census proved Sophia correct but infuriatingly, place of birth was only stated as 'Ireland', Thomas having been born there circa 1842 and Margaret circa 1847. Their eldest son was born in Yorkshire in January 1881.

"Wasn't the Irish Famine in the 1840s?" Thomas asked. "Maybe they had to emigrate because of it?"

That evening at her flat, they went back to the 1901 Census on the internet. Both Thomas and Margaret were still alive and their years of birth were again circa 1842 and circa 1847 in Ireland.

Then Sophia found a link to the 1861 Census for Yorkshire and found a Thomas O'Hara in the town born circa 1842 and his five brothers and sisters. His father was yet another Thomas O'Hara born circa 1818 and his mother Eleanor born circa 1820. All the family were born in County Kilkenny, Ireland, except one child who was born in Yorkshire circa 1849.

"Is it the right family?" she wondered aloud and went back to the 1881 Census.

Both Thomas and Eleanor were still alive in 1881 and were living with their eldest son, Thomas, born circa 1842, and his wife Margaret born circa 1847, and their family in the town.

"It's them." She smiled at Thomas in delight. "They came from County Kilkenny in Ireland."

Thomas was staring at the laptop screen. "Where is County Kilkenny?" A quick search brought up a map of the counties of Ireland. "Ah, I see it. And they moved to Yorkshire between the birth of Gerard O'Hara in 1847 and Andrew O'Hara in 1849."

"We need to verify this, get birth, marriage and death certificates, and print-outs of the various census forms, but you have an ancestor who was a miner and we've traced them right back to Ireland. And we can tie-in the gravestone inscriptions we found, too. Look. Thomas O'Hara, born 1842. He died on the 15th August 1914. His wife, Margaret, nee Milmoe, was born 1847. She died on the 18th September 1919. This is brilliant, we've got the O'Haras right back to 1818 in County Kilkenny in Ireland."

Thomas exhaled slowly as if he couldn't quite take it all in. He watched as Sophia inputted all the information into the genealogy program before clicking on the descendants of Thomas O'Hara born circa 1818.

"They're all called Thomas," he said. "All the eldest sons are called Thomas, except for Danielle's father. He named his eldest son Andrew. Then, I'm called Thomas." He looked at her. "I wonder who named me?"

"Sophia?" Des called up the stairs and she quickly closed the lid of the laptop while Thomas closed his notebook.

"Yes?" she replied. "Come up."

Des climbed the stairs and opened the door. "Oh, you're both here." He sighed. "There's someone in the house."

"What?" Thomas got to his feet.

"I've just seen a light in the house."

Thomas pulled his phone from his jacket pocket, scrolled down to a number and rang it. Listening for a moment, he ended the call while Sophia and Des stared at him curiously.

"Shouldn't you ring the police?" Des urged.

"It's not a police matter. It's Lady Heaton. Right. We have to catch her in the act."

"Lady Heaton?" Des was dumbfounded.

"Sophia and I will go to the front door. Des, you go to the side. She'll be in the drawing room."

Sophia and Thomas hurried around the side of the house and crept up the steps to the front door. As quietly as he could, Thomas unlocked and opened the door and they went into the hall. One of the drawing room doors was open and they could see torchlight inside the room. They crossed the hall and Thomas went into the room first, snapping on the light. Lady Heaton was at one of the china display cabinets, a figurine in her hand. She almost dropped it when the light came on.

"What are you doing?" Thomas asked calmly.

"Thomas."

"Well?"

Lady Heaton looked past him at Des standing awkwardly behind them in the doorway. "Do you really want Des to know?"

"I'll go."

Thomas nodded. "Thank you, Des." He waited a couple of moments before turning back to Lady Heaton. "Well?" he asked again.

"It's for Danielle."

"What is?"

"The money. You don't think she's interested in this, do you?" She put the figurine on top of the cabinet. "Danielle has been asking for money for years."

"You've been stealing items for years?"

"No, only the last year or so, when she threatened to go public."

"And you believed her?" he demanded. "You really think she'd go public? She's got far too much to lose. Her children know nothing about this."

"I couldn't take that chance. She said she wanted to try and dry out, too, in some clinic or other."

"That figurine will give her at least a month in the most expensive clinic in the country. You've been in contact with her all along, haven't you?"

Lady Heaton grimaced. "She wouldn't leave us alone. Letters. Phone calls. Did you never wonder why we changed the house number so often? Threatening that she'd come here and demand to see you. At first, her husband was able to reason with her but as her drinking got worse she started to disappear for days on end and he would ring here and tell me to be on the lookout for her. Now I've had enough. I'm too old for all this."

"So you're just going to give her what she wants?" Thomas asked.

Lady Heaton gave him a little smile. "I can never do that. It's you and Stephanie she wants."

"But we're not children anymore."

"She calls you her 'babies'. Always has done."

Thomas sighed. "If I were to meet her? Would that satisfy her?"

"It might."

"Then suggest it to her. And tell her if she looks for any further money there isn't any and if she persists, her eldest son will have to make himself known to his half-brother and sister. See how she likes that. There will be no more stealing, no more money. Now, please leave."

Lady Heaton walked past them without a word and they heard the front door close.

Thomas went to the cabinet, picked up the figurine, and put it back inside.

"Will I ever finish paying for Stephanie and me? God knows what all she's stolen because of me and for me."

"Do you think meeting Danielle is really a good idea?" Sophia asked. "What if she blurts something out to Michelle about meeting you?"

"Well, what can I do?"

She sighed. "I honestly don't know."

A week later, Thomas followed Sophia up the stairs to her flat.

"Lady Heaton's gone to bring Stephanie home from hospital and Danielle and her husband are coming up here to visit the family. I've agreed to meet her at the Royal Hotel in Leeds on Thursday. Will you come with me? Her husband is coming with her."

"I'll come."

"You don't have to," he added quickly.

"I know, but I'll come."

"I won't row with her. At least, I'll try not to."

That evening, Thomas' phone rang while they were searching the online General Register Office birth, marriage and death indexes.

"It's Stephanie," he told her, swiped the screen to answer the call and listened for a few moments. "Just a minute," he said and pressed the mute button. "Stephanie's very bored and she's wondering why we haven't been to see her. We're going to have to go over there." Sophia pulled a face and he pressed the mute button again to unmute the call. "Stephanie, we'll be over tomorrow morning. Yes, both of us, I promise." He ended the call and rolled his eyes. "We're going to the apartment for coffee in the morning. How cosy. I can't wait."

"At last." Stephanie opened the door to them. "I was beginning to think you were avoiding me."

The farmyard apartment had been finished and furnished to a very high standard and Sophia followed Stephanie to a cream leather sofa and sat on the edge.

"Where's Mother?" Thomas asked.

"Making the coffee. She won't let me do a thing."

"Good."

"But I'm going mad. She watches all the soaps and all the reality TV crap."

"I thought you liked that sort of thing?"

Stephanie glared at him then turned to Sophia. "So? Been out on any further dates?"

"No, not yet…" She tailed off as the door opened and Lady Heaton came in with a tray.

"Here we are. Milk and sugar, Sophia?"

"Milk, one sugar, please."

"Biscuit?"

"No, thank you."

"Thomas?"

"No, thank you."

"Well, I'll have one." Stephanie took a chocolate biscuit. "It doesn't cost any extra to sit down, Thomas."

He gave her a weak smile and sat down on the opposite sofa.

"Sophia and I are going to Leeds on Thursday," he announced and Sophia saw Lady Heaton's face pale.

"Shopping?"

"No, just some galleries and museums."

"Good grief, Sophia, bring him shopping," Stephanie urged her.

"I might do if there's time."

"Well, at least you've got him out of those terrible suits." Stephanie eyed Thomas' jeans and shirt.

"He managed that himself."

"Better late than never. I bet half your clothes were moth-eaten."

"Mothballs," he replied drolly. "Don't you like the scent?"

Having somehow managed to talk about nothing in particular for well over an hour, Sophia was greatly relieved when Thomas made their excuses and they left.

"Small talk," he said as they walked back to the stable yard. "I don't know how the queen puts up with it day in, day out."

Standing outside The Royal Hotel, Sophia could feel Thomas' trepidation. He clasped her hand, his was freezing and squeezed it.

"Am I doing the right thing?" he asked at last.

"I can't answer that," she replied softly.

"I know." He took a deep breath. "Okay, here goes."

They went into the lobby. Danielle and Don were seated in a corner to their right. Sophia nudged Thomas and nodded to them just as Don spotted them and touched his wife's arm. They got up as she and Thomas approached. Danielle couldn't tear her eyes away from Thomas but Sophia was mightily relieved to see that the older woman was sober.

"Thomas," she said softly.

"Mrs Armstrong." He put out a hand.

Danielle's face fell but she shook his hand. "Danielle. This is my husband."

"Don."

"Thomas."

"Shall I order some coffee?" Don looked at Sophia and she smiled and nodded. "I won't be a minute."

"Shall we sit down?" Sophia went to one of the sofas arranged at right angles around a coffee table.

"I'm sorry," Danielle began. "About…before…"

"Before?" One of Thomas' eyebrows rose. "Which 'before'? The before when I saw you for the first time and you were drunk? Or the before where I learned that Lady Heaton had been stealing from the house in order to feed your alcoholism?"

"Both." Danielle glanced up as her husband returned.

"Good. I believe Lady Heaton has been in contact with you?"

"Yes."

"So you understand that there will be no more money?"

Danielle swallowed noisily. "Yes. I'm sorry. Don didn't even know."

Thomas looked at him. "So where did you think the money was coming from? Alcohol isn't cheap."

"You've never lived with an alcoholic, have you?" Don replied shortly. "They will do anything for their next drink and—"

"It's all my fault, I know," Thomas finished.

"No," Danielle hissed.

"So when did you start drinking, then?" he asked and Danielle looked at the floor. "What would it take for you to stop drinking?"

Danielle slowly raised her head. "To have my babies back," she whispered.

"Stephanie and I aren't babies anymore. And Stephanie knows nothing. I only found out by accident. Her blood group meant that there was no way Lady Heaton could have been our mother."

"Will she ever be told?"

"I don't know. She's home from hospital and in a couple of weeks she'll return to her apartment here in Leeds."

Danielle nodded. "You were such beautiful babies. You're still beautiful."

Thomas smiled self-consciously. "I don't know about that."

"I asked your father to call you Thomas. Since the year of dot, all the eldest O'Hara boys were called Thomas. Apart from my father. He was called Andrew."

"I know."

"How?"

"I was curious, so Sophia and I looked into the O'Hara family tree."

Danielle's face brightened. "I've been meaning to do that myself. Grandad always said that they came from a place called Kilkenny in Ireland."

"Well, we traced them back to there. They left during the Famine."

"That's right. They walked to the nearest town, got the Mail Coach to Dublin and sailed to Liverpool. Have you met Michelle?" she asked suddenly and looked at Sophia.

"No, he hasn't," Sophia replied. "And she knows nothing about this."

"And that's the way it's going to stay," Don added firmly. "What happened was…" He tailed off as their coffee arrived and Sophia passed the cups and saucers around. "It was illegal, Danni, I've told you a million times that it was."

"What did you do with the money?" Thomas asked.

"Bought our house in London. Do you hate me?"

Thomas looked startled. "To be honest, I don't know how I feel towards you yet."

"They say you work very hard."

"Yes. It takes a lot of effort to keep the place going."

"And Sophia?"

"I love Sophia very much," he said, giving her a little smile.

"Did you meet her mum?"

"No, sadly, I didn't."

"She knew, didn't she?" Sophia asked.

Danielle nodded. "I had to tell someone, and she was my best friend."

"You mean, you didn't know?" Thomas turned to Don. "When did you find out?"

"On our honeymoon," Danielle answered. "I got drunk and it all came pouring out. I told him to leave me but he wouldn't. The number of times I've told him to leave me."

"Michelle told Sophia that you'd tried A.A.? Will you try it again now?"

"I don't know."

"Please?"

She stared at him. "I told them what I'd done. Their faces…"

"Please?"

Slowly Danielle nodded.

"Thank you."

"Will you do something for me?" she asked.

"If I can."

"Send me the stuff you have on the O'Haras. I'll see if I can add to it and I'll write down some of the family stories I've heard."

"Of course I will. Thank you."

"Got to do something now I'm a recovering alcoholic."

"I have something for you." Thomas reached into the inside pocket of his jacket and extracted a photograph. "It's Stephanie and me…I don't know where you're going to hide it but…"

Danielle took it and finally burst into tears. Don gently extracted the photograph from her fingers and put it in his jacket pocket.

"I'll keep it safe," he said and Thomas nodded. "We should go…I'll just pay for the coffee."

"No, I'll pay, it's fine."

"Thank you, then."

They stood up and Danielle took Thomas' hands. "Will I see you again?"

He nodded again. "When you're up from London again we'll arrange something."

"Thank you." She stood on tip-toe and kissed his cheek before following her husband out onto the street.

Thomas exhaled a long breath. "I need some air."

Chapter Twelve

Sophia and Thomas lay on their backs in the stone circle. White clouds were bouncing across the sky above them. Sophia reached into the pocket of her jacket, pulled out a piece of paper and passed it to him.

ASK ME TO MARRY YOU

Thomas sat bolt upright. "Are you sure?"

She smiled, sat up, and turned the paper over in his hands.

JUST ASK!

They got up and he immediately got down on one knee. "Sophia Nelson, will you marry me?"

She smiled. "Yes, I will." He opened his mouth and she quickly covered it with her fingers. "Don't you dare ask, 'Are you sure?'"

He laughed. "I won't, then." He bent and kissed her. "Thank you."

"I love you," she said simply. "Can we tell my father first?"

"How will he take it?"

"Well, I hope."

Luckily, William Nelson smiled. "I've seen this coming for weeks. I'm happy for you, lass."

"Thanks, Dad." She hugged and kissed him. "I kept Thomas waiting a long time."

"There were a lot of things to consider."

"Yes, there were," Thomas replied.

"Well, I know you love her, and I know you'll take care of her." Mr Nelson put out a hand. "Congratulations, son."

Thomas smiled and shook his hand warmly. "Thank you, William."

Stephanie admitted them to the farmyard apartment and stared at them in delight. "Engaged? At last. Mother?" she shrieked into the kitchen. "Thomas and Sophia are engaged."

Lady Heaton came into the living area and smiled knowingly. "How wonderful. Congratulations."

"So, when is the wedding? Where is the wedding?"

"We don't know yet and St Margaret's in the town."

"Are you going to have an engagement party?"

Sophia and Thomas glanced at each other.

"No," he replied. "The wedding reception will be party enough."

"Have you told your father, Sophia?" Lady Heaton asked.

"Yes, and he's very happy for us."

"Good," the older woman replied simply.

They left at the earliest opportunity and eyed each other wryly.

"I need to go and tell Michelle now before the news gets out," Sophia told him as they returned to the stable yard. "And indirectly Danielle." Thomas nodded. "I'll find you when I get back."

Michelle smiled when she opened the front door fifteen minutes later. "Oh, hi."

"Is this a bad time?" Sophia could hear laughing from inside the house.

"No, the exact opposite, actually. You'll never guess but Mum's just announced that she's off the booze and is going to start A.A. again."

"That's great."

"Come in."

"Thanks. I have an announcement to make myself."

"You're engaged, aren't you?" Sophia nodded. "Oh, that's fantastic." Michelle gave her a hug. "Come into the lounge."

"Sophia." Cathy ran to her for a kiss. "I haven't seen you for ages."

"I know, I'm sorry. Hi, everyone."

"Sophia's got an announcement to make," Michelle cried.

Sophia shot a glance at Danielle, who bit her bottom lip.

"Well, um, Thomas and I got engaged today."

"Congratulations." Danielle hugged and kissed her. "Your mum would have been so happy."

"I know."

"Why didn't you bring him?" Tony demanded. "You're engaged and I haven't even met the bloke."

"He's hardly a bloke," Michelle protested and Sophia began to squirm. "Baron Heaton of Heaton Abbey House.

Tall, dark, handsome, and a complete sex god by all accounts."

"I'll bring him the next time, I promise."

"But Mum and Dad won't be here," Michelle added.

"Oh, well, you'll meet him soon enough."

Danielle nodded while Don just looked at the floor.

"Where will you get married?" Danielle asked.

"St Margaret's, but we don't know when yet."

"How's your dad taken it?" Tony asked.

"Very well. He likes Thomas a lot."

"Well, that's all right, then. How about his mother?" Sophia froze. "I mean, I've seen her in town and she looks terrifying and she'll be your mother-in-law."

"I don't see her an awful lot now. She moved out of the house and into one of the new farmyard apartments."

"Tea, everyone?" Michelle asked, and there were murmurings of approval.

Danielle followed her daughter out of the living room. Sophia heard her go upstairs and followed her, muttering something about the bathroom. She found Danielle in the spare bedroom pacing up and down.

"I couldn't bring Thomas," she said softly. "It would have been too awkward."

"I know. He doesn't regret meeting me?"

"No, not at all."

"And Stephanie? How is she?"

"Getting stronger all the time. I'd say she'll be moving back to Leeds soon. Michelle said you announced that you were stopping drinking and going to A.A." Danielle nodded. "When are you going home?"

"Tomorrow. I'm going to start A.A as soon as I can. I

299

announced it to everyone, so I'll have to do it now."

"Good." Sophia gave her a hug. "You're being really brave. Keep it up, won't you?"

Driving back to the abbey, she saw Stephanie on the drive ahead of her, stopped and lowered the window.

"Want a lift?" she called.

"Thanks." Stephanie opened the passenger door and got in. "Drop me in the stable yard and I'll walk back to the farmyard."

"No problem. Look, could you do me an enormous favour?" she asked as she parked outside the flat.

"Of course, what?"

"Come up to the flat." Stephanie followed her upstairs and Sophia went to the bedroom, returning with the corset. "Help me on with this?"

Stephanie's eyes bulged. "Where did you get that?"

"Long story, but I can't put it on by myself."

"It's beautiful. I wish I had the figure for something like that. Come on, let's get you into it."

She returned to the bedroom with Stephanie following her, got undressed and Stephanie eased the corset over her head. "Not too tight," she cried, watching in the wardrobe mirror as Stephanie pulled on the strings and then tied a bow. "Thanks."

"Let's see." Stephanie turned her around. "That's amazing. Good thing it's summer or you'll freeze to death in the house."

"I'm wearing a blouse, anyway. What if I meet Helen?"

Stephanie laughed. "When I was in the flat, I heard all sorts of amazing things from their flat."

Sophia pulled a disgusted face. "Thanks for that. Are you

sure you don't need a lift back?"

"No, I can make it. I doubt if you could drive in that, anyway. Now, go and wow Thomas."

Sophia let herself into the house via the side door and pulled off the note stuck to it.

COME TO THE DINING ROOM
THOMAS

She climbed the stairs, wriggling a little in the corset, and walked along the corridor to the dining room.

"Thomas?"

"Come in." She pushed open the door and found him lighting the candles on the long table. It was set for two. "I hope you haven't eaten?"

She smiled. "No."

"Good. Now, it's nothing special – shepherd's pie – I mean, Helen wasn't to know. She still doesn't know, actually. I thought we'd tell them in the morning. Anyway, it's in the oven, all I need to do is bring it up here. Hungry?"

"Yes, I am, actually."

"Good. If madam would like to be seated?" He held her chair and she eased herself down. "Won't be long."

She wriggled again. It wasn't cold in the room but what it would be like in January, she had no idea. Come to think of it, she had no idea what the house as a whole would be like in January.

"Is it cold?" she asked, as he returned and set the dish down on a placemat. "The house, I mean, in winter?"

"Freezing. The heating is on in five rooms – my bedroom, what was Lady Heaton's bedroom, my sitting room, what was her sitting room, and the kitchen. In the rest of the house, the heating is on for an hour a day, but it barely takes the chill off the air. Any more and we'd need our own oil well. I should be in *The Guinness Book of Records* for the quickest showers and baths ever. Are you cold now?"

"No, I'm fine." She watched as he dished out the shepherd's pie. "I managed to speak to Danielle alone. She had announced to everyone that she was giving up alcohol and going back to A.A. She's happy for us."

"Good."

"Michelle and Tony want to meet you."

"Oh. Is that wise?"

"Probably not but what can we do? Danielle and Don are leaving tomorrow, so we'll go over maybe the next day?"

He nodded and put a plate down in front of her as she wriggled again. He frowned.

"Are you all right?"

"Yes, just a bit…sorry…I wanted to save this for later but I need to get more comfortable…"

She pushed her chair back and got up and began to undo her blouse. Thomas' eyes widening with every button. She slipped the blouse off and his eyes bulged as they took in the corset.

"How did you get it on?"

"Stephanie helped. She's tied it a little bit tight, though. I just need to—" She wriggled again. "Oh, God, that's better."

"I won't be able to eat a thing now."

"Well, you'd better, you're going to need all your strength for later on."

He roared with laughter. "Oh, really?"

302

"Yes, really. I mean, when I sit down, my breasts end up right under my chin."

"And very nice they are, too."

"Just eat for now, Lord Heaton."

He laughed again and sat down with his plate, watching as she seated herself and wriggled.

"Wine?"

"Yes, please."

He poured. "Is it very uncomfortable?"

"A bit. It just forces everything up…"

"I know what you mean."

"Ha, ha."

"My great-great-grandparents had eleven children. I wonder what it was – corsets or the cold?"

"How many children do you want?"

"Two?"

"That's a relief."

"A boy and a girl. There's no other sort."

"That's true."

"There's something I want to ask you. It's always been that Lord and Lady Heaton have had separate bedrooms and separate sitting rooms – well, if you could call the library a sitting room – but that's what my father and all before him used it as. I broke with tradition when I took over Grandmother's sitting room for myself. The question is, do you want your own bedroom and sitting room or not?"

"No," she replied immediately. "And I'm sure."

"Good." He smiled.

They finished their meals and she got up and stretched.

"That's better."

"I'll just bring this lot down to the dishwasher."

Her eyebrows shot up. "Do you know where it is?"

"Ha, ha."

"I'll blow out the candles then I'll be in your living room."

She was closing the curtains when he closed the door behind him and she felt hands close around her waist and lips touch her shoulder.

"Turn around," he whispered. She turned and he retrieved a box from his jacket pocket. "This was my great-grandmother's," he added, opening the box and revealing an emerald and diamond ring. "I hope you like it."

"I do, it's beautiful."

"Really?"

She nodded and he slipped it on and kissed her hand. He ran his hands over the corset examining the lace and embroidery before bending and kissing the swell of her breasts.

"Want to go upstairs?" she asked and he nodded.

"No condoms down here."

They left the room and kissed their way up the stairs, along the corridor, and into his bedroom.

"Do you want to take this off?" she indicated the corset.

"No," he replied, running his hands over it again before adding quickly, "but if you're finding it uncomfortable...?"

"Not for now." She smiled as they quickly got undressed in record time. "But I'd like to be on top."

"I'd like you to be on top, too," he murmured, ripping open a condom and rolling it on. He sat on the bed before moving back further as she climbed over him.

She sank down, taking him fully inside her. Relaxing her muscles, she began to rock on Thomas' lap. Her hands were holding his shoulders while his were clasping her corseted waist as she moved slowly up and down over him, controlling their pace. Her head fell back once she found a rhythm, rolling her hips in slow circular movement, letting her feel all of him inside her. She could feel herself coming, the building tingling warmth low in her stomach, and could hear her inability to hold back her gasping moans of pleasure. Her body tightened, her fingers gripping his shoulders, pulling herself as close to him as she could get. The corset rubbed against his chest with each roll of her hips, chasing the increasing bouts of pleasure pulsing through her. Her body jerked around his before finally going limp. Thomas bucked his hips, still chasing his release, before groaning and dropping back onto the bed, bringing her down with him.

She couldn't bring herself to roll off him, was still savouring the feel of him inside her and wasn't ready to let go of it just yet. Sweeping her hair back off her face, he kissed her lips.

"I love you," he whispered.

Two days later, Michelle opened her front door to them and stared at Sophia then at Thomas before smiling.

"At last, we've been dying to meet you. Come in."

"Thanks," Sophia replied as they went inside before making the introductions. "Michelle – Thomas. Thomas – Michelle."

"Do I curtsey?" Michelle asked cheekily, closing the front door. "Or call you milord?"

"God, no." Thomas forced a laugh. "Just Thomas. Good to meet you."

"And you. Come and meet Tony and Cathy."

"Sophia." Cathy ran to her for a kiss then stopped and stared rudely up at Thomas. "Who's that?"

"This is Thomas. We're getting married."

"When?"

"Oh, we're not sure yet."

"Say hello to Lord Heaton," Tony instructed and Cathy's eyes bulged.

"A lord?"

"Just Thomas." He smiled.

"Tony, you kind of met Thomas at Mum's funeral."

"Yes. Hello again." The two men shook hands. "Congratulations, again, Sophia." Tony kissed her cheek. "And you, Thomas."

"Thanks."

"You're really a lord?" Cathy was amazed.

"I'm afraid so."

"You're afraid of what?"

Thomas laughed kindly. "Oh, lots of things. What I meant was is that being a lord isn't all it's cracked up to be."

"Why?"

"Lots of things."

"Tea or coffee?" Michelle asked him.

"Coffee, please."

"Coffee all round, then." Michelle went to the kitchen and Sophia followed. "Bloody hell, Soph," she hissed. "He's gorgeous." Sophia flushed. "Would you mind if I took a photo of the two of you to send to Mum?"

"Why?"

"Because she'd love to see you and him. Go on."

"Well, okay…"

She and Thomas stood awkwardly in the back garden as Michelle beeped away with her digital camera.

"Mum's finally mastered the internet so I'll be able to email these to her."

"Has she started A.A. yet?"

"Yes. She says it's going well. Let's have that coffee."

"Are you going to have a bridesmaid?" Cathy demanded.

"Cathy," Michelle scolded but Sophia just laughed.

"Well, yes, I am. And a matron of honour…?" She raised her eyebrows enquiringly at Michelle.

"Really?" Michelle laughed. "We'd love to, thank you."

"You and me?" Cathy squealed.

"You and me."

"Oh, thank you, Sophia." Cathy ran to her for a hug.

"It's probably not a good idea," she said as Thomas drove home. "But I had to ask them."

"I know."

"Now, don't kill me for suggesting this," she added. "But Stephanie for the other bridesmaid?"

Thomas threw her a horrified glance before sighing. "Can we elope? Or get married in the Bahamas or something?"

"My dad would never forgive me," she replied sadly.

"I know. But it's going to be a nightmare."

"What can we do?"

"Not a lot."

A date for the wedding was set – the 15th August – and another date was set for a meeting to discuss specifics. Stephanie and Michelle would meet there for the first time. Sophia asked Michelle to come a bit early and met her in the stable yard.

"Is Lady Heaton not coming to the meeting?" Michelle asked.

"No, there'll be just the four of us. Want a quick tour?"

"Yes, please."

Half an hour later they sat on the main stairs and Michelle rubbed her forehead.

"What?" she asked.

"You're going to freeze to death here in wintertime."

"I know. Thomas and I will just have to have lots of sex to keep warm."

"In that four-poster bed?"

"No, it's supposed to be really uncomfortable. Wherever takes our fancy, I suppose. I quite fancy doing it on the dining room table."

Michelle squealed with laughter then clapped a hand over her mouth as Thomas appeared.

"Hello, again."

"Hi," Michelle croaked.

He looked curiously at Sophia and she smiled.

"Just discussing how to keep warm here in the depths of winter."

"Oh. Well, I do put the heating on every now and again. It won't just be sex, Ms Nelson," he added with a wink and carried on to the living room.

They roared with laughter, followed him, and were just about to sit down when door opened and Stephanie came in.

"Sorry, I'm late."

"I think I was early," Michelle said.

"Michelle – Stephanie. Stephanie – Michelle." She made the introduction nervously, feeling Thomas' eyes on them.

"Good to meet you." Stephanie smiled at her. "God, I so need to find a man. Soon I'll be the only person I know who isn't married."

"Shall we get started?" Thomas suggested and they sat down on the sofas. "Right, the date is set and the church is booked. The reception will be here. Should it be in a marquee or shall we make use of the house?"

"Both, I say," Stephanie replied. "Meal in the dining room. Drinks and nibbles in the drawing room. Dancing in a marquee on the lawn?"

Sophia nodded and looked over at Thomas.

"Yes. Good. Now, caterers? A firm from the town preferably."

"Halls?" Stephanie suggested.

"I've heard good things about them," Michelle spoke up. "Or, if not them, there's Powell's?"

"A band or a disco?" Thomas continued.

"A band who can play a bit of everything," Michelle added.

"I know a few," Stephanie said. "I'll narrow them down a bit then you can go and listen and take your pick."

"Okay, good."

"Now the dress," Stephanie added, with a smile. "Which I will be making as my present to you."

Sophia reached out and gave her hand a grateful squeeze. "Thank you. But it will only be discussed when my fiancé is not here. But I know exactly what I want."

A month later, she hung the dress up in the wardrobe in Michelle's loft conversion and grinned at her.

"I've always known exactly what I wanted. I never

thought I'd actually get it made for me."

"Well, it's fabulous. All the dresses are. I can't wait."

"You can't wait?" She laughed. "Right, I have to go. Thomas and I are going to see band number two."

"What was the first lot like?"

She pulled a face. "My gran would have loved them."

They were very late back to the house after seeing the band who were surprisingly good and were looking forward to a lie in on Sunday morning when Thomas' phone rang just as they were about to put out the light.

"It's Don," he told her. "Don? Yes. Sorry, we were out, I had it switched off…what? But I thought it was going well? Is there nothing we can do? Shit. Thanks, Don." He ended the call and slowly put the phone down.

"What?" she cried.

He turned to her, his face snow white. "Danielle's sold her story to a newspaper. It'll be front page news in about…now."

Sophia stared at him, unable to speak.

"She managed to go to two A.A. meetings this time. Don thought it was all going well but…he's leaving her, he says he's had enough. This is the final straw. He's on a train on his way up here to try and explain to Michelle."

"What are we going to do?" she whispered as Thomas got out of bed.

"I have to ring Lady Heaton and you…"

"Need to ring my dad."

"Oh, God, Sophia." He clutched his head with both hands. "I am so sorry. I should never have gone to see her."

"But she promised…she promised that she'd go to A.A."

"I'm sorry."

She shook her head, got out of bed and went to get dressed.

"I'll ring Lady Heaton," he told her. "Then I'll go and wake Des and Helen. God knows who might turn up. We'll have to figure out a way of keeping them out."

"I'm going to see Dad. This isn't something I can tell him on the phone. And if he's agreeable I'll bring him back here?"

Thomas nodded, kissed her lips and went out, pulling a t-shirt over his head.

Fifteen minutes later, she rang her father's doorbell, her heart pounding. She had absolutely no idea how he would react. She had to ring it again before she heard a noise in the hall.

"I'm not opening the door at this bloody hour. If you've got identification you can put it through the letterbox."

"Dad, it's me."

The door opened slowly and her father stared at her. "What is it? Is it Thomas?"

"No, he's fine. Can I come in?"

"Yes. What is it?" he asked again as she followed him into the living room. "It's half past four."

"It's about Danielle Armstrong."

"Michelle's mum?"

"Yes." She clenched and then unclenched her fists. "She's Thomas's mother."

She watched his reaction. He frowned and shook his head.

"Say that again?"

"Danielle is Thomas's mother."

"I don't understand…" He went to his armchair and sat down heavily. "Explain."

She sat on the edge of the sofa. "I heard Thomas and Lady Heaton arguing. Stephanie was in hospital, she'd just had a miscarriage and lost a lot of blood. Thomas had offered to donate but was told that his blood group didn't match. He then learned that Lady Heaton had already offered to donate but that her blood group didn't match either and because of her blood group it was impossible that she could be Stephanie's mother. Or his."

"I don't believe this."

"Lady Heaton is infertile. She offered her husband a divorce but he refused. Instead, they looked for a surrogate mother. One who would have to go about it the old-fashioned way."

Her father's eyes bulged. "Now you are having me on?"

"No. Stephanie was born first. She couldn't inherit the title or the estate so they had to give it a second go. Thomas was born the following year."

"And you've known all along?"

"Since my first day there."

"So why are you telling me now?"

"Danielle's an alcoholic. She agreed to go back to A.A. but she's sold her story to a newspaper. It's on sale now. It's all going to come out. Don's left her. He's on his way up to Michelle's. I want you to come back to the abbey with me."

"Why?"

"Because you are the father of the woman who is going to marry the man whose mother was paid to have him. Journalists could turn up. TV. Please, Dad."

"Bloody hell." He got up and went out. She heard him open his wardrobe door and rolled her eyes in relief. "I'm not sleeping in a bloody four poster bed," he told her as they left the flat.

"You won't be," she assured him, taking a holdall from him.

She drove into the stable yard and saw Lady Heaton's car parked outside Thomas' office. Going in the side door she heard voices in the kitchen. Thomas, Lady Heaton, Stephanie, Des and Helen were standing around one of the tables. On it was a copy of *The World on Sunday*. Its headline screamed:

I sold my babies for £10,000!

Thomas looked over at them. "Come in. I nipped down to the all-night petrol station on Moorland Road."

She nodded and glanced at Stephanie. She was pale but surprisingly calm.

"I closed the gates after me."

"Thanks." Des nodded. "I'm off down there to lock them but if they want in, they'll get in."

"Has Don rung again?"

"No," Thomas replied. "He's probably got enough to cope with."

"Coffee," Helen announced and went to the cupboards for mugs.

"What do we do now?" she asked.

"Be prepared for the media to turn up. Be prepared for all hell to break loose. I've rung the police and explained – well, tried to explain. They're sending some constables over."

"Drink this." Helen set a tray down on top of the newspaper.

"Thank you." Lady Heaton took a mug.

Des managed to gulp the scalding coffee down and went out.

"Would you like to go to bed, Dad?" she asked.

"Yes, but I wouldn't be able to sleep. I'm Sophia's dad, by the way." He introduced himself.

"Sorry, Dad." She groaned. "I meant to…"

"It's okay," Stephanie said quietly. "Drink your coffee. Mr Nelson, I'm Stephanie and this," she turned to Lady Heaton, "is Lady Heaton."

Lady Heaton nodded to him.

"And this is Helen Fields."

"We've met before." Helen smiled. "Good to see you again, Mr Nelson."

"And you."

"You knew Danielle O'Hara, as she was then?" Lady Heaton queried.

Her father turned to her. "No. But my late wife did. She knew, didn't she?" He looked at Sophia.

"Yes. Those pictures of Blackpool – Danielle was pregnant in them – despite her doing her utmost to conceal it."

Thomas' phone rang and he went into the pantry with it. Her father pulled the paper out from under the tray and began to read.

"Must you?" Lady Heaton cried in disgust.

"Stop it," Stephanie warned.

Mr Nelson put the paper down. "I think I will go to bed, Sophia, if you don't mind?"

"No. Come on, Dad."

Thomas peered out of the pantry as they passed and she pointed out to the stable yard. He nodded.

"Where are we going?" her father asked.

"My flat. It'll be easier for you." She quickly changed the bed and left him out some towels. "Bathroom is here. I'll leave a light on out here so you don't lose your way. Tea and coffee are up here. Bread is here. Anything else, just hunt for it. I'll leave you my phone just in case. You remember how to use it?"

"Yes. Sophia, I can't believe any of this. And your mum knew, too."

"I know. Dad, I'm sorry."

He shrugged. "What could you do? When your mum and Danielle ended their friendship, I never really knew why. Don't take this the wrong way but you know what some women can be like, falling out over the slightest thing. But not your mum. Now I know what it was about."

Thomas met her in the stable yard. "That was Des on the phone. The police are down there so he won't lock the gates. Is your father all right?"

"Yes. I just thought the flat would be easier for him."

They returned to the kitchen and Sophia went straight to Lady Heaton.

"My father is seventy-eight years old. I will not have you look down your nose at him or make any snide remarks. Is that understood?"

"Perfectly."

"Where's Steph?" Thomas asked.

"She went out a couple of minutes ago," Helen replied.

Sophia met Thomas' eyes and followed him out of the room, up the stairs and along the corridor to the library. Stephanie was at the decanters pouring herself a gigantic whisky.

"Is that wise?" he asked. "You probably won't sleep it off."

"I don't care."

"Okay." He closed the door. "Put the glass down and shout. Scream if you want. But just do something. I'm starting to get worried."

"So was I," she murmured. "I was beginning to wonder if it would ever come out."

"What?"

"You heard."

"How long have you known?"

Stephanie shrugged. "Since I was about ten. I heard 'Mother' and Father arguing. They were having to change the house telephone number again."

"I can't believe you never said anything."

"Oh, for God's sake, Thomas," she cried. "And say what? Oh, by the way…?" She sighed. "I never knew who she was, though. Our real mother. Michelle's mum, eh?"

Sophia nodded. "Yes."

"I'm sorry."

"What for?" Thomas asked.

"For never being here. I just couldn't bear seeing you in that bloody office day in, day out working your arse off to pay for me and you and all of this bloody estate. And I'm sorry for always nagging you to act differently, dress differently. I just thought that it would make you think, 'To hell with this,' and get out of here and meet someone. I didn't think you'd have to wait until you were forty for someone to literally turn up on your doorstep."

"I didn't really turn up," Sophia told her. "Lady Heaton chose me."

Stephanie's eyes bulged. "Oh, bloody hell…" she began but tailed off and Sophia pulled what she hoped was a comical face. "But aren't you angry?"

"Been there, done that, got the t-shirt," Thomas replied dryly.

"Is that one of the reasons Mo…Lady Heaton moved out?"

"Yes."

"Thought so. No wonder you didn't want to come over to the apartment. Okay, what do you want to do? We can't just stay here and wait to be surrounded."

"Well, I'm not going anywhere." Sophia went to the window. "The press are probably at Michelle's, too, and I'm not having them see her knock me out."

"She wouldn't…?"

"She would. She's my best friend and I've kept this from her for months." She turned and gave them a bleak smile. "So, it'll probably be just you, me and Dad, walking up the aisle. Actually, my side of the church will probably be pretty empty now. The Bahamas mightn't be such a bad idea now, you know."

"Sophia…" Thomas came to her and kissed her temple. "Look, if the worst comes to the worst, we can always get married here."

"In the chapel?" Stephanie asked and Sophia's heart sank. "Why not?"

"Because I wanted to leave my bouquet on Mum's grave," Sophia replied. "Because I wanted to get married knowing that she wasn't too far away." She burst into tears and swore.

"I hope it won't come to it," Thomas whispered.

"So do I."

The media were kept at bay at the gates to the abbey and Sophia went to the flat at nine o'clock to see if her father was up. He was at the electric kettle.

"Did you sleep?" she asked.

"I did, for an hour. Your phone rang. It was Michelle."

"Oh, God."

"Don't worry, the wind went completely out of her sails when she realised that it was me, not you."

"Was she very upset? Hysterical?"

"Shouted a lot." Mr Nelson reached for the teabags. "Called you a lot of names. Called her mother a lot of names. Can't blame her, really. Her father then took the phone. Asked how you all were, which was good of him, considering. Said he'd try and calm Michelle down and explain. But he won't be going back to Danielle. Peter's on his way to her."

"Is this it? I mean, there won't be more in next week's paper?"

"No, this is it, according to Don. But it's more than enough for him, poor bloke. Said that he found out that Danielle was an alcoholic and why on his honeymoon." He shook his head as the kettle clicked off and he poured the boiling water into the teapot. "Have you slept?"

"No. Stephanie, Thomas, and I have been in the library. Stephanie knew all along."

Her father's head jerked up. "No?"

"Yes. She overheard when she was ten. Knew that her mother wasn't her birth mother but not who her real mother was."

"And Thomas?"

"Dazed. He…" She tailed off as her phone rang. It was Michelle.

"Don't answer it," her father advised.

"No, I have to speak to her." She picked it up and swiped the screen. "Michelle."

"Not hiding behind daddy now?"

"It wasn't like that."

"You've known all along, haven't you?"

"Yes."

"And that Mum drank?"

"No, not about that."

"Were you ever going to tell me?"

"No."

"Dad's left Mum and there are all these journalists outside."

"They're here, too."

"Not right outside your window. You've got a mile long drive and eight foot high gates to keep them out."

"Yes. Where is your mum?"

"On the train. Peter's bringing her up here. Dad's furious but we want her to explain herself. Oh, God, I don't believe this."

Michelle hung up abruptly and Sophia put the phone down.

"Peter and Danielle are on their way up on the train."

"Here." Her father passed her a mug of tea. "I'd love to be a fly on the wall when she arrives."

Sophia rolled her eyes. "A fly wearing protective armour." She went to the window to open it and saw Thomas in his office. She put her mug on the table and went to him. "Dad's just made a pot of tea. Come up."

"Thanks."

"Danielle and Peter are on their way up on the train," she told him as she poured him his tea.

"Bloody hell, is that wise?"

"I doubt it," her father replied.

"Michelle rang just now, that's how I know. She rang earlier but Dad managed to deal with her."

"Good. Thanks, William. We're not on the news, are we?"

"Haven't had the TV on. I'm more of a radio man in the mornings but I can't work the radio here at all. It's one of those digital ones."

"Well, read that instead." Thomas threw the newspaper onto the breakfast bar. "Makes for quite interesting reading."

Mr Nelson turned the paper around and Sophia and he both read the article.

Suburban housewife, Danielle Armstrong, has revealed how she was approached by Lord William Heaton of Heaton Abbey House in Yorkshire to become a surrogate mother when it was discovered that his wife was infertile. Danielle agreed and after negotiating a fee of £5,000 bore Heaton a child. The child was a daughter, Stephanie, and unable to inherit the Heaton Abbey Estate. Following receipt of a further £5,000, Danielle bore Heaton a son — Thomas, the current Baron Heaton, who will shortly marry miner's daughter Sophia Nelson.

What makes this story even more extraordinary is that back in 1975 and 1976, test tube technology was not yet developed so Danielle would have had to sleep with Heaton in order to conceive!

He was a handsome man…

"Yes, I had to sleep with Lord Heaton," Danielle admits. "I had to sleep with him a number of times, in fact, but he was a handsome man…"

Danielle used the £10,000 to purchase a house in north London following her marriage to Don Armstrong, an accountant, with whom she has two children – Michelle and Peter. But that is not the end of the story. Turn to page 5!

Giving up my babies made me hit the bottle!

"It was only after I had handed my babies over that I realised the enormity of what I had done," Danielle says quietly. "Those babies were my flesh and blood. I'm afraid that is when I started drinking really heavily."

Danielle freely admits that she is an alcoholic.

Sometimes I just feel like ending it all…

"I've tried Alcoholics Anonymous and had such a bad experience that I swore I would never go back but then I promised Thomas that I would try again but it is so hard. I've been to two meetings but when I saw Thomas in an article in a tourist brochure promoting Heaton Abbey House, I'm afraid I just reached for the bottle. He is my son and I've missed seeing him grow up. His sister doesn't even know I exist. I know I've failed everyone, especially myself. Sometimes I just feel like ending it all…"

Danielle was reunited with Thomas a few months ago but, as she says, his sister, Stephanie, knows nothing.

"Thomas gave me a photograph of himself and Stephanie and I treasure it. They are so beautiful, my babies."

Is she relieved that her secret is now out in the open? Danielle shrugs.

"Well, I am, but no-one else will be. But I just couldn't live a lie any longer."

"She's clearly not thought it through," Mr Nelson said. "She could go to prison for this. Surrogacy was illegal, wasn't it?"

"Yes, but all she was worried about was where the next drink was coming from."

"Where's Stephanie?"

"She's cut across the park to the apartments for a shower and a change of clothes. Lady Heaton's gone back there, too. There's nothing else we can do except sit this out. There's still time to cancel today's tour?"

Sophia shook her head. "As long as the police know that there's a coach coming this afternoon. I don't want them being turned away."

"You sure?"

She smiled. "Positive."

"Okay, get some clothes, go to my bedroom and sleep until I wake you."

"What about you?"

"I'll have an early night tonight."

She retrieved some clothes, kissed them both, and went out.

Chapter Thirteen

Thomas woke her at half-past one.

"Brunch is served," he whispered and kissed her lips.

"Any updates?"

"No. Nothing."

Thankfully, the Australian tour group weren't avid readers of *The World on Sunday* and the tour passed off uneventfully. She went to the flat and found her father watching a DVD.

"Any news?" he asked.

"No. With a lot of luck, the journalists will clear off soon."

"But then what?"

"I've no idea."

"Sophia?" She heard Thomas' voice in the stable yard and went to the window.

"Up here."

"You're not going to believe this." He stood at the door and nodded to her father. "They're all coming over here. The whole lot of them. Michelle rang the office and told me that as soon as Danielle and Peter arrive they're all coming over here to thrash it out."

"Bloody hell, we might as well go and sell tickets at the gates."

"This needs to be sorted out, Sophia," her father told her patiently.

"Yes, but not while everyone is still in shock and furious about it."

Thomas' phone beeped a text message and he grimaced.

"They're on their way up the drive."

"Where are Stephanie and Lady Heaton?"

"Waiting in the drawing room. Come on, let's get this over and done with."

Sophia and Thomas stood at the front door as Michelle, Cathy and Don got out of one car and Tony, Danielle and Peter got out of another. Thomas squeezed her hand and went forward.

"Come inside, please."

Stephanie got up as they all went in and Lady Heaton turned away from the window. Danielle took one look at Stephanie and burst into tears.

"Oh, for God's sake, woman," Don snapped. "You brought all this on yourself so shut up."

"Listen," Thomas shouted. "The first thing we are going to do is close the curtains. The press saw you drive in and I know the police are there but, well, you know what they're like."

"I don't but my so-called wife does."

Sophia went to one window and Stephanie to the second and Lady Heaton switched on the lights.

"Good," Thomas went on. "Now, we are going to try and discuss this without any further shouting. Is that clear? Can we all sit down, please?" Everyone did as he asked and he nodded. "Thank you. Now, Lady Heaton is going to explain how all this came about."

For the first time, Sophia saw Lady Heaton look startled.

"Oh, that's right, blame me for all this."

"Explain please."

Sophia glanced at everyone's faces as Lady Heaton explained the circumstances which led to Stephanie and Thomas's births. Her father and Michelle were astonished. Poor Cathy looked bewildered. Tony and Peter were disgusted, Don furious and Danielle ashamed.

"…And she kept ringing us up," Lady Heaton continued. "At all times of the day and night. Drunk more often than not. Then she began to demand money. Eventually, Thomas caught me having to steal items from my own home to sell so that she would have money for alcohol."

Everyone looked at Danielle who shrugged.

"I wished I hadn't given my babies up…"

"You sold your babies," Michelle snapped. "Jesus, Mum."

"Sophia and I met Danielle and Don in Leeds," Thomas explained. "I told Danielle that there would be no more money for alcohol and Danielle agreed to start going to A.A. again."

"Bloody hell, Thomas. Surely you know that an alcoholic has to want to stop drinking of their own accord not be pressurised into it."

"Michelle, she wasn't pressurised," Sophia told her.

"And you can shut up."

"Michelle," Don warned and she rolled her eyes. "Sophia's right, your mother wasn't pressurised, and I honestly thought that she was going to the meetings. I just should have bloody gone with her."

"I bet there was consternation when I was born," Stephanie spoke and everyone turned to her. "A girl – shock, horror."

Sophia looked at her father who pressed his lips together.

"When you were born, we knew that we would have to try again," Lady Heaton said crisply. "We had to have an heir. We approached Danielle again and she agreed to have another baby."

"Christ," Peter whispered.

"And Thomas was born the following year. He was a beautiful baby. He and Stephanie both were. I have no regrets over what we did. Danielle was given time to consider our offer both times and both times she agreed."

"She agreed because you dangled a wad of money in front of her face," Tony cried.

"Well, she was hardly going to do it out of the kindness of her heart, was she? I'm sorry, who are you, exactly?" she asked in an imperious tone and Tony flushed.

Sophia got up. "This is Michelle and Peter, Danielle and Don's children. Tony is Michelle's husband and Cathy, here, is their daughter."

"I see. Well, I'm pleased to meet you." She rose. "Now, if you'll excuse me…?"

"No," Thomas snapped. "We're not finished here. Sit down. Now." Lady Heaton jumped and retook her seat. "Thank you. Now, we have to try and decide how best to deal with all this. Firstly," he turned to Danielle, "will there be more revelations in next week's paper?"

"No," she whispered.

"Well, that's something at least." He looked at the others. "I would like to get to know you. We're family whether we like it or not—"

"And he's not as scary as he looks," Stephanie interrupted. "And I'm not quite as stupid as people make out."

"Why would they think that?" Peter asked.

"My ex-boyfriend used to hit me and it was months before I left him. He almost killed me first but I did leave him eventually."

"Where is he now?"

"Descended into hell with a bit of luck. He took an overdose a few months ago."

"Good," Peter replied and Stephanie gave him a little smile.

"We also mustn't forget that Sophia and Thomas are getting married soon," Stephanie added. "And nothing is going to bugger that up. Are we clear on that? Sophia's had to put up with a hell of a lot here and we are not going to ruin her wedding."

"Hear, hear," Mr Nelson called. "Maria knew, didn't she?" he asked Danielle. "Maria was Sophia's mother," he explained to the others.

"Yes, she knew. I had to tell someone. She begged me both times not to do it but I wouldn't listen. It's all my own fault. How she kept it to herself, I don't know."

"She wrote it down in her journals," Sophia told her. "But it was a miracle that it didn't come out when she became ill."

"Yes. Poor Maria. I'm so sorry for everything. I'm...I'm not going to drink all the money I got from the paper. I've decided that I'm going to book into a clinic."

"Don't make promises you won't keep," Don said harshly.

"I'm not. I'm going to book into a clinic and I'm going to get off the booze once and for all. I overheard the journalist on his phone." She gave a little humourless smile. "He called me a wrinkled old alky." There was a shocked silence and she shrugged. "And I looked in the mirror and I saw a wrinkled old alky. I have to do something before I end up a dead wrinkled old alky. I want you back and I don't want people to pretend that I don't stink of booze anymore. And I want to get to know all my children and know that they aren't ashamed of me. The first time Thomas saw me I was drunk. I'm not proud of that. So I'm booking into a clinic."

"Good," Thomas said softly. "And about the wedding; Sophia and I are going to need your help. You're all invited but there's a chance that it might not take place on the day we intended. It all depends on whether the press are still interested in us then. Sophia and I are going to see the vicar and see what days are free around the original date and ask him to keep those days free for now. Sophia wants to get married in St Margaret's, her mother is buried there as you know, so the date issue will be a family secret."

There were a couple of smiles. Even Michelle nodded.

"Thank you. Now, shall we go down to the kitchen and have some coffee?"

Sophia and Stephanie closed the blinds in the kitchen and Thomas switched the light on.

"Would anyone prefer tea?" Sophia asked. "I can make a pot of tea, too?"

"Yes, please," her father replied.

"I would, too," Lady Heaton added.

"I'll do the tea if you like?" Stephanie offered.

"Thanks, I'll see if I can work the coffee machine."

She set it to produce a huge jug of coffee then went to find something for Cathy. The poor little girl was completely bewildered. She eventually found some small cartons of fruit juice in the pantry and was returning to the kitchen when the back door opened and Helen came in.

"Anything I can do to help?"

"We're making tea and coffee. Come in and have some."

"Thank you."

"Orange or blackcurrant?" She held the cartons out to Cathy.

"Blackcurrant, please," Cathy whispered.

"I'll open it." Michelle took the carton.

Sophia turned away and saw Danielle watch Stephanie make a huge pot of tea before setting out cups and saucers on the worktop.

"It'll be easier if everyone helped themselves," Stephanie told Sophia, who nodded. "Is she staring at me? Danielle?"

"Yes."

"I just don't know what to say to her. Could ask if she takes milk and sugar, I suppose. Keep an eye on Thomas, I think he's running on autopilot at this stage."

"I will. I'll get the coffee jug."

"Tea and coffee," Stephanie called. "Can everyone help themselves please?"

Sophia poured two coffees and passed one to Thomas.

"So far so good."

He gave her an exhausted smile. "Yes. Thanks. Do you think she will check into a clinic? Danielle?"

"Who knows? But I think this has frightened her a hell of a lot. She's got a lot to do: try and get Don back, and try and get to know you and Stephanie."

She watched as Stephanie produced a packet of chocolate biscuits from somewhere and offered one to Cathy before putting the rest on a plate. She then took the plate, went to Danielle and offered her one.

"Thank you," Danielle said quietly. "Your boyfriend used to hit you?"

"Yes. I, um…I lost a baby. And my spleen. It took a long time for the penny to drop and for me to realise that one day he would kill me if I didn't leave him for good." Stephanie closed her eyes for a moment. "I don't know if I should be talking to you like this. I mean, I've only just met you, but if I can leave Simon, you can stop drinking. And now I'll shut up."

"No," Danielle replied softly. "No, you're right. I am going to stop drinking, I promise."

"Good."

"Cathy needs the toilet." Sophia hadn't heard Michelle approach and jumped.

"I'll take you." She put her cup down. "There's a toilet under the stairs."

"Under the stairs?"

"Under the half-landing," Thomas explained. "Give the chain a good pull, it's a bit temperamental."

They went up the stairs and along the corridor to the hall.

"Here we are." Sophia opened and closed the door for Cathy before looking around for Michelle, who was at the portraits. "He's Thomas' father." She pointed.

"Right."

"And I'm sorry for deceiving you. The corridor to the kitchen is over there."

"Sophia, wait."

"What?"

Michelle shrugged. "I don't hate you. I just…I just don't know how I'm ever going to get my head around all this; how I'm ever going to explain it to Cathy; how I'm going to face people…"

"Mummy?" Cathy called and jumped as her voice echoed around the hall. "I can't reach the chain."

"I'll lift you up," Michelle replied and they went back across the hall to the toilet. "Pull hard. Good."

"Wow." Cathy ran into the middle of the floor. "Are you really going to live here, Sophia?"

"Yes. With Thomas."

"You're still getting married?"

"Yes, why?"

"I thought something had happened; that you weren't anymore."

"Something has happened," Michelle told her. "We found out that Thomas and Stephanie are my brother and sister and Peter's brother and sister."

Cathy stared at her mother then at Sophia and then back at Michelle again. "How?"

"Stephanie and then Thomas were born before Peter and me."

"And you didn't know?"

"No. It was before Granny Danielle married Grandad Don so it was a bit of a surprise. That's why we're all here so we can talk about it."

"But Thomas is a lord?"

"That's right. But he's your uncle, too, now."

They returned to the kitchen and Cathy went straight to Thomas and tapped his arm. "Are you my uncle now? I thought you were a lord?"

He crouched down. "I am, but I'm your uncle now, too. You don't have to call me Uncle Thomas if you don't want to. Do you want to be called Aunt Stephanie?" he called across the room to her.

"Stephanie is just fine."

"Oh, good." Cathy smiled. "Because I don't call Peter Uncle Peter."

"Made me feel ancient." He came to them. "So it's just Peter."

"I had to pull the chain very hard, Thomas."

"I hope you didn't break it?" he teased.

"No, not that hard. Can I have another biscuit?"

"I think Stephanie has them."

"Okay."

"Peter." He put out his hand.

"Thomas." They shook hands.

"Big brother, eh?"

"Looks like it. Although, I've been the little brother up to now."

"Like cars?" Peter asked.

"Well, yes, I suppose so. I haven't really thought about it."

"What have you got?"

"My father's old Jaguar. I'll show you soon."

"Cheers. Your…um, Lady Heaton doesn't look too happy," Peter added and they turned. Lady Heaton was seated at a table in a corner. "I kind of feel sorry for her, to be honest. What do you think she'll do now?"

By the blank expression on Thomas' face, he clearly hadn't given it much thought.

"I don't know. She's living in one of the farmyard apartments. I'm not going to evict her, I'm not a heartless bastard. When all is said and done, she was my father's wife, she ran this house and she brought Steph and me up."

"Somehow I doubt if she'll want anything to do with us." Michelle joined them. "No matter how sorry you feel for her."

"No, but at the same time she must be relieved that all this isn't top secret anymore."

"I'm going to have to go soon. Cathy needs a proper dinner and Dad looks out on his feet. I don't think he got any sleep last night."

"Join the club," Thomas smiled weakly. "What about the press?"

"Sod them."

"What are you going to do about Danielle and your father?"

"I don't know. If Mum really is intent on this clinic idea then, maybe, he might forgive her. But for now, it's separate rooms." She pulled a face and looked around for Cathy. "Cathy? Come on, we're going home."

"Now?"

"Yes, now." Michelle turned back. "I'm glad that this didn't end up in one big fight. Thanks for that, Thomas."

"Is the shock wearing off yet?" he asked.

"That might take a while. Mum's always been full of surprises. Usually drink related. But this…"

"Well, if you ever need any help? I mean it, Michelle."

Michelle nodded. "Thanks."

"And if you want me to take Cathy for a few hours, ring me?" Sophia added.

"I'll probably take you up on that."

"I'll bring you up to the front door."

"We won't be long behind you," Tony told his wife, who nodded.

"How many times have you got lost here?" Don asked Sophia as she pulled open the huge front door.

"A few times, even with a map."

"I suppose you're glad in a way that it's all out in the open."

"Yes," she admitted. "But not the way it happened."

"You're right there." He took Cathy's hand and they went out to Michelle's car.

"I apologised to your dad," Michelle told her. "For being hysterical on the phone."

"Well, if you need to be hysterical again sometime you know where I am."

Michelle laughed. "I'll probably take you up on that, too. Chuck the rest of them out soon, you and Thomas look knackered."

"Will do."

Returning to the kitchen, she found Stephanie and Danielle deep in conversation with Lady Heaton watching them stony-faced. Thomas was pouring himself yet another coffee.

"We should go, too." Tony put his cup on the worktop. "Thanks for refereeing, Thomas."

"I'm not sure whether we actually resolved anything, I mean Danielle and Don haven't resolved anything, but we've all met now so that's something at least."

They watched Tony drive away and Thomas gave her an exhausted smile.

"Thank God that's over."

"For now, anyway. Bed?"

He nodded. "In a few minutes."

She followed him down to the kitchen where Helen and Stephanie were loading the dishwasher. Lady Heaton was still seated in the corner but got up when she saw them.

"I suppose you'd like me to move out now you've found your mother's family."

"No, not at all," Thomas replied. "You're quite welcome to live in the apartment."

Lady Heaton was taken aback but retaliated quickly. "But think of the revenue you're missing out on."

"Well, if it concerns you that much, you choose. The apartment or Sophia's flat in the stable yard?"

"I think...Sophia's flat in the stable yard. We didn't spend an inordinate amount on the farmyard apartments for family to then occupy them."

"No. Thank you." He stifled a yawn.

"You're exhausted. We'll discuss it when we've all had a good night's sleep."

"Do you need a lift back to the farmyard?"

"Thank you, no. Stephanie and I will take the short cut across the fields again."

"I'll talk to you tomorrow." Stephanie gave them a smile and followed Lady Heaton out.

"Are you two hungry?" Sophia asked. Her father and Thomas looked at each other then back at her. "I could rustle up something lightish before we go to bed? Beans on toast?"

The two men smiled.

Half an hour later she left her father in the flat preparing for bed and returned to the house to find Thomas.

"I've just rung Des," he told her. "He's just been down to the gates. He thinks the press are getting fed up. A couple got over the wall somewhere but when they got up here all the curtains were closed. Same story over at Michelle and Tony's."

"Good. Let's just go to bed."

It was midday before they stirred and headed downstairs to the kitchen. Sophia was frying bacon and sausages before Helen and Des arrived.

"Have you eaten?" Sophia asked.

"We had some cornflakes."

"Bacon sandwich?"

Both grinned and Thomas began to butter some bread.

Sophia did her best but still felt as though she had guided a group of senior citizens around the house as if on autopilot. Luckily there were no complaints or any copies of *The World On Sunday* in their possession.

Retrieving her phone she opened a text message from Michelle.

Mum gone home. Going 2 book herself straight in2 a clinic

Sophia smiled and replied;

Good. Give her our best wishes

"Good news?" Thomas came into the kitchen and helped himself to a cup of coffee.

"Danielle's booking herself straight into a clinic."

"Let's hope she stays the course because she's on the wedding guest list. She and Don are getting individual invitations. Whether they turn up together or separately is up to them. A hundred guests; it's not a huge amount, is it?"

"No, but we decided on family and close friends only. We don't want to be going around our own wedding reception asking, 'Sorry, who are you, again?'"

Thomas laughed. "That's true."

Sophia paced up and down the bathroom floor, smoothing sweaty palms down her jeans. Stopping at the sink, she blew out her cheeks and picked up the pregnancy test. It was positive. Bright colours danced in front of Sophia's eyes and for an awful moment, she thought she was going to faint. She placed it back in the sink, put the toilet seat down and sat on it. Reaching for the glass on the shelf above the sink, she lifted the toothbrush out and ran water into it. She gulped the water down and wiped her mouth before standing up, hoping her legs would hold her. Putting the glass back, she picked up the pregnancy test and left the flat.

Thomas was in his office so she tapped on the door.

"Are you busy?"

He smiled. "It's nothing that can't wait."

"Good." She closed the door and pulled down the blinds.

"What's this?" Thomas' smile broadened into a grin.

"I need to show you something," she said and put the test on the desk. "I've missed a period and I'm usually like clockwork." Thomas' jaw dropped but she plunged onwards. "I wondered if I'd missed because of the stress of all that's happened but I thought I'd better buy a pregnancy test all the same. I plucked up the courage just now and did it and it says I'm pregnant," she said, pointing to the window in the test kit.

Thomas stared at the test then at her in complete bewilderment. "Pregnant?"

"This test is 99% accurate. One of the condoms must have ripped or burst. And we do have sex a lot." She couldn't help but laugh.

"Oh, my God," he whispered. "Oh, my God." He grabbed her around the waist and pulled her into an embrace. "Oh, my God."

"You're happy?"

"Are you?"

"Shocked," she admitted. "Stunned. But happy."

"Good. So am I."

"Really?" she asked quietly. "Because this is so sudden."

"Really. Oh, my God, I love you."

"Can we tell my dad first?" she asked and Thomas grinned and nodded.

It took an age for her father to come to the front door and open it. Sophia stared at him in surprise, it was only four o'clock in the afternoon but he was in his dressing gown.

"Dad, are you all right? Are you ill?"

"No, no, I'm fine. You didn't say you were coming round."

"Do I need to make an appointment?" She laughed then clapped a hand to her mouth as a woman in a nightdress appeared behind him in the hall.

"Everything all right, William?"

Her father shuffled awkwardly. "Yes, fine."

The woman gave Sophia and her father a puzzled glance before retreating in the direction of the bedroom.

"Looks like I should have made an appointment, Dad."

"Sophia…"

"Let me know when it's okay to call round. Bye, Dad."

She turned and pushed past Thomas and headed for the car on wobbly legs. A moment or two later, he got into the driver's seat.

"I'm sorry," he said simply and she gave him a humourless smile. "Do you know who she is?" he asked.

She shook her head and he leaned over, kissed her forehead, started the car and drove them back to the abbey.

In what was now their living room, she sank down onto one of the sofas and rested her face in her hands for a moment.

"I can't face Lady Heaton just yet."

"No, of course not." He exhaled a laugh and she raised her head in surprise. "Sorry, I was just going to offer you a whisky."

"How about a cup of tea instead?"

He smiled and nodded. "Won't be long."

It was stupid to be angry but she couldn't help it. Good grief, how long had it been going on? Since before her mother had died?

She dropped her head into her hands. Her mother had thought him dead for months. She had been astounded when her mother had casually referred to her husband in the past tense for the first time and even more astounded when he had paid little or no attention. Bloody hell, she should have known something like this would happen.

"Here we are." Thomas pushed the door open and then closed it with his foot.

"Thanks." She took a mug from him and put it down on the coffee table. "I feel such an idiot for not expecting something like this to happen."

"Your mother was ill for a long time."

"Yes. It was just a bit of a jolt, especially when I haven't a clue who she is."

She jumped as the front doorbell jangled.

"Drink your tea, I'll go." Thomas squeezed her shoulder and went out.

He returned a couple of minutes later and she got to her feet when she saw who was with him.

"Dad?"

"I had to come and explain. Can I sit down?"

"Yes, of course. Here." She pushed her mug towards him. "Tea."

"Thanks, Sophia." He seated himself on the opposite sofa and took a sip of tea while Thomas stood behind her. "Well, her name is Sylvia. We've been – how do you young people put it – seeing each other for a while now. I'm sorry, I should have told you sooner, I just didn't know how to. I know how devastated you were when you lost your mum."

"Yes, but you lost her a long time ago. When I came back from London she was already referring to you in the past tense."

Her father nodded. "When I came out of hospital after I broke my arm and had to have the pin put in your mother assumed I was dead and sadly I stayed dead. Sophia, your mum was the love of my life and always will be, but I was lonely and so was Sylvia when I met her."

"When did you meet her?" Sophia asked.

Her father shifted uncomfortably in his seat. "I'm not going to lie to you, lass. I was introduced to her at the club after your mother's funeral."

Sophia inhaled and then exhaled a shaky breath. "I see. Is that why you told me to go home?"

"No," he shouted, making her jump. "No, I could see how difficult you were finding it all and I knew Thomas would look after you."

Sophia glanced up at Thomas, who was standing behind her father's chair, he pulled a sympathetic expression and she sighed.

"I'm sorry, Dad, it's just a bit of a shock."

"I know, lass. Was there something you'd come to see me about?"

Sophia glanced up at Thomas again and he nodded.

"Dad, Thomas and I are going to have a baby."

"You're pregnant?" Her father's eyes almost popped out of his head. "I'm sorry, it's just a bit of a shock."

"Yes, it is, but we're both absolutely delighted." Thomas smiled and to her relief, her father's face broke into a smile and he nodded.

"A grandad."

"Yes." She leaned over and kissed his cheek.

"Who else knows?"

"No-one yet."

"What do you think Lady Heaton will say?" he asked and her heart plummeted.

"Who knows?" Thomas replied. "But we are delighted and that's what matters."

"When are you going to tell her?"

"This evening."

"Good luck."

"This evening?" Sophia enquired.

"We don't have to. We can leave it until the morning if you'd prefer?"

"No." She sighed. "We'd better get it over and done with."

"You sure?"

"Positive."

"Okay." He reached over and squeezed her shoulder but it did little to reassure her.

Two hours later, she climbed the stairs with Thomas to what had once been her flat on leaden legs. He knocked at the door.

"Who is it?" Lady Heaton's voice asked.

"Thomas and Sophia. Can we come in?"

"Yes."

Thomas opened the door. Lady Heaton was seated on the sofa. She had been watching *Emmerdale* but had muted the sound. There wasn't a floral pattern in sight and she looked completely out of place in the modern surroundings.

"Settling in?" Thomas asked.

"Yes."

Thomas cleared his throat. "May we sit down?" Lady Heaton extended a hand and Sophia took the armchair leaving Thomas no choice but to sit at the other end of the sofa. "Thank you."

"Was that your father I saw earlier, Sophia?"

"Yes, it was."

"Nothing wrong, I hope?"

"I was telling him I was pregnant," Sophia announced. Thomas' eyes widened but instead of being shocked or taken aback, Lady Heaton simply nodded.

"We're absolutely delighted," Thomas added.

"Will you be bringing the wedding forward?"

"No. There's no need."

"You'll be wearing an Empire-line dress, then, to hide your condition?"

"Lady Heaton, I am only a few weeks pregnant. I'm not going to be waddling down the aisle next month."

"Well, you have my congratulations."

"Thank you."

"Have you told Stephanie?"

"Not yet. You are only the second person we've told."

Lady Heaton inclined her head, reached forward and opened one of the drawers in the coffee table. She extracted some sewing and placed it on the table. In the bottom of the drawer, Sophia saw some condom packages with needles threaded through them. She struggled to her feet, sure she was about to throw up.

"Sophia?" Thomas frowned.

She pulled the drawer open further, reached for the condoms, and threw them onto the coffee table. "You bitch."

Thomas reached for one and held it up with a hand which began to shake. "After choosing Sophia for me, I thought you couldn't possibly sink any lower." He threw it down. "How bloody wrong can I be? What if it hadn't been Sophia? Eh?"

"It was only ever going to be Sophia, Thomas. She may

not have a title and ancestry but, as we all now know, she is more than capable of breeding an heir." Lady Heaton smiled at her little joke. "And now, thanks to the two of you, there will be new blood in the family."

"Thomas." Sophia reached for his hand. "Come on."

She led him out of the flat on wobbly legs and they went slowly down the stairs, across the stable yard, and into his office. Thomas closed the door and then the blind before turning to face her.

"I'm sorry," he whispered. "I'm so sorry."

"My father is never to know."

"No. Sophia—"

She shook her head and covered his lips with her fingers. "I want to marry you. And I want to have our baby. She'll have to come to the wedding for appearance's sake but I want her moved back to the farmyard apartments. I don't want to see her any more than is absolutely necessary."

He nodded. "She can go in the small corner one."

They jumped as someone began knocking at the door. "It's Stephanie. Are you decent?"

Thomas went to the door and opened it. "Come in."

"What on earth's the matter?" Stephanie looked from Thomas to her. "You both look awful."

"Sophia's pregnant," Thomas told her. "Thanks to Lady Heaton."

Stephanie's face creased in bewilderment. "I don't understand. Unless you're telling me that's she's really a man?"

"Lady Heaton replaced my condoms with some she had taken a sewing needle to."

His sister's eyes bulged. "I don't know what to say."

"Well, that's a first," Thomas muttered.

"What are you going to do?"

"Move her to the small corner apartment in the farmyard so we don't have to see her unless it's absolutely necessary," Sophia told her.

"Is that all?"

"I want to marry Thomas and I want to have the baby. I don't know what else we can do."

"Have her locked up."

"And explain why, exactly?" Thomas demanded.

Stephanie sighed. "I don't know."

"My father is never to know," Sophia added.

"No, of course not. Do we need to change the date of the wedding?"

"No."

"Okay, good. Well, can I now congratulate you both?" she asked with a little smile.

"You can," Thomas nodded, and she hugged him before kissing and hugging Sophia.

"Have you told Michelle?"

"No. I'll go round tomorrow morning."

Michelle sat on the sofa in her living room, mug of coffee in her hand, staring at her open-mouthed. "No, of course, I won't tell your dad. Bloody hell, Sophia."

"Yeah."

"How are you?"

"Fine, considering. I haven't had any morning sickness, thankfully."

"And how's Thomas?"

"He feels terrible, even though it's not his fault. If I'd gone on the pill this wouldn't have happened. I mean, we did want children, just not this soon."

"Are you bringing the wedding forward?"

"No, there's no need. Stephanie's really relieved, she's put a huge effort into it all. She was dreading having to move the date and me the church because of the press but they seem to have left us alone. You haven't had any more trouble?" she asked and, to her relief, Michelle shook her head.

"No, there's been nothing. Will your dress need altering?"

"No, I doubt it."

"So, who's going to tell Lady Heaton she has to move again?"

Sophia grimaced. "Both Thomas and me. Strength in numbers, and all that."

Lady Heaton took the request to move surprisingly well. "The corner apartment with the oddly-shaped rooms? Quirky, I think the television property programmes would call it. Yes, it will suit me. I will ask Stephanie to help me pack. I take it she knows?"

"Yes," Thomas replied. "Please speak to Des Fields about the furniture."

"I will."

Thomas nodded and they turned to leave.

"Thomas?" Lady Heaton called and he spun around.

"No. Nothing you say will ever make up for what you've done. We don't expect to see you before the wedding."

"So you are going ahead?"

"Of course," he replied and they went out.

A week before the wedding, the rehearsal was held at the church. If the vicar wondered where the groom's mother was, he kept it to himself.

Chapter Fourteen

Sophia spent her last night as a single woman on a camp bed in her father's living room. The bed was uncomfortable but it was better than the lumpy couch. Stephanie and Michelle arrived at nine in the morning and the hairdresser half an hour later. By a quarter past ten, Sophia was ready and went to the kitchen to be out of the way as the others got dressed.

"Dad?" she called softly from the door and he turned. She smiled. He was wearing a grey morning suit, and she'd never seen him so smartly dressed.

"Oh, lass," he whispered. "I wish your mother was here to see you…"

"Become a baroness?" she finished and he chuckled.

"She'd have liked Thomas."

"I know."

The cars arrived at a quarter to eleven for the short drive to St Margaret's Church. In the graveyard, Stephanie gave The Dress a final once over then grinned.

"Perfect. All set to marry my little brother?"

"I am."

"I still can't believe you're going to Ireland on honeymoon. It'll rain."

"I know, but we're still going."

"All right. Now, let's take our places."

As the bridal party neared the top of the church, Thomas turned and Sophia smiled. He was wearing a black morning suit and had never looked more handsome.

"Hello," he whispered.

"Hello," she replied.

Half an hour later they were married and, after greeting the congregation at the door of the church, the new Baroness Heaton took her husband's hand and led him to her mother's grave. She carefully crouched down and laid her bouquet on the grave.

"I hope you like the flowers, Mum. White roses were always your favourite. This is Thomas, Mum. Your new son-in-law. Oh, and I'd better tell you now – you're going to be a granny. I'll come and see you when Thomas and I get back from Ireland. We're going to see where Thomas' ancestors lived. Love you, Mum."

She straightened up and Thomas kissed her forehead.

During the group photographs, Lady Heaton stood stiffly next to an equally rigid Thomas on the front steps of Heaton Abbey House, before she went back to the marquee as the more informal photographs were taken. She was seated next to Thomas at the meal but apart from exchanging pleasantries about how well the day was going, in order to keep up appearances, they didn't speak.

"Happy?" he whispered to Sophia as they began the dancing.

"Tired," she admitted. "But happy."

"Tell me when you want to go to bed."

She smiled. "I will."

"You look so beautiful. Is that really one of Stephanie's dresses?"

"Yes." She laughed. "We did experiment with a more Renaissance style but I looked like a Pantomime Dame."

"Come outside for a few minutes." He took her hand and led her out onto the lawn. "I'm melting in this suit."

"You look gorgeous..." She followed his gaze, watching as Andrew and Stephanie hurried into the wood on the other side of the lawn.

"Well, well," he murmured. "Did you know about them?"

"No. Did you?" she asked and he shook his head. "Well, good for them."

He didn't reply and she frowned then jumped, hearing someone approach. Turning around, her heart sank on seeing her new 'mother in law'.

"I wanted to speak to you both before you left."

"Yes?" Thomas prompted.

"I wanted to say what a handsome couple you make and I hope you'll be very happy."

"Is that it?"

"Thomas." She laid a hand on his arm.

"No. After all you've done – after all you've done to interfere – you can just stand there and hope Sophia and I will be very happy. You bloody-well know we'll be very happy – you wouldn't have matched us up if you hadn't known we'd be very happy."

Lady Heaton nodded. "Have you seen Stephanie?"

"No. We haven't."

"Very well. Enjoy your honeymoon."

Sophia watched as she walked away before turning to

Thomas. "Let's do a circuit of the lawn then go back into the marquee. It's a bit early to go to bed."

"All right." He sighed. "I'm sorry. It's just that I can hardly bear to even look at her now."

"Come on." Taking his hand, they began to walk around the edge of the lawn. Passing the wood, they could hear Stephanie giggling and Andrew shushing her.

"It's all right, it's only the baron and baroness." Stephanie stepped out from behind a tree, Andrew following.

"Sorry," Thomas told her. "We didn't mean to spy on you."

"It doesn't matter. We were going to 'come out', so to speak when you got back from Ireland. We've been seeing each other for a couple of months now."

"Does anyone know?"

"No. Not even Lady Heaton."

"Lucky you," Thomas muttered.

"Now, now." Stephanie wagged a finger at him. "You've just married this beautiful woman, you're going to be a father, and you've never been so happy. So enough of that. Yes?"

He smiled. "Yes."

"Good."

"What time are you off tomorrow?" Andrew asked.

"I'm driving them to the airport at ten," Stephanie told him. "Can you pass me my camera?"

Andrew pulled a pink digital camera from the inside pocket of his morning suit and passed it to her.

"I want to take a couple of informal photos, Sophia," Stephanie added and Thomas groaned. "Mr and Mrs Heaton-type photos, not Baron and Baroness Heaton portraits."

"Thomas." She nudged him. "I can count on one hand the number of photos you actually smiled in. Kiss me?"

He smiled, tilted her face up, and kissed her lips.

"Excellent." Stephanie circled them, her digital camera beeping. "Now, put an arm around her. Good."

"Can I take a couple of you and Andrew?" Sophia offered.

"Wow – photographed by the bride. Thank you." Stephanie handed the camera over and threw her arms around Andrew's neck as Sophia began to photograph them.

"Maybe a couple of you not trying to strangle my best man?" Thomas suggested.

"Okay." Stephanie let Andrew go and planted a noisy kiss on his lips. "Oh, Sophia, you'll never guess?"

"No, probably not."

"Michelle's just told me that your friend Gavin's just been outed by his mum."

Sophia's eyes bulged. "What?"

"Apparently, his mum's known he's gay all along."

"What about his dad?"

"She sat him down and told him when Gavin turned twenty-one."

"I don't believe it. They've known for the best part of fifteen years and not let on to Gavin?"

Stephanie shrugged. "Michelle said the whole thing would be perfect for Jerry Springer. Once we've all been on, of course."

"There you are." Turning, Sophia saw Danielle approaching them carefully across the grass in her high heels and returned the camera to Andrew. "I wanted to see you before you left."

"We'll go back to the marquee." Stephanie kissed Danielle's cheek as she passed. "And chat to you later."

Danielle nodded before turning back. "You look beautiful – both of you."

"Thank you," Sophia smiled, feeling Thomas squeezing her hand. "So do you." She glanced up at him, knowing he wanted to tell his mother about the baby, and smiled.

"While we have you on your own, we want to let you into a little secret."

"Oh?"

"Sophia's expecting a baby," he told her softly.

"Really?" Danielle clapped a hand to her cheek. "Oh, congratulations."

"Very few people know yet," Sophia told her. "We're going to announce it when we get back from Ireland."

"How are you?" Thomas asked.

"Very well. I haven't had a drink in four weeks."

"Keep it up, won't you?"

"I promise."

Returning to the marquee, they mingled and danced for a further two hours before giving Stephanie and Andrew a quick wave and slipping out otherwise unnoticed. Thomas was quiet as they climbed the steps to the front door.

"What is it?" she asked softly as he opened the door.

"Come inside." She did as he asked and he closed the door. He led her out into the middle of the vast hallway before stopping. "I never thought I'd find anyone to share this place with me. Look at it – it's old, it's huge – and it's cold."

"It's also historic, people want to see it, and we need to make the most of that."

"I know. Dance with me?"

She smiled as he took her in his arms and began to waltz her around the floor.

"You're beautiful, Mrs Heaton."

"Mrs Heaton?" she echoed.

"What do you want people to call you?" he asked.

"Just Sophia," she replied and he nodded. "I didn't know what to call you in the beginning," she went on. "Everyone called you, 'Lord Heaton', or, 'my Lord', and you never invited me or them to call you anything else."

"One thing I'll always have to be grateful to Lady Heaton for is bringing you here. You were a breath of fresh air. If it weren't for you, some archaeologist a few hundred years from now would have discovered a mummified me in my office."

Sophia couldn't help but laugh and hugged him. "I love you."

"And I love you." Taking her hand, he led her across the hall and up the stairs.

THE END

Other Books by Lorna Peel

The Fitzgeralds of Dublin Series

A Scarlet Woman: The Fitzgeralds of Dublin Book 1 -
http://mybook.to/ascarletwoman
Dublin, Ireland, 1880. Tired of treating rich
hypochondriacs, Dr Will Fitzgerald left his father's medical
practice and his home on Merrion Square to live and practise
medicine in the Liberties. His parents were appalled and his
fiancée broke off their engagement. But when Will spends a
night in a brothel on the eve of his best friend's wedding,
little does he know that the scarred and disgraced young
woman he meets there will alter the course of his life.

Isobel Stevens was schooled to be a lady, but a seduction
put an end to all her father's hopes for her. Disowned, she
left Co Galway for Dublin and fell into prostitution. On the
advice of a handsome young doctor, she leaves the brothel
and enters domestic service. But can Isobel escape her past
and adapt to life and the chance of love on Merrion Square?
Or will she always be seen as a scarlet woman?

A Suitable Wife: The Fitzgeralds of Dublin Book 2 -
http://mybook.to/asuitablewife
Dublin, Ireland, 1881. Will and Isobel Fitzgerald settle into
number 30 Fitzwilliam Square, a home they could once only
have dreamed of. A baby is on the way, Will takes over the
Merrion Street Upper medical practice from his father and
they are financially secure. But when Will is handed a letter
from his elder brother, Edward, stationed with the army in
India, the revelations it contains only serves to further
alienate Will from his father.

Isobel is eager to adapt to married life on Fitzwilliam Square
but soon realises her past can never be laid to rest. The night
she met Will in a brothel on the eve of his best friend's wedding
has devastating and far-reaching consequences which will
change the lives of the Fitzgerald family forever.

A Discarded Son: The Fitzgeralds of Dublin Book 3 -
http://mybook.to/adiscardedson
Dublin, Ireland, 1881. Isobel Fitzgerald's mother, Martha,
marries solicitor James Ellison but an unexpected guest
overshadows their wedding day. Martha's father is dying and
he is determined to clear his conscience before it is too late.
Lewis Greene's confession ensures the Ellisons' expectation
of a quiet married life is gone and that Isobel's elder brother,
Alfie Stevens, will be the recipient of an unwelcome
inheritance.

When a bewildering engagement notice is published in
The Irish Times, the name of one of the persons concerned
sends Will and Isobel on a race against time across Dublin
and forces them to break a promise and reveal a closely
guarded secret.

Historical Romance

Brotherly Love: A 19th Century Irish Romance -
http://mybook.to/brotherly-love
Ireland, 1835. Faction fighting has left the parish of Doon divided between the followers of the Bradys and the Donnellans. Caitriona Brady is the widow of John, the Brady champion, killed two years ago. Matched with John aged eighteen, Caitriona didn't love him and can't mourn him. Now John's mother is dead, too, and Caitriona is free to marry again.

Michael Warner is handsome, loves her, and he hasn't allied himself with either faction. But what secret is he keeping from her? Is he too good to be true?

Mystery Romance

Only You - http://myBook.to/onlyyou
Jane Hollinger is divorced and the wrong side of thirty – as she puts it. Her friends are pressuring her to dive back into London's dating pool, but she's content with her quiet life teaching family history evening classes.

Robert Armstrong is every woman's fantasy: handsome, charming, rich and famous. When he asks her to meet him, she convinces herself it's because he needs her help with a mystery in his family tree. Soon she realises he's interested in more than her genealogy expertise. Now the paparazzi want a piece of Jane too.

Can Jane handle living — and loving — in the spotlight?

About The Author

Lorna Peel is an author of historical fiction and mystery romance novels set in the UK and Ireland. Lorna was born in England and lived in North Wales until her family moved to Ireland to become farmers, which is a book in itself! She lives in rural Ireland, where she writes, researches her family history, and grows fruit and vegetables. She also keeps chickens (and a Guinea Hen who now thinks she's a chicken!).

Contact Information

Website - http://lornapeel.com
Blog - https://lornapeel.com/blog
Newsletter - http://eepurl.com/ciL8ab
Twitter - https://twitter.com/PeelLorna
MeWe - https://mewe.com/i/lornapeel
Pinterest - http://www.pinterest.com/lornapeel
Goodreads - http://www.goodreads.com/LornaPeel
Facebook - http://www.facebook.com/LornaPeelAuthor
Instagram - https://www.instagram.com/lornapeelauthor

52818225R00221

Made in the USA
Lexington, KY
21 September 2019